PRAISE FOR THE NOVELS
OF ALEC NEVALA-LEE

CITY OF EXILES

"Alec Nevala-Lee creates a dazzlingly detailed and authentic world of intrigue, weaving a harrowing tale that will enthrall readers with an undercurrent of political ambiguity that evokes le Carré and an intricate, continent-crossing plot reminiscent of *The Day of the Jackal*. Delivering a complex mix of espionage, European politics, Old Testament riddles, and Cold War mysteries, Nevala-Lee is clearly emerging as one of the most elegant new voices in suspense literature."

—David Heinzmann, author of *Throwaway Girl*

THE ICON THIEF

"Alec Nevala-Lee comes roaring out of the gate with a novel that's as thrilling as it is thought-provoking, as unexpected as it is erudite. *The Icon Thief* is a wild ride through a fascinating and morally complex world, a puzzle Duchamp himself would have applauded. Bravo."

—national bestselling author Jesse Kellerman

"Alec Nevala-Lee is no debut author; he must have been a thriller writer in some past life. This one has everything: great writing, great characters, great story, great bad guy, and a religious conspiracy to boot. *The Icon Thief* is smart, sophisticated, and has enough fast-paced action to keep anyone up past

—*New York* ... stopher

...ued ...

"Twists and turns aplenty lift this thriller above the rest. From the brutal thugs of the Russian Mafia to the affected inhabitants of the American art world, this book introduces a cast of believable and intriguing characters. Add a story line where almost nothing is as it first appears, and where the plot turns around on itself to reveal startling contradictions, and the result is a book that grips and holds the reader like a vise. I devoured it in a single sitting."

—national bestselling author James Becker

Also by Alec Nevala-Lee

The Icon Thief

CITY

OF

EXILES

✚

ALEC NEVALA-LEE

A SIGNET BOOK

SIGNET
Published by New American Library, a division of
Penguin Group (USA) Inc., 375 Hudson Street,
New York, New York 10014, USA
Penguin Group (Canada), 90 Eglinton Avenue East, Suite 700, Toronto,
Ontario M4P 2Y3, Canada (a division of Pearson Penguin Canada Inc.)
Penguin Books Ltd., 80 Strand, London WC2R 0RL, England
Penguin Ireland, 25 St. Stephen's Green, Dublin 2,
Ireland (a division of Penguin Books Ltd.)
Penguin Group (Australia), 250 Camberwell Road, Camberwell, Victoria 3124,
Australia (a division of Pearson Australia Group Pty. Ltd.)
Penguin Books India Pvt. Ltd., 11 Community Centre, Panchsheel Park,
New Delhi -110 017, India
Penguin Group (NZ), 67 Apollo Drive, Rosedale, Auckland 0632,
New Zealand (a division of Pearson New Zealand Ltd.)
Penguin Books (South Africa) (Pty.) Ltd., 24 Sturdee Avenue,
Rosebank, Johannesburg 2196, South Africa

Penguin Books Ltd., Registered Offices:
80 Strand, London WC2R 0RL, England

First published by Signet, an imprint of New American Library,
a division of Penguin Group (USA) Inc.

First Printing, December 2012
10 9 8 7 6 5 4 3 2 1

ALWAYS LEARNING   **PEARSON**

I do not talk in details—people who knew them are all dead now because they were vocal, they were open. I am quiet. There is only one man who is vocal and he may be in trouble: [former] world chess champion [Garry] Kasparov. He has been very outspoken in his attacks on Putin and I believe that he is probably next on the list.
—Former KGB general Oleg Kalugin, quoted in *Foreign Policy*, July 25, 2007

"The unacknowledged legislators of the world" describes the secret police, not the poets.
—W. H. Auden

PROLOGUE

And it came to pass by the way at the inn, that the Lord met Moses, and sought to kill him.

—Exodus 4:24

Manuel was watching the man with the books. For most of the past week, he had waited outside this man's home and office, studying his habits and quiet routine, and by now, he thought, he had come to know him rather well. All the same, he still had trouble believing that this was the person he was supposed to kill.

Tonight, his target was dining at a restaurant near La Plaza de los Naranjos. Watching from the van across the street, Manuel could see the man in question, whom he generally thought of as the translator, seated at a table with his books and a glass of red wine. Next to him sat an attractive young woman, her head bowed over a book of her own, following along intently as the translator pointed to the page.

The van was parked before a whitewashed hotel. Behind the wheel, looking out at the restaurant, sat a pale, thin man in his twenties. Manuel did not know his name. "It would be easier to do it here."

Manuel shook his head. "No. Your employers may not have to live with these people, but I do. Are we clear?"

The pale man lifted the flap of his jacket, revealing the grip of a pistol. "We're clear."

"Good. And don't forget this." Opening the bag at his feet, Manuel pulled out a sawn-off shotgun, uncovering it just enough for the younger man to see. "Bring this to the Calle Lobatas. And when you get there—"

A few minutes later, the translator left the restaurant. Every night, as the other tables cleared, he spent an hour tutoring this girl, a waitress, in English. When the lesson was over, he accompanied her to the door, where they parted ways with a smile. As the translator headed off, the girl looked after him for a moment, then turned aside. Reading her dark eyes with ease, Manuel reflected that if he had been in the translator's place, he long since would have taken to walking her home.

From the glove compartment, Manuel removed a pint of rum in a paper bag, which he slid into his pocket as he climbed out of the van. Closing the door behind him, he waited as the pale man started the engine and pulled away. Once the van had rounded the corner, Manuel headed after the translator on foot. Under his coat, resting against the bottle, was his gun.

Manuel followed the translator into the labyrinth of streets to the north of the plaza, careful to keep well back. He was good at this sort of work, if somewhat slower than in his prime. As a young man, he had survived many bloody years in Marbella, but now he was almost fifty, the world had changed, and he was taking orders from a stranger less than half his age.

Beyond the plaza, the winding streets grew narrow, the balconies to either side heavy with flowers. Up ahead, the translator, little more than a shadow in the darkness, moved quickly along the sidewalk. He was a slender man of medium height, his age hard to determine. As usual, he was neatly but unremarkably dressed, his brown suit simply cut, a leather satchel slung across one shoulder. His face was intelligent but nondescript, the kind that was easy to forget.

And then there were his books. Manuel knew that he worked as a translator for a firm on the Calle Ricardo Soriano, and could often be seen with books in both English and Spanish, as well as a third, unfamiliar language, perhaps Hebrew. Yet for all his close observation of the translator's unassuming life, he still had no idea why anyone would want this man dead.

Caught up in these thoughts, Manuel belatedly noticed that the translator had turned onto a different street than usual. He quickened his pace. If the target was taking another route home, it would upset his plans. For a second, he considered calling his partner, then decided to wait and see where the other man was going. From his pocket, he withdrew the rum, which would allow him to pose as a drunk, if necessary. Taking a careful swig, he spat it out, then continued into the night.

A short time later, some distance away, the pale man was waiting on the Calle Lobatas, in a doorway across from the villa where the translator lived. In his right hand, well out of sight, he held his pistol, and he had stashed the shotgun nearby, tucking it into one of the heavy planters that lined the sidewalk.

As he lurked in the shadows, waiting for the translator to appear, he was startled by a noise at his side. His cell phone was ringing. Cursing softly, he pulled the phone from his pocket and checked the display. It was Manuel. Turning away from the street, he answered. "What is it?"

There was no response. He was about to speak again when he felt something cold and hard press against his back. A voice came in his ear: "You should always turn the volume down."

The pale man did not move. Out of the corner of his eye, he saw the man behind him close the phone he was holding, put it away, and take something else from his pocket. It was Manuel's pint of rum. He tossed the bottle to the ground, where it shattered to pieces on the curb.

As the pale man closed his eyes, the other man took away his pistol and phone, then checked him for weapons. At last, he withdrew the gun. "Take a step forward and turn around."

The pale man obeyed. When he turned, he found himself facing the translator, who was holding Manuel's pistol. He had removed his shoes and was standing in stocking feet. In his other hand, he held the phone. "If I were to check the call history, what would I find?"

"*Nada,*" the pale man said. "We wouldn't be stupid enough to carry our real phones."

The translator seemed to grant this point. He slid the phone into his pocket. "Where are you from?"

"London," the pale man said. "But it doesn't matter. I could be from anywhere."

"I know." The translator raised the gun. "You were in a red van. Where is it?"

"Around the corner." The pale man jerked his head. "If you want it, it's yours."

"First, we're going for a ride." As he spoke, the translator reached over with his free hand and undid the flap of his satchel. The pale man watched with interest as the translator slid the pistol into the bag, still holding it, then motioned for him to go first. "Hands away from your body."

The pale man turned obligingly, his hands raised, and stepped onto the pavement, his eyes scanning the deserted street. Across from him stood the villa. The van was parked around the corner, just out of sight.

And up ahead, a few steps in the same direction, was the planter with the gun inside.

He went slowly forward. The planter was directly in front of him. As he walked on, straining to hear the translator's faint footsteps, his eyes remained fixed on that cluster of flowers. A single quick movement forward and down, and the gun would be in his hands. It would be easy.

Another step. Now the planter was within reach. It seemed to fill his entire field of vision. And he was just about to walk past it when, from overhead, there came the sound of a shutter being drawn back.

Behind him, the translator looked up at the woman who had appeared at the window of the villa. The pale man saw his chance. Falling to his knees, as if he had stumbled at the curb, he found himself at eye level with the planter. His hand plunged into the flowers and closed at once on the shotgun's grip.

The translator had no time to draw his own gun. As the pale man brought the shotgun around in a flurry of leaves, shouting, the translator simply raised the hand in his satchel and fired, blowing a hole in the bottom of the bag.

Silence. The pale man looked down at the wound in his chest, the gun tumbling from his fingers. For a second, he seemed inclined to retrieve it, but evidently decided that it wasn't worth the effort, and fell back against the whitewashed wall. Then he slid to the ground.

Coming forward, the translator kicked the shotgun away, then reached down and tore open the dying man's shirt, revealing a gout of arterial blood, which came in waves with each slowing heartbeat.

He looked into the pale man's face. His voice was a whisper. "Tell me who sent you."

The pale man only stared back. A moment later, the flow of blood slackened, then ceased altogether.

From above, voices were rising. Ignoring them, the translator checked the dead man's pockets, finding nothing but a set of keys, which he took. Then he parted the man's shirt more carefully. On the pale chest, through the blood, he could make out a tattoo. It had been etched in white ink, the lines raised, and depicted a bird, perhaps an eagle, with a pair of outstretched wings.

The translator studied the tattoo, memorizing it, then pulled the shirt shut again. From overhead, he heard more voices. He pocketed the keys, then headed up the block, leaving the pale man lying among the flowers.

Rounding the corner, the translator, whose name in another life had been Ilya Severin, and in darker times the Scythian, moved quickly through the shadows. He was angry with himself. At first, Marbella had seemed safe, but he should have known that it was still too close to home. He had grown careless. And it would not be enough to simply vanish once more.

He looked back over his shoulder at the villa, thinking of the shelves of books he had collected over the past two years. It was a shame to leave them behind. The books were a part of him, in ways that few others would ever understand, and now he would never see them again.

But even as he disappeared into the darkness, he knew that there would be others.

I

✠

November 28–
December 14, 2010

I will not serve that in which I no longer believe, whether it call itself my home, my fatherland, or my church: and I will try to express myself in some mode of life or art as freely as I can and as wholly as I can, using for my defence the only arms I allow myself to use—silence, exile, and cunning.

—James Joyce, *A Portrait of the Artist as a Young Man*

The photographer is an armed version of the solitary walker reconnoitering, stalking, cruising the urban inferno, the voyeuristic stroller who discovers the city as a landscape of voluptuous extremes.

—Susan Sontag, *On Photography*

1

"This isn't working," Renata said, glaring through the camera viewfinder. "I don't know what it is, but I'm not convinced by this."

The models reclining on the stage said nothing. One was wearing a diaphanous Dior gown, the other nearly nude, both with wet hair and skin so pale that it photographed as almost translucent. If it weren't for the second girl's eyes, which had been darkened with charcoal shadow into deep raccoon rings, even Lasse Karvonen, who was very good with faces, would have had trouble telling them apart.

Karvonen was seated at a wheeled cart at one edge of the studio, his laptop covered with a plastic shade. The stage itself, set against a gray backdrop, was lit bright and hot, and the fans only pushed the air around without making the room any cooler. Music droned from a stereo on the wall: *Rave on down through time and space, down through the corridors—*

Renata thumbed the shutter release lever a few more times, as if taking out her frustration on the mechanism itself, then stormed over to the laptop, almost twisting herself up in the tether that snaked between the camera and the computer. Stylists and assistants scattered out of the way. Karvonen was aware of their eyes on his face, pleading silently with him to make it stop.

He glanced over at the photographer as she came up beside him. Renata Russell was a lean woman in her late forties, her long mane of hair shot through with silver. She was wearing a man's brown silk shirt with damp patches under the arms, and as she leaned over the laptop, he found that he recognized her smell. "I don't know what to do. They're dead on camera."

As a stylist ran over to the models, hurrying to repair the damage caused by trickles of sweat, Karvonen pointed to the screen. "It isn't them. We need a stronger side-light. I told you this before."

"And I told you before that it's already too bright. We're blowing out the detail."

Karvonen enlarged the image on the laptop. The photo had been laid out to account for the magazine's gutter, which was invisible, but had to be treated like another person, lurking unseen at the heart of the shot. "If it's too bright, we can darken it later. But if it's too dark—"

"You see, that's the thing," Renata said. "You want to fix everything in the computer. I'm trying to get it in the goddamned camera."

Karvonen, opening up a contrast curve, said nothing. On any other day, he suspected, she would have been fine with his approach, but tonight was different. This wasn't an assignment, but an audition piece, and everything from lights to craft services was being paid for out of her own pocket. He chose his words carefully. "Even if you're right about the girls, the detail is killing us. We need to fuck it up a little. If we pump up the contrast here—"

He finished adjusting the curve. At once, the shadows

were deepened and the highlights increased. "Look. If we put in a sidelight, we lose detail, but think about what we gain. All we see are those burning eyes."

Renata looked at the screen. At last she nodded. "All right. But I won't do this unless we can do it for real. Get an umbrella from the van. I'll change formats. Somebody want to give me a hand?"

As an intern ran up to Renata, Karvonen headed for the door to the street. At thirty, he moved with an athlete's grace, although he had nothing but contempt for most sports. For a photographer's assistant, he was muscular and tall, with long, nearly white blond hair that made a sort of halo around him in pictures whenever he was caught against any kind of light.

Outside, the van was parked at the curb. The studio, which was rented for the night, lay on a quiet side street in Holland Park, not far from Renata's home on Pottery Lane. Karvonen unlocked the van's rear doors and fished through the jumble of equipment, finally unearthing a silver photographer's umbrella. Closing the door, he was about to head inside again when, glancing down, he saw the symbol that had been chalked on the pavement.

It was a red crosshairs, drawn, as if by a child, on the rough stone of the curbside.

Karvonen studied it for a moment. Stepping onto the curb, he erased the chalk circle with the heel of his boot, then slung the umbrella over one shoulder and went back into the studio.

The rest of the shoot took less than twenty minutes. When they were done, Renata handed the camera to an intern and applauded herself. The crew, relieved, clapped politely, then began packing up the equipment.

As Karvonen put away his laptop, he became aware of two female presences hovering at his side. Turning, he found himself facing the models, their makeup gone, changed into matching hoodies and jeans. The taller one nudged the other, who gave him a smile. "Hi, there."

"Hi," Karvonen said, winding a length of cable around his arm. "What do you want?"

"So we're staying at a model apartment with a girl from our agency," the smaller one said shyly. "It's not too far from here. We're heading out for a drink soon, if you wanted to join us—"

Karvonen set the cable aside. "I have plans. And I don't know if you should be going out anyway. Renata was right. You're dead on camera. Ask yourself if this is something you want to celebrate."

Before they could respond, he picked up his laptop case and turned away. As soon as they had wandered off again, hurt, he looked at his watch. Half past seven. He was about to head for the door when a woman's voice came from behind him. "Don't tell me you didn't want to fuck either of them."

"You know better," Karvonen said without turning. "I don't sleep with little girls."

"These days, it seems, you hardly sleep with anyone." Renata sauntered into his line of sight. She had changed into a cashmere overcoat with a long, witchy scarf, a Birkin bag over one arm. "Am I going to see you later?"

As the lights of the studio went down, Karvonen headed for the doors. "I'm busy."

"I see." Renata drew the coat around her as they went outside. "Well, if your plans change, maybe we can do another session tonight."

They reached the van, which was yellow, but seemed white under the sodium lamps. Karvonen handed her the laptop, then watched as she climbed inside. "I'll do what I can. Should I bring the girls?"

Renata only shut the door in his face. Karvonen, grinning, put on his gloves and went over to his motorcycle, which was parked at the curb. Climbing onto the bike, he pulled on his helmet and roared off without looking back. He would need to push it to get to the meeting on time.

A quarter of an hour later, he was at a pub in Highgate, not far from the cemetery. The interior was a warm cave in dark wood and leather, fringed lamps hanging from the ceiling, the lintels picked out in damask. Karvonen went up to the curved green bar and took a spot at the end, next to an elderly man in a suit who seemed absorbed by his mobile phone. The bartender came up to him and smiled, her braids pinned up on the top of her head. "What can I get you?"

"Lapin Kulta, please." Karvonen waited as she brought the beer, then gave her a five-pound note, telling her to keep the change. Turning away, he raised the bottle to his lips and took a long draught.

At his side, the man in the suit spoke quietly without looking up from his phone. He was missing part of the first two fingers on his right hand. "What name did Achilles use when he hid among the women?"

"Pyrrha," Karvonen said without turning. "Because of his red hair." He took another swig of beer. "What is it, then?"

"Three men in London," the man said. "One delivery. And a bit of retouching."

In the corner, where the window seat was heaped with

games, two men were playing chess, their eyes lowered in concentration. Watching them, Karvonen replied softly. "I'll see what I can do."

The other man said nothing. A second later, he gathered up his things and left the bar, having never looked up from his phone.

Once the man was gone, Karvonen finished his beer, then headed for the men's room, which lay at the rear of the pub. Going inside, he found himself alone in a cramped, dank room lined with black and white tile. An industrial sink ran along the far wall. On the door of the toilet stall, nearly lost among a scrawl of other graffiti, was chalked a red crosshairs.

Karvonen went into the stall, closing the door behind him. Leaning down, he reached behind the toilet tank, where his fingers brushed a taped bundle. He pulled it loose, then brought it into sight.

Inside the plastic bag, there were three items. The first was a roll of film, which he slid into his jacket pocket. The second was an encrypted phone and charger. He switched the phone on, then pocketed this as well.

The last item was a pistol. Removing it, Karvonen ejected the clip and examined the cartridges. Then, sticking the magazine into his back pocket, he pulled back the slide and checked the chamber, which was empty. He pressed the release, sending the slide forward again. Raising the gun, he looked down the sights at the graffiti on the inside of the door, then pulled the trigger. *Click*.

Satisfied, he slid the magazine back into the grip and tucked the gun into his belt, under his jacket. He flushed the toilet, then opened the door and emerged from the stall. After washing his hands, he left the bathroom.

A minute later, he was back on the street. As he went over to his bike, he checked his watch and smiled. He had a number of things to do in the meantime, but if he hurried, he could be in bed with Renata by ten.

2

Even before the constable said a word, Rachel Wolfe knew what was coming. The officer at the door seemed like little more than a boy in a woolly pully, his face red and cheerful beneath its foolish helmet, as he studied her warrant card and returned it with a grin. "An American, then, are we?"

Wolfe smiled as gamely as she could. Somehow, no matter what she did in this city, they always sensed that she was a stranger. "Yes, I'm from New York. But I think I'm in London now. Are you going to let me in?"

"Afraid I have orders to limit the number of individuals on the scene," the officer said apologetically. He gestured to the other side of the barrier tape, which was strung at the level of his waist. "Perhaps you can wait outside?"

Wolfe only pursed her lips and took a step back, as if to get a sense of her surroundings. She was in Stoke Newington, standing before one of the many garages and hand car washes that lined these dingy streets. A pair of panda cars was parked across the way, along with the green van of the scenes-of-crime unit.

Off to one side, next to the door where she was standing, lay the garage itself, its windows covered in steel mesh. Through the dirty glass, Wolfe could make out two men in white suits moving like ghouls around the interior, one with a camera, the other with a clipboard.

Turning back to the officer, she handed him a business card. "Listen, can you do me a favor? Give this to the crime scene manager, the one in the garage, and tell him I'm here to see Alan Powell. It's an urgent personal matter."

Wolfe sealed the deal with a bright missionary smile, the kind that had opened doors for her before. The officer looked uncertainly at the card, which bore the unfamiliar insignia of the FBI. "Well, all right. Hold on."

He disappeared down the corridor, his shoes clicking rapidly against the linoleum. As soon as he was out of sight, Wolfe glanced over her shoulder to make sure that no one else was watching, then simply stepped over the blue-and-white barrier tape and entered the building.

Inside, she found herself in a foyer that smelled strongly of smoke. The front door had been knocked off its hinges, the bolt still intact in the frame, and was leaning against the wall to her right. As she moved forward, keeping to the approach path, splinters of wood crunched beneath her feet.

Going upstairs, she followed the sound of voices into what turned out to be the bathroom. In the far corner, near the tub, a plainclothes detective, probably an inspector, was examining something on the floor, his ample body blocking her line of sight. Kneeling beside him was a dark, lanky figure in a surgical mask, evidently the Home Office pathologist. From here, she couldn't see what they were studying, but it seemed to be the source of the smoke.

Standing a few steps away, his back to her, was Alan Powell. When she entered the room, he glanced around to see who it was, then gave her a nod. "Morning, Wolfe. Interesting, isn't it?"

"Very interesting," Wolfe said. Looking him over, she saw that he was even more disheveled than usual. With his thick glasses and high forehead, he did not cut an imposing figure, but a year ago, when he had requested her as a liaison, there were good reasons why she had said yes. And although he seemed abstracted now, when she looked at him more closely, she saw a familiar gleam in his eyes.

In any case, she knew better than to bother him here. Instead of crowding around whatever was beside the tub, she began going over the rest of the bathroom, knowing that there was no need to hurry.

The room was small and stuffy, the ceiling and walls covered in soot. Above the sink, a mirror gave back a tarnished version of her own face. It looked washed-out and faded, which was not entirely the mirror's fault. Over the past year, she had adopted a more severe style, tying back her blond hair and using only a civilized minimum of makeup, as far as possible from the perfect Molly Mormon. As she studied her face now, though, it seemed to her that she had succeeded all too well.

She put on a pair of gloves to check the wastebasket under the sink, which contained a few rags coated with grease. A bar of abrasive hand soap lay next to the faucet. Inside the rim of the basin, there were several brown stains. Examining them, she found that they were relatively fresh.

Behind her, the inspector's cell phone rang. Answering it, he moved into the hallway, clearing a space. Wolfe straightened up at once and, trying to seem casual, went over to the spot he had vacated, where she got her first good look at what had been left here for them to find.

Kneeling on the bathroom floor, propped against the tub, was a man's body. He had been shot in the head, then set on fire. His flesh was blackened into a shiny shell, the skin of his chest, arms, and legs split by the heat. The body's pose was particularly striking: the arms raised and elbows bent, the burned fists at the level of the face, as if in rage or supplication.

The pathologist, who was still crouching on the floor, seemed to notice her for the first time. He prodded the body's flexed joints with a gloved finger. "Pugilistic attitude. Heat tightens the muscles and gives you this pose. Looks like he's praying, right?" He turned to Powell, who was standing nearby. "As I was saying, he was dead before he was lit up. Burned to destroy trace evidence. And before rigor set in, which means within two hours of death."

Powell made room for Wolfe to approach. "Any ideas about the accelerant?"

"Something that burned clean and hot," the pathologist said. "When the fire truck arrived, it was already out. Could be a number of things—"

Wolfe spoke up. "It was potassium permanganate. I saw traces of it in the sink."

The pathologist, who had turned back to the body, pivoted around to face her. "What was that?"

Wolfe heard a trace of amusement in his voice but saw that it was too late to retreat. "Potassium permanganate. It burns when mixed with glycerol. I recognize the stains from my Boy Scout survival kit."

Powell smiled faintly at this, but the pathologist seemed to be taking the idea seriously. Before anyone could reply, footsteps sounded from outside, and the scene manager appeared at the door, followed by the officer Wolfe had encountered on the way in. The officer pointed to Wolfe. "That's her."

"Sorry, everyone," the scene manager said. "She didn't have authorization. Does she have permission to remain?"

The pathologist glanced at Wolfe, then turned back to the body. "She's your protégée, Alan. I'll leave it to you."

"I wouldn't call her anyone's protégée," Powell said, not unkindly. "She can stay."

As the others resumed their inspection of the dead man, the scene manager took down Wolfe's name, saying, "Watch where you step, or we'll take your shoes. Maybe best not to go anywhere at all—"

"Actually, I'm almost done here," the pathologist said, rising from beside the body. "I can show her around." He gave a nod to Wolfe, who followed him into the hallway, sensing that she was being excluded from the scene.

When the pathologist pulled down his mask, however, she saw that he was surprisingly young and rather handsome, a West Indian who was the only person of color at the garage, aside from the victim. He flashed her a charming smile. "The name's Lewis. Shall I show you around downstairs, then?"

Wolfe, who was in no mood to be charmed, made a strategic choice not to smile back. "Personally, if you don't mind, I'd like to see the guns."

Lewis seemed surprised by her abruptness. For a moment, his smile faded, only to be replaced by another, which, like its predecessor, was seductive and apparently genuine. "Of course. Follow me."

They went down the hallway to the bedroom, a cluttered space with windows facing the street on both sides. The pathologist led her to the bed in the corner. "So what is it that brings you to London?"

"I'm a liaison officer," Wolfe replied, ticking off the usual points. "Technically I'm a legal attaché with the Bureau's embassy office, but they've given me a desk in Vauxhall. I'm here to assist with investigations pertaining to international organized crime. Powell brought me in."

"I've heard that the two of you go back some time. What's he like to work with?"

"Oh, he's clearly brilliant," Wolfe said, stepping around a scene investigator who was dusting for prints. "But he's also the kind of man who can't close a case without opening two others."

On the unmade bed, an array of guns had been laid out on a plastic sheet. Each had its own label and exhibit number on a white card, placed there for photographic reference. Reaching out with a gloved hand, Wolfe examined the guns, turning them over to get a better look. Two Uzis, a Skorpion submachine gun, three pistols. She looked away. "This is all you found?"

"Yes, so far," Lewis said, following her as she went to the window. "So what's your interest in this man?"

"We were watching him. Unfortunately, we missed the part when he ended up dead." Wolfe looked at the restaurant across the street, its sign lettered in Turkish. She wondered if the officers stationed upstairs could see her.

At her side, Lewis looked out at the silent neighborhood. "A gunrunner, I hear?"

"An armorer," Wolfe said. "Aldane Campbell. A machinist who lived in Dalston, although he also kept a flat above this garage. We believe that he was a leading armorer for the Yardies."

"So what are we talking about? Conversion of starter pistols into guns, or what?"

Listening to Lewis's questions, Wolfe wondered whether he took any personal interest in the dead man, who had been a member of the dominant West Indian gang in London. "That's how it began. But he was a mechanical prodigy. If a shipment of guns came from overseas, he inspected them and returned them to working condition. A man with good hands."

"Looks like he got more than he expected. But at least you have the guns, right?"

Wolfe did not reply. A second later, the scene manager approached, saying that Lewis was needed in the next room. Excusing himself, the pathologist gave her another smile, then headed off. Wolfe watched him go, feeling surprisingly sorry, but instead of following, she crossed to the other side of the bedroom, where a second row of windows opened onto the alley at the rear of the building.

A voice came from over her shoulder. "He must have entered the building through the back. You can't see it from across the street. We were probably watching the whole time he was here. Rather lucky of him."

"Maybe." Wolfe turned to look at Powell, who was standing a few steps behind her. "Or maybe he knew the place was being watched, which means we have a leak. Rather unlucky for us."

"I know," Powell said. A faint odor of smoke was wafting off his clothes, and Wolfe suspected she smelled the same way. "But if our man was killed for a reason, he may be more interesting dead than alive. Nice work, by the way, on the potassium permanganate. Lewis says it was a good call. He's a clever one himself—"

Wolfe accepted the praise, but she still smarted from before. "So what now? You've seen these flipping guns. This isn't the shipment we expected. We were hoping for something big. Abakans. Kalashnikovs. I could go on."

"I'm aware of that." Powell removed his glasses and, in a gesture she had come to recognize, polished the lenses one at a time. "But to tell you the truth, I was never particularly interested in the guns."

He put his glasses back on, smiling slightly, and headed out of the room. Wolfe let him go, then glanced down at their pathetic haul. Picking up the Skorpion, she hefted it expertly, then looked down its sights at the view outside. It was typical, she thought, lowering the gun again. The operation had failed, their best lead was dead, and Powell was returning to the body as if meeting an old friend.

3

From the window of the loft, which stood on the third floor of an apartment building in the Shoreditch Triangle, the flats across the street seemed like a grid of dioramas, opening onto slices of discrete lives. Most were artists' studios with easels, racks, and shelves of books and journals. In one of the windows, a woman was sculpting something in clay, her profile outlined against the light.

Karvonen looked out at the view for a moment longer, then drew the drapes. A warm, muscled creature was pressing against his legs. He stroked its downy head, then went into the kitchen. As the cat mewed at his feet, its tail beating back and forth, he opened a can of fish and set it on the floor. Then he took a beer from the refrigerator and brought it over to his work area.

The loft in which he resided was carved out into two roomy halves, the work and living spaces separated by a tiny kitchen. The living space was divided by bookshelves into a sitting area and bedroom, while the work area included a computer with two flat-screen monitors, a pair of large printers, and, through a door at the rear of the studio, the darkroom.

Taking a seat at the computer, he brought it out of

sleep mode, then opened a file. It was a shot of the models from earlier that week, taken from very close, one girl turned to face the camera, the other with her lips against her double's throat. He dragged the window onto the larger of the two screens, then put on the music from the shoot: *Rave on, John Donne, rave on, thy holy fool—*

Karvonen opened his beer and got to work. At this point in his career, when he had been working as a photographer's assistant and retoucher for many years, he did his work with fluency and skill. He knew that there were elements of the craft that could never be taught, no matter how carefully one trained. Which was also true, as it happened, of the other things he did so well.

He began with a straight print, on matte paper, at one-quarter size. Removing it from the printer, he compared it to the version on the screen, checking the image profile. On the print itself, he circled a number of areas with a grease pencil. Then he began the absorbing work of improving on reality.

Half an hour later, the shadows were sharper, the highlights more intense, giving the women a glossy, inhuman sheen. Karvonen flattened the adjustment layers, then printed a proof on cold-tone paper. He made a few more changes, using a separate curve to account for the qualities of the paper itself, then took out an uncut sheet and prepared to print the full version.

As he was printing the final proof, the bell of his flat rang. Rising, he went over to the intercom. "Yes?"

A female voice came over the speakers: "Let me in. It's fucking freezing out here—"

Without replying, Karvonen held down a button to unlock the door downstairs. Then he went back to the printer. Removing the finished print, he hung it beside the others, securing it to the wall with refrigerator magnets.

As he stood back to regard the full portfolio, there was a knock on the door. Closing the file on his computer, he went to the door and opened it. Renata stood in the entryway. "Am I intruding?"

"Always," Karvonen said. As she kicked off her shoes, he took her coat, his hands brushing her shoulders. Underneath, she was wearing a mannish suit with a Hermès scarf knotted carelessly at the neck. The suit was wrinkled and seamed, as if she had retrieved it from a pile on her bedroom floor.

Renata let her bag drop, then reached down and scooped up the cat, which was pushing itself against her legs. Cooing, she held it close, getting gray hairs across the front of her jacket, and went over to the desk, her eyes caught by the posted photographs. "Are these ready?"

"Yes, I just finished the last." As Renata studied the pictures, Karvonen went into the kitchen and took a bottle of white wine from the refrigerator. He poured two glasses, then went back to the desk, handing one to Renata.

Releasing the cat, Renata took a sip, then turned away from the proofs. "Good. Send me the files by tomorrow. I've already shown a few shots to Dior. They're excited, but they want to see the rest."

She went into the living area. As Karvonen followed, he wondered whether she suspected how much he knew about her situation, and why she wanted this contract so badly. Using his own considerable resources, he had determined that Renata had gone deeply into debt since her divorce. Her air of glamour had been maintained with multiple mortgages, forcing her to consolidate her debts with an art investment fund, using her portfolio as collateral. At the moment, she owed close to half a million pounds, which, if unpaid after six months, would cost her the rights to her own work.

At her worst, Renata had grown paranoid, accusing her own staff of passing information to her creditors. More recently, her fears had eased, and there were even moments when he suspected that she welcomed her predicament. Debt was a clarifying force, editing away everything that wasn't essential, like the retoucher's brush. And he sometimes had the feeling that Renata, wearying of the complexities of her own life, had subconsciously courted this purification.

A bottle of wine later, the cat had been banished to the balcony, and they were in the bedroom together. Renata, her clothes in a heap on the floor, was prowling around like a tiger, stripped down to her panties and bra. "Those fuckers," she said, her voice slurred. "I can't believe they bailed on me like this—"

Karvonen removed a key from his pocket and unlocked the lowermost drawer of his bureau. "What did they say?"

"Nothing. They're like a bunch of little girls." Renata ran her fingers through her hair, taking a fistful in each hand. "So get this. Two years ago, I did a photo spread of the top businessmen in London. A hundred traders in suits—"

Karvonen took a small plastic bag from the drawer. "Yes, I remember that shoot."

Renata continued to pace. "The next year, the magazine did the same thing, but with a revised list of names. Then, yesterday, they tell me they're canceling this year's spread. It was just too hard, they said, to explain to fund managers why they were dropped from the list. It's fucking ridiculous for them to treat me like this. Like they don't even know who I am—"

Karvonen laid out two lines of white powder, then said, rather slowly, "It seems to me that this might be an opening."

Renata came over and lowered her face to the bureau, drawing her hair back. A second later, she raised her head, her fingertips fluttering before her nose. "What do you mean?"

He watched as she breathed deeply through her nostrils, then lowered her head again. "We approach a different magazine. Tell them we want to do a portfolio of the city's top business leaders. The ones who survived the downturn. Not a group shot, but a series of portraits. Then, after we take the pictures, the magazine throws a party for everyone involved—"

"—and we sell them copies of the prints. I get it." When Renata came up from the bureau the second time, her eyes were gleaming. "Large format, signed and numbered, five thousand pounds each—"

Karvonen stripped off his shirt and pants. He slid the bag back into the bureau, locked it, and got into bed. "Exactly. A quarter of a million right there. Round it down, and call it two hundred thousand. You see?"

Renata peeled off her panties in one quick movement and straddled him. Reaching back, she unhooked her bra, revealing her small pointed breasts, but seemed caught up in his proposal. "I even know who to ask first. Not just the rejects from this year's list, but the traders who are still making deals. Like the guy I met last year, James Morley. He's always had a thing for me—"

Karvonen, his hands on her slender hips, paused. "I don't think I remember him."

"Hey, it doesn't matter. You just leave it up to me, kid." Renata ran her hands across the hard surface of his chest, her fingers cool against his breastplate of skin. "God, look at you. You're so perfect. Just a flawless piece of stone. There's so much that I could teach you—"

Reaching out, she turned off the light. As she sank slowly onto him, he glanced over at the bureau, which was barely visible in the darkness. In the lowermost drawer, in a secret compartment, were the prints from the roll of film he had retrieved. When developed, they had turned out to consist of some documents, a few photo-copied diagrams, and the names of three men.

Thinking of these names, Karvonen was struck by the coincidence of a moment ago, but he quickly dismissed it from his mind. There were more important things to consider. The armorer had been easy enough, but the next task would be more difficult. He had already begun acquiring the things he would need, including the con-struction gear at the back of his closet, next to the box with the gun.

Karvonen looked coldly at the woman above him, her face in shadow, and reminded himself that he had to stay focused. Much remained to be done, and his deadline was only three weeks away.

4

Wolfe began every day on her knees. Mormons were taught to pray for half an hour each morning and night, asking to be opened up to the Holy Ghost, but these days, this meant waiting uncomfortably for a voice that never came. When she was younger, God had spoken to her directly, or so she had once believed. Now the divine had passed out of her life altogether, and she was left wondering why God didn't just come out and show himself, without all the needless mystery.

After another moment, Wolfe rose from her bedroom floor. They had put her up in a serviced flat in Vauxhall, the space scrupulously clean, almost sterile, its windows looking out onto the dirty sky. She went into the kitchen, where a lump of bread dough covered in plastic was rising on the counter, next to her wallet and keys. Wolfe slid them into her purse, then slung her laptop case over her shoulder, feeling, as usual, the absence of a gun.

Outside, moving past two wings of gray concrete and green glass, Wolfe headed for the river, pausing for a moment to regard the listless ditch of the Thames. A few seagulls were perching on the mud of the bank. At first, she had been excited by the prospect of a river view, but its sodden reality had been yet another case of this city refusing to meet her expectations.

A year ago, Powell's call had come at a time when she was already hungering for a change. The Bureau's glass ceiling was no worse than any other, but as in most organizations built on mentorship, it was hard for a young woman to find a sponsor. Powerful men were wary of the rumors that inevitably accompanied such relationships, and while a female patron could sometimes be found, Wolfe, who had never outgrown certain mother issues, had quietly blown several of her best chances. As a result, after a brilliant start out of Quantico, she had been stranded in an endless stream of warrants and wires. Which was why she had jumped so eagerly at Powell's offer.

And now it had all come to nothing. Walking along the river, she tried to consider the situation as objectively as possible. In less than two months, on completion of her stint as a liaison, she was scheduled to go home. She had hoped to return with a major operation to her credit, and until yesterday she had seemed very close. Instead, she had been left with nothing but a dead armorer and a few reactivated guns, which made it all the more crucial that she find something to use now.

Powell, she knew, would want to press onward with the case, but perhaps it was best to cut their losses and make whatever arrests they could. As she continued along the river, though, Wolfe felt further from a decision than ever. And her mood was not helped by the realization, which had gradually grown over the past few months, that sooner or later she was going to leave the Church.

Her destination was only ten minutes away. Unlike the

Metropolitan Police, with its ostentatious building and rotating sign, the Serious Organised Crime Agency kept a studiously low profile. The agency's headquarters were located in an industrial office park, its three nondescript brick buildings trimmed with aluminum, with a high steel fence surrounding the campus.

Wolfe went inside, giving the guard a smile. Continuing along the concrete walk, she entered the building on the left, its interior walls painted an institutional gray, and took an elevator to the third floor. When she emerged, she found herself in a cubicle farm where rows of other officers, mostly men, were breakfasting on bacon rolls and cups of steaming tea.

Her own workstation, as always, was the neatest desk in sight. Hanging up her coat, Wolfe glanced to either side. The two chairs next to hers were empty. She paused. "Oh, no—"

From behind her came the sound of efficient footsteps. Turning, she found herself face-to-face with Maya Asthana, the officer tasked with tracing the financial side of the weapons trade. Even with glasses and a ponytail, Asthana was a knockout, and the smartest person Wolfe had met here so far, even if she could sometimes be seen flashing a greedy eye at her own engagement ring. "We've been wondering where you were. The briefing started ten minutes ago."

Wolfe, dumping her things on her desk, followed Asthana across the crowded floor. "I thought it wasn't until this afternoon."

"Rescheduled," Asthana said briskly. "Now that our best lead is dead and barbecued, we need to decide what to do next."

"That's why I'm here," Wolfe said, wishing mostly for a cup of cocoa. With a sinking feeling, she realized that she would probably be asked to give an opinion at the briefing, but was still as undecided as ever.

They reached the conference room. Inside the windowless space, eight officers sat at a long table, with others hovering at the edges. Although several empty chairs remained, Wolfe hung back at the doorway.

At the head of the table sat Dana Cornwall, the deputy director of the intelligence directorate. Cornwall was in her late fifties, her hair layered in silver feathers, and as one of the highest-ranking women at the agency, she was a major reason why Wolfe had asked to be assigned to this division. At her elbow lay a tabloid with a red masthead, the angle making it impossible to read.

Powell, who was seated at the deputy director's side, glanced up at Wolfe, then continued his briefing. "Firearms have been sent to Lambeth for comparison. We're working our way through the prints, although smears indicate that the killer wore gloves. Cameras are being checked from nearby estates, but—"

Cornwall interrupted. "So what you're saying is that we have nothing. We don't even know why this armorer was murdered. And until we find out who killed him, we all look like bloody idiots."

She held up the newspaper. On the inside page Wolfe saw an image of the armorer's garage, along with a smaller photo of the late victim, apparently taken from a police mug shot. The headline, in all capitals: *YARDIE ARMORER TORCHED IN STOKE NEWINGTON*.

"The case has already hit the papers," Cornwall continued, throwing the paper down. "In half an hour, I need to explain to the Home Office how a notorious criminal and potential informant was killed right under our noses. Either we were inexcusably careless, or . . ."

Cornwall trailed off. Wolfe knew that she was reluctant to mention the possibility of a leak, although it was clearly on everyone's mind. At last, she spoke again. "You all know that this agency is facing problems. If we don't show results, we may not exist by the end of the year. So what do we get if we move now?"

A stocky, balding officer spoke up. This was Arnold Garber, Wolfe's other desk mate, his sleeves rolled up past his meaty forearms. "A dozen arrests, maybe more. We can shut down the greater part of the arms trade in Dalston and Stoke Newington. If nothing else, we'd get these guns out of the hands of the Yardies—"

Asthana, who had taken a seat on the other side of the table, broke in. "But then we're just leaving an opening for someone else. If we don't smash the larger system, there's no point to any of this."

"Especially these days," Powell said. "With the end of the art trade, Russian state security is weaker, but only on the civilian side. Their rivals in military intelligence, which is a separate world from the Chekists, are stronger than ever. Now that the war in Georgia is over, there's a whole new source of guns headed this way unless we can shut down these networks first. And the arms trade wouldn't exist at all if it weren't approved at the highest levels of the Russian government—"

The room erupted. In the corner, Wolfe was tuning out the clamor of voices when she saw the deputy director's eyes on her own. "Wolfe, you're our liaison," Cornwall said. "What do you think?"

At once, the conference room fell silent. Feeling thrust into the spotlight, Wolfe took a breath, sensing nothing resembling divine inspiration, and spoke slowly. "The Bureau's official stance remains unchanged. We've seen an explosion in armed crime on both sides of the ocean, fueled by Russian guns. To stop the flow of illegal weapons, we need to go to the source."

"Yes, yes, I know all that," Cornwall said irritably. "But what about *this* operation?"

Wolfe saw Powell waiting for her response. Before she knew what she was going to say, she heard herself speak: "If we wait any longer, we'll lose our chance. We need to move in now."

Across the room, Powell sank back into his chair, the disappointment visible on his face. Cornwall nodded. "All right. I think I have enough to go on. I'll inform you of my decision soon."

The meeting ended. As the other officers left, Wolfe went up to Powell. "Alan, I—"

Powell ignored her and turned to Cornwall, who was heading for the door. "We need to talk about surveillance. My guys at the Met want to watch the garage until the end of the week, in case anyone else shows up."

"A bit like locking the barn door, isn't it?" When she stood, Cornwall revealed herself to be startlingly small, coming only to the level of Powell's chin, but there was no doubt as to who was in charge. "They're only interested in the red-ink time. Shut it down. We'll talk later about what comes next."

She left the conference room. Once they were alone, Wolfe turned to Powell again. "Alan, don't kill me."

"It's all right," Powell said. He reached up to remove

his glasses, then, as if thinking better of it, lowered his hand again. "I don't blame you. If I were in your position, I might have stabbed myself in the back as well."

Wolfe followed him to the door. "If I wanted to stab you in the back, I'd have to get in line. This is the right call."

"You're wrong. This isn't when you shut a case down. It's when you break it wide open." Powell paused at the door. "I expect that Cornwall will listen to your recommendation. She likes you, and it's safe to say that she's lost patience with me. But when this is all over, you'll see that I was right."

Turning off the lights, he left the room. Standing in the darkness, Wolfe found herself thinking of a pilgrimage she had made soon after arriving in this city. Baker Street had turned out to be nothing but a line of shops and fast food restaurants, and she had sensed, even then, that this city was only going to frustrate her ambitions. There were no great detectives here, and she was far from one herself, just a hopeless exile, alone, from the country of the saints.

5

The agent at passport control, an attractive woman in a blue head scarf, studied the document in her small hands, then looked up at the traveler before her. "And what is the purpose of your visit?"

"To see a few sights," the traveler said. "And perhaps to look up some friends."

The agent's eyes met his own, their expression cool but oddly teasing. "And how did you choose this city?"

He smiled. "I used to live here. I am curious to find out how things have changed."

"I see." She held his gaze for another beat, then stamped his passport and handed it back. "Welcome to London, Mr. Muromets."

"Thank you." Ilya Severin tucked the passport into the inside pocket of his suit jacket, then continued on through customs. After changing some money, he bought a newspaper and prepaid phone at the airport drugstore, then went down to the lower level, where he gave a taxi driver an address in Golders Green. As they drove away, he set his watch an hour back, looking out at the overcast sky. Then he opened the paper and began to scan the headlines.

It was strange to be back in London. After the attempt on his life, he had driven to Málaga, where he had retrieved cash and documents from a locker at María Zambrano Station, along with his last clean passport. The drive had given him plenty of time to think. It was impossible, he had seen, simply to fade away again. He had to learn more. Which was why he had returned to this city.

In Marbella, he had tried to disappear into books, believing that this was the life for which he had been intended. It was only now, with the clarity of hindsight, that he saw that he had really been trying to become something he was not. And he was still brooding over this fact when he opened the newspaper to the next section, nearly turning past an article about the death in Stoke Newington.

A second later, the face of the dead man, which appeared in an inset at the bottom of the page, caught his attention. Ilya frowned, then began to read the story more closely. It was not a long article, with most of the page taken up by a photo of the scene, and when he was finished, he read it again.

At last, he set the article aside, trying to decide what it meant. Aldane Campbell was a name he knew well, but there were other details, such as the use of potassium permanganate, that disturbed him even more deeply. The article implied that the armorer had been killed by one of his own associates or by an underworld taxman, but the more Ilya considered the situation, the more convinced he became that something else was at work here.

Looking out the window, he saw that they had left the highway and were moving north through a drab section of Ealing. He leaned forward to speak to the driver. "I'm sorry. But I just remembered that I need to stop somewhere else. Shacklewell Lane. Off Kingsland High Street."

"Stoke Newington?" The driver did not seem pleased by the change of plans, but finally grunted and eased the cab ponderously onto Uxbridge Road. As they headed east, Ilya settled back in his seat. The article had not given the garage's address, but he knew very well where it was.

Half an hour later, the taxi arrived at its revised destination. Ilya paid the driver, then got out. As soon as he shut the door, the cab roared off, leaving him with his luggage on the damp curb.

Taking an umbrella from his suitcase, he looked around. One side of the street was occupied by a looming council estate, all brown brick and dead windows. Across from it rose a construction site, long since abandoned, its plywood fence covered in graffiti and peeling flyers.

He opened his umbrella and headed north. This neighborhood had never been particularly lovely, but it had also been hit hard by recent austerity measures. The downturn had been only the latest in a long series of local disasters, the most visible of which had revolved around drugs and guns. Ilya had never concerned himself much with the former, but guns were another matter entirely.

As he went up the street, he passed rows of ethnic restaurants and salons, their signs the brightest colors on the cheerless block, and entered an area given over to even greater desolation. Aside from a few car washes, the buildings he saw, with their soaped or dirty windows, seemed to have been shut up for ages.

Rounding the corner, Ilya found himself on a familiar stretch of road. Up ahead, he saw the garage. Instead of approaching it at once, he continued to the end of the block, pausing in front of a Turkish restaurant. Glancing up and down the street, he saw only a few cars and buses passing along the avenue in the distance. Satisfied that he was alone, he retraced his steps to his destination.

He studied the garage. From the level of his eyes upward, it was shabby brick, but lower down, the outside wall had been painted canary yellow, curiously free of graffiti, as if spared out of respect. To his right, a mural depicted a row of brown people in wide hats working in a wheat field, presumably in an idealized Jamaica, far from the real squalor of Kingston.

Approaching the entrance, Ilya found that the front door had been replaced by a sheet of plywood, a police seal fixed across the edges. To the left stood the garage itself, set against a small paved lot, with a steel gate and two brick walls topped with loops of razor wire. Through the dusty windows, which were covered in mesh, he could make out a workbench and tool chest.

Ilya had seen this place before. Years ago, he had come to negotiate a purchase for Vasylenko, his old mentor, in the days when they had been expanding their operations from Bayswater out into the beckoning city. Brodsky, he recalled, had given them the name. According to the terms of the deal, only one man had been allowed into the garage, and Ilya had volunteered at once.

He had been expecting a disdainful Yardie, and had been surprised by Campbell's intelligence. After confirming Ilya's identity, the armorer had taken him inside, where he had removed the lid from a packing crate. Inside had been a number of welder's gloves, and inside each glove had been a gun.

Ilya had examined the weapons carefully. Most had been deconverted pistols or revolvers, but there had also been two glistening submachine guns. Ilya suspected that the armorer had included the Uzis to tempt him into expanding his purchase, but he had kept to the original order, selecting four Glocks and two Tokarevs at three hundred pounds each. He still remembered the armorer's clever hands, and how gently, almost lovingly, he had handled the weapons.

And now he had been murdered. Looking into the darkened garage, Ilya sensed that this death had not been random. He knew an intelligence operation when he saw one, and he could already discern the outlines of a plot. There were cabalists, he recalled, who spent hours gazing into water, seeking something divine in the reflection, and it was this sort of distorted image that he was contemplating now.

Even as he weighed the next step, however, he became aware of a voice in his head, soft but insistent, telling him to walk away. If he got involved, it argued, it would mean exposure, perhaps death, when he had already taken an enormous risk by coming back at all. Far better, it whispered, to leave now, while it was still possible, and bury himself in his books.

But there was another voice, a stronger one, that told him that he had been brought to this place for a reason. The more he considered it, the more it seemed to him that the timing of this murder, coming so soon after the attack in Marbella, could not be due entirely to chance.

As Ilya turned away from the garage, he found himself thinking of the image, so dear to the cabalists, of scripture as a mansion with many locked passages. In front of each door was a key, but the key did not open the door next to which it was placed. It was the task of the scholar, working diligently, to find the key for the door he wanted. And when he reflected now on his current problem, it occurred to him that he knew of at least one place where such a key might be found.

A moment later, Ilya noticed that the patter of drops above his head had fallen silent. Glancing up, he saw that the rain had ceased. And as he passed the restaurant on the corner, he closed the umbrella, allowing the unseen camera in the upstairs window to get a good shot of his face.

6

"Activity is the genius of this church," Wolfe's mother said, the brightness of her voice undiminished by five thousand miles. "If a missionary works, she gets the Holy Spirit. Which is the case with most other things in life."

"How true," Wolfe said, the telephone receiver wedged between her shoulder and left ear. She was seated at her desk in Vauxhall, eyes aching from staring at her computer for the past three hours. On the cubicle wall above the monitor, she had posted photos of the guns from the armorer's garage. Next to her keyboard was a copy of the ballistics report from Lambeth, which said that the serial numbers on each gun had been erased, and none had ever been linked to a crime.

"I was just talking to Sister Beth about this," her mother continued, speaking rapidly as always, her words tumbling out in a nonstop stream. "She asked if you'd had a chance to visit the temple in Newcastle."

"It's at the top of my list. And my friends are dying to see it. Unfortunately, I don't have a car." As she spoke, Wolfe studied the website on her screen, where dealers could sell deactivated weapons to local collectors, the guns rendered useless by the removal of crucial components. For most citizens in the United Kingdom, these were the only kinds of firearms that could be legally purchased.

The problem, Wolfe knew, was that such weapons did not always remain deactivated. Guns that operated on the blowback principle, like Uzis, Stens, or various crude automatics from Eastern Europe, could be restored to working order by any machinist with a minimum of skill. And although the guns at the garage had been carefully erased of any sign of their provenance, it might still be possible to determine who could have sold similar guns in the past.

All the same, it was a long shot, and at a time when she had expected to be closing a major case, it felt stingingly like grasping at straws. Wolfe realized that she had missed her mother's last sentence. "What was that?"

"I said you need to be careful. I know it's exciting to be away from home, but you can't get distracted by work, at least not without a higher purpose. As your grandmother might say, it can be dangerous there in Babylon."

This last statement was punctuated by a quick laugh, as if her mother was lightly mocking her own sentiments, but Wolfe knew that she really wasn't joking at all. She noticed that Asthana, who was seated at the next desk, was looking over at her curiously. "Funny, but they don't call it Babylon here. It's London. Like how they call an elevator a lift—"

Clicking onto a new page, she broke off. The image here was that of a submachine gun set against a gray background. It was a deactivated Skorpion, the same model, as far as she could tell, that had been found in the armorer's garage. And looking at the description, she saw that it was being offered, promisingly, by a dealer based in Islington, not far from Campbell's neighborhood.

"Well, I'm just glad you'll be coming home soon," her mother said. "Anyway, I know you're super busy, so I'll let you go. You know that your dad and I will always be proud of you—"

"Thanks, Mom. I know." After saying goodbye, Wolfe hung up, then wrote down the dealer's information. Out of the corner of her eye, she saw Asthana looking at her. "Don't say anything."

"I wouldn't dream of it," Asthana said, typing away at her terminal. "You should talk to my mother sometime. We've barely spoken since I told her that I wasn't going to get married in Lucknow. When I told her I wanted a green wedding, she thought it meant I'd be wearing an emerald sari."

Wolfe smiled. "She'll forgive you in the end, even if it kills both of you first."

"Yes, I know." Asthana spun around in her chair. "Which reminds me. You're leaving in two months, and you still haven't met Devon. We're having a drink with some friends at the Lavender Pub on Friday. Garber will be coming, and maybe a few others. Interested?"

"I'd love to, but I have a lot going on," Wolfe said evasively. In fact, she had been dodging Asthana's invitations for months, having never come to terms with this city's pub culture, where it seemed that everyone was constantly drinking. "I've got a hot date with some reactivated guns."

"Oh, but you need a break." Asthana's face took on a sly expression. "I've even asked Lester Lewis to join us."

Wolfe closed her web browser and rose from the desk, notebook in hand. "Who?"

"You know who. *Lewis.* The Home Office pathologist you fancied at the garage—"

Wolfe, feeling a hot blush spread across her face, hoped that Asthana didn't see it. "I don't recall saying those words."

"You said you thought he was handsome. Well, it turns out that he's single. Devon knows him from work. Apparently he's a real rising star at the Home Office. So are you coming?"

Opening her mouth to decline the invitation, Wolfe heard herself saying the opposite. "All right. But only to meet this man of yours."

"I knew you'd say yes." As Asthana turned back to her computer, smiling, Wolfe decided to make her retreat. Heading across the floor, it occurred to her that it might be a good thing to go out with her fellow officers, just this once. Maybe, she thought wildly, she would even have a beer.

Powell's office stood at the far end of the floor. When she poked her head inside, she saw only a mountain of papers in the vague shape of a desk. Turning away, she was about to head back to her cubicle when she ran into Arnold Garber, who was carrying a stack of files that reached to his stubbly chin. "Any sign of Powell?"

"Cornwall's office," Garber said, not slowing down. "I think they wanted to see you."

"Thanks," Wolfe said to his retreating back. She walked across the floor to the deputy director's office, which occupied most of the southwest corner. When she got to the door, she saw a paper sign on the knob: DO NOT

DISTURB. She considered it for a moment, then knocked. A second later, a voice told her to enter.

Inside, the deputy director's desk stood under the window, which looked out onto the nearby office park, with half the remaining space in the room given over to a conference table. On the wall behind the table was an Anacapa chart, a family tree of relationships between various parts of the arms trade.

Cornwall was seated at her desk, along with Powell, studying what appeared to be some surveillance photos. Going closer, Wolfe saw that there were three shots in all, evidently taken from the post across from the garage. Then she realized that she had seen the man in the pictures before.

"You've got to be kidding," Wolfe said, staring at the man's face. It was Ilya Severin.

"I'm afraid not," Powell said, all but vibrating with excitement. "Surveillance was never called off. The order was lost in a pile of action requests. Yesterday afternoon, the team saw our man. The Scythian himself."

"Powell has been walking me through his background," Cornwall said, removing her reading glasses, which hung from her neck by a fine chain. "I want you to be honest with me. Could this be our killer?"

Wolfe tried to get her head around this. Ilya had been an assassin, yes, but something about this murder seemed out of character. He had never burned the bodies of his victims, and his last few killings had all been motivated, at least in part, by a clear sense of retribution.

A second later, her doubts were swept away by a thought that rendered all else meaningless. This was the break that she needed. Ilya's reappearance would shake

up the entire division, and she was one of only two officers at the agency who had dealt with him before.

In the end, Wolfe only nodded, her face perfectly
calm. "It's possible. We know that he was responsible for
at least two deaths in the United States. Before that, we
believe that he was one of the leading enforcers in London."

Cornwall frowned at the photos. "But you were saying
that he's turned on the mob?"

"That's my understanding," Powell said. "Look at his
story. A Russian Jew and model student, but convicted at
eighteen of dealing on the black market. He was sent to
prison in Moscow, where he fell in with Grigory Vasylenko—"

"A piece of bad news," Cornwall said. "Leave it to the
Russians to put a boy like that in the same room as a *vor*.
What then?"

"We believe that both were freed in Primakov's general amnesty, although the details aren't clear. When
Vasylenko came to London, he brought Ilya with him.
Ilya became a major asset, until he was betrayed after an
assignment in New York. He's been on the run ever
since."

"But not without doing some damage first," Wolfe
said. "We know he went after the men who double-
crossed him. One died; another lost an eye. And we think
he was the one who killed Alexey Lermontov."

"Lermontov," Cornwall said. "The man you thought
was in charge of the art trade?"

Powell's face darkened. "We know he was in charge of
it, but never had the chance to make our case. A year ago,
we found him in Fulham, shot once through the head.

Someone texted the police with the location of the body. Ballistics linked it to a revolver that Ilya had used in the past. We know for a fact that he had it when he disappeared. It was a message."

Wolfe could understand the bitterness in his voice. Lermontov, who had financed intelligence operations using art transported by the mob, had been their best proof of a link between the Russian secret services and organized crime, but his death had left them unable to prove it. Vasylenko, his leading contact among the *vory*, or brotherhood of thieves, had been arrested and sentenced to twenty years on a range of weapons and conspiracy charges, but at the trial, there had been no mention of Russian intelligence.

Cornwall was looking out the window, taking in the gray block of the office park. "A dangerous man. But why would he go after this armorer? Is there a connection here I'm not seeing?"

"Given the nature of the underworld in London, it wouldn't surprise me if their paths had crossed," Powell said. "It's even possible that Ilya sees it as an extension of his mission."

Cornwall turned away from the cheerless view. "And what sort of mission is that?"

Wolfe saw that the question was directed at her. "Ilya was betrayed by the intelligence services. Killing Lermontov and destroying the art trade was his way of striking a blow in return. So if we're right, and Russian intelligence is involved with the arms trade as well—"

"—then your man will want to bring it down before we can," Cornwall finished. She fell silent, as if considering her options. Finally, she said, "All right. I'm postponing the raid until we can take this new factor into account. Until we know more, the details stay in this room. What else?"

Wolfe did her best to hide her sense of triumph. "I can request Ilya's file from the Bureau. If we cross-check it with his record here, we can get a sense of his haunts, his associates, the places he might visit—"

Even as she spoke, she saw that Powell was staring at the Anacapa chart on the wall. Following his gaze, she realized that he was looking at one particular photo, and as he turned back, his eyes bright, she knew at once what he was going to say: "And we need to see Vasylenko."

7

In Finsbury Park, beneath the overcast sky, a row of adjoining townhouses stood below the railway tracks. A construction worker in a hard hat and vest was strolling along the sidewalk, a canvas satchel at his side. Anyone watching from the bus stop on the corner would have seen him go without pausing past the house with the iron fence, but as he went by, he glanced over once without turning his head, taking in its reinforced door and windows.

Continuing onward, he approached another building six houses away, closer to the end of the block. This second townhouse was under renovation and apparently vacant, a scaffolding of plywood laid across its face like a cruel orthodontic device. It was separated from the sidewalk by a low brick wall the height of a man's waist. The worker stepped over it easily, then went to fetch the wooden ladder that was leaning against the side of the house.

Setting the ladder against the lowest platform of the scaffold, which was eight feet off the ground, he climbed up. He had been watching this house for several days. According to public documents, it was unoccupied, and although weeks had passed since any work had been done, he was fairly sure that the sight of a construction worker would not attract undue attention.

When he reached the final level of the scaffold, he climbed onto the flat roof, which was lined with crinkling tar paper, with a raised ledge on all four sides. He looked at the area behind the building. Past the overgrown rear yard stood a tumbledown of dead branches and leafless trees, followed by a strip of muddy grass. Beyond that, there was a wire fence, and finally the train tracks themselves.

Lowering himself to a seated position, Lasse Karvonen settled down on the roof, his back to the ledge. From here, he could not be seen from the street. He removed his hard hat and vest, laying them on the rooftop. Under the vest, he was wearing a black sweater and dark jeans.

From his pocket, he removed a single yellow apple, then took the *puukko* knife from the satchel at his side. It was a beautiful sheath knife with a birch handle and steel blade, the back of the knife flat so that one could push a thumb against it while carving wood, the tip curved upward for skinning.

Using the knife, he cut up and ate the apple, listening to the National Rail trains rolling by every few minutes as he waited for the sun to go down. The knife had belonged to his grandfather. Karvonen had brought it with him to the army, where it had been the only civilian item allowed in his paratrooper's kit. Other soldiers had often asked to see it. They knew, of course, who its owner had been.

Karvonen had been eight years old when his grandfather died. During the war, the old man had taken a Soviet bullet through the cheek, shattering his jaw, so his face was oddly misshapen, a large lump protruding from one side. With his goblin ears and eyes, he had been a frightening figure, but Karvonen had always inched closer, prompted by his parents, whenever his grandfather spoke about the war.

"Suomussalmi." All the stories began with this one word, a kind of invocation, as if to summon back the ghosts of the north: "You can picture it, the men on skis, dressed all in white, coming down to destroy the Russians section by section. When the snow fell, it covered dead and wounded alike. Men would lie bleeding on the ground, but even if the blood stopped, they froze to death. You see?"

Karvonen, still his mother's favorite child, had nodded rapidly. His grandfather had sucked back the spit from his gums and smiled, saying, "We could hear the Russians over the radio. The Swedes had broken their codes. They would beg for food, saying that they were starving, or that they had shot their last horse for meat. Once, over the radio, they said that they would set up a triangle of fires near their camp, so that the air force could drop food and bullets. We made our own triangle a mile away and watched as the airdrop was lost in the snow—"

Years later, long after his grandfather was dead, Karvonen would learn that because of the Winter War, Stalin had resolved never to invade Finland again, knowing that the result would be a bloodbath. It had kept their country safe for generations. Yet there was one figure who was strangely absent from the old man's stories, and for the full account, Karvonen had been obliged to ask his parents, who had finally told him what his grandfather had done.

Using iron sights that would not fog up in the cold, keeping snow in his mouth so the vapor of his breath would not give him away, his grandfather had racked up four hundred kills as a sniper, the second highest total of the war. The kills had taken place over the course of a long year, but when Karvonen pictured the men his grandfather had slain, it was always as a single mountain of bodies, lying there in the snow, ready to be consumed in a funeral pyre.

After his grandfather died, leaving him his *puukko* knife, Karvonen had begun to hunt on his own. In the woods behind their house, one could find hares, squirrels, sometimes even deer. He had not used a rifle. Instead, he would set snares and wait beside them for hours. Sometimes, depending on his mood, he would torture the animals as well. Regardless of what he did, he would always burn the bodies afterward, clearing a circle of dirt for a small bonfire.

Looking into the flames, a boy of eight already becoming something that his parents could not understand, Karvonen had seen that he would never be as great a sniper as his grandfather. Better, he had thought, to go in close with a pistol, or even a knife, as the ghosts of the north had done with the Russians, creeping up through the snow and cutting their throats. Hunting, he had found, was the only time he truly felt alive. It also silenced the voices in his head.

He suspected that his grandfather had heard those voices, too. One morning, he had gone into the bathroom, loaded a shotgun with his trembling hands, and blown off the top of his skull. He had been eighty years old. Some time afterward, Karvonen's father, a children's photographer, had done the same, but with a noose instead of a gun. In those days the suicide rate in Finland had been the highest in the world, four times higher than that of Britain, caused by some indefinable combination of darkness, drink, and the dead whiteness of the sky.

Thinking of these things now, still on the roof, Karvonen saw that the sun had gone down. He had been waiting for almost three hours. Taking his hard hat and vest, he wadded them up, then went over to the edge of the roof and tossed them into the tumbledown. The apple core he flung into the darkness.

Slinging his canvas bag over his shoulders, he crouched out of sight again, waiting for the next train to come. Less than a minute later, exactly on schedule, it passed by. As the train thundered along the row of houses, drowning out all other sounds, he began to creep silently across the adjoining rooftops, slipping over the ledge from one house to another, counting the chimneys as he went. As the sound of the train faded, he halted. The roof he wanted was six houses away.

Karvonen waited in the darkness for the next train. When it came, he repeated the process, allowing the noise to conceal the sounds he made. After the train passed, he paused again. Working this way, moving only with the trains, it took him forty minutes to cover the distance. At last, however, he reached the final house, the one he had passed earlier that evening.

Crouching down on the last rooftop, he settled in to wait as the sky grew gradually darker. Finally, at close to eleven, his watch told him that it was time to move. As soon as he heard the next train coming, he lowered himself silently from the rear ledge of the rooftop, hanging from the edge by his fingertips. Two feet below him was the flat roof of an extension, which thrust itself into the rear yard. Next to it, he knew, was a window. As the train was passing, he waited until the noise had reached its height, and then, carefully, he let go.

He dropped two feet and landed softly on the second roof, next to the window at the rear of the house. Pressing himself against the outside wall, he listened. All was silent. When he was sure that he had not been overheard, he set to work, knowing that ten minutes were left until the next train.

Karvonen examined the window. As he had expected, it was held shut with a flimsy catch. From his canvas satchel, he took a short pry bar and wedged it noiselessly between the frame and sill. He tested it gently, gauging the pressure on the latch, and saw that it was ready to give.

For nine minutes, he waited, one gloved hand motionless on the pry bar, until he heard the approach of the train. He held back until it was almost upon him, the rumble of the wheels building to a roar, and then put all his weight onto the bar.

The latch broke. Karvonen raised the window, moving quickly now, the pry bar falling to the yard below as the train thundered along the tracks. Drawing his pistol, he went into the house.

Outside, the noise of the train rose in a trembling wave of sound, then began to fade. Just before it ceased entirely, there was a scream and two muted gunshots. A second later, the train was gone, and across the rows of slumbering houses, nothing remained but silence.

8

"Vasylenko isn't a man you want to underestimate," Powell said, locking up the sedan. "A *vor* doesn't survive for long if he isn't intelligent. He'll be cautious, and he'll have his solicitor there. And he doesn't like women, especially Americans, although I think we can make use of that."

Wolfe, the case file in hand, matched him stride for stride as they walked along the car park. "What about you?"

Powell looked ahead at the hulk of Belmarsh Prison. "He doesn't like me, either."

Crossing the road, he glanced over at Wolfe. She was dressed as severely as usual, an attractive young woman determined to be taken seriously, which implied that she didn't know that she was taken very seriously indeed. He had hoped that her talents would find a more suitable outlet in London, and he was angry with himself at having failed to provide it.

As they approached the prison, he took cold comfort in the fact that it wasn't entirely his fault. SOCA had always been a troubled organization, founded as an uneasy hybrid of five different agencies, but over the past year, it had grown even more dysfunctional. A series of failed operations, as well as the recent change of government, had left everyone scrambling for funds, and a proposal to reorganize the entire agency under a new name had only made things worse. As a result, Powell had been forced to play a political game that, as a rational creature, he deeply disliked.

All the same, if the timing had been bad for him, it had been even worse for Wolfe. After falling out of touch for almost a year, he had impulsively proposed her for the liaison role, based on little more than a memory of certain qualities she had shown in New York. Now, after months of budget cuts and infighting, they had finally been granted an opening, so it was easy to understand the intensity he saw in her face. "What about the solicitor?"

"You've read the transcripts," Powell said. "He's young, but smart. At Vasylenko's trial, he managed to exclude all testimony about the intelligence connection. So he's very good at what he does. And he won't let Vasylenko talk unless he thinks we have something to offer him."

They ascended the curb on the other side, approaching the prison entrance, an orange brick building guarded by a row of short metal posts. "But we don't have anything to offer."

Powell nodded grimly as they passed through the doors to Belmarsh. "Yes, I know."

They went under the coat of arms and entered a reception area. Inside, Owen Dancy, Vasylenko's solicitor, was signing in with the guard. Dancy was not yet forty, but at the top of his profession, and very fat. When they shook hands, however, his palms were dry, and there was something in the plump cushion of his fingers that radiated confidence. "Good to see you, Powell. And you must be—"

Wolfe shook his hand. "Rachel Wolfe. I'm a liaison officer with the Federal Bureau of Investigation."

"I see." Dancy's smile pushed up the rolls of flesh around his eyes. "A bit out of your way, aren't you?"

"Lucky for me you have such interesting clients," Wolfe said. The guard, who had already searched the solicitor's briefcase, examined her purse and flipped carefully through the file folder for contraband. He was a bulky man with a shaved head, wearing the usual blue jacket, white shirt, and black tie. Powell knew that the guard's tie was a clip-on, to keep prisoners from strangling him with it.

After the search, they were escorted by a second guard into a deserted concrete courtyard. At this hour of the morning, the prison was quiet, except for the barks of patrolling Alsatians in the distance.

They headed into the nearest of the four housing blocks. Each block was in the shape of a cross, with a common central area surrounded by four spurs. Going inside, they went down a corridor of lavender brick until they reached a pair of metal gates. The guard took a key from his belt, unlocked the first gate, pulled it heavily aside, and ushered them in. Once they were through, he shut the first gate and opened the second with a different key. Then they continued onward.

Now the walls were green, indicating that they had entered a secure area. Every few yards, they passed through another set of gates, repeating the same process as before. As they went on, the smell of the prison, which had been faint at first, gradually grew riper, a thunderous mingling of body odor and unwashed laundry. Powell saw that Wolfe noticed it, too.

When they reached the last corridor, its bricks painted blue, it was deathly quiet. This was the lifers' spur, populated by men who would never leave prison again. Contrary to what one might have expected, it was also the most settled wing. Unlike the majority of prisoners, who were awaiting trial, most lifers didn't want trouble, merely a chance to serve out their sentences in peace.

They entered the interview room, which had thick glass on all four sides, like a fish tank. The guard let them in, then turned to leave. "Wait here, if you please. It will only be a moment."

Once they were alone, Dancy lowered his bulk carefully into a chair. "I'm looking forward to hearing what this is about. I assume you wouldn't be here without a good reason. Or are you going to make me guess?"

Even as the solicitor spoke, the door was unlocked from the outside, and a guard led Vasylenko into the room. As the old man, his eyes on Powell, took a seat next to Dancy, the guard told them to knock if they needed anything, then left, locking the door on his way out.

Powell looked at Vasylenko. At seventy, the *vor* was smaller than he remembered, his hair and mustache a shade whiter. He was dressed in jeans and a gray pullover. While on remand, he had been allowed to keep his own clothes, but now only his trainers were his own. All the same, he retained an aura of power, as if these earthly garments were merely a shell, ready to be discarded at the right moment.

When Wolfe introduced herself, Vasylenko regarded her coolly, then turned his eyes to Powell. His voice was almost accentless. "We haven't spoken in a long time. It makes me wonder why you are here."

"We don't intend to keep you from your other engagements," Powell said, taking the case file from Wolfe. He found himself looking at the edge of a tattoo visible above the collar of the old man's shirt, a hint of something pointed, like barbed wire. "But there's something we thought might interest you."

Opening the folder, he removed the surveillance photos and pushed them across the table. Vasylenko picked them up carefully, studied the shots for a moment, then set them down again. "So?"

Powell saw a challenge in the old man's eyes, which were fixed disdainfully on his own. "Those pictures were taken this week in Stoke Newington. An armorer named Aldane Campbell was killed. Two days later, this man showed up at the scene. We're hoping you can tell us why."

Vasylenko did not drop his eyes. "And why would I know anything about this man?"

"I expect that you know a great deal about him," Wolfe said. "Ilya Severin killed for you in the past."

Vasylenko smiled, but kept his eyes on Powell. "You must be mistaken. He wasn't a killer. He was a righteous man. Or so he thought. If he killed anyone, he must have been deeply confused."

Powell felt the old man daring him to look away, and resolved not to give him the satisfaction. "So you know him. But you don't know what his interest in this armorer would be?"

"No," Vasylenko said. "If anything, I am more curious about you. It seems very fortunate that you obtained these photographs. I wasn't aware that the police kept a crime scene under such close surveillance, long after the murder itself. Or did you have it under surveillance already?"

Powell saw that Vasylenko had lost none of his cunning. "Did you know Campbell?"

"I never met the man." Vasylenko turned aside, as if bored. "As for Ilya, if you find him, you can ask him yourself. He is no longer any concern of mine. All I remember is a dreamer with his head in books. He did not understand how the world really worked. Or what he really was."

"Which was what, exactly?" Powell asked. "A tool of Russian intelligence?"

Dancy interrupted. "If you're only going to dredge up that old issue, I see no point in continuing with this interview. In any case, I don't see why you're asking my client about a man he hasn't seen in years—"

Powell only smiled. If there had been any point in doing so, he might have told them the truth, which was that two years ago, when ballistics linked Ilya to the gun that killed Lermontov, he had seen it as a message meant for him. This was not a reasonable conclusion. It was doubtful that Ilya even remembered him at all. But the more time passed, the more convinced he became that the art dealer's death had silenced the one voice capable of providing the answers he had spent most of his career trying to find. And all because of one man.

In the end, of course, Powell said none of this. Instead, he glanced at Wolfe and said, "You know, that's a good point. You haven't seen him in a long time. So perhaps we can remind you of a few things."

Seeing her cue, Wolfe spoke up, producing a sheaf of pages. "Two years ago, your dreamer put down his books long enough to take out a very powerful man in New York. After he was betrayed, he went after his former collaborators. One died. The other had his eye burned out. Later, he was disabled with a stun gun and left for the police. It seems that Ilya then went to London, where he took out a leading paymaster. Which makes me wonder what else he has in mind."

Powell took up the thread. "You see, it would be one thing if he were killing upstanding citizens. At the moment, though, he seems much more interested in taking down everything your kind has worked to accomplish. So when you come right down to it, he isn't dangerous to us. He's dangerous to you."

Vasylenko had listened to this speech in silence. "So what are you trying to say?"

"If you don't want to cooperate, it's your call," Wolfe said. "But I suspect that you'd rather make life hard for Ilya. Before you refuse, then, you should ask yourself how safe you really feel with a man like this on the street."

Vasylenko did not reply at once. Although nothing in his expression betrayed what he was thinking, Powell thought he could sense the wheels turning rapidly in the old man's head.

At last, Vasylenko spoke again. "As I said before, I take no interest in this man. I do not know where he is or care what he does." He paused. "But if I did care, I would look at Marbella."

"Marbella?" Wolfe looked at Powell, then back at the *vor*. "What's in Marbella?"

Vasylenko only turned to his solicitor. "If you don't mind, I would prefer to end this now. These two have wasted enough of my time."

The old man signaled for the guard. After a beat, when it became clear that the interview was truly over, Powell rose from the table, followed by Wolfe. As Dancy stayed behind with his client, Powell knocked on the other door, which was opened a moment later by the guard in the hallway.

Wolfe remained silent until they were back in the corridor. "So what do you think?"

"We got more than I expected," Powell said, waiting as the guard unlocked the first set of gates. "You did good work back there."

"Unless he was only playing with us." As they went through the gates, moving away from the lifers' wing, Wolfe seemed to grow thoughtful. "Vasylenko said that Ilya didn't know what he was. What did he mean by that?"

Powell followed the guard outside, passing through the concrete courtyard. "Look at Ilya's background. He was brought up to hate the civilian intelligence services, and he believed that by working with the mob, he was undermining the system that the Chekists had created. In fact, though, he was working for them all along. Everything he knew was a product of their training."

Wolfe seemed satisfied with this. As they signed out, though, Powell found himself further considering this point as well. Ilya, he saw, wanted to destroy the forces that had turned him into a killer, but such a man could never really escape his past. Even as he exacted his revenge, he continued to think and act in a certain way, using the set of skills he had acquired. He was the enemy of the secret services, but also their greatest creation. And to anticipate his next move, it was necessary to consider how his training had taught him to think.

As they left the prison and walked silently to the car park, Powell realized that he already had access to much of this information. There was one man, he knew, who had spent his entire life contemplating these matters. Which meant that, as painful as it might be, he had to go back to Canterbury.

He was still coming to terms with this when his mobile phone rang. Unlocking the car door, he answered it. "Yes?"

It was Arnold Garber. He was excited. "Get back here now. We've got another body."

9

At first, when the dead man's face was revealed, Wolfe thought it was sheathed in a kind of translucent membrane, like a caul. A second later, as the sheet was pulled farther back, she saw that the pathologist had covered it in a plastic bag, as well as both of the hands. The arms were bent and slightly raised, in the pugilistic position, and nearly all of the flesh had been burned away.

Lester Lewis, the Home Office pathologist, removed the plastic sheet, then took it to the countertop to check for trace evidence. As he examined the sheet, he smiled at her. "I hope you aren't easily sick."

"Only when I breathe," Wolfe said, blushing slightly. In point of fact, she wasn't feeling particularly well. She had never liked the morgue, with its waxy smell of death, like furniture polish, laid over a deeper odor of decay, which reminded her uncomfortably of some underlying truth about the body.

To distract herself, she tried to list the differences between forensic procedure here and what she remembered from New York. Back home, the bags around the corpse's hands would have been paper, not plastic. And there was no central morgue in London. Instead, each body was brought to the nearest hospital mortuary, in this case a somewhat grimy room in Whittington Hospital in Archway, a few miles from where the dead man had been found.

She looked around at the others. For continuity of intelligence, officers who had observed the scene in Finsbury Park were encouraged to attend the postmortem, with the inspector assigned to the case standing at the head of the table. At his side was Powell, who had accompanied her to the dead man's house earlier that day. Wolfe could still smell the smoke in her own hair.

Lewis finished examining the plastic sheet, then removed the bags from the body's head and hands. As his assistant took pictures of the body, climbing onto a stepladder to get a better view, the pathologist began to dictate: "The body is that of a normally developed, well-nourished, extremely burned male of indeterminate age. Height is approximately seventy inches, weight eleven stone. Nearly eighty percent of the skin has been burned away. The hair is gone. So are the eyes."

Setting the recorder down, he gently lifted the head from the block on which it rested, examining the wound on the back of the skull. "There is a large defect at the rear of the skull, consistent with a single gunshot wound to the head. No exit wound is visible." He lowered the head again, then counted the dead man's teeth with a steel probe. "All thirty-two teeth are present. And something else—"

He explored the interior of the mouth with a gloved index finger, then removed it and showed it to the others. On his fingertip, there were number of dark purple crystals.

Smiling subtly at Wolfe, Lewis said, "The substance in the mouth is consistent with potassium permanganate." He deposited the crystals in a plastic vial, then spoke quietly to his assistant. "Gary, please bring me some glycerol when you have a chance. Not the silver bottle—the brown one."

After examining the clothes for foreign objects, he began to undress the body. Looking over his shoulder, Wolfe saw that the dead man's shirt was almost entirely burned away. As Lewis laid the blackened remains on a clean sheet of paper, he continued his dictation. "Fragments of brittle material, suspicious of charred clothing, adherent to the left lateral torso. On the thorax, a defect consistent with a gunshot wound at the level of the heart."

The pathologist carefully pulled off what was left of the dead man's jeans. He found that the seat of the jeans, where the body had rested against the floor, was almost intact. Taking it off the rest of the way, he laid it on the counter, then checked the back pockets, first the right, then the left. Looking into the left pocket, he paused. "There's something here."

With a pair of tweezers, he gingerly removed what turned out to be a charred piece of paper, the edges going from chocolate brown to black. He set it on a tray, then examined it through a magnifying glass. "A portion of the text is still visible. I can make out one of the words. *Ainha*."

The detective inspector came for a look. "Ainha? What's that supposed to mean?"

"An Arabic name, I believe." Lewis lowered the lens. "Didn't you say that he was Algerian?"

Powell nodded. "Rachid Akoun, a recent immigrant from Algiers. Unemployed, unmarried. Trained as an electrical engineer, but had been working more recently as a lorry driver. We're still looking into his background."

"I see. Well, perhaps you should also be looking for a woman named Ainha." As the inspector wrote this down, Lewis set the burnt paper aside. "The rest of the note is unreadable, although I suspect that at least a portion can be reconstructed. Gary, please be sure to pack it up for the lab."

The rest of the postmortem was fairly routine. From the dead man's skull, a nine-millimeter slug was removed for comparison to the one recovered in Stoke Newington. Most memorable was a moment near the end, when Lewis tested the substance they had found in the corpse's mouth. Placing some of the dark purple crystals in a glass dish, he carefully added a few drops of glycerol. At once, the crystals began to smoke, and were instantly consumed by a hot burst of flame.

After the postmortem was over, Powell went off with the detective inspector for a cleansing scotch and cigar, while Wolfe returned to the office alone. On the train back, she went over her notes from the crime scene. Akoun had been killed in the bedroom, then dragged to the bathroom to be burned, destroying any trace evidence. So far, aside from the manner of death, there was no sign of any connection between him and the armorer in Stoke Newington.

At the office, it was lunchtime, and the smell of curry drifting across the floor made Wolfe faintly sick. As she approached her workstation, she saw Asthana quickly close a wedding website on her computer, then take a file from her desk. "I've been talking to Marbella," Asthana said, handing her the folder. "They've got a pair of killings that look like Ilya's work."

Wolfe opened the folder, which contained a police report. "Who were the victims?"

"Manuel Fuentes, a local enforcer linked to the drug trade, and a second victim, as yet unidentified. Looks like a hit gone wrong. The intended target took out Fuentes first, then shot the other outside a hotel and boardinghouse. One of the tenants was a foreigner who worked at a local translation firm. He's vanished. Police suspect that he's the one who killed the other two."

Wolfe studied the attached statement. "And we think that this translator was Ilya?"

"The descriptions seem to match. He was living there under the name Daniel Kaverin. A strange place to hide, though. Marbella is a center for organized crime. I'd think he'd want to stay well away—"

"Vasylenko's crew doesn't operate in Spain," Wolfe said, scanning the file. "They've been pushed out by a younger breed of criminal. Maybe he thought he'd be safe there." She noticed that the police had searched the missing man's flat, which, judging from the attached photos, had contained mostly books. "There must have been prints in his apartment. Did they run them?"

"They did," Asthana said. "No hits from the Interpol database. The prints are on file now, though, so if he turns up again, we'll know."

"Good." Wolfe spent the next few minutes going over the report. On an attached witness statement, there was a phone number and email address for a young woman, a waitress at a local restaurant, who had reportedly known the suspect. After thinking it over for a moment, Wolfe picked up her telephone and dialed.

The phone rang twice before it was answered by a woman's voice. "*¿Bueno?*"

Wolfe switched easily into Spanish, which she had learned on her mission to Bolivia. "Hello, am I speaking to Malena Vargas?"

"Yes," the woman said, something cautious in her tone. "How can I help you?"

Wolfe opened her notebook. "My name is Rachel Wolfe. I'm a special agent with the Federal Bureau of Investigation, operating as a liaison officer with the Serious Organised Crime Agency. I'd like to ask you some questions about the man you knew as Daniel Kaverin."

"I only have a few minutes," Malena said warily. "I'm leaving for work soon—"

"This won't take long. I just wanted to clarify a few things. He was tutoring you in English?"

"Yes, as a favor to me. I'm hoping to go back to school, so I need to take the entrance exams. He was a regular at the restaurant, and I knew that he was a translator, so I asked if he'd give me some lessons."

Wolfe noted this down. "You must have talked a lot, then. I was wondering if he ever mentioned anyone he knew in London. Do the names Aldane Campbell or Rachid Akoun sound familiar?"

"No," Malena said. "He never told me about his past. Only about books—"

Something about this caught Wolfe's attention. "What books do you mean?"

"He always had a book with him at the restaurant. Mostly English, but also Hebrew. A lot of titles about

Judaism. Anyway, I'm not sure. He was very private. And I do need to go."

"That's fine," Wolfe said. "I'm sending you my contact information. If anything else occurs to you, you can call me day or night."

"All right," Malena said, then hung up without saying goodbye. Replacing the phone, Wolfe looked again at the photos of books in Ilya's flat. Hebrew text was visible on some of the spines, which reminded her of what Vasylenko had said. Ilya was a dreamer. And his head had always been in books.

Wolfe looked over at Arnold Garber, who was eating a kebab at his desk. "Garber, if I wanted to put together a list of all the good Hebrew bookstores in London, where would I start?"

Garber wiped his mouth with a napkin. "You could ask me. I'm a bad Jew these days, but that wasn't always the case."

"Well, if I needed to visit the best Hebrew bookshop in the city, where would it be?"

"Manor Books," Garber said without hesitation. "It's in the Steinberg Centre, over in Golders Green. A bit out of the way, but it's the best bookstore of its kind. Anyone with an interest in Hebrew will end up there eventually."

"Thanks." Wolfe wrote down the name, then slid open the top drawer of her desk, taking out a rumpled London atlas. Checking the index, she flipped to the map covering the area of Golders Green, which wasn't far, she recalled, from Hendon, a neighborhood where Ilya had once lived.

Garber turned back to his lunch. "So, are we still seeing you for drinks tonight?"

"No," Wolfe said absently, paging quickly through the atlas. "I think I'm going to be busy—"

Even as she said this, something else occurred to her. Wolfe put down the atlas and picked up her notepad. On the top of the open page, above the notes from her recent call, she wrote down the word from the charred fragment in the dead man's pocket. *Ainha*.

She studied the word for a moment. Then, crossing it out, she wrote *Rainham*.

10

"Good night, Roman," the cashier said, taking down his overcoat from its hook near the door. "See you tomorrow."

"Yes, all right," Roman Brodsky said distractedly. He was seated in the office at the rear of the store, going over his notes from the past day, the green hooded lamp casting a white circle on his desk. His notes were written in a fine, barely legible hand, a mixture of Russian, English, and the several other languages that Brodsky had acquired over the course of his untidy life.

The cashier, who had worked the front of the store for ten years without expressing any interest in Brodsky's other activities, smiled and left, the door chiming once as he departed. Brodsky turned back to his notes. A pot of tea sat at his elbow, the third and longest steeping from that day's leaves, so that the final cup, which he drained now, was angry and dark with sediment.

After another minute, he fed some of the notes into the shredder beside his desk, then rose heavily and brought the remaining pages to the safe in the corner. Inside, there was a handgun, never fired, and bundles of money in four different currencies. He set his notes on top, along with a battered address book. Then, donning his coat, he glanced around the office once more before turning off the lights.

In his thick glasses and sweater, Brodsky looked something like a tortoise, or like one of the innumerable mollusks that dwell in caves along the ocean floor. He passed through the store, with its shelves of sweets, smoked fish, and pickles, and went outside. Locking the door, he lowered the security gate, then headed up the street for home. He easily could have afforded a car and driver, but he liked these solitary walks, which gave him time to think.

Whenever Roman Brodsky bothered to consider the shape of his own life, which was not very often, he saw himself as one of those necessary men without whom much of the world's business would grind to a halt. In a city of immigrants and exiles, especially one in which almost nothing was written down, his role was as essential as it was misunderstood.

Back in Russia he would have been known as a *tolkach*, or fixer. In his youth, as a recent arrival in the city, he had established himself as an accomplished lock picker and entry man, but after a bit of time in prison, he had concluded that he had no taste for it. Instead, sensing an opening, he had invented a role for himself, becoming a broker for services that were otherwise unable to advertise. Which only meant, in a way, that he had continued to open doors for a living.

As he walked down the street now, he reviewed the day's events in his head. He had managed to arrange employment for five Russian illegals in the East End, who would soon set to work making souvenirs at a Turkish sweatshop. Another situation had turned out to be rather more delicate. A group of thugs had tried to extort a stall owner in Petticoat Lane, only to find that he was the cousin of a very powerful man. Brodsky had been brought in to negotiate a settlement that would allow both parties to save face, and was scheduled to meet with them later tonight.

He turned onto his own block, which was surrounded on all sides by the white masses of hotels and garden squares. A creature of habit, he had lived for most of his London life in the same housing estate, although he had moved out of his old flat a few years ago to a larger one on the top floor. Entering the lobby, Brodsky took the lift up, then trudged to his own flat. The door had a pair of heavy locks, which he unlocked with two separate keys.

Inside, the foyer was dark. Brodsky was closing the door, noticing in passing that it seemed to stick oddly in the frame, when he felt something heavy descend on the back of his head. He must have blacked out at once, because in what felt like the blink of an eye, he found himself seated upright in a hard chair, as if he had somehow fallen forward into this position.

His head was aching. As his vision cleared, he became aware of a number of things. He was in his own kitchen. Behind him, the bulb above the sink had been switched on. In the faint yellow light, he saw that he was naked except for his glasses, and that his bare arms and legs were bound to the chair with loops of wire. When he tried to move his head, he found more wire encircling his throat.

A shadow fell across his body. Someone was standing behind him. Before he could speak, he felt something like a coarse powder being poured onto the crown of his skull, as if in a strange benediction. The powder, which had the consistency of sand, slid down the back of his neck and fell on his shoulders like dandruff, flakes of it adhering to his sweating skin.

Looking down, he saw the powder gathering in a heap on his lap, and saw that it consisted of many small crystals. It was hard to determine their true color, but they seemed dark purple, almost black.

Brodsky recognized them. At once, the fear that had been lurking at the back of his mind rose sickeningly to the surface.

The trickle of powder ceased. A second later, a darkened figure came into his line of sight. The area beyond the chair was in shadow, so he could not see the man's face. In the light from above the sink, however, he saw that there was a squeeze bottle of colorless liquid clutched in the man's right hand.

Brodsky stared at the bottle. A single choked word escaped from his lips. "Wait—"

The man sat down in a second chair that had been placed just out of the circle of light. His face remained in darkness. Raising the bottle in his hand, he spoke softly. "You recognize this?"

Brodsky said nothing, his heart thumping damply in his chest. Looking to one side, he saw that the kitchen drapes had been drawn. There was a clock above the refrigerator, but he couldn't see it from here. If he didn't show up for his meeting, which was scheduled for nine, the men he was supposed to see would quickly suspect that something was wrong. All the same, he didn't know how long it would take for them to come looking for him at home.

He swallowed, feeling the dull itch of crystals on his body. His clothes had been left in a heap on the floor. "Listen," Brodsky said hoarsely, trying to sound as reasonable as possible. "There's five thousand in cash in the bedroom. I have even more at the store. If you let me go now—"

The man in the darkness cut him off. "I am going to ask you a question. I advise you to think very carefully before you respond. You know who I am. Do you understand why I am here?"

An image of a blackened body in a bathroom appeared in Brodsky's mind. He found that his exposed manhood had shriveled, as if trying to draw back into his body. "I think you're here to kill me."

"Not necessarily," the man said. "I'm here to have a conversation. Nothing more."

The man settled back into his chair. Brodsky saw that there were gloves on his hands. He was unable to take his eyes from the squeeze bottle, and felt the cups of tea from earlier that day pressing against his bladder.

"The police are closing in," the man continued. "They've started asking questions about the armorer in Stoke Newington. Some of their questions are good ones. Which makes me suspect that they have an informant. I want to know if you have any idea who this informant might be."

Brodsky tried to shake his head, then stopped, feeling the wire cut painfully into the area under his chin. "I told them nothing. I have no reason to inform on anyone. It's bad for business—"

The man squeezed the bottle in his hand. Brodsky saw a stream of colorless liquid arc out of the nozzle and splash against the floor at his feet, only a few inches from where the largest pile of crystals had collected. Seeing this, he began to flail, trying to rise from the chair, only to feel the wire dig into his wrists and ankles. At last, he sank back again, the sweat running down his sides.

"Let's try again," the man said, settling back into his own chair. The stream of liquid stopped. "Perhaps we can even talk like men. I know how someone like you stays in business. You throw the police a shipment, a robbery, a name, so that they'll look the other way when it counts. I want to know what you've told them about me. And I want to know it now."

He raised the bottle again, aiming higher. Before he could squeeze it, Brodsky spoke, the words spilling out in a rush: "Wait, wait, *wait*—"

The man kept the bottle where it was. Brodsky took a breath, looking down at his arms and legs, which were furred with the black crystals. "All right. I've grassed a few times. I've given up a shipment or two. But only for men who were going to get caught anyway. I have nothing to gain by informing on you. I know what kind of people are involved here—"

The man spoke quietly. "And what do you know about these kinds of people?"

Brodsky backtracked, seeing his mistake. "Nothing. I don't even know their names. Or yours. But if I inform on them, my life is worthless. And there's nothing I can tell the police. All I've done is make some introductions."

"I'd like to believe you," the man said, almost gently. "But you're the only one."

"That isn't true," Brodsky said, suddenly glimpsing a way out. "If anyone went to the police, it's the guy from

Cheshire. James Morley. For all I know, he's having second thoughts. Maybe he knows that someone took out the first two names. After what happened to Akoun—"

The man's voice remained cold. "And how could he have figured this out?"

"Maybe he reads the papers." Brodsky groped for an answer. "If he wasn't afraid, he wouldn't have altered the meet. He knows you can't touch him at Olympia. But maybe he wants to call the whole deal off. He's a businessman, he gets scared, he drops a line to the police, right?"

For a long moment, the man seemed to consider this. Brodsky, still sweating, heard the ticking of the clock above the refrigerator. He found that his glasses were about to slip down the bridge of his nose.

Abruptly, the man stood. Brodsky flinched, his eyes on the bottle, but the man only turned away. "Fine. I'll talk to Morley. But if I find out that you've lied to me, the next time we meet, you won't even hear my voice."

Going into the next room, the man unlocked the door of the flat, opened it, and went out into the hall. The door closed. Alone in the kitchen, Brodsky sucked in a trembling breath. As he did, his glasses fell off.

Outside, the man continued down the darkened corridor. As he headed for the exterior stairs through which he had entered the building, one of the overhead lights briefly illuminated his face. It was Ilya Severin.

He opened the door to the stairs, sliding the bottle into his coat pocket. Tucked into his waistband was the pistol he had found in Brodsky's bedroom closet, along with two boxes of cartridges. Like its counterpart in the office safe, it had never been fired, but Ilya had confirmed that it was in good working order.

In his other pocket, liberated from a drawer in the bedroom, was a set of lock-picking tools, left over from Brodsky's former vocation. These would also be useful. Possession of the tools was a crime in itself, though, so if he was going to carry them, he would need to be discreet.

Reaching the stairs, he descended, the night air cool on his face. Half a minute later, he had climbed down to ground level, and then he was out on the street. It was a quarter past eight.

As he walked away from the housing estate, he considered what the fixer had said. From the papers, he had already learned about the second victim, but the other name had come as a surprise. It had a familiar ring, but he wasn't sure from where, so he resolved to look into it further.

At the station, Ilya consulted the map on the wall, confirming the location of a stop at the end of the District Line. Before passing through the turnstiles, he paused at a trash container, where he threw out his squeeze bottle of water and the plastic shaker in his other pocket, with its last remaining handful of coarse black salt. Then he headed underground.

11

When Renata awoke that morning, she found herself suddenly aware of two things. The first was that she was going to get clean. No more drugs or drinking. The second realization was that her financial troubles would soon be over. Dior would come through, along with her upcoming side project, and at that point, it was only a lucky break or two before she was back on her feet.

Upon her arrival at Golden Square, her mood was only slightly dented by the tactless guard at Cheshire, who insisted on searching her bag with his bulky fingers. "Be careful there. I don't like people touching my stuff—"

"Very careful, yes," the guard said, stuffing a hardened hand down between her neatly packed flashes and lenses. He was in his middle forties, with the accent of a Cold War villain, and after performing everything short of a full body search, he shoved the gear back into her bag and led her to a brushed metal door at the end of the hall. He knocked, then pushed the door open. As he ushered her inside, he caught her eye. "I will see you before you go."

He shut the door, leaving her in the office. Renata looked around the sterile space, which was not particularly

CITY OF EXILES / 85

promising. Like the corridor outside, it was stark white, with a burnished black floor. A chessboard had been set up in one corner. The only spot of color was a painting on the opposite wall, a pop art portrait of a man in his fifties. It was clearly just a silk-screened photograph, daubed with bloody reds and oranges, and she recognized it at once as the work of a celebrated artist of the sixties who had cheerfully embraced Thatcherite materialism.

At the far end of the room sat James Morley, the man in the portrait, stationed before an array of trading terminals. Rising from his desk, he approached Renata. "Pleased you could make it," Morley said, extending a hand. "I've been looking forward to seeing you again."

"Glad to be here," Renata said, setting down her bag for the handshake. The manager of the Cheshire Group's activist fund was trim and tan, wearing a wool suit and worsted tie, and would have been quite handsome were it not for his eyes, which were startlingly like those of a vulture. Renata wondered how much he knew about her situation. She was convinced that her creditors had sources everywhere, and although she had recently taken precautions to ensure that her staff remained loyal, it was impossible to silence the rumors entirely.

As Morley took a seat behind his desk, she thought back to their first meeting, at an assignment just over a year ago. It had been a photo shoot for titans of finance, but even in that group, Morley had stood out for his drive and ambition. After the shoot, they had spoken over cocktails, his vulture's eyes undressing her. There had even, she recalled, been a hint of sexual attraction, although her own tastes, then as now, skewed mostly toward younger men.

The portfolio manager checked something on his computer. It appeared to be a list of standings for the London Chess Classic, which had begun earlier that day. "How long do you expect this to take? I only have half an hour—"

"Oh, that's plenty of time," Renata said, although given half the chance, her sessions could last sixteen hours or more. Today, however, she was ready to compromise. "We can start right away, if you like."

Morley nodded absently, turning back to his terminal. From her bag, Renata took out a folding reflector and expanded it to its full size, about three feet across. She wheeled a chair into position and set the reflector across its arms, gold side showing, so it softened the contrast on Morley's hard features.

Opening the other bag, she removed her camera and attached a Speedlite flash. Turning it on, she took a test shot, then tilted the camera to check the screen. As she adjusted the flash, she sensed Morley watching her. "Remind me of what you're doing," the portfolio manager said. "It's part of a series?"

Renata took another shot and studied it. This one was better. "Oh, you know, just portraits of traders, the ones who survived the downturn. Could you tilt your head a bit forward, please?"

Morley turned back to the monitors. "I'm surprised that you got anyone to agree to it. Most managers are keeping a low profile these days—"

"Honestly, you're the first one who said yes." As she continued taking shots, Renata began to fall into the rhythm of the shoot, and found that she was glad to be here alone. For vaguely defined security reasons, she hadn't been allowed to bring an assistant, and although she had been annoyed at first, it felt strangely satisfying to return to a simpler way of working.

Her best photography had always been done in solitude. A camera, as everyone knew, was a sublimated gun, and the purest emblem of her art was that of the photographer as a hunter, alone against the world. With a staff of assistants, though, this element was diminished. Retouching took uncertainty out of the equation, but there was also a loss of resourcefulness. And perhaps she would have kept control of her life, she thought, if she had gone out on her own more often.

She noticed that her memory card, which also held pictures from the Dior shoot, was nearly full. Sliding it out, she replaced it with one from the pouch hooked to her belt, saying, "Listen, maybe you could get away from the desk? The light will be better on the other side of the room."

Morley tapped a key, closing the chart on-screen, then turned away from the monitor. Rising from behind his desk, he went over to the table with the chessboard in the corner. "Here?"

"Yes, perfect." Coming up behind him, Renata saw that the new location gave her a chance to put the pop art painting in the background. "Quite the portrait you've got there. You're like Dorian Gray—"

Morley smiled. "My story isn't quite as interesting. The artist has a nice little scam going. He'll paint a portrait for anyone who donates twenty thousand pounds to a given charity, meaning that his assistants silkscreen your face on a canvas and he splashes some paint around—"

"A good business model." She lowered herself to one knee. "Mind fixing your tie?"

Glancing down, Morley complied. "Later, when you pick up the canvas, you find that he's done *four* portraits, arranged in panels so they all bleed together. He'd be glad to sell you only one, he says, but it would be a shame to break up the composition. Invariably, you agree to fork over another sixty thousand. The original twenty goes to charity, as agreed, and he simply pockets the rest."

"That's quite wicked," Renata said, although, as she continued to take shots, she found herself wondering if she could do something similar. "How did you end up with just the one?"

"A year ago, he tried to extend his scam by painting traders for a Russian investment journal. But it's a mistake to try and outfox men like us. We don't like being cheated, whether it's by Putin or someone else. Only five portraits out of sixty were sold. Nobody paid full price. I bought one for a thousand pounds, nine hundred more than it was worth. But I wanted it, you see."

Renata lowered her camera. What he was describing, she realized, was almost exactly what she had in mind for her own project. "But why?"

"So I could tell you this story," Morley said. "You don't invest in Russia without iron in your heart. You're staring down thieves who would gladly cut your throat, so you won't be bullied by some *artist*. Besides, most traders don't want themselves painted. You don't flaunt your wealth. Not now—"

"Fair enough," Renata said, her face burning. "So why let me take your picture, if it's such a bad idea?"

He seemed to consider the question. "I don't know. Perhaps it's because the world is changing. I want something to remember this moment in my life, before it's gone for good." Morley glanced at his watch. "In any case, I'm afraid that's all the time I have. I hope you got what you needed."

Renata stood slowly. "I should be able to pull something out of it. As for the rest—"

"My assistant will contact you about payment." Morley rose as well, then watched as she packed up her gear. "All the same, I wouldn't count on many others saying yes. You should have tried it a few years ago. Still, it was good seeing you again. Perhaps we could have dinner sometime?"

Renata forced herself to smile at this. Then she turned and fled as Morley sat down at his desk again, immersing himself in the more lucrative world that her desperation had only briefly interrupted.

Outside the office, the security guard was nowhere to be seen. Renata walked quickly past the receptionist, who looked up as she walked by. "Excuse me, but if you could wait a moment—"

Renata ignored her. She took the elevator down, a pulse ticking on her forehead. For a moment, looking down at her camera bag, she had the urge to erase all the photos she had taken. It had been stupid to come here, stupid to tell him what she had in mind, stupid to pretend that this was a way out.

She arrived at the lobby, then marched blindly into the square, bags banging against her side. It wasn't even noon, but she needed a drink. Or something more. Because in the light of day, it came to her why Morley had asked her out to dinner. He was a vulture. He invested in the bankrupt and undervalued. And he knew a distressed asset, like her, when he saw one.

12

Powell's ankles were swallowed up by the grass as he crossed the garden. As he approached the figure in the wooden chair, he noticed that the lawn was turning brown and dry. The last gardener, he recalled, had been fired, and he reminded himself to hire someone to take care of the house and grounds.

He reached the man in the chair, who was facing away from him. As he came around for a better look, he was surprised to see that the old man's eyes were open. He spoke quietly. "Hello, Dad."

His father looked up. At that first unfocused instant, his eyes seemed wild, like those of an animal startled out of sleep. "Eh?"

Powell crouched down beside his father's chair. "Dad, do you know who I am?"

A second later, some of the wildness departed, and his father's face grew more organized, as if he was gathering his wits by an effort of will. He glanced away, as if embarrassed. "Yes, yes, hello—"

Powell studied his father. He was bundled up in an ancient overcoat, the collar of his sweater askew. His face, which had once been angular and severe, had grown fat, almost leonine, the result of years of childlike nibbling on sweets and chocolate. "How are you feeling?"

"Fine, perfectly fine," his father said irritably. He looked down at his knee, where his right hand was pawing nervously against the fabric. "They've been watching both of us, you know. They aren't going to let you go."

"Who?" Powell asked, although he had grown used to these bouts of paranoia. "Who is watching us?"

A vacant look stole into his father's eyes. He made a vague gesture, then turned to the trees, as if the conversation were no longer worth the effort. Decades ago, this garden had been planted with fruit trees, where the birds still made their nests, but these days the apples were left on the ground to rot.

Powell rose, then put a gentle hand on his father's shoulder. "Dad, is it all right if I go into the study?"

After a beat, his father gave him a quick nod. Powell stood there for a moment longer, wondering whether the old man would speak again, then headed back toward the house where he had been born.

The house was in Canterbury, a few miles from the cathedral. Whenever he returned, he was surprised to find that the house was not actually in the cathedral's shadow, which was how he remembered it. Having seen his father's personality depart completely, he no longer believed in a soul, but this had not led to a crisis of faith. Indeed, the soul's absence was almost a relief, although he still dreaded the day, which he was secretly sure would arrive, when his own mind would start to fade.

Powell went onto the porch, slid open the latticework door, and entered the house. Inside, it was dark but fairly clean, with a lingering odor of pipe smoke, although his father hadn't smoked in a long time.

Leona, the nurse, was in the kitchen, looking out the window at the garden. In her powder blue uniform and white trainers, she radiated competence, and Powell liked her, even as he felt guilty for not visiting more often. As he went into the kitchen, she gave him a bright smile. "How did it go?"

"Well enough," Powell said, taking the glass of water she offered. "He seems to be doing better these days."

Leona turned back to the window, through which his father's hunched form was visible. "He likes it best in the garden. It's the only place where he can sit still. He must have loved it before—"

"Yes, I suppose." As Powell drained the glass, it occurred to him that he had never seen his father in the garden before his illness. These days, it had become a place of refuge, or exile, allowing his father to retreat from the house, with its shelves of books that he could no longer read. "And he's been sleeping?"

"Only during the day," Leona said. "He's always dozing or napping. But he wanders at night. Looking through drawers and cupboards. I try to make sure he doesn't turn on the stove, or leave the refrigerator open—"

"I know how he can be." Powell set down the glass. "I'm going to be in the study. Just knock if you need anything."

"Oh, we should be all right." Leona indicated a sandwich on the counter. "This is for you, if you like."

"Thank you—that's very kind." Powell picked up the plate and left the kitchen. Passing down the corridor, he approached the closed door of the study. Going inside, he set the plate on the desk, then shut the door behind him.

The first thing that struck him was the smell of old books, which brought him back to his childhood at once. As a boy, Powell had been thrilled by the sight of Cyrillic characters on the leather spines, with their air of sinister mystery, and even today, he wouldn't have dared to enter this place without permission.

He scanned the shelves, which lined three of the four walls. Many of the volumes were in Russian. Glancing over the bookcases, he saw some of his father's most treasured possessions, like the unfinished Russian translation of the *Encyclopédie*, which had been canceled before it was halfway done, and the Soviet encyclopedia whose subscribers had been instructed to remove the article on Beria with a razor blade, replacing it with one for the Bering Strait.

The fourth wall was the one he needed. It was occupied by a set of filing cabinets, the drawers carefully labeled and classified, containing what seemed like thousands of documents. Powell was daunted by the amount of material, but knew that he had no choice but to plunge in. Taking a bite of his sandwich, he opened the nearest drawer and began to flip through the files.

An hour later, his eyes aching and sandwich gone, he emerged with a stack of folders ten inches high. The oldest files, he had found, were the most organized. As you neared the end of the archives, they grew more and more chaotic, until, by the final drawer, they were essentially random. The last few folders contained a great deal of peculiar detritus, including unopened mail from three years back, and, in one case, the empty, flattened bag from a packet of crisps.

Powell brought the selected files back to the desk, where he sat down. The desk, he knew, had never been touched, leaving a snapshot of his father's life from three years ago. Next to the lamp was a slip of paper. Looking at it, Powell saw his own name in his father's unsteady hand, and next to it, what seemed like a guess at his birthday. The date on the page was wrong.

He switched on the lamp. Beside it stood a bronze sculpture of Felix Dzerzhinsky, the first director of the Cheka. A larger version of this statue had stood in Lubyanka Square, its fate reflecting that of the nation itself. Twenty years ago, after the fall of the old regime, it had been toppled with a noose around its neck, then left in a park to be stained with urine. More recently, in a fit of nostalgia, it had been raised again. And a similar sculpture sat on the desk of Vladimir Putin.

Considering the statuette now, Powell saw it as an emblem of how nothing in Russia ever really changed. The files were another reminder. His father had spent years building these dossiers on Russian intelligence activity, the files bulging with newspaper and magazine clippings, his own notes, and original case files, most of them heavily redacted. And even after his retirement from Thames House, he had continued to compile this material, persisting in his belief in Russia's dark destiny.

Powell opened the topmost folder and laid the pages out on the desk. As he began to sort through the material, he reminded himself of what his father had taught him. You had to approach things systematically. Reason alone wouldn't solve every problem, but until you had exhausted its possibilities, there was no excuse for failing to apply it carefully, even if it led to more questions than answers.

What he had, on the most basic level, were two bodies. One was a Yardie armorer, the other an unemployed Algerian engineer. The victims seemed to have nothing in common aside from the method by which they had been killed. So it was with method that he had to begin.

The folders that he had extracted from his father's files contained information on assassinations, successful or otherwise, conducted by Russian intelligence outside its own borders. Ilya Severin had been brought up in this tradition, even if he had not been aware of it. In his killings, Powell could see signs of his training, much as a connoisseur could recognize the hand of a particular artistic school.

And yet something about the recent deaths continued to bother him. When you got right down to it, the secret services weren't very good at assassinations in foreign countries. At home, they held the power of life and death, but overseas, they were less capable. Their only successful killings tended to be public poisonings, like those of Markov and Litvinenko. It was very hard to kill a careful man in his own house. Which was why these last two murders were so unusual.

But there was at least one recent assassination where the victim had been poisoned at home. Anzor Archvadze had been one of the most carefully guarded men in the world, and yet, two years ago, Ilya and an accomplice had managed to slip into his mansion and expose him to a binary poison, leading to his death the following week. Powell still remembered his first glimpse of the oligarch in the hospital, his skin peeling away, a shell of a man occupied by dementia and paranoia.

Clearly, then, Ilya was more than capable of taking out

a target at home. In the case of Archvadze, though, there had been a good reason. He had gone to the house to retrieve something, a painting that he had been ordered to recover. But in the cases of Campbell and Akoun—

Powell sat up in his chair. For a moment, he sensed an insight lurking just outside his field of vision, ready to be grasped if he could only pin it down. Then, at once, he saw it clearly, and knew why these men had been killed.

He stood, his pulse suddenly high. His first inclination, oddly, was to tell his father, who once had been the only audience that mattered. These days, though, if he shared the news, the old man wouldn't remember it for long.

In any case, he thought, there was someone else who deserved to hear it first. Taking the phone from his pocket, Powell retrieved a number from the list of recent calls. Then he dialed Wolfe.

13

"I forgot to mention that we saw Jane at dinner," Wolfe's mother said over the phone. "You wouldn't believe how enormous she is. And for such a tiny thing! But she was positively glowing—"

"I'll bet," Wolfe said absently. She was behind the wheel, on the road to Rainham, her cell phone's headpiece in one ear. At the moment, she was feeling tired and irritable from spending the past three nights staking out a Hebrew bookstore in Golders Green, following a hunch that she had yet to share with anyone at the office. And now, on top of everything else, she was lost.

At some point in the past few minutes, it had begun to rain. To one side of the road, there was a weedy field; on the other, rows of flat metal roofs. She had borrowed the Peugeot, which smelled strongly of perfume, from Asthana, who had been glad to get the mileage reimbursement. By now, she should have arrived at her destination, but it was becoming increasingly obvious that she had taken a wrong turn somewhere in the last mile or so.

As her mother continued to prattle on about Jane, her youngest brother's saintly wife, Wolfe turned into an office parking lot that had conveniently appeared on her right. Pulling into a space, she put the car into park and took the road atlas from the glove compartment.

Looking at the jumble of roads on the map, Wolfe saw that she had, in fact, gone the wrong way at the last roundabout. She also realized that her mother had switched to one of her favorite topics: "—and we'd be so happy if you found someone. No pressure, of course, but your father and I have been talking, and—"

Wolfe slid the atlas back into the glove box. "Mom, I have some bad news. As far as I can tell, there are no single Mormon males in the entire city of London. They're all gone. The sex-in-chains case scared them away. And I'm not going to Newcastle to see what I can round up among the missionaries."

Her mother gave a brittle laugh. "Ha, ha, yes, of course. But, you know, I'm serious. This isn't just about finding a boyfriend. Remember, dear, the highest calling of all is family—"

"Mom, stop it," Wolfe said. Looking out the windshield at the dirty rain, she heard herself blurt out these words: "The reason I'm not going to the temple is that I'm leaving the Church."

There was an ominous pause. Then, mortifyingly, her mother began to cry. "Don't *say* that," she said between sobs. "I know you've had a rough time in London, but if you want to stick a knife in your father's heart—"

"Mom, you're breaking up," Wolfe said quickly. "I'll call you back later. Love you."

She hung up. Then, for good measure, she removed her headpiece, turned off her cell phone, and set it on the dashboard, regarding it warily, as if it might somehow find a way to ring again.

CITY OF EXILES / 99

"Shit," Wolfe said aloud, swearing for the first time in the better part of a year. It felt good. A second later, catching sight of herself in the rearview mirror, she felt compelled to ask herself whether her mother might be right. She was almost thirty years old, single, still a virgin, and, for some reason, seated in a borrowed car in a parking lot in Rainham, not even sure what she was doing here at all.

If her mother had been there, and willing to listen, Wolfe might have said that it was one thing to deal with the absence of God, once his voice had fallen silent, when the rest of your life still testified that you were one of the chosen. But after honor and advancement had slipped away, leaving you neither blessed nor cursed but merely ordinary, the silence grew unbearable. It was hard to believe in God, she thought, if you were no longer sure that he believed in you.

For a moment, Wolfe thought about calling her mother back and telling her some of these things. In the end, though, she simply put her car in reverse and wheeled out of the parking lot.

Ten minutes later, having managed to avoid thinking about anything else in the meantime, she saw her destination up ahead. It was the industrial estate whose address had been recovered from the scrap of paper in Rachid Akoun's pocket, the text revealed under infrared light.

Wolfe parked around the corner and got out of the car, taking a softcover book and some printed leaflets from the front seat. Opening her umbrella, she headed for the industrial estate, where an open steel gate led onto a concrete driveway. Past the fence, she saw a forklift and some trucks parked in front of a yellow portal frame warehouse, joined to an office of brown brick. The door of the warehouse was open, but there was nobody in sight.

She went through the gate, her shoes clicking wetly against the damp concrete, and approached the warehouse. The open door revealed a rectangle of darkness. She peeked inside. Just beyond the door, there was a row of shipping containers, followed by a mountain of irregular blocks swathed in layers of plastic. Farther off, she could hear voices coming from the rear of the building.

Going closer, she saw that the objects wrapped in plastic were pallets of old computer monitors. In a rolling bin to one side was an equally massive pile of electrical waste: a jumbled heap of wires, circuit boards, printers, and processing units, once state-of-the-art, now nothing but junk.

A second later, her perspective shifted, and she saw the warehouse as it would have appeared to a man like Rachid Akoun. And as she studied the mound of electrical scrap, seeing it instead as a gold mine of components, she understood at once what had brought him here.

She went up to the nearest shipping container, which was taller than she was. On its corrugated metal side, there was a printed label with a serial number. Eighteen digits, but she knew that just the company prefix counted. It took only a second for her to commit the seven digits to memory.

Turning, she left the warehouse and began to walk around the property. Up ahead was the office block. The lights on the ground floor were lit, and through the translucent glass, she could make out a pair of shadows.

She was about to go closer when she heard a voice. "What are you doing here?"

Wolfe turned. Standing behind her was a man with dark

hair and stubble, his skin nut-brown, the sleeves of his rain slicker tight on his bulging arms. She sized him up quickly. Six feet tall, maybe one hundred and eighty pounds. She noted this in the blink of an eye. Then she smiled.

"Good afternoon," Wolfe said, launching easily into a string of words as familiar as her own name. "After centuries of being lost, the original Gospel of Jesus Christ has been restored by a loving God through a living prophet. I have evidence of this that you can hold in your hands, ponder in your heart, and pray about to learn its truth for yourself. Will you allow me to share this message with you?"

The man took a step back, startled. He took in the book and stack of leaflets in the crook of her arm, then glanced back up at her face. In his eyes, she saw an expression that she had often encountered, the look of someone who had already decided she was insane but wasn't sure whether she was dangerous. "I am sorry, but you cannot stay here," the man finally said. "This is a place of business."

"Okay, I understand," Wolfe said. She took a step forward. "Would it be all right if I came back another time?"

The man shook his head. "No, no, we are working here. You need to leave, please."

He reached out to her, as if about to take her by the arm, then seemed to think better of it. Beckoning her forward, he led her back toward the front gate. Wolfe went out, giving him a smile, then headed around the corner.

Getting back into the Peugeot, she switched on her phone, seeing in passing that she had two new messages from her mother, which wasn't too bad. The third message was from Powell. She returned the call.

Powell sounded excited. "I know the connection between our victims, and why they were both killed at home. Campbell was a machinist. Akoun was an electrical engineer for an energy firm in Algeria. Our killer wouldn't have gone after them at home, instead of someplace easier, if there wasn't something he needed there. You see? He took something from each of the crime scenes."

"I think you're right," Wolfe said. Fishing out her notebook, she wrote down the serial number that she had seen on the shipping container. "I just got back from the address in Rainham. It's an electrical waste recycling plant."

She described what she had observed, then said, "Technically the waste is supposed to be recycled here, but it looks like they're illegally shipping it overseas. I've seen this kind of thing before. They dump broken equipment into shipping containers, put working computers on top to disguise it, then label the whole thing as functional and ready for export. Then they send it to Africa or China, where kids strip it down for gold, copper, steel. It's a big business for organized crime—"

"And for scavenging electrical parts," Powell said. "You think Akoun came here?"

"It's possible." Wolfe started the car. "If he was working on something when he died, maybe he used the warehouse to scrounge components. And if our killer took something from him and Campbell—"

"—then maybe he's trying to build something, too," Powell finished. "But what?"

"I don't know." Wolfe pulled into the street, then rounded the corner. The conversation with her mother seemed very far away. "But if he's building something, it raises two questions. What is it? And what else does he need?"

14

Karvonen was seated at his desk when the phone rang. Spread across his work surface was a sheet of newspaper on which a pair of mechanical objects had been placed. Next to the two parts of the device, beneath the magnifying lamp, lay one of the prints he had developed from the roll of film recovered in Highgate, consisting of a diagram and a set of instructions.

After a moment, he stirred himself and rose from the desk, following the sound of the phone to the bedroom. The ringing was coming from the lowermost drawer of the bureau next to the bed. Taking the keys from his pocket, he unlocked and opened the drawer. Inside was the phone that he had found in the restroom at the pub, charging on its adapter cord, which snaked out through a small hole at the rear of the bureau. He answered it. "Yes?"

The voice was cautious. "There has been a change in plans. We need to move up the timeline. Perhaps one or two days. Is that a problem?"

Karvonen glanced over at his workstation. "No. As long as I get the materials."

"The meeting will take place as arranged," the voice said. "But he wants to know how to recognize you."

"Tell him that I will be wearing a green coat. And that I will be carrying a camera."

Without replying, the man on the other end of the line hung up. Karvonen was about to put the phone back into the bureau when the bell of his apartment sounded. Frowning, he rose and went over to the intercom, phone still in hand, and pressed the button to talk. "Who is it?"

Renata's voice came over the speaker. She sounded hoarse, as if she had been crying. "It's me. Please, let me come up—"

Karvonen hesitated for a second, then pressed the button to open the door downstairs. Going back to his desk, he gathered the components of the device and brought them to the bureau in the bedroom, which was still open. He put the device inside, along with the phone, and slid the drawer shut.

As he was locking up the bureau, there was a knock from outside. He pocketed the keys and went to the foyer of the loft, glancing at himself in the mirror by the door before opening it.

Renata did not look good. As she came in, she seemed even more rumpled than usual, the shirt under her coat partly unbuttoned, her eyes rimmed in red. "Dior canceled the project."

"I'm sorry." Karvonen arranged his face in a look of sympathy. "What did they say?"

"That they didn't like the fucking *pictures*." Renata twisted free from his attempt at an embrace, then marched over to his desk without taking off her coat. The proofs from the shoot were still posted on the wall above his computer. Renata tore down a handful and began to rip up the glossy paper, the faces of the models crumpling under her hands. "Those mother*fuckers*—"

Karvonen closed the door. "You need to calm down. There will be other clients."

"You don't understand." Turning away, Renata wandered over to the sitting area and flung herself onto the couch. "Without this assignment, I'm ruined. This fucking art fund has me over the table. If I don't pay in six months, they own my entire portfolio. They wanted this all along. They had people watching me. I know it. They always planned for me to default. *Shit*—"

She buried her face in her hands. Karvonen, who had already poured a glass of wine, handed it to her silently. Renata took the glass and downed most of it at a gulp. He refilled it, seeing her old paranoia return. Even now, he felt the first faint stirrings of boredom, and sensed that it would be a long time before he could get her out of the house. "You have other options. What about the portraits?"

Renata shook her head. "It isn't happening. Two years ago, maybe, we would have had a shot, but now it's unseemly. These guys don't want their pictures taken, not in a downturn. The press would have a field day. Christ, who knows. Maybe I can take pictures of my fucking lenders. What do you think?"

She laughed bitterly, the tears leaving snail tracks on her face. Karvonen put his arm around her, sneaking a glance at his watch. Then he looked down at the crown of her head, which she had tucked up against his chest, like a baby, and decided that after one more drink, he would send her on her way.

Before he had a chance to put this plan into action,

however, she was kissing him, her right hand already groping at his fly. Karvonen briefly considered pushing her away, but he sensed that this would only lead to more tears, so in the end, he took the path of least resistance.

An hour later, alone in the shower, he began to give serious thought to the prospect of breaking things off. Looking down at the fresh scratches on his upper arms, it seemed to him that Renata had become more trouble than she was worth. There had been a time, not long ago, when he had hoped that her connections would be valuable. As a photographer, she had access to many leading celebrities and politicians, and Karvonen and his handlers had seen this as an opportunity. In fact, though, such contacts were usually meaningless, at least when it came to real information.

Karvonen turned off the water, then reached out for a towel to dry himself. It was best, he finally decided, wrapping the towel around his waist, to end things now. The next two weeks would be demanding enough, and the last thing he needed to worry about was a woman.

His decision made, Karvonen emerged from the bathroom, his body slick with steam. He saw that Renata was seated, naked, on the edge of his bed, her back turned. It was still a good body, sleek and lean, and for all his recent resolve, when he looked at her now, he felt himself stir again.

A second later, Renata turned around. She had the device in her hands. "What's this?"

Karvonen glanced at the bureau. The lowest drawer was open, the keys that she had taken from his pants pocket still dangling from the lock. A small bag of coke had been removed and left on the bureau's surface.

He turned back to her and smiled. "It's something I've been meaning to show you. Give it here."

Renata rose from the bed, the device still in her hands. The look on her face was curious, nothing more, and he could tell at a glance that even after their lovemaking, she was still a little drunk.

Karvonen extended his left hand. After what seemed like a moment of hesitation, she handed over the device. He took it, and almost in the same movement, he drove his right fist into the pit of her stomach.

She doubled over, the air whooshing out of her lungs. Before she could take another breath, Karvonen set the device on the bed, reached down, and put one hand on her chin and the other on the back of her skull. He pushed her head to the left, then snapped it hard to the right.

It was over in less than a second. When he released his grip, her body slumped to the floor. Her head was bent strangely to one side, as if she were looking at something under the bed. Around him, the loft seemed very quiet.

Karvonen saw that the towel had fallen from his waist. Bending down, he snatched it up and put it back on, then crossed to the other side of the flat. Along the far wall, a row of windows ran from floor to ceiling. The curtains were open. He drew them. It was impossible, he knew, to see into the bedroom from here, but all the same, it was necessary to think very carefully about what to do next.

For a moment, he considered calling someone. In some ways, it would be easier to let them handle this. Then he reflected that with this new complication, they might decide to take him off the assignment altogether, and having brought things so close to completion, he did not want to give up control now.

More important, he wasn't sure that he trusted them to take care of it. He had never been especially impressed by their competence, and knew that he could do a better job on his own.

Going back toward the bed, he found the cat sniffing around the body. He bent down and scooped up the cat, who mewed in protest, and brought it over to the balcony. Opening the sliding glass door, he tossed it out, then shut the door and headed back to the bedroom.

After a moment's consideration, he took the body by the ankles and dragged it into the bathroom, which was still steamed up from his recent shower. Reaching down, he slid an arm under Renata's naked shoulders, another under her knees, and laid her in the tub, her head lolling back. Then he returned to the bedroom, where he gathered up her clothes, her shoes, and her Birkin bag, went back into the bathroom, and tossed them into the tub as well.

Only then did he get dressed. Removing his towel, he pulled on his underwear, then put on a work shirt, socks, and an old pair of jeans. From the closet, he took a sturdy pair of shoes and slid them on, lacing them tightly.

On the top shelf of the closet, next to the box with the pistol, there was a long rectangular case. He brought it down, set it on the bed, and opened it. Inside, there was a Sami knife in a sheath of reindeer leather. The blade was carbon steel, sixteen inches long, the tang running all the way down the birch handle. Removing it from its sheath, he brought it into the bathroom and laid it on the sink.

After retrieving a few more things from the kitchen, Karvonen took a canvas bag that was hanging on a hook next to the front door, then went out into the hallway.

Locking up the flat, he headed downstairs to the basement. A look at his watch told him that it was close to eleven.

The basement of his building had a common area with a laundry room. From a shelf above the washing machine, he took some garbage bags and a bottle of bleach. Next to the dryer, someone had left a pair of work gloves, which he also took. Tossing them into his bag, he headed back upstairs.

When he returned to his own floor, he saw that one of his neighbors, a painter whom he knew only slightly, was heading into her flat. She was young, freckled, and attractive, a folded kerchief holding back her red hair. As she opened her door, she smiled at him. "Hey, there."

Karvonen returned the smile as he passed, heading for his own door. He was about to go inside when he heard his neighbor speak again from behind him. "Hey, my friends and I are throwing a party tomorrow night, and we'd love it if you could come. Think you can make it?"

He turned. His neighbor was standing half in her doorway, half in the hall, her face in shadow, waiting for his response.

"I'll do my best," Karvonen said. Then he went into his own flat and shut the door.

15

Three days later, a man sat alone on a park bench in Golden Square, holding a paper bag. It was a quiet area at the heart of the city, not far from Piccadilly, the graying garden otherwise occupied only by a pair of teenage girls, eyes lowered separately to their mobile devices. A king's mournful statue kept watch over the enclosed flower beds, which were surrounded by stately buildings on all four sides.

From his position on the bench, Ilya kept an eye on the building on the northeast corner. It was seven stories high, faced with red brick and limestone, an iron fence running along the ground floor. Although it was outwardly nondescript, he could see the wires of a security system, and the windows on the top floor had the faint green tinge of bulletproof glass.

As he watched, a sleek black town car rolled up the street and parked at the curb by the building. He had seen this car before. Rising from the bench, Ilya picked up his paper bag and walked unhurriedly across the square. Inside the bag, tucked beneath a folded napkin but still readily accessible, grip upward, was the gun he had taken from Brodsky's flat. He did not expect to use it now, but he also knew that you rarely expected such a moment before it came.

On the other side of the square, across from the building he was watching, there was a cycle hire station with five bicycles lined up at their docking points. Ilya went up to the kiosk, where users could rent bikes with a credit card, and pretended to study the terms of use. From here, he was only a few steps away from the car, which was idling at the building's entrance.

He studied the car out of the corner of his eye, noting its wide, reinforced pillars and the slight distortion of its thick windows. As he watched, the driver, wearing a wireless headpiece, emerged from behind the wheel, leaving the engine running, and went around to open the rear passenger door.

As soon as the door was open, a slim, tanned man emerged from the building, talking into a mobile phone. He was in his fifties, conservatively but expensively dressed, a Halliburton briefcase in his left hand. A second man in a charcoal suit followed one step behind.

Ilya watched as they crossed the sidewalk. He recognized the first man from photographs, but was more interested in the figure behind him. The second man was dark and muscular, with something of a wrestler's stance and quickness. As he headed for the car, he swept his eyes up and down the street, his gaze lighting briefly on Ilya, then moving on to the rest of the square.

If anything was going to happen, it would happen now. Ilya watched, his gun at the ready, as the first man slid into the rear of the car, leaving the door open. Even as he pretended to read the text on the kiosk, he remained intensely aware of his surroundings, a sensation he remembered well from his old life, the level of intention and clarity required for prayer—

From somewhere to his left came a scream. The second man, who had lowered his head to enter the car, spun in the direction of the noise. Ilya glimpsed an earpiece in the man's right ear as he turned toward the sound as well, and saw that the girls he had noted earlier were exchanging screeches of greeting with a third. His hand, which had tightened on the paper bag, relaxed.

Seeing that the shriek was a false alarm, the second man slid into the rear of the car. The driver closed the passenger's door, then went back around and got behind the wheel. A second later, as they pulled away from the curb, Ilya watched as the car carrying James Morley, senior activist manager of the Cheshire Group, headed for the corner and disappeared.

As soon as the car was gone, Ilya turned and left the bicycle docking station, his pulse easing. He had spent much of the past few days in the reading room of the British Library, looking into Morley's investments, and had been struck by what he had found. Studying the financial statements and magazine profiles, he had received an impression of an intelligent businessman, investor, and chess player, but one whose entire career was based on a fundamental misunderstanding.

According to published reports, Cheshire had over two billion dollars of capital under management, down from three billion before the downturn. Most of it, as far as Ilya could tell from public filings, was invested in Russia, India, and other emerging markets. Yet Russia was not simply another emerging economy making its way to a more stable form of capitalism. It was, in fact, something altogether different, a vast machine concerned only with maintaining its own power, and to treat it as anything else was to misread the situation entirely.

Of course, such a mistake was easy to understand. It was tempting to assume that Russia operated by the same principles as the rest of the world, and that one could deal with it as one would approach any other rational government. The real question was whether Morley, after finally glimpsing the country's true nature, was now seeking a solution outside the rules.

As Ilya turned and headed across the square, he found himself thinking of his own ancestors. For a certain kind of Jew, the earthly regime was a reflection of the kingdom of heaven. Moses, they said, treated even Pharaoh with respect, and to rebel against the state was a crime deserving of death.

The result had been a widespread submission to a policy of spiritual strangulation. Russia rarely had any use for the Jews, but it had decided that it was more important to control and contain them than to assimilate them entirely. Faced with such official disregard, most had tried to survive on the state's terms, including his own parents, who had made the long journey from Chita to Moscow without seeing that this merely drew them deeper into the game.

Hence the wisdom of those who had chosen instead to exile themselves in the Torah. There had never been very many, but they had been grudgingly tolerated by the state, which had failed to grasp their true significance. Once you allowed one group to set itself apart, others would inevitably follow. And the one thing that these first tentative movements had in common, for all their visible differences, was nothing more revolutionary than the study of Hebrew.

As Ilya walked along the square, which was empty aside from the teenage girls and a man taking pictures of the king's statue, he found himself missing his books. In his rented room, he had kept the shelves bare, as if books themselves were a sign of weakness. Yet they had also been a source of strength for greater men, which was something he could never allow himself to forget.

Ilya hefted the bag in his hands, feeling the weight of the gun. He knew that tomorrow would be difficult, and that it would be easier to call the police. In the end, though, he also knew that one system could not be brought down by another. The broken vessels could only be restored by one man working in solitude. And it made no difference whether the man himself was shattered in the process.

Regardless of what happened tomorrow, he thought, tonight would be one of the last quiet moments he would ever have. Perhaps, then, it was best to spend it in a way that honored what he still saw as the fundamental realities.

As he headed across the square, caught up in these thoughts, he nearly bumped into the man who was taking pictures of the statue. Ilya stopped short, then continued on his way, apologizing. "Excuse me."

The photographer stood aside, lowering his camera. "Not at all," said Karvonen.

16

"I just don't see how anyone so smart could get into that much debt," Asthana said, glancing over the newspaper's inside page. "It says she owed half a million pounds to a shady art fund, which stands to get the rights to all her work if she defaults. Now she's picked up and left town. Not even her best friends know where she's gone, unless she's thrown herself off a bridge. Want to see?"

Asthana handed the paper to Wolfe, who skimmed it briefly before sliding it onto the already cluttered dashboard. Looking at the head shot of Renata Russell that illustrated the story, her first reaction was a very Mormon disapproval at the idea of so much debt, a reminder of how much her identity was still tied up with the Church, as perhaps it always would be.

They were parked on a side street in Golders Green, on a quiet corner that gave them a good view of the Steinberg Centre. Wolfe had been watching the front gate for a week and a half. Every day after work, she would duck out early and sit here for hours until the bookstore inside closed. In order to go through the main entrance, you had to sign in with a guard at the desk, and although she had considered involving the security team directly, she had finally decided against it.

At first, she hadn't told anyone at the office, either, but when it became too hard to obtain an agency car, she had convinced Asthana to let her use the Peugeot instead. Now, as the light grew too faint to read small print, Asthana exchanged the newspaper for a bridal magazine as thick as a phone directory. "Honestly, I can't believe you've been doing this every day."

Wolfe reached into the backseat for a cup of lime gelatin, which was her preferred sustenance on a stakeout, along with copious amounts of diet soda. "I don't mind work like this, if it's for a good reason. Of course, unlike a few officers I could mention, I don't plan on making a career of it."

Asthana turned down the corner of the current page, which displayed a dress by Dior. "Do I detect a dig at Powell?"

Wolfe peeled back the foil from the gelatin cup, then scooped up a green spoonful. "It isn't a dig. It's an observation. The more I get to know him, the more I think he's exactly where he wants to be." She popped the spoon into her mouth. "I've been watching Alan for years, and you know what I've decided? He's afraid of answers. All he wants are questions. And if that's all you need, then Russia is the country of your dreams. You never get to the bottom of it, no matter how much you try."

"I know. The irregular verbs alone will kill you. And you don't approve, I take it?"

Wolfe finished the gelatin cup. "I don't want to find myself alone at forty because I spent my life chasing shadows. Which isn't to say that I won't end up alone anyway. But at least I'll have had a career. Otherwise, I might as well have listened to my mother and had six babies in Provo."

"I have some bad news for you. Sooner or later, we all become our parents." Asthana closed the magazine. "Have you talked to her?"

Wolfe smiled tightly. "I'm screening her calls. Clearly I'm the daughter of the year."

She tried to keep her tone offhand, but in fact, this was the longest she had ever gone without calling her mother. Wolfe knew that her silence was only making things worse, but even so, she wanted to put off this particular conversation for as long as possible, ideally forever.

Asthana glanced out the window. "Join the club. I don't think my mother even knows what I do for a living, except—"

She broke off. Wolfe followed her eyes. Coming up the sidewalk, heading for the entrance to the Steinberg Centre, was a man in a long coat, a paper bag in one hand. It was Ilya Severin.

"Oh, *shit*." Asthana's bridal magazine fell to the floor. "What do we do now?"

Wolfe sat upright, staring, as Ilya went through the gate. Even now, she couldn't believe that her hunch had paid off. A second later, he was gone, as if his appearance had been nothing but her imagination, and she finally found her voice. "Call Powell. Tell him we've found our man."

Opening her door, she slid out. Asthana watched in disbelief. "What are you doing?"

"Checking out the situation," Wolfe said, feeling as if

she were observing her own actions from a distance. "Wait here."

Wolfe closed the door. Her heart was still clocking away, so she had to remind herself to follow her own advice and take this one step at a time. Going to the curb, she waited for a car to pass, then crossed the street.

Just inside the entrance, a guard was seated behind the counter, images from security cameras displayed on a bank of monitors. Before he could say a word, Wolfe took out her warrant card and held it up, a finger on her lips. Then she pointed to the door that led into the Steinberg Centre itself. Behind his glasses, the guard's eyes widened, but then he seemed to understand, and nodded.

Turning away, Wolfe went through the second door, which led to an enclosed courtyard. Up ahead was the bookstore, which she approached with caution. At the entrance, a bargain bin was piled high with moldering volumes. Beyond this, a window in the closed door looked into the store's interior.

Wolfe peeked inside, seeing rows of shelves, tables heaped with leather-bound books, and racks crowded with menorahs and dreidels. A man was standing before one of the bookcases, studying the spines, his back turned to her. It was Ilya. She had crossed paths with him just twice before, and only once from up close, so it was strangely unsettling to see him like this.

It was hard to guess his age, but he seemed under forty. A dark suit and coat. His face was nondescript and lean, his figure gaunt, with a student's slender fingers and wrists. From this angle, she could not see his eyes, but from their one previous encounter, she remembered them as the most striking thing about his appearance, penetrating and almost black.

A moment later, he began to turn aside from the shelf he was studying. Before he could turn all the way, Wolfe took a step back, bringing her out of sight of the door. She waited for another second to see whether he would emerge, then withdrew and went back to the security desk.

The guard was standing behind the counter, awaiting her return. "What's going on?"

Wolfe indicated one of the monitors, on which Ilya was visible from above. "The man in the bookshop. You recognize him?"

The guard turned to study the screen. "Don't think so. Not sure if he's been around before. What's he done, then?"

Wolfe ignored the question. "Is there another way out from the bookstore?"

The guard shook his head. "No, this is the only way in or out. If he wants to leave, he needs to get past me."

"All right. Give me the number for your phone." Wolfe waited as the guard wrote it down, then took the scrap of paper, saying, "I'm going to be watching from across the street. When he leaves, just let him go. Don't let on that anything is out of the ordinary. Can you do that?"

"Yes, of course." The guard seemed nervous. "Tell me, though, is he dangerous?"

"No," Wolfe lied. Then she left the security counter and headed back to the street.

At the curb, she paused as another car passed, its headlights slicing through the night. As she went to where

Asthana was parked, it occurred to her that she had forgotten to see what name Ilya had used to sign in.

In the car, Asthana had a phone to her ear. As Wolfe opened the door, Asthana said, "She's back. I'm putting you on speakerphone."

Asthana set the phone on the dashboard. A second later, Powell's disembodied voice emerged. "What the hell is going on?"

Wolfe climbed inside and pulled the door shut. "It's Ilya. He's in the bookstore now. We're keeping an eye on the only way out. I've told the guard to let him go if he tries to leave."

Asthana opened her own door. "Look, I say we grab him. We can handle one man—"

Wolfe put a hand on her arm. "*Wait.* We don't know if he's armed or not. He's carrying something in a bag. I couldn't tell what it was."

After a beat, Asthana shut her door, and Powell's voice came over the phone again. "I agree. I'm not authorizing an arrest without backup. I can have an armed mobile team out there in ten minutes."

"Hold on," Wolfe said forcefully. "You're missing the point. I don't think we should grab him at all. If we take him now, we won't know what he's planning. It's better to follow him and see where he goes—"

A flurry of heated debate ensued. Wolfe kept an eye on the gate across the street, afraid that Ilya would reappear at any moment. After a second, she managed to retain control of the conversation. "Listen to me. The two of us can follow him. Asthana, you can shadow him on foot, in case he gets on a train or bus. And I can track you both from the car."

Even as she spoke, she saw a darkened figure emerge from the Steinberg Centre. A couple of books were tucked into the crook of his arm, and the bag was still in his other hand.

"*Shit,*" Wolfe said, swearing without realizing it. She turned back to the phone. "He's leaving. If we're going to do anything, we need to do it right now. Powell, you're the lead officer. You make the call."

Silence on the other end. Wolfe and Asthana watched as Ilya continued up the street. Every step, Wolfe knew, took him farther out of reach, and if they lost him now, they might never find him again.

At last, Powell spoke. "All right. Listen carefully. Here's what we're going to do—"

17

The following morning, at a few minutes before eleven, Ilya emerged from the train at Kensington. Above the outdoor platform, outlined against the sky, a barrel roof loomed in the distance. Ilya regarded it for a moment, then headed toward the exit, along with the remaining passengers. Over his shoulder was slung a bag containing one of his recently purchased books, although he did not expect to need it. Under his coat he carried the gun from Brodsky's flat.

It was only a short walk to his destination. Crossing the street, Ilya continued along the sidewalk, moving parallel to the Grand Hall of the Olympia exhibition center. It was a soaring event space of red brick and stone dressings, the roof fashioned of iron and glass. On any other day, he might have paused to study it more closely, but at the moment, his attention was fixed on a second building up the road, which was where most of his fellow passengers were going.

At last, he arrived at the conference center, an Art Deco block of gray stone. Arrivals in ones and twos were already passing through the doors facing the sidewalk, but instead of heading inside at once, Ilya went to the other side of the street and entered the grocery store across the way.

Picking up a basket from the rack by the door, he pretended to shop, moving slowly down the nearest aisle. He took a box at random, then glanced through the window, which disclosed a view of the conference center. A flock of schoolchildren in polo shirts was being led inside by a teacher in a white blouse. Farther up the block stood a pair of traffic officers in peaked caps and fluorescent vests. Otherwise, there did not seem to be any police.

He watched and waited for another fifteen minutes, occasionally taking another item from the shelves and placing it in his basket. Then, just as he was beginning to fear that he had been mistaken about the timing, he saw a familiar town car pull up at the opposite curb.

A second later, the driver slid out and opened the rear door. James Morley emerged, carrying a silver briefcase and a rolled tournament program, followed by his bodyguard. The two men exchanged a few words with the driver, who nodded and got back behind the wheel. After a moment, the car pulled into the street, driving away as Morley and his bodyguard went into the building.

As soon as they were inside, Ilya left the grocery store, abandoning his basket on the floor of the nearest aisle. He quickly crossed the street, moving past the two traffic officers. As he joined the throng heading into the center, he did not see the white van parked around the corner.

Passing the security desk, where a single guard was seated, he followed the other attendees to the elevator bay, where he went up to the third floor. When the doors opened, he stepped out into the lobby, and found himself in the middle of the London Chess Classic.

Ilya looked around the room. It was a vast beige space with rows of tables set up for casual games. In the lounge area to his right, surrounded by a set of soft brown benches, an oversized chessboard had been laid out on the floor, its pieces the height of small children. In each of the corners stood flat television screens, ready to show live footage of the main tournament, which would take place beyond the closed doors of the auditorium directly ahead.

At the moment, there were perhaps six dozen people milling around the lobby, a mixture of chess players, schoolchildren, journalists, and staff. Standing near the bookstall at one end of the room were Morley and his bodyguard.

Keeping them in his peripheral vision, Ilya went up to the information desk, where a woman was seated next to a stack of tournament programs. To either side stood a pair of oversized rooks, which made her look something like a pawn. She glanced up. "Can I help you?"

"I'd like to buy a ticket for today's tournament," Ilya said, placing his bag on the countertop. "Are there still passes available?"

"Yes, of course." Plucking a form from the stack to her left, the woman slid it across the counter, along with a pen and a square of cardboard for a visitor's pass. "Admission is ten pounds."

"Fine, thank you." Opening his wallet, Ilya handed her a bill, then filled out the form. "It's more crowded than I expected."

She slid the visitor's pass into its transparent sleeve. "Well, it's the next-to-last day, and Magnus Carlsen always draws a crowd. And Victor Chigorin is scheduled to make an appearance—"

"Is he? I didn't know." Ilya took the pass and slung it around his neck. Picking up one of the programs, he turned away from the desk, looking out across the main floor. "Thank you very much."

He headed into the crowd, opening his program but not bothering to look at it yet. Chigorin's presence was an unexpected element. He did not think that it would affect his plans, but knew it would change the dynamics in the room, so he reminded himself to be aware of it.

Glancing around the lobby, he saw that Morley and his bodyguard had left the bookstall and were making their way toward the center of the crowd. Ilya noted their position, then began to walk slowly around the periphery of the floor, keeping them always in the corner of one eye.

Across from the information desk, near the elevator bay, was a South Asian woman talking quietly to a burly man in a nylon parka. As soon as Ilya had passed, she detached herself from her companion and took the elevator to the ground floor.

Leaving the building, the woman crossed the street, moving against the flow of the crowd. A white panel van was still parked around the corner from the conference center. The woman tapped twice on the van's rear doors, one of which swung open, and climbed into the darkened interior. "He's definitely staying," Asthana said. "So what do we do now?"

Inside, Powell and Wolfe were seated in the rear compartment, which was cramped and rather cold. Across from them sat a pair of Flying Squad officers from the Met's armored response unit. Both were in their early thirties, decked out in matching mustaches and polycarbonate armor, the Velcro grabbing at the upholstery whenever they shifted in their seats.

As Asthana shut the door, Wolfe glanced over at Powell. They had hurried here as soon as surveillance, which had kept a continuous eye on Ilya since they had followed him from the bookstore the night before, confirmed that he was bound for the final stop on the Kensington line. "What do we think he's doing?"

"Not playing chess," Powell said flatly. "He wouldn't have scoped out the location like this if he didn't have something in mind. Garber, what can you tell from where you are?"

The radio in front crackled as Garber responded. "Ilya's checking out the room. He's got a program in his hands, but isn't looking at it. It seems to me that he's watching the crowd."

A second later, Dana Cornwall's voice came over the radio. Wolfe knew that the deputy director was listening in from her office in Vauxhall. "You think he's here for a meeting?"

"It's possible," Powell said. "If this is anything like the chess tournaments I've seen, there will be plenty of Russians and other expatriates. We need more eyes on the crowd. I want to go inside with Wolfe."

"That's a bad idea," Asthana said. "Ilya has seen you before. Garber and I can cover him on our own—"

"But you don't know him like we do," Wolfe interjected. "And there are hundreds of people inside. Any one of them could be here for a meeting. Powell has the best chance of recognizing a familiar face. Anyway, Ilya only saw us for a minute, in a group of other officers, over two years ago—"

Before anyone could respond, Cornwall's voice came over the radio. "All right. But I want Asthana in there first. Once she's in place, Garber will consult with security. After they confirm that the coast is clear, Powell and Wolfe can check out the crowd. But make sure you stay well back."

One of the two Flying Squad officers spoke up. "What about armed support?"

"We've got bystanders to worry about," Cornwall said. "I don't want this turning into a firefight. We'll keep an eye on our target and see what he has in mind. Until then, nobody moves. Agreed?"

"Agreed," Powell said. "Asthana, you head back inside. We'll await your call."

"Got it." Asthana opened the door and slid out. Watching her go, Wolfe found herself thinking of the name on the bookstore register, the one she had returned to check after tracing Ilya to his room in Golders Green. Where every visitor was supposed to sign his name, he had written *Ilya Muromets*.

Wolfe hadn't recognized the reference, but Powell had. It was the name of a Russian saint, he had told her, who had remained immobile for thirty years before rising to carry out deeds of heroism. "A strange choice for a Russian Jew," Powell had said. "I'm not sure what he means by it—"

At the time, Wolfe had been equally mystified, but now she thought she understood. Since his last appearance, Ilya had gone dark for two years, which must have seemed like much longer. Now, after his prolonged exile, he had returned under a new name. And as Wolfe waited in the van for the signal to move, she wondered what he could possibly have in mind.

18

At that moment, the woman at the information desk inside the conference center glanced up as a shadow fell across the countertop. Standing before her was a tall, rather handsome man in a long overcoat, the strap of a camera bag crossing his chest. He smiled. "Is this where I pick up a press pass?"

She looked at the driver's license he was holding up. Next to his head shot, the name on the card read TREVOR GUINNESS.

"Right, just a second," the woman said. She ran her eyes down the names on the press list, which she had printed out and placed next to her computer. The name was there. She crossed it off, then handed him a pass with a gray neckband from the pile at her side. "You're all set."

"Thank you," the photographer said. Accepting the pass, he slung it around his neck, then headed off into the crowd.

At the big board that had been set up on one side of the room, several children were playing with the over-sized chessmen, wrapping their arms around the pieces to shift them randomly from square to square. The photographer paused here, setting his camera bag on the nearest bench. Opening the bag, he took out his camera and screwed on a telephoto lens. Then he shut the bag, slung it over his shoulder again, and began to look through the viewfinder at the room.

Karvonen surveyed the crowd. At the moment, he estimated, there were roughly two hundred people, a number that could be expected to double before the end of the day. On the far wall hung eight oversized portraits of the players in the main invitational tournament, the next round of which would be starting in a few minutes. Framing the wall in his viewfinder, he took a photo of it, although he was more interested in the fire doors that stood to one side.

For the past few days, he had been researching this tournament, wanting to be ready for anything that happened. The London Chess Classic was only in its second year, but it was already the most important annual chess event to be held in the city for decades. It consisted of an invitational match between eight top grandmasters, along with several open and junior events. The tournament took place over the course of seven days, of which this was the next to last.

On his left, two doors led into a pair of conference spaces, including the commentary room, where a panel of experts would be analyzing a live feed of the invitational. To his right, another set of doors led to a hall where the open tournament was now taking place, with chessboards and clocks set up on rows of long tables. Directly ahead was the auditorium itself, where, according to his watch, the invitational tournament would shortly begin.

A second later, as he was sweeping the lens across the

room, he saw a familiar face. Karvonen lowered the camera. It was Morley. He was standing in a corner of the lobby, looking across the floor. Following the fund manager's eyes, Karvonen saw another man, his bodyguard, emerging from one of five doors at the opposite end of the room. He tracked the bodyguard through his viewfinder, then took a picture of the two men as they met halfway across the floor, conferred, and finally headed for the doors of the auditorium.

Once they were out of sight, Karvonen moved quickly across the room, making his way to the row of doors from which the bodyguard had emerged. When he was a few steps from the door he wanted, he paused and looked back. Here and there, scattered throughout the crowd, he saw members of the conference center staff, recognizable at a glance by their matching black shirts. None seemed to be looking in his direction. As soon as he was sure that he was not being watched, he turned the knob of the door, then slipped inside.

Karvonen closed the door behind him. Switching on the lights, he looked around. He was alone in a small seminar room, one of several that lay at this end of the conference center. An oblong table with eight chairs took up most of the carpeted floor, with a blank whiteboard on the far wall. Ahead of him, on the other side of the table, was a second door with an illuminated exit sign.

Going over to the table, he took one of the chairs and wedged it beneath the knob of the door through which he had entered. Then he crossed the room and opened the second door. Poking his head out, he saw that it led into a darkened stairwell, and it could only be opened from this side. After a moment's thought, he unslung his camera bag, set it on the floor, and removed his overcoat. Rolling the coat, he stashed it behind the stairwell door.

From his camera bag, he removed a roll of gaffer tape. He tore off a piece, then used it to tape down the lock of the door, in case he needed to come back in from the stairwell. Going down one flight of steps, he peered over the edge, noting that the stairs led to an exit on the ground floor. Then he returned to the seminar room, closing the door carefully behind him.

He went up to the conference table and set his camera bag down. The bag had a false bottom, a flap of stiff nylon fabric that looked identical to the bag's actual base. Lifting the flap, he extracted something from underneath, then used two strips from the same roll of gaffer tape to secure the object under the table, near the edge, where it could be easily retrieved.

Last of all, he removed a folded green jacket from the bag's outside pocket. It was a cheap plastic coat that could be rolled into a ball. He shook it out, put it on, then picked up his camera bag and headed for the door.

As he removed the chair that he had wedged beneath the knob, he reflected that Morley had been more careful than his first two targets, but not careful enough. Because such men could leverage a portfolio, they believed that they could take risks in other ways. Sooner or later, however, they always discovered that they didn't understand what risk meant at all.

After replacing the chair, Karvonen glanced around the room one last time, checking that everything was in place. At last, satisfied, he turned off the lights and went back into the lobby.

Closing the door behind him, he walked quickly away

from the seminar room. As he passed into the crowd again, he became aware of a growing air of excitement, and that a group of attendees had gathered around the elevators, which they were watching with anticipation.

Standing to one side was a staff member in a black shirt. Karvonen caught his eye. "What's everyone so excited about?"

"Victor Chigorin," the staff member said. "The grandmaster. He's on his way up."

"I see," Karvonen said. Looking around the lobby one last time, he confirmed that Morley and his bodyguard were nowhere in sight. Then he turned and headed for the auditorium, where he knew they would be waiting.

19

When the elevator doors opened, Powell's first reaction was alarm at how many children were here. Looking around the lobby with Wolfe at his side, he saw a line of grade school students heading for the junior tournament, with a handful of even smaller children romping around the pieces on the big board. He spoke softly. "Christ, look at these kids. We need to be careful here—"

His second impression, following hard on the first, was that a number of people were watching him. For a moment, he thought that he had been spotted. As always, whenever he was out on surveillance, he felt conspicuous, and almost glanced down to see if his radio harness was showing. A second later, he realized that they weren't looking in his direction at all, but staring past him toward the elevators, as if waiting impatiently for someone else.

Wolfe gave him a nudge. "Garber's here. Come on. Let's get away from this crowd."

Turning, he saw Garber coming their way. They left the elevators and met him halfway across the room, where Garber handed them a couple of visitor's passes. "Here, put these on."

Powell donned his pass, then followed Garber across

the crowded floor. Wolfe spoke quietly at his side. "How does it look so far?"

"A nightmare," Garber said. "Kids everywhere, and at least two hundred attendees, probably with more to come. Ilya hasn't moved from the auditorium. Asthana is covering him now."

Powell glanced over at Garber as they passed through the lobby. He knew that a concealed Glock was tucked under the officer's jacket, drawn from the armory that morning. "Any sign of who he's trying to meet?"

Garber shook his head. "Nothing. He hasn't spoken to anyone. It's possible that he's waiting for somebody, but—"

He broke off as a smattering of applause came from the other side of the room. Powell turned to see a powerfully built man in an unbuttoned overcoat emerging from one of the elevators, accompanied by the tournament director and what looked like a contingent of three bodyguards. Powell recognized him at once. It was Victor Chigorin, grandmaster, activist, former world champion, and on the short list of the greatest chess players of all time.

"Well, great," Garber said, staring as Chigorin strode purposefully across the room. "As if things weren't already bollocks enough."

Powell only studied the grandmaster in silence. Like computer scientists or mathematicians, who tended to look down on anyone who didn't know code or number theory, chess enthusiasts often assumed that they were more intelligent than anyone who didn't play, which meant that Chigorin had ample reason to consider himself the smartest man in the world. He was no longer the young dynamo of his classic period, but with his trimmed gray hair and bristling eyebrows, he was still a striking figure, and he carried himself like a sports star.

Watching him, Powell couldn't help but wonder whether they had misread the situation, and whether Chigorin might be in danger. As Garber turned aside to call security, Powell spoke into his headpiece, using the standard radio term for an individual under surveillance. "Mobile one, has India moved?"

Asthana's voice came over his earpiece. "Negative. He hasn't budged from his seat."

"Tell me the second he does." As he spoke, Powell watched Chigorin cross the room, shaking outstretched hands as the tournament director steered him into the corner, where two chairs had been set before a bank of cameras.

Garber pocketed his phone. "I've checked with security. Chigorin will do an interview and book signing, then head to the commentary room. Personally, I don't like this. I think we should grab Ilya now."

"We can't go yet," Wolfe said. "If we take him down now, we won't learn anything."

"But what if he goes after Chigorin?" Garber gestured around the lobby. "Look at the bloody situation. What do you say, boss?"

Cornwall's voice came over the radio: "I'm going to let Powell make the call. Do we think that Chigorin is at risk?"

"I don't know," Powell said into his headpiece. "Something about it feels wrong. I'm going for a closer look. Wolfe, come with me."

As Garber stayed behind to watch the entrance, Powell

and Wolfe headed across the room, moving toward where Chigorin and his interviewer had taken their seats before the cameras. Wolfe turned to Powell. "I'm afraid that I never joined chess club. What's this guy's story?"

Powell continued toward the far end of the lobby, where the crowd was rapidly growing. "He's one of the greatest players in the world. They used to call him the Turk, after the famous chess automaton, but he hasn't played competitively in a long time. At the moment, he's among the most prominent critics of Putin. The rumor is that he's going to run for president in two years."

Wolfe frowned. "So why would Ilya care about him? If he's a critic of Putin—"

"I know," Powell said. "It doesn't fit his profile. Nothing about this adds up."

As they drew closer to the crowd near the grandmaster, Powell reflected that a great deal of Chigorin's recent career had failed to add up as well. Chigorin had been a tireless opponent of the intelligence services, pressing for official investigations into kidnappings, assassinations, abuses of power. Yet for all his popularity overseas, he was no real match for the forces at home. There was no advantage to being a chess master in a game where your opponent could change the rules at will.

All the same, Chigorin had proven himself a perpetual irritant to the current regime, leading demonstrations against state security and working to build a viable opposition, which had obliged him to take certain precautions. Powell pointed toward the elevators, where a bodyguard had taken up position, while two more stood just out of camera range, all of them tough Turkish types. "Chigorin's received death threats and harassment at home, so he's very careful. There's no way anyone could take him down here and hope to get away with it."

They reached the rows of attendees pressing against the circle described by the cameras. Chigorin, a microphone clipped to his lapel, was seated across from his interviewer, a slim, dark man with a wide forehead. Behind them, a table was piled high with copies of Chigorin's latest book, which promised to share the secrets of chess tactics in the boardroom.

As Powell and Wolfe found a vacant place to stand, the interview began. The interviewer introduced himself and his guest, then turned to Chigorin. As they began to discuss the tournament, Powell kept his eye on the crowd. There were perhaps fifty people watching. Near the front of the group stood an attractive young woman in a red dress, her lips parted slightly, her body seeming to vibrate with the thrill of being so close to the great man.

After a few more questions about the tournament, the interviewer shifted gears. "Obviously, you've spent most of the past decade focusing on politics. Would you say that chess has influenced your political views?"

"Chess has shaped everything I've done," Chigorin said at once. "If you want a pretentious answer, which I think you do, I refer you to Tolstoy's conception of the calculus of history, which says that world events are composed of countless tiny factors that the historian must integrate into a coherent whole. This is not so different from what a chess player does."

"What about Putin?" the interviewer asked. "What is the calculus of his regime?"

Chigorin's face took on a serious expression, although Powell sensed a certain relish as well. "It doesn't take a genius to see the disregard for human rights, the growing gap between rich and poor, the oppression of the press. This isn't a government. It's a corporation run for the benefit of a handful of former intelligence agents. Nabokov had it right. Russian history can be understood as the continuous evolution of the secret police. This is just the latest incarnation."

"I see," the interviewer said, expressing little interest in the turn the conversation had taken. "So do you intend to run for president?"

Chigorin leaned forward in his chair, his powerful shoulders straining against his suit. "I haven't thought about it. At the moment, the challenge is to build a coalition. The state doesn't mind the existence of opposition parties as long as they're too divided to get anything done. This is why I'm working to bring these groups together. It's the only way to permanently crush the Chekists."

The interviewer smiled. Powell sensed him mentally reviewing the transcript of the interview, wondering what could be pulled out for fifteen seconds on the evening news. "And how are you finding London?"

As Chigorin replied, shifting easily into a discussion of his favorite local restaurants, Powell saw that the interview was winding down. He spoke quietly into his headpiece. "Looks like he's going to start the signing soon. I'll stick with him until he heads for the commentary room."

Wolfe was still watching the crowd, which had grown restless when the talk turned to politics. "Where do you want me?"

Powell looked across the lobby. "There's a good observation point near the auditorium doors. Plant yourself there. When Ilya comes out, we'll need more than one pair of eyes."

"Got it," Wolfe said. She touched him lightly on the arm. "You be careful, all right?"

"I will." Powell turned back to the interview. As the taping ended, Chigorin thanked his interviewer and removed the microphone from his lapel. He set it down on his chair, then headed for the table where his books were displayed. And it was at that moment, unnoticed by anyone, that the woman in the red dress detached herself from the rest of the crowd and began to move in his direction.

20

Inside the auditorium, the invitational tournament had been under way for thirty minutes. Sixteen rows of seats were packed with spectators watching the four games taking place simultaneously on a stage at the front of the room, the action unfolding on the quadrants of an overhead screen. It was so quiet that one could hear nothing but the occasional faint click of cameras.

On the stage itself, which was framed with brown curtains, eight grandmasters were paired off at the tables. They ranged in age from twenty to over fifty, with little in common aside from their neatly pressed shirts and air of intense concentration. After placing each piece, they noted down the move on their score sheets, then tapped the clock. As they played, arbiters flanked them on either side, with photographers moving silently around the stage.

Ilya was seated near the back of the room, one row behind Morley and his bodyguard, who occupied a pair of seats across the aisle. From here, he could see the briefcase on Morley's lap, beneath the rolled tournament program in the fund manager's hands. And although he kept his eyes mostly on the games in progress, he continued to consider the briefcase from time to time.

If the situation at the tournament was a game, Ilya thought, it was one he had entered halfway through, without knowing what the earliest moves had been, or even the names of the players. Still, there were certain things that he could determine merely by studying the board. The fact, for instance, that the killer had gone into the houses of the first two victims, when Ilya knew from his own experience that it was always easier to catch one's target away from home.

He looked over at Morley, who seemed to be watching the games with absorption, although the way his hands clutched the program told a different story. Morley had been more cautious. He had chosen a public place for the meeting, changing the location at the last minute and bringing his own protection. Clearly he suspected that he was taking a risk by coming at all. Yet this transaction, whatever it was, was important enough for him to see it through, rather than calling it off altogether.

Ilya wasn't sure what was supposed to take place here, but he had a few ideas. The first two deaths had all the marks of an intelligence operation. Either they had been carried out to destroy evidence, or they had been intended to retrieve something. And the more he looked at the case on Morley's lap, the more he suspected that the second possibility was correct.

Which left him with no choice but to disrupt the exchange. And the best way of doing this was to get the briefcase first.

He thought of the pistol under his jacket. If necessary, he could take the case by force. Perhaps he could even escape with it. But the last thing he wanted was more blood on his hands. And as he looked at it now, something about the briefcase itself seemed strange. It was too obvious, like a prop from a movie, as if—

Before he could finish this thought, he was distracted by a murmur from the crowd. When he looked up at the screen, it took him only a second to see what had happened. A player in the fourth match had blundered in the twelfth move, giving up a knight. Glancing at the stage, Ilya saw that the aging grandmaster, normally so impassive at the table, was clenching his fists in frustration, while a tremor of anticipation went through his younger opponent's body.

As the reality of the situation became clear, the photographers moved in like sharks, trying to capture the moment without disrupting the game. Ilya watched the stage for another second, then turned back to the audience. Only then did he see that Morley and his bodyguard had risen from their seats.

Ilya felt his pulse accelerate, but he forced himself to remain where he was. He waited as the two men edged into the aisle and headed toward the exit, moving away from the action onstage. Morley was still carrying the briefcase. Ilya watched them go, tracking them without moving his head, and was about to follow when his eye was caught by something else.

At the edge of the auditorium, in the far aisle, another man was heading for the doors. He wore a green coat and had a press pass around his neck, along with a shoulder bag. A camera with a telephoto lens was in his hands. And for some reason, even as the drama unfolded on the stage behind him, he was the only photographer in the room not taking pictures.

Ilya looked more closely at the man's face. A second

later, in a rush of understanding, he saw who it was. It was the photographer he had encountered in Golden Square, taking pictures of the king's statue, or pretending to do so, only a few moments after Morley had left for the day.

Gathering up his bag, Ilya rose slowly from his seat. As he headed for the aisle, his awareness drawn into a tight point, he felt a number of facts fall into place. Two victims had died so far, both skilled craftsmen. But not everything could simply be made. For certain items, you needed something else. You needed access. Which was precisely what a man like Morley could provide.

Then, glancing at the photographer again, he saw that the other man had halted. And that he was looking back at him.

Before Ilya could turn away, he felt their gazes lock. The other man's eyes were clear and very blue. For a moment, the two men stood across from each other, separated by half the auditorium, but close enough to see everything that counted. They looked at each other, feeling the rest of the world fall away. And each man recognized the other for what he was.

At last the photographer turned and continued toward the exit. Ilya darted a glance toward the doors leading out to the lobby, which swung closed as Morley and his bodyguard left the room.

The photographer headed for the same set of doors. Just before he was about to slip outside, he turned back for one last look at Ilya. Then he disappeared through the doors as well.

As soon as he was gone, Ilya followed, his heart thudding. When he was a few steps from the exit, he undid his jacket, giving him easier access to his gun. Then he pushed the door open and went outside.

At the other end of the room, watching the doors, Asthana spoke into her headpiece: "He's out. Wolfe, where are you?"

21

Wolfe had taken up position outside the auditorium a few moments earlier. From here, by the doors, she had a good view of the lobby, where the crowd that had gathered around Chigorin was starting to disperse, with handfuls of onlookers clustering around the television screens in the corners.

A second later, she heard a shout from the part of the floor where the interview had taken place. Turning, she saw that a pretty young woman in a red dress had gone up to Chigorin, who was about to begin his book signing. Recognizing the woman from earlier, Wolfe noticed for the first time that she had one hand in her purse. With her other hand, she waved at Chigorin: "Excuse me, sir—"

Chigorin, who had been chatting with the tournament director, turned in her direction. "Yes?"

Before anyone could react, the woman's hand slid out of her purse and threw something in Chigorin's face. Wolfe started with surprise. From where she was standing, it looked like a wad of dollar bills, and as it hit Chigorin in the forehead, it burst apart into bits of paper, which fluttered to the ground.

As a gasp went up from the crowd, the woman screamed at Chigorin, her voice loud and hectoring: "Judas! Political prostitute! You're a tool of the Americans! You should be ashamed to call yourself Russian—"

The room erupted in confusion. Wolfe, still looking across the floor, stood back, her palms outward, as a wave of people, many with cameras, rushed toward the source of the conflict. She spoke into her headpiece, back to the wall: "Stay focused, everyone. Powell, what's going on?"

Powell was still standing near the bank of television cameras. She heard his voice in her ear: "—just a protester. Looks to me like a member of the Young Guard. I'm going to try and—"

He broke off. Wolfe saw him take an involuntary step forward, shoved from behind as one of Chigorin's bodyguards rushed the protester, who was still shouting. He seized her by the arm, pulling her back, as another bodyguard led Chigorin away from the melee. The woman's voice rose above the din: "This man is not Russian! He is an American citizen! He has taken an oath to undermine our country in the name of the State Department—"

Cornwall's voice crackled over the radio: "What the bloody hell is going on?"

Wolfe saw that Powell had forced his way to the edge of the crowd, dusting himself off. "It's a protester," Powell said in her earpiece. "A member of a Putin youth group that has harassed Chigorin in the past. I can see the money that she threw in his face. Thirty-dollar bills."

A second later, his voice was drowned out as the woman lunged for Chigorin again. Everyone in the crowd seemed to be shouting at once. The television crews scrambled to get footage of the protester, as well as Chigorin, who was being hustled toward the elevators by his bodyguards. Raising his arms, the tournament director assumed a stance at the center of the confusion, his face shining in the camera lights: "Ladies and gentlemen, *please*—"

Wolfe looked over at Chigorin, who was standing by the elevators, apparently arguing with his security detail over whether or not to leave. She was about to go closer when Asthana's voice came over the radio: "India is on the move. Wolfe, please tell me you're watching the doors."

"I'm here," Wolfe said, turning in time to see the doors open. She braced herself, taking a step back, then saw that it was only a press photographer in a green jacket, who turned away and headed for the far end of the lobby. Something about him caught her eye, but before she could put this impression into words, the doors opened again, and Ilya appeared.

"He's out," Asthana said in her ear. "Wolfe, where are you? You need me to follow?"

"Wait." Wolfe drew back, keeping out of Ilya's line of sight, and watched as he took a step forward. He glanced for a moment at the commotion on the other end of the floor, then headed in the opposite direction. As he moved past her, his jacket swung open, and she saw the grip of a pistol.

Wolfe whispered into her headpiece. "I have eyes on him. And he's got a gun."

Garber's voice came over the radio at once: "A gun? You're sure about that?"

Wolfe's eyes tracked Ilya across the lobby floor. "Yes. I only saw it for a second. It's in a shoulder holster. Tokarev, maybe."

Cornwall cut into the conversation. "All right, that's enough. Take him down now."

"Got it," Powell said. Wolfe turned to find him standing at her side, his face flushed from the recent excitement. Behind them, the noise of the crowd was rising in waves. He gave her a nod. "Let's go."

They moved in together. Ilya was twenty paces ahead, walking toward the far end of the lobby, where attendees were watching the commotion from a distance. Wolfe saw a handful of children standing a few steps away, staring at the uproar with wide eyes, and began to pray that nothing would happen here—

Behind her, there was a fresh round of noise. Turning, Wolfe saw that the woman in the red dress had managed to break free from the man who had taken her by the arm. She stumbled forward, eyes on Chigorin, who was still standing at the elevator bay. Then, trying to elude the bodyguard, who was one step behind, she turned and collided with a television camera. It went crashing to the floor, tripod legs extended, lens shattering with a plastic crunch.

Wolfe turned back to Ilya. She saw that he had halted in response to the noise as well. And that he was looking straight at her and Powell.

In his dark eyes, she saw recognition. She flashed back two years to the basement of a club in Brighton Beach, the only time the three of them had ever been in the same room together—

Then time snapped back, and Ilya ran for the door leading to the stairs. The number of onlookers in the lobby had swelled, so he had to push his way through the crowd to the stairwell, which was twenty yards away.

Wolfe, running with Powell at her side, saw an opening between two groups of attendees. She took it, then found herself stumbling across the big chessboard, scattering the oversized pieces like bowling pins. She nearly tripped over an overturned pawn, but managed to right herself as she shouted into her earpiece: "He's heading for the stairs. Cut him off, cut him off!"

She and Powell moved separately across the floor. Powell timed it right and managed to squeeze through a gap in the crowd, making it to the elevator bay before Ilya could close the distance.

Ilya saw that the path to the elevators was blocked. Without a pause, he turned and headed in the other direction, where a set of doors led to the hall where the open tournament was in progress. As Wolfe watched, he slammed into the doors and pushed through to the other side. She followed, arms pumping, and plowed through the doors just before they closed. Powell entered a second after she did, puffing from the unaccustomed exertion.

Inside, row after row of chess players were seated in pairs, looking up in surprise as Ilya ran down the hall, threading his way between the long tables. At the other end of the room, there was a door with an exit sign. Ilya would be there in a few seconds. Wolfe yelled into her headpiece: "Armed unit, we need you on the ground! He's heading for the eastern stairs—"

As a member of the Flying Squad said something unintelligible over the earpiece, she broke off. Garber had appeared at the exit. Wolfe saw the flash of something metal in his hand. For a second, it looked like a gun, and she thought wildly that this couldn't happen now, not with so many people—

Then she saw that it wasn't a gun at all, but an expanding steel baton. Garber extended it with a flick of his wrist, and as Ilya neared the door, he swung it savagely, taking the other man off his feet.

Ilya fell, colliding with one of the tables on his way down. Chessmen went flying. As the players backed away, clearing a space, Garber yanked the gun from its concealed holster and pointed it at Ilya, who was lying on the ground, facedown: "Don't move! Don't you fucking move!"

Wolfe slid to a halt, her breath coming in ragged gasps. Looking down, she saw Ilya on the floor, his hands held away from his body, his face impossible to read. She couldn't believe it was over.

Powell appeared at her side, his glasses slipping down his face. He pushed them back up the bridge of his nose, then took a set of handcuffs from his pocket. Kneeling, he cuffed Ilya by the wrists, reciting the standard caution between lungfuls of air, something unreal in the tone of his voice: "You do not have to say anything, but anything you do say may be given in evidence—"

A crowd was gathering around them. Wolfe was doing her best to keep them back, her warrant card up in the air, when she realized that Ilya was speaking, his face pressed against the floor: "—James Morley. He's the target. I'm not the one you want. It's the photographer. You understand?"

Hearing this, Wolfe remembered the man in the green coat, the one she had seen leaving the auditorium a second before Ilya. It occurred to her now that although he had entered the lobby just after the protester's attack on Chigorin, he had barely even glanced at the confusion, which had drawn every other photographer in sight. Instead, he had calmly gone the other way.

Without a word, Wolfe turned and headed back toward the lobby, moving in a fast walk at first, then breaking into a run. Powell's voice crackled over her earpiece: "Wolfe, what the hell are you doing?"

"The photographer," Wolfe managed to say. She reached the doors leading out to the lobby and burst through, hoping blindly that she wasn't too late. "It's him. We've got the wrong man—"

22

Karvonen had observed the chase from a distance. Standing at the far end of the lobby, a few steps from the door to the seminar room, he watched warily as the man he had seen in the auditorium took off across the floor, followed by a man and woman who did not seem entirely ready for the pursuit. It struck him as a piece of good luck, but he didn't yet know how it would affect his plans.

As he turned away, ignoring the commotion behind him, he asked himself who the first man could be. He had seen him before, in Golden Square, and might not have remembered him had he not been trained, in both his professions, to scrutinize every face he saw. When he considered who else might be watching him, he thought briefly about walking away, but did not. Even if this was a trap, he would not escape by turning from his purpose now.

Looking over his shoulder, he saw that everyone in the lobby was staring at the confusion unfolding at the opposite end of the hall. Satisfied that no one was even facing in his direction, he went up to the door of the seminar room, turned the knob, and went inside.

The first thing he saw was Morley, standing next to the conference table, on which his briefcase had been set. A rolled copy of the tournament program was clutched in his right hand.

An instant later, Karvonen felt someone strong seize him by the shoulders. He was shoved and spun around so that his face pressed against the smooth surface of the dry-erase board on the wall. A voice whispered in his ear, a threatening rumble with a thick Russian accent. "Don't move, *suka*."

Karvonen smiled, his face squashed against the whiteboard. "I wouldn't dream of it."

Keeping one hand pressed against the small of Karvonen's back, Morley's bodyguard shut the door. Karvonen laced his fingers behind his head as the bodyguard began to frisk him, searching his pockets and jacket for weapons. A rough hand ran up and down his legs, pausing only to feel his groin. Karvonen patiently endured the search, saying, "A strange meeting place, with Chigorin himself only a few steps away. Or is that the reason you chose it?"

In response, the bodyguard only yanked away his camera bag. He unzipped the cover and rooted around inside, checking all the pockets, examining the camera and lens, even uncovering the false bottom. Finally he shoved the bag back into Karvonen's hands and turned to Morley. "He's clean."

Karvonen slung the camera bag over his shoulder. "Now is it my turn to search you?"

"You're lucky we agreed to meet you at all," Morley replied. "Let's get it over with."

"Of course," Karvonen said. As he went up to the

conference table, he kept an eye on the others. The bodyguard, who braced a chair under the doorknob as easily
as he might have thrown a prisoner around an interrogation room, was straight from the Lubyanka, but Morley
was a more polished presence. When he undid the clasps
of the case and lifted the lid, he seemed to be playing a
role he had seen in movies, and Karvonen thought the
case itself was also a bit much.

Morley turned the suitcase around, indicating its contents. "Are we satisfied, then?"

Karvonen looked inside. Lying on a layer of molded
foam padding were two brushed steel cylinders, sleek,
beautiful, and no larger than a couple of CO_2 cartridges.
He reached down and picked one up. It was heavier
than he had expected. Turning the cylinder over, he
studied the base, comparing the socket to the one in the
plans that he had examined so carefully. At once he saw
the trap that had been set. "No. I want the real ones.
Where are they?"

"Good," Morley said. "I wanted to be sure that you
were the man I was told to meet."

Unrolling the tournament program he held in one
hand, he gave it to Karvonen, who opened it to the first
page. Beneath the list of players in the invitational, two
small, not very impressive ceramic canisters had been secured with translucent tape. He undid the tape and examined them. This time they were what he had expected.
"All right. We're good."

"Then we're done here," Morley said. "You have everything else you need?"

Karvonen pocketed the canisters. As he did, he wondered whether this question meant that Morley was igno-

rant of what had happened to the others. He shut the case, then allowed the fingers of his right hand to wander under the edge of the conference table, brushing what he had taped there earlier. "Yes. I'm ready."

"So this concludes our transaction." Morley picked up the case, then looked into Karvonen's eyes. "You won't see or hear from us again. And I don't want to hear from you. Not until this is over."

Karvonen, holding the businessman's gaze, saw a grain of fear there. "You won't."

The bodyguard, who was standing to one side, stretched out a muscular arm. With the tip of his finger, he prodded Karvonen in the chest. "And if you depart from our arrangement, you answer to me. You understand?"

"I do," Karvonen said. Then he reached under the table and pulled out the gun.

Before anyone could react, he brought the silenced pistol up and around and thrust the barrel against the bodyguard's chin. For a fraction of a second, their eyes met. Then Karvonen pulled the trigger.

The gunshot was like the sharp sound a man makes with his teeth pressed against his lower lip. Morley's bodyguard staggered back, blood streaming from his throat, and slumped against the wall. Karvonen could hear the steady pulse of liquid. Everything around him seemed lit from within, his movements precise, deliberate, perfect.

Karvonen turned to Morley. He saw the businessman's eyes widen, his mouth falling open, but before he could say anything, Karvonen shot him twice, two taps in the chest, and watched as he fell to the floor.

All was quiet. Karvonen looked around the seminar room. There was blood everywhere. No time for the purifying fire. Tucking the pistol into his waistband, he took off his green coat, which had caught most of the blood spatter, and let it drop. Then he tore the metal case from Morley's hands, not wanting to leave any evidence behind, and headed for the exit at the rear of the room. The real canisters were still in his pocket.

He opened the exit door, the lock of which he had taped, and went out to the stairwell. His other overcoat was rolled up at his feet. Leaning down, he scooped it up, then quickly descended the stairs.

Back in the seminar room, nothing, except the faint push and pull of a man breathing.

Morley lay on his back, in a pool of his own blood, staring at the light fixtures on the ceiling. Dimly, as if the noises were being filtered through layers of fine cloth, he heard shouts, then a splintering sound as the door was forced. A moment later, the light from overhead was blocked out as a woman leaned over him, her hair backlit, a shadow falling across his face.

Wolfe looked into the eyes of the man on the ground. She said something that Morley could not understand. He drew air into his lungs one last time, then forced out two words before the darkness descended.

"Dyatlov Pass—"

II

✠

December 14–21, 2010

The kingdom of the father is like a certain man who wanted to kill a powerful man. In his own house he drew his sword and stuck it into the wall in order to find out whether his hand could carry through. Then he slew the powerful man.

—The Gospel of Thomas

Tell me where all past years are,
Or who cleft the devil's foot . . .

—John Donne

23

Through the window of the custody room, Ilya seemed otherworldly, seated in a folding chair, his pale face sticking out through its plastic shroud. Wolfe knew that it was only a blue forensic suit, a sterile wrap-around sheet given to prisoners to lock in trace evidence, but to her eyes, it still made him look like a ghost.

She glanced at her phone, hoping that Asthana had checked in without her noticing, but saw no missed calls. Then she looked again at Ilya, who was being photographed by a constable with a digital camera. She wanted to talk to him now, but there was no halting the booking process, even though every passing second reduced their chances of finding Morley's killer.

The police station stood in Kensington, where Ilya had been brought immediately after his arrest. At two in the afternoon, the officers were nearing the end of the early turn, but many had lingered to stare at their new celebrity. Wolfe had been particularly interested to hear what name he would give. In the end, he had simply identified himself as Ilya Severin, replying in the same tone he used for everything else, quiet, brief, and with a prisoner's regard for the circle of his integrity.

On the other side of the glass, a scenes-of-crime officer finished swabbing Ilya's hands, then ran a comb back and forth through the prisoner's hair. Ilya leaned forward obediently, but as he did, he raised his eyes to the window. For a second, his gaze seemed to latch on to Wolfe's, although she knew that there was no way he could really see her. Then he turned away again.

At the far end of the room, Powell was speaking to the detective inspector, who had arrived five minutes ago. Wolfe checked her phone one last time, hoping in vain to find that Asthana had called with an update, then headed over to where the two men were standing.

"The firearms charge is enough to hold him," the inspector was saying. "We have the gun he was carrying when he was arrested. It doesn't look like a match for Campbell or Akoun, but we'll run it against the database—"

"Yes, that's fine," Powell said absently, his eyes fixed on the view through the window. Wolfe could sense his impatience to begin the interrogation. "In the meantime, we have an outstanding warrant for his arrest on suspicion of the murder of Lermontov, which means that we can question him without a solicitor present. I want to talk to him alone."

As Wolfe looked into the next room, where the scenes-of-crime officer was preparing yet another swab, she knew that they had to move quickly. A description of the man from the tournament had been issued to all available units, but for now, Ilya was their best source. And as she watched him sit stonily as a cheek sample was taken, Wolfe saw that he was already retreating into himself.

She turned to the others. "Listen, the rest of the process can wait. The longer we let this go on, the less cooperative he's going to be. He was tracking our killer. We need him to work with us."

"Unless he and the killer were in collusion," the inspector said. "We can't rule out that possibility. Frankly, it's easier for me to accept than the idea that he was planning to disrupt this assassination—"

"But we won't know until we ask him. And we need to ask him now." Wolfe pointed into the next room. "I know how the process works. They'll take his blood and confiscate his clothes. By the time they're done, he won't want to cooperate. He'll tell us to go to hell."

Wolfe nearly blushed at the unaccustomed profanity, which seemed to hang in the air, though she knew that the others wouldn't even notice it. Finally, the inspector said, "Fine. Give me one minute."

The inspector went into the custody room, closing the door behind him. As soon as he was gone, Wolfe turned to Powell. It was the first time they had been alone together since the arrest. "How do you want to handle this?"

"I'll lead," Powell said. "I know Ilya best. Which is to say I don't know him at all."

Wolfe heard a certain bitterness in his tone, which unsettled her. "Alan, listen to me. I know you've been hunting this man for a long time, but we can't get sidetracked. We've got to find this killer. If Ilya knows who he is, we need to convince him to help. Anything else is a distraction."

Powell headed for the interview room. "I'm aware of that. And to be honest, I'm not convinced that he knows much of anything. At the most, he has a knack for turning up at just the wrong time—"

"I know," Wolfe said. "Which means the three of us have something in common."

Inside, the interview room consisted of a table and four chairs, the walls lined with acoustic padding. Wolfe pulled out a chair, then decided that it was better to be standing. She tried to convince herself that she was extraordinarily calm, and yet she was also very aware of her heartbeat.

When the door opened again, Ilya entered the room with the detective inspector at his side. The forensic sheet was gone, taking away some of his ghostly aura, but his eyes remained distant and veiled. When he saw them, his face did not change, although Wolfe thought she saw a flicker of recognition.

As Ilya took a seat at the other end of the table, the inspector loaded a disc into the player on the wall, pressed the *RECORD* button, and gave the standard cautions. Powell sat down as well. Only a narrow table stood between him and the man he had pursued for so long.

After a beat, Powell shook out his handkerchief and began to polish his glasses. "Ilya, my name is Alan Powell. Do you remember me?"

Ilya said nothing, but he gave a short nod, as much with his dark eyes as with his head.

"Good." Powell put his glasses back on. "It's been a long time coming. I've been trying to find you for years, ever since you showed up at that club in Brighton Beach. We were both foreigners there, but now we're home. And I know you must have returned for a reason."

He paused, as if waiting for Ilya to speak, but the other man said nothing. Powell continued, unperturbed: "I don't know how much you've been told so far, but James

Morley is dead. So is his bodyguard. They were shot at the tournament, as you expected, just as we were taking you into custody. The killer, the photographer, is gone. We're currently in the process of tracking him down, but I think you know more about him than we do. Am I right?"

Ilya listened to this speech in silence, his eyes brightening only slightly at the news that Morley and his guard had been murdered. Wolfe noticed that his most striking features, aside from his eyes, were his hands, which were those of a lens grinder or other fine craftsman.

Powell, for his part, kept his attention focused on Ilya's face, which remained neutral. "Ilya, I know you've been tracking this man. I know that you went to the armorer's garage and the other crime scenes. I also know that none of this would interest you without reason. I've followed you long enough to suspect what this reason might be. Was this an intelligence operation?"

For the first time, Ilya seemed to take an interest in what Powell was saying. A challenging gleam appeared in his eyes, but when he spoke at last, his voice was soft: "The signs were there."

"And what signs were those?" When the other man did not respond, Powell smiled tightly. "Let me tell you what I think. You saw that an intelligence operation was under way, and you resolved to disrupt it, because this is what a man like you does. You did it in Brighton Beach. And you did it with Lermontov."

If Powell had been hoping for a reaction to the art dealer's name, Ilya disappointed him. He only sat in the same attitude as before, looking silently across the table, as if waiting for something more.

"There's no point in denying that you killed Lermontov," Powell said, his voice hardening. "The gun used to kill him was last seen in your possession. You brought it across the Atlantic, which couldn't have been easy, but it was intended to send a message. You wanted your enemies to know who had done this. And they do. But now it's time to send a message again."

Powell paused. "I know you don't trust me or the system I represent. You prefer to work on your own. But at the moment, the system is all you have. So I'm asking you, if you still hate the Chekists, to help us find this man."

Even before this entreaty was over, Wolfe saw that Ilya had tuned out. Powell, she realized, had taken the wrong tack. Before anyone could speak again, she was surprised to hear her own voice: "Ilya, what is the Dyatlov Pass?"

It was the first time she had ever spoken to him directly. Wolfe saw Ilya turn toward her, sizing her up, and for a second, she saw a trace of interest in his expression, a single spark in those black eyes. Then, as swiftly as it had appeared, it was gone, and Ilya turned back to Powell.

"Let me tell you a story," Ilya said. "Four men entered the king's orchard. When they saw what was there, one of them died at once. Another went mad. The third cut down all the shoots. And only one departed in peace." He paused. "You see, you had your chance. When the time comes, you'll see that you should have let me go. I have nothing more to say."

Ilya turned aside. Mentally replaying his words, Wolfe thought that she had heard this story somewhere else before, but couldn't remember where. Before she could ask him about this, Powell rose from the table. She saw that he was angry. "We're done, then. But this is far from over."

He left the room. The inspector glanced at Wolfe, then spoke for the benefit of the audio recorder: "Interview terminated at three fifteen."

With that, Wolfe left the room as well, glancing back once at Ilya, who remained in his seat. A moment later, a pair of constables appeared to escort him back to the custody area.

She joined the others in the hallway, where they discussed what the next steps would be. "We'll keep him at the station overnight," the inspector said. "I'll consult with Crown Prosecution about the rest. We'll start by charging him with Lermontov's death, and take it from there."

"Fine," Powell said. Wolfe could see for the first time how drained he was. "I'll want to talk to him again, but not until we've had more time to prepare. There must be a way inside—"

Powell broke off. Following his eyes, Wolfe saw that Garber was coming up the hall, a camera in one hand. "Just got this from a photographer at the scene. It's our best set of pictures so far. Wolfe, I need you to take a look."

"Be right there," Wolfe said. She glanced over at Powell. "Anything else you need?"

The real question, buried in her words, was whether he was doing all right, but Powell seemed to take it literally. "Not right now. I'll call you when I know what we're doing next. Go on, then."

He turned away, resuming his conversation with the inspector. Wolfe regarded them for a moment, then followed Garber to the station entrance. She saw that he was on edge, as if the high of taking down Ilya had already dissipated in the heat of the chase. "What else have we got?"

"Nothing. That's the goddamned problem." Garber led her out of the station and toward the van at the curb. "The killer chose just the right moment to make his move. Four hundred people, and nobody saw a bloody thing."

He slid open the doors of the van. Wolfe climbed into the rear, where a laptop had been set up on a plastic crate. As she sat down, Garber took the camera, hooked it up to the computer, and began loading the photos. "Shots cover the past four hours. Tell me if you see our guy."

In the darkened interior, Wolfe studied the pictures, scrolling quickly past the earlier shots. Most were close-ups of the players, but a few took in the larger crowd. She pointed one out. "Look here. You can see Morley and his security chief. Ilya is right behind them. And—"

She frowned. In Morley's lap, obscured by the chair in front of him, there was a hint of silver. "He's carrying some kind of briefcase. It wasn't there when we found him, was it?"

"No," Garber said. "The killer must have taken it. So maybe this was a robbery."

"Or an exchange." Wolfe scrolled to the next set of pictures, focusing on the faces in the crowd, especially the photographers. Finally, in one of the very last shots, she saw a familiar figure in the corner of the image, a tall blond man with a green jacket and camera. He was not looking at the lens, but the light made a sort of halo around his face, which was one she would never forget.

"Here we are," Wolfe said. She pointed at the screen. "That's him. That's our man."

24

Karvonen was heading up the ramp from Old Street station when his phone rang. The underground terminal stood in a noisy roundabout, the bicyclists chiming their bells as they sped past, so he had to hold the phone close to his ear to hear the voice on the other end. "Yes?"

"You've been blown," his handler said. "The police already have your picture."

His head lowered, Karvonen strode quickly up the sidewalk, moving past rows of cafés and kebab stands. He was carrying only the shoulder bag with his camera and gun. The silver case had been left in an alley three blocks from the convention center, after he had disposed of the fake canisters and padding in two separate trash bins. "How did it happen?"

"Our source says an officer saw you at the tournament. We're still trying to figure out how she identified you. And it gets worse. They've found Renata's body. Or most of it. It won't be long until they put the rest together." His handler's voice grew cold. "Did you really think we wouldn't find out?"

As he listened, Karvonen found himself swept up by a wave of anger. He had been coasting on a kind of high, and he resented being brought so abruptly down to earth. Still, he knew that his state of mind had been a dangerous one, so he did not entirely begrudge the wakeup call. "I did what had to be done. And you've kept things from me as well. Who was the man I saw?"

His handler hesitated, then said, "A nobody. An outsider showing his face where it wasn't wanted. We'll take care of him ourselves. It wasn't necessary for you to know who he was—"

"And it wasn't necessary for you to know about Renata." Karvonen touched the canisters in his pocket. "If you want what I have, you'll let me see this through. Otherwise, you'll never hear from me again."

There was silence on the other end. When his handler spoke again, his tone was all business. "Fine. But we need to regroup. The police will be looking for you. You have half an hour, maybe less, to close everything down."

"Done," Karvonen said. "But I'm going to need a few things. When can we meet?"

"I'll need time to prepare. Come and find me two hours from now." The handler gave him an address in Highgate. "Do you know it?"

Karvonen recognized the location. "A barber shop. You going to give me a shave?"

"And a haircut." A note of grim humor appeared in his handler's voice. "If you're going to make it out alive, you'll need a new face."

His handler hung up. Karvonen pocketed his phone, then rounded the corner into the Shoreditch Triangle, the kebab stands giving way to pubs and art galleries. The street was narrow and paved in cobblestones, and after a few steps, the noise of the roundabout fell silent.

As he drew closer to his own building, which was half-way up the block, Karvonen crossed the street, heading for a Vietnamese restaurant on the other side. Above the door, an overhang cast a rectangle of shade. Karvonen halted in this area of shadow, then looked across the way.

He studied the entrance to his building. On the ground floor was an architectural firm with scale models of houses displayed behind plate glass. His own motor-bike was parked at the curb. Raising his eyes, he found the row of windows that belonged to his studio. From where he was standing, he could tell that the curtains were drawn, and he saw no sign of movement behind the drapes.

Karvonen remained there for another minute, watching the windows intently. It was not just the police he was concerned about. He knew it was possible that his handler, concerned by his ability to complete the project, had sent someone else to retrieve the canisters. Granted, there were not many men left with his particular set of skills, which meant that his handler might not want to dispose of him so casually. But the possibility could not be dismissed.

In the end, he emerged from the shade of the over-hang, crossed the street, and went around to the other side of the building. Beneath the rows of hanging air conditioners, the stairs were accessible through a rear entrance. Unlocking this door, Karvonen let himself in, glancing back once before going inside.

The stairwell was silent and dark. Karvonen shut the door behind him, then crept quietly upstairs, checking each landing as he went, one hand on the pistol in his camera bag. When he reached his own floor, he stationed himself to one side of the doorway, then peeked carefully through the pane of frosted glass that looked into the corridor beyond. It was empty.

Karvonen opened the door, hand still on the gun, and stepped softly onto the fourth floor. He checked the door leading to the opposite stairwell, confirmed that it was clear, and finally went back to his own flat.

Placing an ear against the door, he listened. Nothing. He drew the gun and took out his keys, inserting one into the lock. Listening intently, he turned the key, then pushed the door open.

He swung inside, leading with the gun. His flat was dark, with only a narrow line of sunlight shining through the gap in the curtains. Leaving the door ajar, Karvonen rapidly checked the entire loft, going from one room to another, and found that everything was as he had left it. Only when he had confirmed that the loft was clear did he close and lock the door again.

As he was sticking the gun into his belt, Karvonen heard paws against the floorboards as his cat came running to meet him. Bending down, he tried to scoop the cat up with his free hand, then felt sharp teeth sink into the web of flesh between his thumb and forefinger. He cursed and flung the cat away, watching it scamper on skittering claws into the kitchen.

Sucking on his injured hand, Karvonen set his bag on the floor and made his way into the loft, leaving off the lights. He began by changing his clothes, tossing the ones he had been wearing into the empty bathtub. A packed bag already stood at the rear of his closet. From the lowest drawer of his bureau, where the device had once resided, he extracted the charger for his encrypted phone, sliding both charger and phone into the bag's outside pocket.

The device itself was no longer here. A few days earlier, after checking the components one last time, Karvonen had taken the device apart and mailed it in two packages to an address he knew by memory. Traveling by regular mail, it would take several days for the parcels to reach their destination, which gave him just enough time to get there as well.

Back in the main loft, he removed the memory card from his camera and slid it into his pocket. Kneeling by his desk, he removed the plastic cover from the computer tower, undid the screws holding the hard drive in place, and yanked it away from its cables. A stack of printouts from the desk went under his arm. Returning to the bathroom, he threw everything into the tub, along with his wallet, his passport, and, after removing the clip, his gun.

In his darkroom, tucked neatly among a shelf of other chemicals, stood two glass jars of potassium permanganate, as well as a soft plastic bottle of glycerin. He took them into the bathroom, where he smashed the jars in the tub, scattering the dark purple crystals. Then, squeezing the bottle, he sent a colorless stream of glycerin arcing over the rest. After a few seconds, the crystals flared into flame, cooking the metal and plastic and burning the paper to ashes, the words on the page disappearing like a photo developed in reverse.

When the paint above the bathtub had begun to blacken, Karvonen left the bathroom, the fire still burning, and looked around the studio. The cat was in the corner, yowling, but he ignored it as he slung the bag over his shoulder, canisters tucked in his pocket, and left the flat.

As he was locking the door behind him, a voice came from over his shoulder: "We missed you the other night—"

Karvonen turned. It was his neighbor from across the hall, her hair tied back in a ponytail, her work shirt spattered with paint. He gave her a smile. "Sorry, but something came up at the last minute."

Wagging a finger, she headed for her own flat. "Well, I forgive you this time. But you won't get a second chance." She paused, listening, then arched an eyebrow. "Is that your *cat* I hear?"

Karvonen's smile grew wider. From behind the door, the cat's faint howling could still be heard. In his mind's eye, he saw the fire spreading in the bathtub, and knew that it would not be long before the smell of smoke spread into the hallway. "He misses me. But he'll quiet down soon."

He gave his neighbor a wave, then headed for the stairs as she went into her flat. Behind him, the first few strands of smoke were beginning to seep out from under the studio door.

Taking the rear stairs, he was out on the street in under a minute. Going back around to the front of the building, he passed his bike without pausing, feeling only a twinge of regret at the thought that he would never ride it again. From his coat pocket, he took a knit cap, which he pulled down over his head.

As Karvonen went up the street, heading for the underground station, he heard a two-tone siren, then saw a pair of panda cars coming in his direction. Passing him, they drove on without pausing, heading for the triangle. Karvonen continued onward, moving into the crowd near the roundabout, and when nobody was watching, he took the keys from his pocket and flung them away.

25

"Request for bail is denied," Mr. District Judge Roundhay said, looking down from his long oak bench at the man installed in the dock. "The accused shall be remanded into custody until the date of his next court appearance, provisionally scheduled for one week from today, at which time—"

It was the day after his arrest. Ilya was seated in a wooden chair at the center of the dock, a Securicor officer beside him, only a step away from the bench with his advocate and the prosecution counsel. Above the courtroom ran a cramped public gallery. Along with a number of unfamiliar faces, he could see Powell and Wolfe.

Ilya turned back to the courtroom. As his advocate, a small, bearded man with whom he had spoken only briefly, went over the timetable for the trial, he began to tune out. The police had laid out their case quickly and efficiently. Somewhat to his surprise, he had been indicted for the murder of Lermontov. He guessed that this was due to Powell's influence.

A moment later, he was informed that the hearing was over. Rising, he allowed himself to be escorted out of the courtroom by a guard, who led him downstairs to a long yellow corridor. At the end of the hallway stood a row of cells. The Securicor man unlocked the nearest steel door and eased it open. "Here we are, then," the guard said. "End of the yellow brick road."

Ilya went inside. It was a small room, about ten feet by five, with two plastic chairs, a cheap table, and walls covered in graffiti. Despite its lack of charm, it represented a step up from his most recent accommodations, a cell at the Kensington police station with a mattress infested with lice.

Behind him, the guard withdrew, saying, "You have visitors. Won't be a moment." Then he shut the door. There was no need for him to lock it, because there was no handle on the inside.

Ilya remained standing in the cell, waiting for whatever was coming. Over the past twenty hours, he had carefully considered his situation from all sides. He had never expected to receive bail, meaning that he would be sent to prison, on remand, until his trial. This in itself was not a cause for concern. Ilya had spent years in the worst prisons in the world, and there was no question in his mind that he would survive. But he knew, even now, that there would be complications.

He was still standing in the middle of his cell when the door was opened a second time. As Powell and Wolfe entered, the Securicor man pocketed his keys. "Door open or closed?"

"Open," Powell said. He pulled out a chair, then gestured at the other. "Have a seat."

After a beat, Ilya sat down. He saw that Wolfe remained standing, as she had at their earlier interview. Turning to Powell, he thought back to their first meeting. Even in a mob of men with guns, something about the Englishman had caught his attention. This was no less true today, which was why he was slightly annoyed when Powell began by laboriously explaining the situation to him yet again.

"Let's not waste time," Powell said, laying a file on the table. "You're being sent to Belmarsh. You know what that means."

Ilya said nothing. The news was not a surprise, but it gave him a peculiar satisfaction to hear it. This, he saw clearly, was the test he was meant to receive. Anything less would have been a disappointment.

"Vasylenko is there," Wolfe said, speaking for the first time. "Along with many of his men. We know that he wants you dead. And you've certainly given him reason enough to call for your blood."

"Which presents us with a problem," Powell said. "We need you alive. We're doing our best to transfer you to a safer location, but the process can take weeks or months. And we might have better luck if you agree to cooperate."

Ilya, remaining silent, saw immediately that this offer was less straightforward than it seemed, and was sorry that they evidently thought so little of him. Still, he sensed that further information was forthcoming, so he only inclined his head, as if inviting them to continue.

Powell opened the case file, removed a photograph, and slid it across the table. "This is Lasse Karvonen, the man who killed Morley and his bodyguard. We also believe that he murdered Campbell, Akoun, and a photographer named Renata Russell, for whom he was working as a retoucher. He's missing. We've been to his flat, but it's cleaned out. He burned everything before he left."

Ilya looked at the picture, which was of the man he had seen at the tournament. It was a handsome face, but as he looked it now, he saw an underlying coldness that was apparent even in this unguarded shot.

Powell took the photo back. "We don't know where he's gone, but whatever he's doing, it isn't over yet. Based on the evidence, he was gathering the components for some kind of device. And we suspect that the plot involves Russian intelligence." He paused. "If you know anything about this man, you should share it with us. Then, perhaps, we can get you out of the lion's den."

Ilya looked evenly at Powell. He saw the depth of intellect there, but also a man who had too much confidence in the system, and wondered whether Powell realized how little power he really had. "You speak Russian?"

Powell glanced at Wolfe. "Not very well, I'm afraid. But I know enough to get by."

Ilya saw that he was downplaying his expertise, but decided to let it pass. "You know the *netovtsy*?"

"Yes," Powell said. "A schismatic movement in the seventeenth century. They gave up all worldly speech except for the word *no*."

"Very good," Ilya replied. "Then you already know what my answer will be."

Powell looked at him for another moment. Then he rose, scooping up the case file. Heading for the door, he signaled to the guard, who had remained outside. "We're done. Wolfe, let's go."

He left the room. For a moment, as Wolfe turned away, Ilya sensed that she wanted to say something else, but in the end, she only followed Powell into the corridor. As soon as she was gone, the door of the cell clanged shut, and Ilya was alone once more with his thoughts.

A few minutes later, the door opened again. The guard grinned at him. "It's time."

Rising from his chair, Ilya went into the hall, where he was handcuffed to a second guard and led outside to a prison van. It had ten windows, all opaque, so that it was impossible to see inside.

Climbing into the van, he was uncuffed from the guard and locked into a separate cubicle. Next to him, in the adjacent sweatbox, a tattooed man in a donkey jacket was muttering to himself in an unintelligible stream, which only rose in intensity when, a minute later, the van lurched forward and trundled clumsily out of the court-yard.

It was forty minutes to Belmarsh. During the trip, Ilya did not look out the window once. Instead he scrutinized the faces of the men around him, only one of which really caught his attention. This was a prisoner close to his own age, his hair long and stringy, who seemed to be sleeping, his head leaning against the window of his cubicle. Every now and then, however, there was a faint flash of white between his lids, like the visible slit of a reptile's eyes.

At last, the van slowed. Turning to the view outside, Ilya saw a gate open to let them in, then close heavily behind them. After passing through a second gate, the van entered a concrete courtyard, where it halted, engine idling. Then the prisoners were led out one at a time.

Ilya was one of the last to disembark. As he descended the steps of the van, he took a moment to survey his sur-roundings. The courtyard was girded by a brick wall, thirty feet high, topped with razor wire. Overhead stretched a flat white sky. From the line of prisoners to his side, he heard a short bark of laughter.

They filed into the receiving spur, where their first stop was a kind of transparent cell with walls of thick glass. Ilya sat down, ignored by the others. The man he had seen earlier on the van, pretending to sleep, was standing apart from the rest, who were pointedly not looking in his direction.

A second later, his name was called. Ilya went into the reception area, where he was told to complete a form by a guard seated behind the counter, who asked him for his name, age, and weight in stone. The guard noted his answers, then inquired after his religion. When Ilya replied, the guard wrote it down, saying, "Don't see many Jews, now, do we?"

From there, he passed into the next room, where an arc lamp hung from the ceiling. Ilya stood in the white circle, feeling the heat on his shoulders, and was ordered to strip. He complied, handing his clothes to the guard at his side, aware at all times of the video camera on the wall.

The guard looked him over, taking note of the pale scars that tattoos, now erased, had left behind. Then, after declining the option of keeping his own clothes while on remand, Ilya was brought into the next room, where he was given a blue striped shirt, jeans, a gray pullover, and a black donkey jacket.

Ilya dressed, then went to a nearby room for a medical interview, at the end of which he was informed that he would be spending his first night in the hospital wing. He knew that this was standard procedure for prisoners on remand, and that it meant he would be kept on suicide watch.

Carrying his bedding in his arms, Ilya followed another guard upstairs, climbing three flights to a long corridor. This guard, a heavyset man with glasses, was less careful than the others, and he did not glance back as he unbolted two doors and led Ilya into the hospital ward: "Here we are, then—"

Ilya went inside. Around him, gradually rising in volume as he neared the heart of the ward, there were stifled screams, shouts, the sound of weeping. He saw pale faces, skinny legs, the eyes of countless exiles.

As he and the guard approached the door of his cell, Ilya became aware of two things at once. The first was that he could feel Vasylenko's presence. Vasylenko, he suspected, could sense him as well. Sooner or later, the old man would come for him. It was only a matter of time.

His other realization, as his cell door was unlocked, was that while he was here, a man on the outside was readying something in perfect freedom. And with every passing second, Ilya sensed, the plan that he had failed to prevent was drawing ever closer to completion.

26

An hour earlier, a ticket agent at the Eurostar desk at St. Pancras had looked up as a set of footsteps came to a halt at her counter. Standing before her was an attractive man with short dark hair and a pronounced widow's peak. He gave her a nod. "Good morning. I'd like to buy a ticket to Brussels. One way, please."

The agent glanced him over appreciatively, then looked down at her terminal, typing with her lacquered nails. She was South Asian and twenty, with a manner poised between brisk and flirtatious. "And when will you be leaving?"

Unslinging the bag he was carrying on his shoulder, the traveler set it on the floor. "The next available train, please."

"Let's see what we have, then." The ticket agent studied her computer screen. "You're in luck. The next train will be departing in forty minutes. I can get you a good seat for sixty-four pounds."

"That sounds fine." As the traveler smiled, the agent saw that the only flaw in his otherwise faultless looks was his teeth, which were crooked and pronounced. British smiles, she thought, could be so unfortunate.

He handed her his credit card, which the agent swiped through the reader on her terminal. *DALE STERN*, it said. As the transaction went through, she took a brochure from her desk. "Check in straight to your left here, all the way down the hall. You have about ten minutes before boarding starts." She took the ticket from the printer and set it on the counter, circling the relevant information in ballpoint pen. "Here you are, then. St. Pancras to Brussels Midi, one way only."

The traveler smiled again as he accepted the ticket. "Thank you very much."

"You're quite welcome," the agent said. She kept her eye on him as he turned away, passing through the glass doors into the station beyond. Then she went resignedly back to work.

Outside, on the main floor of the station, Karvonen headed for the platform, his paper ticket in hand. At the entrance, he fed the ticket into a slot, which spat it out again as the gates opened to let him through. Up ahead, a sliding door of frosted glass led to the security line.

At the front of the queue, which had only a handful of other travelers, he put his bag on a conveyor belt, watching as it disappeared through the curtain of the scanner. As he placed his wallet and other personal items into a plastic bin, a guard politely asked him to remove his jacket, although he was allowed to retain his thick sweater. Underneath his shirt, the canisters were secured between his shoulder blades with a cross of medical adhesive tape.

Karvonen passed through the metal detector. It did not register the canisters, which were ceramic, with only a few small metal components. He picked up his bag at the other end. As he did, he passed a young woman, also coming out of security, who was gathering her things while talking into a mobile phone: "Hold on. I'm just going to put my bits away—"

Beyond security, there was a second line at passport control, where two French border agents in identical blue uniforms were stationed in a glass cube. Karvonen pushed his passport through the opening in the window. The nearest agent picked it up, glanced at it briefly, then stamped and returned it. Karvonen thanked him, then headed for the departure lounge.

His passport had not been scanned into the larger border control system, but even if it had, it would not have presented a problem. The passport was real. Karvonen had picked it up from his handler the day before, along with other items in the name of Dale Stern. He had not asked where this identity came from. Nor had his handler volunteered the information.

Karvonen entered the departure lounge. In the old days, he knew, the city had been full of documentation agents, their only function to obtain birth certificates and passports to support legends for illegals. In a pinch, documents could also be bought from various undesirables, such as addicts looking to score money for a fix, although the Yardies had cornered that market these days.

Once you had obtained the essential pieces of paperwork, you could begin to construct the legend. Some were quite elaborate, with flat rentals and pay stubs meticulously documenting an entire fictional life. Others consisted of little more than a driver's license, a passport, and a credit card with occasional purchases. Dale Stern was of the latter kind. The legend would not hold up to sustained scrutiny, but it was more than enough for his present needs.

At the news kiosk in the departure lounge, Karvonen bought a copy of that morning's paper, noticing that the seller's eyes strayed down to his bad teeth. He still wasn't used to his new face. Because the legend had been obtained at the last minute, it had forced him to change his appearance more than he would have liked, although it was nothing that could not be reversed.

Yesterday, after arriving at the meeting with his handler, he had been understandably reluctant to get into the barber's chair, especially with a man holding a razor nearby. His handler's response had been curt but reasonable: "If we wanted to kill you, you would be dead already."

Karvonen had granted the wisdom of this observation. He was also reassured by the fact that he had hidden the canisters beforehand. With that, he had climbed into the chair, where his hair had been cut and tinted, and his hairline and eyebrows reshaped with electrolysis. A dental plate and colored contact lenses had completed the picture. The result was far from perfect, but it would do.

As he tucked the newspaper under his arm, he saw that the departure platform for his train had been posted. He followed a stream of families and schoolgirls with rolling suitcases up an escalator ramp, which was walled in with glass. Arriving at the next level, he moved down the platform until he reached the carriage whose number was printed on his ticket. He found his seat and put his bag in the overhead rack. Then, sitting down, he unfolded the paper and began to read.

On the front page, there was an article about the killings at the tournament, which had shocked the entire city. There was also a picture, not very good, of Karvonen's face. He was more interested in the inside article about the discovery of Renata's body. So far, the press had failed to connect the two incidents, although he knew that this was simply a matter of time. He read both articles with care and looked up only as the train began to glide smoothly out of the station.

Outside, it was overcast, and the sides of the track were heaped with pink gravel. After pausing at another station, the train began to pick up speed, and before long, it was barreling serenely through pastureland, with dots of cows cropping the grass beneath the white sky. It reminded him, faintly, of a journey he had taken many years ago. At the time, it had not seemed especially important, but when he looked back now, he saw that it had determined nothing less than the course of his life.

It had, of course, been a trip to Russia. Karvonen had booked the ticket with a pack of his college friends, the train taking them from Helsinki to a faraway city whose name he had not heard before or since. For his friends, as for many young men, the trip had been an excuse to get drunk as the snowy landscape unspooled outside the window. Karvonen, meanwhile, had found himself changed forever.

For the first time in his life, looking at the expanse of this country pressing against the borders of his own, he had glimpsed the destiny inherent in geography. Land had its own inexorable power. Russia, with its sheer massiveness, could hardly be other than central to the future of the world. By comparison, Finland, its icy appendage, seemed like a nation of mist and shadows.

Until that moment, Karvonen had not known what kind of man he would be. Taking picture after picture through the window, he had seen how constrained he had been by his homeland. Finland was too complacent, too marginal, and even if it produced great assassins, their names would remain unknown.

Karvonen, instinctively, had wanted the greatest possible stage for his talents, and the view from the train had told him exactly what that stage should be. Russia was his country's oldest enemy, and he had been raised from the cradle to see it as such, but it also defined its neighbors by its gravitational pull. There were also times, like it or not, when your enemy was the one you wanted to impress.

In the end, then, he had approached them with his services. His audition, which he had planned carefully, had been the murder of a business chief for a Russian news agency. After stabbing the reporter to death at home, using his grandfather's knife, he had gone to the intelligence services with proof of the killing, obtaining an introduction from a military contact. Their own ranks, as he would soon find, contained surprisingly few true killers, so they had gladly taken him on.

Even then, however, they had not fully understood his reasons. Like all Finns, Karvonen had loved his country deeply, in some ways more than his own life. Yet it was impossible, looking across the border, not to feel that his homeland had fallen short, or had never been given a fair chance at all. More than anything else, he had wanted to prove to his handlers that, left to his own devices, he could play this game better than any Russian. Which was exactly what he had done.

Then, two years ago, after he had notched up a number of successes, his handler had come to him with a new assignment. The situation was shifting rapidly within the intelligence services, his handler had explained, so he was being given the chance, if he wanted it, to keep up with the changing times.

Now, at last, the project was reaching completion. He had done well. And throughout it all, he had operated under one condition. He had never spilled a drop of Finnish blood. And he never would.

As the train entered the tunnel that led underwater to the continent beyond, Karvonen settled back into his seat. Although he was glad to be leaving the city, he still felt the absence of his tools. Foolishly, and inexcusably, he had left his grandfather's knife behind, a loss that stung painfully whenever he thought of it. He had been forced to give up his gun as well. But both, he expected, would soon be replaced. Brussels, after all, was only two hours away.

27

"We believe that Karvonen has left the city," Wolfe said, standing before a packed conference room in Vauxhall. "We've asked for all transit out of London to be kept under high alert. Police forces in other countries have also been notified, although the suspect seems to have a substantial support network already in place, possibly aided by Russian intelligence."

"A serious allegation," Cornwall said. She was seated at the head of the table, with Asthana and Garber stationed to either side. Ten other officers had squeezed themselves into the room, listening intently to updates on what was already the most important manhunt in the history of the agency. "Before I bring this to the Home Office, I'll need something more."

Powell, who was standing at Wolfe's side, took up the briefing. "An intelligence connection is consistent with Karvonen's background. There's a long history of illegals posing as artists. It's easier to create a cover story within an artistic community than to find a more conventional job."

"But he murdered his employer, possibly because she found out too much," Wolfe continued. "He was also able to clean out his apartment, so it's possible he received advance warning from the inside—"

Garber broke in irritably. "Listen, we don't know that. And the intelligence angle is pure speculation. We need to focus on what we can prove. There's more than enough to connect him to Campbell and Akoun, as well as the tournament killings. What more do we need?"

Cornwall removed her glasses. "That may be enough for you, but at the moment, the press isn't asking about two bodies in Stoke Newington and Finsbury Park. They want to know how one of the city's most prominent businessmen was gunned down thirty yards away from a major police operation. It's a bloody embarrassment. What else do we have on Morley?"

"I'm speaking with Howard Archer, the founder of the fund, tomorrow," Powell said. "He might be able to shed some light on Morley's activities. I also plan to ask him about Boris Levchenko, the bodyguard. I can't be sure yet, but he looks like Dignity and Honor to me."

Cornwall nodded, evidently recognizing the name of an association of former Russian intelligence officers. "And Ilya Severin?"

"We're trying to transfer him from Belmarsh," Wolfe said. "Vasylenko will be out for blood. They're in separate blocks, but he's still at risk. We've tried using the situation to convince him to talk, but—"

"It's a dead end," Powell finished flatly. "Ilya Severin is not going to cooperate."

"So let's sum up," Cornwall said. "Karvonen has killed five people that we know of so far. He may have intelligence contacts ready to help him on his way. And he wouldn't have been activated so abruptly without a reason."

The deputy director looked around the room. "Listen very carefully. I want him found and contained. If he's planning something else, we can't let him slip through our hands. Right, then, back to work."

With the scrape of chair legs against carpet, the meeting broke up. Wolfe gathered her notes, suddenly drained from operating on less than four hours of sleep. As she headed for the door, however, she noticed that Asthana was eyeing her with amusement. "What is it now?"

Asthana pointed toward the cubicle farm outside. "Looks like you've got a visitor."

Wolfe turned to see that Lester Lewis, the pathologist, was seated near her desk. She walked briskly ahead. "I've asked him to work with the investigation. I need his professional advice."

"I'll *bet* you do," Asthana said. "Watch out, though. I hear that pathologists only want you for your body—"

Wolfe responded with what she hoped was an icy look. As they neared Lewis, she extended a hand. "Lester. Good to see you."

Lewis rose and took her hand in a gentle grip. "Glad to be of service. Though I don't know how helpful I can really be."

As Asthana smiled at them from her desk, Wolfe headed for the spare office she had cadged for the meeting. "I need whatever you can tell me. I've looked into some of this already, but it's hard to know what to believe. More than anything else, I'd like your opinion as a pathologist."

Lewis followed her into the tiny room, closing the door behind them. "My opinion? It's bloody strange. So you'll understand if I'm unable to give you a definitive answer, or even any answer at all."

"Let's start with the mystery, then," Wolfe said. "Tell me about the Dyatlov Pass."

They took a seat at the table, where Lewis removed a hefty file from his briefcase. When he opened it, she saw that it contained maps, diagrams, and printouts an inch thick, but nothing, she feared, even resembling an answer to the question posed by Morley's last words.

"Before we start, there's something I wanted to say," Lewis said, sifting through the documents with his fine hands. "In my own experience, a man will talk about all kinds of things before he dies. We don't know what goes through the mind at such moments. Just for the record, then, we need to consider the possibility that what Morley said was merely a case of dying delirium."

"I'm aware of that," Wolfe said. "But it must have been on his mind for a reason. It isn't something he would just happen to know."

"Not necessarily. What happened at the Dyatlov Pass has received little attention in this part of the world, but it's one of the most famous unsolved mysteries in the history of Russia, even fifty years after it took place. Someone like Morley could easily have heard of it. So I'm just saying, on the evidence, that there's no reason to believe that the story was of any special significance."

Wolfe nodded, although part of her resisted such an easy explanation. "Duly noted. But let's go through it from the beginning. I want to make sure that we agree on the basic facts of the case."

"All right, then." Lewis paused, as if uncertain of where to start, then finally turned to the first page in the file. "The incident took place on February 2, 1959. What we now call the Dyatlov Pass lies in the Urals, on the east shoulder of Kholat Syakhl. Mountain of Death, or so I'm told."

"I've heard that, too," Wolfe said. "Unfortunately, I took Spanish instead of Mansi."

"I'm surprised. I was under the impression that there wasn't much you didn't know." He looked down at the page, missing her sudden blush, and continued. "The incident involved nine hikers. Most were students or graduates of Ural Polytechnic, and all were experienced mountaineers. They were led by a man named Igor Dyatlov, who planned a challenging route. Take a look."

Lewis handed her a stack of black-and-white photos. Wolfe examined the snapshots, which showed hikers in parkas and fur hats grinning into the camera. One of the women, not too far from her own age, reminded Wolfe of herself. "Is it all right if I take notes on these?"

"Go ahead," Lewis said. He indicated one of the earliest shots, a picture of a second woman carrying skis at a railway station. "After arriving by train, they took a truck north to the last inhabited settlement and started walking along the valley. On the second day, one of the hikers became ill and had to turn back. Once the others reached the edge of the highland zone, they began making their way through the forest. That night, they set up camp on the slope to wait out a severe storm. And that's where they remained, until they were found by a search party a few weeks later."

He spread a second set of photos across the table. These shots were from a different camera, carried by a rescuer at the scene. Lewis pointed to a picture of a collapsed tent. "The tent was the first thing the searchers discovered. It was badly damaged, with a line of footprints leading into the woods, and it seemed to have been cut open from the inside."

Lewis showed her another shot of the site. "At the edge of the forest, the searchers found the remains of a fire and the first two bodies. They were in their underwear, without shoes, although the temperature that night would have been twenty degrees below freezing. Three more bodies were found across a distance of several hundred yards. It looked as if they were trying to return to camp but never made it. All had died of hypothermia, and one had a fractured skull."

He turned to a photo of a snowy ravine. "It took the searchers two more months to find the last four. They were discovered under twelve feet of snow, in a ravine deep in the woods. One had died of hypothermia, the rest of physical trauma. Two had chest fractures, one had skull damage, but there were no external injuries. And one of the women was missing her tongue."

Wolfe felt a passing chill, the same she had felt after first looking into the story. "So what about the theories?"

"All over the map, as you might expect," Lewis said. "At first, they thought that the Mansi, the indigenous tribe of the north, had attacked the hikers, but there were no signs of a struggle, and only the victims' footprints were visible on the ground. The evidence implies that they were forced to leave the tent at night, a few hours after their last meal. They tore the tent open and fled barefoot across the snow. The four in the ravine were dressed warmly, some wearing parts of the others' clothes, but the rest, as you saw, wore almost nothing."

Wolfe studied the photographs. "But it looks like they managed to build a fire."

"Yes, although there are strange details about this as well. Traces of skin and tissue were found on the trees, which implied that they broke off wet branches until their hands were raw, even though there was dry kindling nearby. Some take this as evidence that they had gone blind."

"Or were acting less than rationally. Could they have been disoriented by the cold?"

Lewis nodded. "Possibly. Hypothermia can cause confusion, and there's a symptom called paradoxical undressing, which may account for the condition in which the bodies were found. But now we get to the wilder stories."

He turned to the stack of printouts. "One allegation is that traces of radiation were detected on the bodies. Scrap metal was also found nearby, which made some suspect that military testing was taking place in the area. After the bodies were prepared for burial, a few relatives claimed that the victims had strange tans, and that their hair had gone gray. And, inevitably, another group of hikers saw orange lights in the sky that night, in the direction of the pass."

Wolfe glanced over the pages. "Could it have been the result of a weapons test?"

"Nobody knows," Lewis said. "Which hasn't stopped anyone from speculating."

Wolfe only continued to look at the pictures. She was about to hand the photos back when her eye was caught by one particular shot, which depicted a line of rescuers with prods in their hands. "You know, this is a probe line. It's used to explore the scene of an avalanche. If I were in a tent and heard an avalanche start, I'd get out of there as fast as I could and head for the largest tree I could find, outside the runout zone. Which is exactly what these hikers did."

Lewis examined the shot. "It's possible. But as far as I know, there's no mention of an avalanche in any of the contemporary reports. And there's still the question of why they didn't return to the tent after the danger had passed. I can look into it, though, if you like."

"Good." Wolfe glanced at her watch. "Listen, I know you've got work to do. Let me walk you out. Thanks so much for this."

"My pleasure," Lewis said, gathering up his files. "And if there's anything else—"

"I'll let you know." Wolfe steered him toward the main floor, seeing that Asthana, while pretending to work, was watching her out of the corner of one eye. After saying goodbye at the elevator, she went back to her desk, still not sure what Morley had been trying to say.

A second later, the memory of the hikers in the woods shifted into another image, one that had been on her mind frequently in recent days. Four men had entered the king's orchard, she recalled, and only one had returned unharmed. And as she thought of this story again now, she saw what she had to do next.

In her cubicle, Asthana was smiling saucily at her. "I *knew* that you fancied him."

Wolfe decided not to dignify this with a reply. "Listen, can I borrow your car tomorrow?"

"I'll need to ask Devon," Asthana said. "But it should be fine. Why do you need it?"

"No special reason." Wolfe turned on her computer, waiting as the screen flickered into life. "There's just someone I need to see."

28

Karvonen arrived in Brussels shortly before noon. Leaving the newspaper on his seat, he retrieved his bag from the overhead rack and followed the other disembarking passengers to the end of the platform. There was no passport control on this side of the border, so he was able to head directly for the central terminal of the station, which lay down a flight of steps.

On the level below, set among the gray pillars and steel benches, there was a row of car rental stands. Going to the kiosk of the largest agency, he rented a small Citroën using the international driver's license and credit card in the name of Dale Stern. From there, he drove to a hotel half a mile from the station, where he booked a room for the night and stopped at the café for lunch.

As he was about to leave, he saw that another customer had left a newspaper on the table next to his. Glancing down, he noticed that his picture had made the papers in Belgium as well, although this article was on the inside page. It was the same picture that had appeared in the London papers, of his old face, so he was not unduly concerned. All the same, he scooped the paper up from the table as he headed for the door, tossing it into a trash bin as he left.

By one in the afternoon, he was driving out of the city. Before heading for the main highway, he paused at a couple of shops in the suburbs. At a hardware store, he bought a shovel, a canvas bag, a pair of work gloves, a package of nails and a compass. Going across the street to an electronics shop, he picked up a screwdriver, some wire cutters, a pocket torch battery, and a number of other odds and ends. He also purchased a road map from the rack alongside the cash register.

Getting into his car, he unfolded the map and studied it for a moment. After locating the village he wanted, he headed south on the highway toward Namur. The day was overcast and chilly. Around him stretched miles of flat, pleasant country, the forest slowly thickening to either side as he neared his destination, which was one hundred and fifty kilometers away.

A few hours later, just after passing the village whose name he had seen on the map, he saw a narrow track off the side of the road, leading into an area of forest. He slowed almost to a stop, checked that there were no other cars in sight, and turned onto the track, moving deeper into the woods.

Karvonen drove for another minute, the shadows of branches running their fingers across the hood of the car, and parked at the side of the road. A footpath ran up a hillock, threading its way beneath the trees. He shut off the engine, got out of the car, and took his equipment from the trunk.

As he did, he listened to the sounds of the forest, hushed but strangely charged in the silence, which reminded him of his own boyhood. Growing up, he had spent hours in the woods behind his house, hunting, fishing, building snares. And as he looked around the forest now, he felt more fully himself than at any time since leaving the barber's chair in Highgate.

Slinging the shovel over one shoulder, he headed up the trail. After a few paces, he found himself, as he had expected, at a small forest chapel. It consisted of a wooden cross fitted with a peaked tin roof, like a hat, and a brass figure of Christ no larger than a toy soldier. Around the cross, to protect it from animals, a coop of chicken wire had been raised.

This chapel, he knew, was the first marker. From here, the road forked, with a narrow trail weaving to either side. Karvonen took the path to the left, counting off sixty paces, until he arrived at a large stone sunk into the ground under an elm tree. He had thought that he might encounter some hikers or picnickers, but evidently the day was too cold and damp.

Pausing at the stone, he took a reading with his compass, then went another forty paces east. Up ahead, among the other trees, he saw a pair of beeches standing apart, like estranged brothers at a family reunion. This, he knew at once, was the location that his handler had described.

When he arrived at his destination, Karvonen propped his shovel against the trunk of one of the trees and laid his bag at the base of the other. He removed his coat, folded it up, and set it on the ground. Then he pulled on his work gloves, took the shovel in hand, and began to dig at a spot between the beeches.

The soil was fairly hard, so it took him a while to break through the surface, but once he was a few inches down, the work became easier. After about a foot, he felt the shovel strike something and heard the soft clink of glass. Reaching down to clear away the soil, he found an empty glass jar and a length of metal pipe, its ends choked with dirt. He set both of these aside, knowing that they had been left there to indicate if the cache had been disturbed.

After another couple of feet, he hit something else. It was a wooden board. Karvonen knelt by the hole, which by now was substantial, and brushed the loose soil away. Glancing around to make sure he was still alone, he found the edges of the plank with his fingers and pried it up.

Underneath, there was a metal lid with a handle. Below the handle, there was a lock. A key was conveniently attached to the handle itself with a fine chain, but Karvonen was not tempted to use it. Instead, he cleared away the rest of the dirt, careful not to strike the handle, and considered what lay before him.

What he had uncovered was one of many weapons caches that Russian intelligence had placed throughout Europe over the past fifty years. These caches were designed to be used by a solitary illegal agent, working alone, to sow destruction behind the lines of an enemy country in case of war. Although the possibility of such hostilities seemed remote these days, the stockpiles had been quietly updated and maintained, with similar caches still in existence in Europe, Israel, and Turkey.

Karvonen set his hands on the cool metal of the container. The key that hung from the handle was a deliberate provocation. This particular cache, like most of its counterparts, was wired with an explosive device that would destroy both the container and anything nearby if it were opened incorrectly. Disarming it would not be especially difficult, but there was always the possibility that the explosive had become dangerously unstable in its years underground.

Rising from the hole, he went back to the beech tree where he had left the canvas bag. Crouching down, he removed the spool of wire and used the wire cutters to snip off two lengths about twelve inches long. After connecting pieces of wire to each of the leads of the pocket torch battery, he opened the package of nails, removed two, and attached one nail each to the exposed ends of the wires. Then he brought this unlikely science project back to the hole, along with the rest of his tools.

Karvonen leaned down over the cache, then carefully used one of the nails to scratch away the paint at a spot on the body of the box. Keeping the nail in place, he used the other nail to scratch away some paint on the lock fitting, so that both of the contacts were touching metal.

From inside the box, there was a soft click. Karvonen exhaled. The explosive device had been disarmed, or so he hoped. Still, he remained respectful of the container as he inserted the attached key into the lock, turned it, and took hold of the handle with both hands.

He had to tug hard at the lid to remove it, but at last it came away with a low hiss, as the rarefied atmosphere inside the container met the air outside. Karvonen lifted off the lid and looked into the cache. There was a small metal casing secured to the inside of the box. He used his screwdriver to remove the four screws holding the casing in place, then took it off.

Inside was the detonator, attached to an explosive charge by a pair of wires. Karvonen pulled the cutters from his pocket and slid the jaws around the first wire.

After a beat, he squeezed the handles and cut the wire in two.

Nothing happened. He cut the other wire, and like that, he was done. Reaching down, he pulled out the detonator and set it aside. Only then did he take a good look at what was inside the box itself.

The first thing he pulled out was a green plastic bag that had been closed with a twist tie. He undid the tie and pulled off the bag, revealing a nine-millimeter SIG Sauer pistol. Examining it, he found that it seemed to have suffered no ill effects from its long sojourn underground. The bag, he knew, was polyethylene infused with a corrosion protectant, and the gun itself had been further treated with a rust preventative that he would need to remove.

He slid the pistol into his belt, then reached down for a second, bulkier bag, which he lifted out of the container. Removing the polyethylene, he found a composite Remington shotgun that held six rounds. He checked it carefully, and found that it, too, was in good working order.

Karvonen slung the shotgun over his shoulder and rapidly went through the rest of the cache's contents, which consisted of ammunition, a holster for the pistol, and spare clips. A can of methyl chloroform for degreasing the guns sat at the bottom, among a few scattered packets of silica gel.

After clearing out the cache, Karvonen cleaned up the site, tossing his tools into the vacant box, along with the explosive charge. Sliding the lid back into place, he locked it again, then loaded the equipment he had retrieved, including the shotgun, into the canvas bag. The pistol he left in his belt.

Around him, the woods had grown darker. Taking the shovel, he tossed the glass jar and pipe into the hole again, then filled it in, tamping down the dirt with care. He dragged a few dead branches over the spot, taking a step back to consider it. Finally he flung the shovel into the underbrush, put on his coat, picked up the bag, and went back the way he had come.

It took him only a few minutes to return to his car. Karvonen unlocked the trunk and carefully put the canvas bag, as well the pistol, in the space beneath the spare tire. He got behind the wheel, started the engine, and began the long drive back to the city. To his right, the sun was going down.

29

On the wall above the desk, there was a map of Napoleon's retreat from Russia. It began with a fat line representing four hundred thousand soldiers marching out from the Neman River. As the line went east, it diminished, until only a hundred thousand men arrived at Moscow. Then, on its way back, it dwindled further, until finally, when it returned to its starting point, fewer than ten thousand remained.

It was a famously remorseless image, and Powell knew it well. Studying the version above the desk of Howard Archer, founder of the Cheshire Group, however, he noticed a small but telling difference. In front of all the numbers on the map, someone had drawn a dollar sign.

Archer looked wistfully at the map. He was a small, tidy man whose demeanor had grown even more subdued in the aftermath of Morley's death. "The map tells most of the story. Until recently we were one of the largest foreign portfolio investors in Russia. The idea was to invest the fund in public companies, then conduct our own investigations to uncover inefficiency and corruption. If the government took steps to address these issues, the share price went up, benefiting everyone involved. That's the theory behind activist investing, anyway."

Powell saw an ironic gleam in the fund manager's eyes. "And how did it work out?"

"Rather well, for a while. At first Putin was on our side. We were fighting the same thing, oligarchs who were buying up state companies and channeling funds into their own pockets. Then, five years ago, everything changed."

"I've read something about this," Powell said. "You were detained at the airport?"

Archer nodded. "I was flying back to Moscow, where I had been living for more than a decade, when I was told that I could no longer enter the country. I was held for a day, then sent back to London, under the pretense that I was a threat to state security. I've been banished ever since."

"Along with Morley, I hear. And what was it that caused such a sudden change?"

"The short answer? Gaztek. The most powerful natural gas company in the world, and the largest company of any kind in Russia. Five years ago, it was put under state control, meaning that the government stood to benefit from the same internal corruption we had been trying to fight. Suddenly our presence in Russia became very inconvenient. In the end, our offices in Moscow were raided, and the men behind it secured a massive payoff from the Russian government."

"So one part of the state was stealing from another," Powell said, knowing that such transfers of wealth were not unusual. "And when your lawyers contested this, they were arrested?"

"Only one. The rest were smart enough to leave the

country. The one who remained was thrown into prison, where he was beaten and denied medical attention. Six months later, he was dead." Archer smiled grimly. "If you want to understand Morley, you need to begin there. He was furious about it. I was aware of this, but I hoped he would channel this rage into his work."

Powell looked down at the file in his hands. On the first page was attached a snapshot of the painting in Morley's office, the fund manager's face spattered with orange and red. "So what did his work involve?"

"Most recently, he had been focusing on Gaztek's upcoming move into Spain. Gaztek supplies a quarter of Europe's natural gas, but it has never been able to penetrate Spain or Portugal. It recently began drilling for gas in Algeria, which would allow it to enter this last region, completing its stranglehold on the continent. Morley was watching this development closely."

Powell wrote this down. "And what was it about this move that concerned you?"

"It should concern all Europeans," Archer said simply. "Gaztek isn't interested in earning a profit for its shareholders, but in furthering the goals of Russian foreign policy. It cut gas supplies in Ukraine after the Orange Revolution, and nearly did the same in Belarus. And it could easily apply such pressure to the rest of Europe. If it were to cut off gas in the winter, half the continent would freeze to death. This is our greatest vulnerability in the area of national security."

Powell sensed that this was a speech that Archer had given many times before. "So if Gaztek enters Spain, its control over the continental gas supply will be complete. And Morley was trying to keep them out?"

"Not exactly," Archer said. "It's too late for that. But we can do our best to hold back the mechanisms of corruption. You see, the major pipelines run through what we like to call the New Silk Route, a criminal highway for arms, drugs, cash. To protect its investments, Gaztek needs to reach an accommodation with various unsavory elements. They subsidize gas for the Transnistrian government, for instance, to the tune of fifty million dollars a year. It's the price of operation."

Powell studied the map. "So at the top of the chain, you have Gaztek. At the bottom, you have criminals who allow it to operate in the worst parts of the world. And to connect those two levels—"

"—you need an intermediary," Archer concluded. "Which is Russian intelligence. Wherever there's money to be made, you'll find them. They take over operations on the ground and siphon off hundreds of millions of dollars. In return, they provide the crucial link between the politicians at the top and the criminals at the bottom. As a result, Gaztek becomes a state unto itself. To protect the pipelines, they can even raise their own military forces."

As Powell listened, he found himself wondering whether he had entered the wrong line of work. He had spent most of his life pursuing such connections in law enforcement, but they could also be followed in the financial markets, where, as in forensics, every contact left a trace. "And what was Morley doing about this?"

"Our assumption is that we can undermine the top of the pyramid by knocking out the foundations. By tracking where the money is really going, we create a climate of transparency that will make it less practical to use the energy supply for political ends. That's what Morley was working on."

"I see," Powell said. "Is that why you had a former intelligence officer on your staff?"

Archer hesitated. For the first time, Powell saw something like wariness in the fund manager's eyes. "How did you know?"

"It wasn't hard. Levchenko's résumé says he worked for years as a diplomatic translator. To me, that sounds like Dignity and Honor."

After another pause, Archer nodded. "Yes. Levchenko had been with us for years, as a security consultant. If you look at other Russia funds, you'll see similar men on the payroll. But I have no reason to believe he was doing anything illegal." He glanced at the clock. "Unfortunately, I have a meeting to attend. We can resume this conversation later. In the meantime—"

"I'll be in touch." Powell closed his file and notepad, then thought of something else. "One last question. Did Morley or Levchenko ever mention something called the Dyatlov Pass?"

"I don't believe so," Archer said. "I can check our records, if you like. What is it?"

Rising from his chair, Powell shook the fund manager's hand. "A ghost story. Thank you again for your time."

Powell left the office. For his own part, he suspected that the simplest explanation for Morley's last words was that they meant precisely nothing. From his own father's illness, he knew that a man could say anything once his mind was gone. In any case, how a man died was rarely as interesting as how he had lived, and Morley's activities had been instructive indeed.

Passing the secretary at the front desk, he thanked her, then took the lift down to the lobby. He was heading out to Golden Square, his mind already turning to his next move, when the phone in his pocket rang. Pulling it out, he saw an unregistered number on the display. "Hello?"

"I see that you've met Howard Archer," a man's voice said on the other end. "Did he have anything useful to say?"

Hearing this, Powell took a step back, scanning his surroundings. A handful of people were visible in the park, none looking his way, but he sensed that he was being watched. He thought he recognized the voice on the phone, but wasn't sure from where. "Who is this?"

"Only someone who wants to help," the man said. "My name is Victor Chigorin."

30

Begin with the cell. It measured three paces by five, the walls painted a dirty green. There was a single bed, a table, a chair. Against one wall sat a steel washbasin and toilet; on the other, a cupboard with two narrow shelves. Beside the cupboard was a window equipped with four iron bars. Through the window one could see only the brick of the opposite block, without a trace of sky.

Across from the window stood the door to the cell, which was made of heavy steel. Its only opening was a Judas hole the size of a large letter box, through which a passing guard would occasionally peer. There was no handle on this side of the door, which was scratched and pitted with layers of graffiti. And that, really, was it, as Ilya had confirmed more than once to his satisfaction.

At the moment, he was shaving. Because the sink lacked a proper plug, he had filled a plastic soup bowl with warm water from the tap, and was using this as a basin. Shortly after his arrival, he had been issued a shaving brush, a cake of soap, and a safety razor. Belmarsh was obliged to provide its inmates with razors, allowing them to maintain a decent appearance, although prisoners were required to hand over the used blade each night before receiving a new one.

Above the sink, a steel mirror, about four inches across, was bolted to the wall. As he lathered up, describing tight circles in the cake of soap with the brush, he reviewed the events of the past day. He had spent the night in the medical ward, in a cell that lacked a flush toilet. Every hour the lights would stutter on in their overhead cage and the Judas hole would slide back, so that the guard on duty could make sure that he hadn't killed himself. The following morning, he had been moved to the induction block, which was where he was currently residing.

He finished lathering his face, then carefully began to shave, the razor leaving a clean stripe of pale skin with every pass. On the table next to the sink stood the remains of his breakfast, consisting of a wedge of stale bread and an egg. The breakfast had been given to him in a bag the night before, along with his supper. Ilya had wanted to avoid the food, but forced himself to chew and swallow it, sticking to the vegetables and potatoes and steering clear of the meat.

Finishing his shave, he rinsed off the razor and brush and splashed water from the tap on his face. He was drying himself off when a bell rang outside. After hanging his towel on the edge of the sink, he pulled on his shoes, then waited until his door was unbolted for the morning's exercise.

When the door swung open, he joined a line of other prisoners from his spur, where he was given a body search by the nearest guard on duty. Then he marched with the other inmates down three flights of steps to the exercise yard. He was very aware of their eyes on his face. For a man accustomed to invisibility, this endless scrutiny had been the hardest part about his new situation.

Outside, in the yard, it was easy to wonder if the destination had been worth the trouble. It was enclosed by a wire fence, a furlong on each side, with a tired lawn in the center. The sky above was like the inside of a skull. All the same, it was his first taste of natural light in almost a day, so he lifted his eyes to it, blinking, like a nocturnal animal brought into the sunshine.

For fifteen minutes, he made a solitary circuit of the yard. Then he noticed that another prisoner was coming his way. This inmate was a few years younger than he was, with crooked teeth and a broken nose, and as the man drew closer, Ilya found that he recognized him. Removing his hands from his pockets, he glanced over at the guards by the gate, who did not seem to be looking in his direction, and wondered whether the crucial moment had already come.

As the inmate continued to approach, Ilya braced himself, then saw the other man halt a few steps away. The prisoner gave a quick bob of his head. "Now, then. You remember me, don't you?"

"Of course," Ilya said, relaxing only slightly. "Grisha. How are you doing?"

Grisha offered up a barely perceptible shrug. The last time Ilya had seen him, years ago, he had been an obliging crook and identity thief, attaching skimmers to convenience store cash registers to snare credit card information. "Six months of porridge. Shit and a shave, really."

He fished out a pack of cigarettes, extending one,

which Ilya declined with a shake of the head. "What do you want?"

"Nothing," Grisha said, igniting his own cigarette with a snap of the lighter. "Just a friendly chat. Heard about you getting nicked in Kensington, after all those years on the run, and for nothing. Bloody shame, innit?" He blew smoke through his broken nose. "As long as you're here, though, you have some friends who want to reconnect. One in particular would like a word."

Grisha motioned with his cigarette toward the fence, his shoulders hunched against the cold. Following his gesture, Ilya found that he could see into the exercise yard of the adjacent block, which was separated from this yard by a second fence and thirty feet of concrete. Standing behind the fence in the other yard was a group of five inmates, all of them looking in his direction. An old man, bundled up warmly, stood at the center. It was Vasylenko.

Ilya felt himself slip, inexorably, into the moment he had been anticipating ever since his arrival. Without looking away from the *vor*, he spoke to Grisha. "What does he want with me?"

"Just a word or two," Grisha said, stubbing out his cigarette. "Come on, then."

He headed for the fence. After a pause, Ilya followed. He tried to retain something of his usual impassivity, but found that it was already gone, and that memories he had long repressed were swiftly crowding in.

It was only twenty paces to the edge of the yard, but the walk seemed to take a very long time. When they arrived, Grisha stood aside, his purpose fulfilled, and turned discreetly away.

Ilya looked through the fence at the old man on the

other side. With only ten yards between them, it was the closest they had been in many years. Vasylenko had aged in the interim, his hair whiter than before, but his face had not changed. For a second, Ilya felt himself back in Vladimir, barely more than a boy. Then his vision cleared, he came back to himself, and he remembered that this was the man who had ordered the death of his parents.

Vasylenko spoke first, in Russian, his voice carrying with surprising ease across the intervening space. "It has been a long time, Ilyushka."

Hearing these words, Ilya thought back to their last conversation, over the phone in a house on Long Island, an ocean and lifetime away. He had to raise his voice to be heard. "A very long time."

"It must come as a shock to find yourself behind these walls," Vasylenko said. "I did not expect to see you again, at least not in such a place as this. How have you been managing?"

Ilya sensed the *vor* circling around the real subject, perhaps because of his men, who were listening closely. The inmates ranged in age from their early twenties to over fifty, and while the older ones had visible tattoos, the youngest, he noticed, did not. "Well enough. And you?"

Vasylenko smiled. "I am an old man. And I have grown older. They say that I am going to die here, although I have no intention of proving them right." He paused. "I was sorry to hear about Marbella. You may not believe me when I say this, but I had nothing to do with it."

"I know," Ilya said. "He had a white tattoo, not a blue one. An eagle. And I know that you no longer have any power there."

He could see the other men react unfavorably. For the first time, Vasylenko's voice hardened. "It has been a trying time for the brotherhood. But I am not so weak here. You would do well to remember this."

Ilya heard the hint of a threat in the old man's tone, which seemed unnecessary. He wanted to ask Vasylenko if his men knew that he had worked for the Chekists. Before he could speak again, however, a bell rang, indicating that exercise period was over. From his side of the fence, he watched as Vasylenko held his gaze for another moment, then turned away with the others. The last man to depart, a pockmarked inmate of thirty or so, spat thoughtfully on the ground before he left.

Watching them go, Ilya heard Grisha's voice. "Not one for making friends, are we?"

Instead of replying, Ilya turned back to the exercise yard, where the prisoners were being called in one block at a time. "Tell me something. Has there been talk of the killing of James Morley?"

"Of course," Grisha said. "Lot of rumors going around. And some of us find you interesting, too. We think you know more than we've read in the papers. You're a bit of a celebrity here."

Ilya studied the other prisoners, who were slowly making their way back to the gate. "Is there someone I can ask about this?"

"A fellow with his ear to the ground, you mean?" Grisha nodded. "Yeah, I know just the guy. A tea boy, a listener, you know. Not much he doesn't hear, I imagine. Want me to arrange it?"

"Yes, if you can," Ilya said. "I'd be interested in hearing what he has to say."

As he spoke, he saw another familiar face. It was the inmate he had noticed on the prison bus, the one pretending to sleep. He was standing at the edge of the crowd, looking at the two of them intently. Ilya eyed him back. Grisha, noticing this mutual inspection, lowered his voice. "I'd watch out for that one, if I were you. Double murder. Nothing to lose at this point—"

Ilya continued to regard the other man. "So why would he care about me?"

"Not saying he would," Grisha replied. "But I'd watch your back when you're near him. And your front as well."

Ilya watched as the prisoner finally turned aside, joining the queue of other inmates. When he drew near the others, they cleared a space for him, as if sensing an unpleasant smell. "What's his name?"

Grisha screwed up his face to remember. "Francis," he said at last. "But everyone calls him Goat."

When their block was called, they filed inside, where they merged into a line of other prisoners. Ilya submitted to a second search, then headed for his spur. Before he could go up the steps, however, he heard someone call his name. Turning, he saw a guard beckoning him closer. "Yes?"

The guard jerked his head to the left. "Visitors' area. Someone to see you. A lady."

31

Wolfe entered the visitors' room, finding herself in a grimy space the size of a small gymnasium. Looking up at the balcony, she saw guards peering down through binoculars, their black ties and white shirts reminding her oddly of missionaries. Five rows of chairs and tables were bolted to the floor. Visitors sat on the right, prisoners on the left, marked off by yellow sashes on their shoulders.

As she walked over to the numbered chair she had been instructed to take, she felt the room's eyes on her face and body. She had driven out alone, in Asthana's car, leaving her warrant card behind. This meeting was off the record. If there was, in fact, a leak at the agency, it seemed wise to keep this visit to herself.

After a body search by a female guard and an examination by a sniffer dog, she had entered the secure waiting area, where she had remained for forty minutes until her number was called. Without her phone or any reading material, she had been given plenty of time to ask herself why she was here. Even now, she didn't really have an answer, only a hunch, or the rumor of one.

All the same, when she saw a guard escort Ilya into the

room, even that whisper of a hunch began to fade, and for one cowardly moment, she found herself wishing that she hadn't come.

When Ilya saw her, his eyes narrowed incrementally. There was a second when he appeared to pause, falling a step behind the guard, and she feared that he was simply going to walk away. Instead, he went up to the table and sat down silently, his blank gaze meeting hers, leaving her to wonder what had prompted him to come this far. Curiosity, perhaps.

Wolfe slid a can of soda across the table, feeling that the gesture was faintly ridiculous. Earlier, after locking up her valuables, she had exchanged her remaining cash for a few plastic tokens that could be used in the vending machines. "Hope you don't mind Fanta."

Ilya set the can aside without looking at it. After holding her eyes for another second, he turned away, his voice flat but not impolite. "I don't see why you're here. I have nothing further to say."

"I know," Wolfe said. "I'm not here to discuss the case. I wanted to talk about something else. About the story of four men in the orchard."

Wolfe thought she saw a flicker of interest in his expression, although this might have been wishful thinking. "What about it?"

"It's a story from the Talmud," Wolfe said. "Four rabbis entered an orchard, or a garden, where they had a mystical vision. One died from the shock. Another became a heretic. A third went mad. Only one, Rabbi Akiba, departed safely. I'm wondering why you told us that story."

Looking into his face, Wolfe felt as if she were back in

Sunday school. As a Mormon, her education had been steeped in the story of Israel, the only history that the church regarded as meaningful, apart from its own. After a pause, Ilya said, "Do you know what they saw?"

"Nobody does," Wolfe said. "Whatever it was, it was secret. Something impossible to describe. And dangerous, at least for anyone who wasn't ready for it. Was that what you were trying to tell us?"

"You still haven't answered my question," Ilya said. "What did the four men see?"

In his tone, Wolfe heard the door she had opened begin to close. "I don't know."

"I didn't think so. The story tells us that a revelation is meaningless if the listener is unprepared. What is truth to one man is heresy for another. I see no point in talking to those who will not understand. Or who give no indication that they will hear what I am saying." Ilya glanced away. Then, after another pause, he said, "You know the work of the chariot?"

Something in his words sent a shiver down her spine. "It's a passage in the book of Ezekiel," Wolfe said. "It's also called the *merkabah*. I'm afraid I don't know much about it—"

"Ezekiel is among the exiles in Babylon," Ilya said sharply. "A whirlwind comes out of the north, the heavens open, and he has a vision of God. He sees four winged beasts, each with the face of a man, an ox, a lion, and an eagle. Then he sees a chariot with four wheels within wheels. Above the chariot is a shape like a man on a throne, made of fire from the waist down. Do you know that much?"

Wolfe bristled at his air of condescension. "Yes. I also

know that students who studied the passage without preparation were burned alive by fire from heaven. Or so the stories say."

"Good," Ilya said. "It was believed that discussing the vision would cause God himself to appear. Fire would come from the sky. So the rabbis tried to prevent the passage from being read aloud in the synagogue. Ezekiel himself received a warning. *And I will make thy tongue cleave to the roof of thy mouth—*"

The image of a woman with a missing tongue passed briefly through her mind. "And this was what they saw in the orchard?"

"Possibly," Ilya said. "But no one knows. That's the point of the story. There are secrets for which the mind is not prepared. It can be dangerous to seek knowledge before you are ready. Otherwise it can destroy you. Or drive you mad. You would do well to remember this."

Wolfe saw that this was the conclusion to which they had been headed all along. "Is that why you won't cooperate?"

Ilya glanced aside. A few seats away, a couple was kissing. "Tell me why you came."

"Because I wanted to talk to you without the police," Wolfe said. "I know you don't trust them. They haven't treated you with respect. But I thought you could be persuaded to help me find Karvonen."

"Why?" Ilya asked. "If you're trying to say that you're different from the Chekists, I see no difference at all."

"Then you're not looking hard enough. Or you're refusing to make the distinction. If you lump me in with the secret police, you trivialize their crimes. I'm trying to save lives, not support an oppressive regime."

"Let me ask you a question. If Lermontov had been arrested, would he have gone to jail?"

"Yes, probably," Wolfe said, even though she already sensed the trap. "Although—"

Ilya broke in. "No. He would have been sent back home. A prisoner exchange, most likely. Nothing can be allowed to upset relations with Russia. Everything works to maintain the system."

Wolfe saw an opening and pounced on it. "But we're trying to take down Karvonen. He's part of the system too, isn't he?"

"Karvonen *is* the system," Ilya said. "He may look like a man. But he's really the expression of an idea."

"Is that how you found him?" Looking into his dark eyes, Wolfe saw she had guessed right. "It was something in the crimes themselves, wasn't it? Something that told you he was working for the intelligence services—"

"As I said to your friend, all the signs were there," Ilya said. "Look at the fires. Why use potassium permanganate?"

"I don't know," Wolfe said honestly. "I thought it might have been one of the chemicals he used in his work. He was a photographer. A retoucher. But there isn't any photographic application that I can find."

"Close, but wrong. Potassium permanganate reacts with glycerin. But it also creates an explosive reaction with cellulose nitrate. Cellulose nitrate is what the secret services use to print code pads. So they can be easily destroyed. Karvonen just turned it to other uses."

Wolfe was struck by how simple this seemed. "And that was what caught your eye?"

"That and other things," Ilya said. "An artist is revealed by the materials he uses. The history of intelligence is a series of layers. One written above another, like a sacred text. Karvonen follows patterns that have existed since before he was born. And like all killers, he has his own compulsions."

Wolfe was about to ask what he meant, then found that she knew the answer. "Fire."

"That's one example. If you want to keep a secret, you don't set it on fire. Fire destroys, but it also draws attention. Like the work of the chariot. The fact that some students are burned alive only attracts others. In this case, Karvonen needs to be invisible, but he also wants to be noticed. He wants his work to be appreciated. Which can be dangerous for a true artist—"

Even as he spoke, a garbled announcement came over the intercom, indicating that visiting hours had ended. Wolfe glanced over at the noise, then turned back to Ilya. "Can I talk to you again?"

Ilya did not answer at once. At last, he said, "If you like. Perhaps next time you could tell me why Ezekiel's vision was so dangerous. Or, at the very least, you could bring me some books."

Wolfe wanted to say more, but found herself being steered politely away by one of the guards. As she headed for the door, she glanced back at Ilya, who was still seated, as instructed, with the rest of the prisoners. His eyes remained on hers until she had left the room.

She passed quickly through the reception area. The encounter had exhausted her, but she was also thrilled that she had found a way in. Ilya had revealed more than she had expected, and she sensed that he was willing to go further. The important thing, she told herself, was to be ready. Ilya had posed a question. And he would only continue to talk if she could venture an answer.

Wolfe thought back to what he had said about Karvonen. An artist was revealed by the tools he used, as much as by his choice of subject. This was all the more true of Karvonen, since he had selected his victims according to the requirements of a larger plan, not his personal inclinations. But his methods were his own. And if she wanted to learn more about a man like this, she had to consider how he had lived and worked, down to the books on his shelves.

In the parking lot, Wolfe got into the car. For a moment, she sat where she was, trying to decide where to begin. Fragments of Ezekiel's vision mingled with images from the Dyatlov Pass, which she reminded herself to discuss with Powell. At last, starting the engine, she headed for the street, and was going over a bump only slightly too fast when the bomb under her car exploded.

32

On the fourteenth floor of the Savoy Hotel, Powell emerged from the elevator and headed for the suite at the end of the hall. Outside, two young bodyguards in good suits were lounging against the wall to either side of the door, chatting about football in Russian. At his approach, they straightened up, and the nearest guard motioned for him to stop. "Must search first."

Powell displayed his warrant card. "My name is Alan Powell. I was invited."

"Sorry," the bodyguard said, in what seemed like a tone of genuine apology. "Must search first."

Returning the card to his inside pocket, Powell raised his arms and allowed himself to be frisked, which the bodyguard did with admirable efficiency and quickness. Then the second guard knocked on the door to the suite, which was promptly unlocked and opened from the inside.

The guards smiled at him as Powell went into the room, where a third bodyguard was standing. It was an opulent space, furnished in a tasteful mingling of Edwardian and Art Deco. The floor beneath his feet was paved in marble, with a chandelier of Murano glass hanging from the ceiling.

On a plush mahogany sofa at the center of the room, Victor Chigorin was seated in his shirtsleeves, looking at something on a tablet computer while breakfasting on yogurt and fruit. At the writing desk by the window, which disclosed a view of the Thames, a shapely female assistant was talking on the phone. Next to her, in a wing chair across from the sofa, sat a man in his thirties with a sharp chin and strikingly bright green eyes. Powell recognized him at once.

Chigorin popped an orange slice into his mouth, then set the computer aside. "Please, sit down," the grandmaster said, gesturing toward an empty chair. "Can we get you anything?"

"I'm fine," Powell said, taking a seat. "Don't let me interrupt your breakfast."

"Thank you. I apologize for eating while we talk, but I'm rarely up before ten." Chigorin indicated the man in the wing chair. "I don't know if you've met Joseph Stavisky, my friend and occasional colleague—"

Powell shook hands with Stavisky. "No, but I know you who you are. I've often been to your website."

Stavisky only bowed his head. He was a lawyer and blogger based in Moscow, the founder of a site devoted to exposing corruption in Russian corporations and government contracts. Powell was surprised to see him here. Two men of such ambition, he knew, would not fit easily within the same four walls.

Chigorin took up a spoonful of yogurt. "We have been speaking about the search for Karvonen. It appears that a dead end has been reached. Stavisky, while I eat, tell him about our interest in this case."

"Of course," Stavisky said, speaking in rapid, nearly

unaccented English. "I assume you know something of my background. As an investor, I had shares in Gaztek, Transneft, all these companies, and wondered where the money was going. Millions of dollars lost every year. So I looked at documents, wrote emails, called for investigations. Before long, people started to listen."

"So it seems," Powell said, although he knew that the site's rapid rise wasn't quite as accidental as Stavisky made it sound. "I hear you've started looking into public contracts as well."

"It was a natural next step. The information was all there, ready to be unearthed, but no one had ever done it before. We found corruption in ministries, regional governments, public works. All I did was put as many eyes on it as possible. Safer, obviously, than doing it on one's own—"

"Those who work alone tend to be murdered, or to simply disappear," Chigorin said with a glance at Powell. "Your friends at the Cheshire Group learned this the hard way, I imagine."

"Which is why I have no fear for myself," Stavisky added. "Nothing would be accomplished by killing me. But this is not the case for certain exceptional men. Someone like Victor, for instance, cannot be replaced. And I have recently come into possession of information that implies he may be in danger."

Powell looked over at Chigorin, who had listened without changing expression. "And you believe this, too?"

After a pause, Chigorin said, "I am not entirely convinced. There have been rumors of plots against my life before. But in the course of looking into this allegation,

Stavisky has uncovered material that may be pertinent to your case. Which is why I advised him to contact you."

"This is the situation," Stavisky said. "Last week, I met with a source who claimed to have knowledge of an intelligence plot aimed against Victor Chigorin. He offered no details, either because he did not know them or was unwilling to share them at once. When I pressed for more evidence, he gave me a number of files, saying he believed they were relevant. When I examined the documents, however, they turned out to be nonsense. Or so I thought at the time."

Chigorin picked up his tablet computer. Turning it on, he opened a file, then handed it to Powell. "You're the first person outside this room to see any of this. We can't give you a copy, but you can read it here."

Powell studied the file, which turned out to be a smudgy photocopy in Russian. He translated the title at the top. "Operation Pepel?"

"*Ashes*," Stavisky said. "We've found references to it in other intelligence sources as well. Apparently it was a special operation of a political nature in Turkey. Originally, it was thought to have taken place in the sixties, but based on this document, the date needs to be pushed back at least to the late fifties. And it says that an agent named Yuri Litvinov was involved."

Powell, scanning the page, recognized the name. "The current director of the FSB."

Stavisky nodded. "He would have been in his twenties at the time, and we know that he was stationed in Istanbul and Ankara. The document doesn't say what the action was, but my source claims it was big. And he says that it somehow relates to a plot to kill Victor Chigorin."

Looking at the grandmaster again, Powell still saw no visible reaction. "And you feel that this source is credible?"

"I've been in contact with him for close to a year," Stavisky said. "All I can say is that he has access to a vast trove of intelligence files. He's leaked documents to me before. All have been authenticated. But such men always have reasons of their own for coming forward."

"I know." Powell turned to Chigorin. "Does Operation Pepel mean anything to you?"

"No," Chigorin said. "But I can see a connection. Have you ever been to Novgorod? The cathedral there has two doors from the twelfth century. One is from Europe. The other is from Istanbul. Russia has always felt that its destiny is to join these two empires. And the place where its eye turns first is Turkey."

As he listened, Powell recalled that Chigorin himself was part Turkish, and that he had been a strong advocate for Turkish rights within Russia. "So you think that this document reflects a covert operation aimed at Turkey. And it has something to do with a plot against your life?"

Chigorin smiled. "As I said before, I have my doubts. If they truly had designs against me, they could have killed me at the tournament. And whatever this document describes took place fifty years ago. Still, these men think in decades or centuries. When it comes to the security services, the past is never gone."

"In any case, my source says that he will have more information soon," Stavisky said. "We're attending a conference on energy policy next week in Helsinki. He indicates that he will deliver additional documents then. Once we see the files, we'll share any relevant materials with you. In return, we only ask that you keep us apprised of developments in the investigation."

Powell saw that he was being offered a deal, although he wasn't sure what it was yet. He handed back the tablet. "I'll do what I can."

"We ask for nothing more." Chigorin gave the tablet to his assistant, who had listened to their conversation without speaking. "If we hear anything further, we'll be in touch. Thank you."

After a closing exchange of pleasantries, Powell rose from his chair and was escorted outside by a guard. As the door closed, he glanced back, and saw Chigorin and Stavisky speaking quietly, their heads close together. Then the door swung shut, hiding them from view.

Powell nodded at the two smiling guards standing outside, then headed for the elevator. As soon as was out of sight, he pulled the notebook from his pocket and began to jot down what he remembered. *Operation Pepel. Ashes—*

As he was finishing up these notes, his phone rang. He almost didn't take the call, but when he looked at the display, he saw it was Asthana. Distracted, he answered it. "What is it, Maya?"

Asthana's voice was shaky. "Alan, it's about Wolfe. Something bad has happened."

33

When Asthana entered the hospital room, Wolfe screwed her face into a smile and delivered the line she had previously rehearsed, with, she hoped, the right amount of toughness: "Sorry about the car."

She had hoped for a laugh, but Asthana looked as if she was about to tear up. "Don't worry about it," Asthana said, coming over to where the others were sitting. "It was all insured, anyway."

"Good thing I am, too," Wolfe said. She was in a hospital room in Woolwich Common, seated in a chair by the window, which looked out at the park across the way. Powell and Garber had squeezed themselves into the tiny space as well. Before the first of her visitors had arrived, she had contrived to wash her face and fix her clothes a bit, but she knew that she didn't look great.

As Asthana sat down, Wolfe had no choice but to regard herself through the other woman's eyes. Her left arm was in a brace. The force of the blast had driven her forward in the driver's seat, wrenching her shoulder and elbow, and her cheek and the back of her neck had been lightly grilled by the heat. She had been lucky to be wearing long sleeves, reminding her of the stories that Mormons liked to tell about the sacred garments, which allegedly protected their wearers from fire.

Wolfe nearly laughed out loud at this, but stifled it. She was feeling more than a little peculiar, a sensation that was partly due to the Vicodin. In the abstract, she knew that she had been miraculously untouched. If the blast had been a few inches forward, it would have taken out the entire front of the car. Still, she couldn't quite process how close she had come. And these days, after years of certainty, she found that she had no particular opinion about what happened after you were dead.

Her ears were still ringing slightly, so she had trouble hearing what Garber said next. "What was that?"

"I was saying that the car has been defused and towed to Lambeth for examination," Garber said, picking up the conversation from a moment before. "Looks like the bomb was attached by magnets under the front and rear seats. A mercury tilt fuse wired to two pellets of Semtex. Serious stuff."

Wolfe nodded at this, although she was still regarding herself and her situation from a comfortable remove. A tilt fuse, she dimly knew, consisted of a plastic tube with mercury at one end and an open circuit on the other. When sufficiently jolted, the mercury flowed to the top of the tube and closed the circuit. If she had been on the freeway when the circuit closed, she would almost certainly have crashed. "So why didn't it take me out the way it was supposed to?"

"We aren't sure," Powell said. "It looks like there was an extra timing device, not part of the original design, meant to activate the circuit after a certain number of minutes had passed. And it seems that it was badly installed."

Garber agreed. "We're still looking into it, but I'm told that the Semtex was wired in relay fashion, like a string of holiday lights. The wiring was bad, so only the charge under the rear of the car exploded. The plastic itself was untagged, meaning that it's at least twenty years old, probably of Czech manufacture—"

"So it's certainly something that Russian intelligence could have done," Powell said. "The incompetence alone makes me suspect them."

Wolfe tried to process this last piece of information. "But not Lasse Karvonen."

"We don't think so," Asthana said. She looked around at the others. "On my way here, I spoke on the phone with prison security. Surveillance footage shows that the bomb wasn't planted at Belmarsh. Which means—" Her voice nearly failed, but she forced herself to continue. "Which means it was probably set when the car was parked outside my house. I'm so sorry, Rachel."

"It could have been meant for you," Wolfe said. "How did they know I'd be driving?"

"That's the big question," Powell said. "It was common knowledge, at least at the agency, that you were using this car for surveillance. The mileage reimbursement forms alone would have told the story. You didn't tell anyone else that the car was being used by Wolfe?"

This question was directed at Asthana, who shook her head. "Only my fiancé."

"We'll need to talk to him, then," Garber said. "If it turns out that he spoke to anyone about the case—"

Asthana blew up at this. "What exactly are you implying? Tell me. I'm *curious*."

Powell broke in. "Calm down, everyone. Garber's perfectly correct. We need to check every possible lead, no matter how unlikely it may be." He looked over at Wolfe. "The real issue is whether you were targeted because of your work. Until we know more, Cornwall wants to transfer you to another case."

Wolfe stared in disbelief. "You're kidding. You can't reassign me now. Not when I'm so close to a break-through with Ilya."

"Which raises questions of its own," Garber said. There was something in his tone that she didn't like. "I'm curious as to what you were doing there at all. It looks strange, especially in light of the concern over leaks—"

Wolfe felt an arrow of anger enter her chemical detach-ment. "Ilya was looking into these deaths when he was arrested. He understands Karvonen in a way that we don't. And I think he likes me."

Garber only turned aside, shaking his head, but Powell had listened with evident attention. In the end, to her relief, he said, "I hate to say it, but I agree. I still don't believe we'll get much out of him, but if he's talking to you, we need to continue. Are you ready to see him again?"

"Yes," Wolfe said at once. "Send me back in. The fact that someone came after me only shows that they're afraid of what I might learn."

"Fine," Powell said. "From now on, though, you'll clear your visits through the usual channels. And you'll have an agency driver. Agreed?"

"Agreed," Wolfe said. She wanted to tell him more of her thoughts on what Ilya had said, but before she could raise the issue, a nurse entered, saying that it was time for her visitors to leave.

As the others rose to go, she watched them enviously. The hospital, to her annoyance, had insisted that she remain under observation until the end of the day. Garber left first, with a muttered farewell, then stalked off into the hallway. Asthana smiled. "Don't worry about him. He's under a lot of stress these days."

"Aren't we all?" Wolfe accepted a hug, then waved as Asthana left the room. As soon as she was gone, Wolfe turned to Powell. "Alan—"

"It's all right," Powell said. For only a second, some emotion he had been repressing appeared in his voice, and she saw how moved he was. Then his usual dispassionate self returned. "You understand, of course, that I'm only allowing you to continue because we need Ilya to talk. In particular, I want you to ask him about Victor Chigorin. I believe his life may be in danger."

"Chigorin?" Wolfe asked. "But if Karvonen was really planning to kill him—"

"—he would have taken him out at the tournament," Powell finished. "I know. But there have been other developments. I'll tell you more soon. In the meantime, Cornwall is hopping mad. She says she expected better of you. I told her to blame it on temporary insanity."

Wolfe smiled at this. "Honestly, it seemed like something you would have done."

"On the contrary. I couldn't have done what you did with Ilya. No one could." Powell paused. "Wolfe, I'm only going to tell you this once. You can be whatever you want. You could be like Cornwall and run your own division. I see it in you. Everyone does. And it would be a terrible waste."

Before she could respond, he set a folder on the table

next to her chair. "Here are the files you wanted, in case you want to do some real work." He headed for the door, where he turned to face her. "I'm glad you're safe. But if you ever go behind my back again, you'll be lucky to end up on mail fraud."

He left. Once she was alone, Wolfe sat in silence, thinking of what he had said a moment ago. Remembering some of the things she had told Asthana, she felt an uncomfortable sense of shame.

In the end, she simply got back to work. Her own notes had been destroyed in the blast, so the first order of business was to reconstruct everything she remembered from her interview with Ilya and to prepare for the next meeting, which she would need to approach as if nothing had happened.

Before she could begin, her cell phone rang. It was Lester Lewis. "How are things?"

Wolfe smiled into the phone. Clearly not everyone had heard the news. "Not too bad. What can I do for you?"

"I have some updates," Lewis said. "I've been looking into reports from the Dyatlov Pass, and there's no sign of an avalanche. It was ruled out by observers at the time, and based on the photos, the slope wasn't steep enough. The snow prods you saw were just standard rescue equipment."

Listening to his words, Wolfe was glad to plunge again into the details of the case, which allowed her to think of something besides her close call. "What about the weapons-test theory?"

"The presence of radiation is suggestive, but it doesn't make sense for the site. One of my colleagues says that most weapons testing would have been conducted farther north, or in the Kazakhstan desert. In the mountains, it's hard to predict where radioactivity will go. But I'll keep looking into it."

"I appreciate that," Wolfe said. After a few more pleasantries, she thanked him and hung up. She wrote down some notes, her shoulder aching, then turned again to the file. Inside was a series of pictures of the shelves in Karvonen's apartment: art books, photographer's manuals, the works of John Donne. Remembering what Ilya had said, she decided to begin here.

As she studied the pictures, her hand strayed to the scorched hair at the back of her head. She would have to cut it off, she realized. And as she considered this, feeling the ache of the burns through her cushion of drugs, she found herself thinking of the work of the chariot, and of the seekers who, in their carelessness, had been touched by the avenging fire.

34

An overnight cruise ship plowed smoothly through the darkening swells of the Baltic Sea, bound from Stockholm to Helsinki. It was a sleek, handsome ferry of thirteen decks, with a beam of just over one hundred feet. In the failing light, its windows gleamed in bright rows, so that from a distance it seemed like a child's toy that had been cast on the ocean, wreathed on all sides by the water.

One of these lights belonged to Karvonen, who was standing in the bathroom of his private cabin, looking into the mirror. Although the changes to his appearance were objectively subtle, his new face was still strange to him, like a mask grafted onto his skull. For a moment, he found himself searching for the telltale signs of the airbrush, as if his features had been retouched by a hand less skillful than his own. Then he turned off the light and left the bathroom.

In the commodore cabin, his bag was on the floor, still packed. Karvonen picked it up and took it to the other end of the room, where he stripped the cushions from the sofa and folded out a hideaway bed. Unzipping his bag, he reached beneath a pile of clothes and removed the shotgun, which he laid carefully on the mattress, followed by the pistol, holster, and ammunition.

It had been a busy two days. The morning after retrieving the guns from the cache, he had taken a train from Brussels to Cologne, and another from there to Copenhagen. After that, there had been an overnight tilting train to Stockholm, where he had checked into a hotel for the day. There he had finished cleaning the guns, removing the coating of rust protectant with a rag saturated in methyl chloroform, the cloying scent of solvent filling his room.

He had also performed a few additional modifications, more as a reflection of personal taste than anything else. Among other things, using the roll of white medical tape that he had employed to secure the canisters to his body, he had laid a strip along the top of the shotgun, an aid to sighting in poor light.

Now he folded up the convertible bed with the guns inside, nestling them snugly between the layers of the mattress. He replaced the cushions, then draped a shirt and pair of slacks on the sofa, memorizing their position, so that he could tell at a glance if the sofa had been disturbed.

When he was done, he felt oddly restless. For the first time in days, he found himself with nothing to do until the next morning. Part of him wanted to examine the guns again, but he knew that checking them once was enough. In the end, he turned out the lights in his cabin, locked up, and headed for the promenade. The canisters, as always, were taped under his shirt.

Karvonen went down the companionway to the centerline mall, which ran along the heart of the ship. For most passengers, this was less a simple ferry than a party boat with its own bars, clubs, and casinos. The central promenade was roofed with glass, protecting tourists from the elements as they drifted in groups through the rows of shops and restaurants.

He began by buying a bottle of Armagnac, which was not entirely to his taste, but would come in handy at his destination. Swinging the heavy round bottle by the handles of its bag, he glanced around at the shops along the centerline. And as he walked past one of the display windows, he was surprised to see, among the other souvenirs, a rack of *puukko* knives.

Going into the shop, he gave the clerk a nod, then examined the knives more closely. The realization that he had left his grandfather's knife behind had been a bitter one. One day, he hoped, it might be possible to retrieve it, but in the meantime, he needed to buy a replacement.

Looking at the knives on display, he saw that there was a respectable selection. Most were tourists' trinkets with cheap plastic handles and stainless steel blades, but there were also a few decent knives with real birch handles and blades of crucible steel. After some thought, he finally selected a good hunter's knife, its tip pointing downward, with a blade the length of his wide palm.

Satisfied, he went for a drink at a nightclub at the fore of the ship. After securing a table for himself, he ordered a pint of Lapin Kulta and settled back into his cushioned chair, feeling the music swell around him in waves of sound. The club had switched twenty minutes ago from a live cover band to house and electronica, and now the floor teemed with a young, sweating crowd.

Karvonen drained his beer rapidly and ordered another. The purchase of the knife had rekindled his good spirits, as if part of his old self had been restored. All the same, whenever he caught a glimpse of his face, with its dark eyes and widow's peak, in the mirror above the bar, it continued to trouble him slightly, and he was haunted by the possibility that he was becoming a different person from before.

As he downed his second beer, he gradually became aware of a conversation taking place at the table to his side. Although the pulse of the music made it hard to hear the words, it was evidently an argument between a man and a woman, conducted mostly in Russian. He eavesdropped idly, catching a few stray syllables here and there, and was about to shift his attention elsewhere when he heard a familiar note in the woman's voice. She was Finnish.

Karvonen turned slightly in his chair. The man, he saw, was young, beefy, and Russian, his arms protruding like sausages from the sleeves of his polo shirt, its collar turned up so it brushed his earlobes. A pair of sunglasses was perched on the bristling crown of his head. The girl, by contrast, was tiny, with too much makeup, but under the paint, she couldn't have been more than twenty.

For the next few minutes, Karvonen kept an eye on them. The argument, it soon became clear, was about money. The Russian, who had grown rapidly pink from the carafe of vodka on the table, grew more belligerent with every word, while the girl replied in a soft voice, taking occasional nervous sips from her glass. Karvonen, even with his good ears, could only make out bits and pieces, but at one point, at a lull in the music, he heard a single word: *"Bliad—"*

The woman turned aside, her lips pressed together. For an instant, her eyes met Karvonen's. Before he could look away, he saw her companion reach across the table and take her by the arm, pulling her halfway out of the chair. Her glass fell over, unnoticed, spilling its contents across the table.

Hauling her to her feet, the man steered her toward the dance floor. As they went by, Karvonen saw that the man's hand was clamped tightly on the girl's arm, and that there were tears of pain in her eyes. For just a second, on the pale flesh of her forearm, he saw the marks of old bruises.

Karvonen watched as they descended the steps to the dance floor. Then he finished his beer, rose slowly from his table, and followed them without haste, keeping a pace or two behind.

On the main floor, he found himself caught up in a crush of bodies. The couple had halted just ahead of him, tears shining on the woman's cheeks. Karvonen turned his head to one side but continued in their direction, as if being pushed that way by the momentum of the crowd. Still keeping his eyes averted, he passed within touching distance of the pair, barely seeming to brush the man as he went.

A second later, the man crumpled to the floor, doubled up, clutching the crotch of his jeans in pain. The bottle of Armagnac, heavy as a bowling ball in its shopping bag, had hit him squarely in the testicles. The girl stared down at him, eyes wide, then turned to look at the man who had just passed.

Karvonen moved on, the bag swinging slightly in his left hand. As he vanished into the crowd, he sensed the girl's eyes on his back, but did not pause to turn around. And as he headed for the door of the nightclub, moving into the cool night beyond, he reflected that in most ways he was still the same man, after all.

35

When Ilya entered the interview room that evening, escorted by a guard, he noticed that Wolfe's arm was in a sling. Wolfe was seated at the table in the center of the room, a paper shopping bag at her elbow. She was wearing a sweater with a neck that came nearly up to her chin, and her hair had been recently cut, so that parts of it stuck out from her head in untidy feathers.

He remained in the doorway of the interview room, regarding her for a moment, then finally took a seat. At his side, the guard turned to Wolfe and asked, "Anything else I can do?"

"No, thank you," Wolfe said, keeping her eyes on Ilya. "I have everything I need."

The guard bobbed his head and left, closing the door behind him. Ilya watched him go, then turned to Wolfe. "I heard what happened."

"I guess the word has gotten around by now," Wolfe said. "Apparently it was quite the sensation around here."

"Yes. But I was glad to hear that you were all right. I didn't expect to see you again."

"Well, I promised to bring you these." Wolfe opened the bag at her side, clumsy with her one good hand, and extracted a pair of books. She slid them across the table. "Here. I'm sorry I couldn't bring more."

Ilya examined the two volumes. One was a hardbound collection of midrashim, the standard rabbinical commentaries on scripture, while the other was Scholem's *Major Trends in Jewish Mysticism*, both of which he had purchased the day before his arrest to replace the copies he had lost overseas. Flipping randomly through the first book, the one he had carried to the chess tournament, he said quietly, "Did you have the chance to read these?"

"Not really," Wolfe said. "I only picked them up from the evidence room today."

"You should at least read Scholem. Halperin and Wolfson are good as well, if you can only read English." Ilya set the books back down. "Thank you. But why else did you come?"

"I enjoyed our conversation from last time. I thought you might want to talk more about Ezekiel."

Ilya knew that she was really here for quite another reason, but he was prepared to indulge her, at least for now. "What about him?"

"I'd like to talk about why his vision was so dangerous. That's why you brought him up, isn't it? You don't think I'm ready to hear what you have to say. But I haven't been burned alive yet—"

Looking at the high collar of her sweater, which concealed the burns on the back of her neck, Ilya reflected that she was braver than he had originally believed. "How old are you?"

"None of your business," Wolfe said. "What does that have to do with anything?"

"A great deal. The rabbis tell us that a student

shouldn't study the *merkabah*, or the work of the chariot, until he's at least forty years old. You don't seem more than thirty. If that."

Wolfe smiled. "I'll be thirty in January. And I know you aren't forty either, at least if your passport can be believed."

Ilya granted the point. "Fair enough. So tell me why the passage was dangerous."

"Because it says things about God that we aren't prepared to consider," Wolfe said. "We're comfortable with a certain idea of divinity, something abstract and unseen, but Ezekiel gives us a version of God who refuses to play by the rules. He sits on a throne, on a chariot drawn by four monstrous creatures, and appears with a human body, as if daring us to fall into heresy."

"But the body of God appears throughout scripture," Ilya said. "God appears to Abraham, along with two angels, on the road to Sodom and Gomorrah. He closes the roof of Noah's ark with his own hands. When Moses asks to see him, he shows Moses his back. Why aren't these passages dangerous as well?"

"I don't know," Wolfe said, with evident impatience. "Why don't you tell me?"

"I thought you came for a conversation," Ilya replied. "If you want to talk, you'll give me your own interpretation."

Wolfe thought for a moment. "It's fine if God appears to Moses. After enough time goes by, even the most outrageous stories become part of the tradition. But when you extend these visions into recent history, like Ezekiel did, they become dangerous again. He's shoving God in our faces, showing us that his body is there in plain sight, and forcing us to deal with the implications."

"Yet the rabbis speak of God wearing the phylacteries," Ilya said. "He drapes himself in a prayer shawl. They weren't disturbed by the idea of his body. God made man in his own image, so there's no reason why he shouldn't take a man's form. You're close to understanding. But you keep missing the point—"

"If I'm so close, then give me something to work with," Wolfe said. "I brought you these books. You owe me that much."

"If you had read the books, you would know the answer." Ilya showed her a page in the collection of midrashim. "Look at the song of the sea. The Israelites pass through the sea on the way from Egypt. Then they sing a song of praise on the shore. *This is my God, and I will glorify him.* It's a vision that cannot be written down. A maidservant at the Red Sea, they say, saw something Ezekiel did not. The real question isn't if God ever showed himself to us. It's why he ceased to do so."

Wolfe studied the page, frowning. "Okay. So why did he stop showing himself?"

"The answer is right here, in front of your face. But only if you've done your reading. Pretend this is a case you're trying to solve. You have the testimony of a witness. In this case, a prophet. But there are aspects of his story that don't make sense. What do you do first?"

"I ask him to tell the story again," Wolfe said. "I look for gaps, inconsistencies—"

"And here your work has been done for you. Ezekiel opens with one account of his vision. Does he describe it again?"

"Yes," Wolfe said after a pause. "Later in the book, he sees the vision a second time."

"So you read more than ten pages. But is there any difference between the visions?"

Wolfe thought for a moment. "When he first describes the creatures, he says that one of the four faces is that of an ox. In the second passage, it's something else. A cherub, I think—"

"Good. Even in Ezekiel itself, you see, the record is being redacted. But we can find traces of the retoucher's hand. The vision is being edited to remove its more dangerous elements. If your first guess had been right, then the editors would have removed any reference to the body of God. But this isn't what they changed. They erased the ox and nothing else. Why?"

"I don't know," Wolfe said irritably. "It didn't strike me as especially important."

"You wouldn't be so careless on a crime scene," Ilya said. "Details are everything. Look at the feet of the creatures. Ezekiel says that they have the feet of a calf. But in the Septuagint translation, this detail is removed."

Wolfe seemed to understand. "So something about the ox makes the rabbis nervous. They're retouching the passage, even in translation, because they're afraid of something most readers would never see."

"But the changes reveal more than they intend," Ilya said. "All retouchers are like this. You should know this by now."

Wolfe, to her credit, understood the allusion at once. "Like the intelligence services."

"Yes. Or your man Karvonen. The rabbis, at least, were respectful of the mystery. But the Chekists obliterated their enemies until nothing was left. Until they grew frightened of poets and painters. But it only made their fears more visible. They erased books, men, nations. Look at Poland and Hungary. Or others that were erased in secret. The traces are there, if you know where to find them—"

As he spoke, Wolfe's eyes lit up, although he wasn't sure why. "How about Turkey?"

Something in this question surprised him. For the first time, he sensed that she had access to information that he did not. He decided to push further. "Yes, perhaps Turkey. Why?"

"Something I recently heard," Wolfe said. "I'll tell you if you tell me about the ox."

Ilya smiled at this. If he pressed further, he sensed he would learn more, but he also knew that it was important not to exhaust all his resources at one meeting. He signaled to the guard, then turned back to Wolfe. "This has been diverting. But I have nothing more to say."

"Just tell me one thing," Wolfe said. "The secret services know how to erase their enemies at home, but overseas, it's harder. It takes a specialist. Is this what Karvonen is doing?"

"I don't know," Ilya replied. "But such a man would only be deployed against a target that could not be taken out in any other way."

Wolfe leaned across the table, her eyes fixed on his. "A target like Victor Chigorin?"

Ilya did not respond, although, in his mind, this name set off its own chain of associations. As the guard unlocked the door of the interview room, Wolfe seemed about to protest, but in the end, she only fished a business card from her pocket. "Fine. But here's my number. They let you make calls here, right?"

He glanced at the card, memorizing the number with ease, and tucked it into one of his books. "Some of us are allowed to make calls. But don't wait for me to contact you. I am not the man you need."

Ilya followed the guard to the door. On his way out, struck by a thought, he paused and looked back.

"Another thing," Ilya said. "A cow's horn cannot be used as a shofar. If you want to talk again, tell me why."

With that, he gave her a smile so grave that it was almost a frown. Then he went back to be locked up in his cell.

36

Asthana was at her desk, taking notes on a stack of invoices, when a man's voice came from over her shoulder. "Working late?"

She jumped a little in her chair, startled, then saw that it was only Garber, who had crept up silently behind her. Turning around, she noticed for the first time that everyone else in the office had gone home. She smiled slightly at her own edginess, which she attributed to overwork, and removed her glasses. "Yes, for the third time this week. Devon is getting annoyed."

Garber sat down on the corner of her desk, which was the only surface that was not covered in papers. "What are you working on?"

"Invoices, mostly." Asthana began to straighten out the untidy heaps of folders. "I'm looking at the military collectibles dealer that sold guns to the armorer in Stoke Newington. Wolfe tracked them down online. They sold Campbell a deconverted Skorpion, remember?"

"I remember," Garber said, leafing through one of the files. "What about them?"

"It occurred to me that they might have sold him components that were used to build whatever Karvonen took from the garage. It's legal, up to a point, to trade in deactivated weaponry, even defused land mines or grenades." Asthana handed him a catalog, printed on rough paper, that she had obtained by writing away to an address in Islington. "See? You can get just about anything, for a price."

Garber studied the catalog, which offered a range of deactivated military equipment, from old black powder muskets to empty canisters of nerve gas. "So you think that these items could be used to make a working weapon?"

"It's possible, if you're good with your hands. Or if you arrange to get a weapon that was improperly deactivated. Someone like Aldane Campbell could have done a lot with this stuff."

He handed the catalog back to her. "I'm surprised that you're the one working on this. Isn't this more Wolfe's area of expertise?"

"Technically, yes." Asthana switched off her computer. "But she's busy tonight with her friend at Belmarsh—"

"Of course. And Powell has signed off on it, too. Sometimes I wonder about the two of them. Don't you?"

"Not really," Asthana said, although the possibility had, of course, crossed her mind. "Powell is married to his work, or at least to his idea of it. He just wants to turn Wolfe into a tiny version of himself. I thought she was too smart to fall for it, but now I'm not so sure."

"I've been thinking the same thing." Garber slid off the desk. "Listen, if you're heading out, I can give you a lift home. I know you've been taking the train since your car blew up. What do you say?"

Asthana hesitated. Strangely, her first impulse was to decline the offer, although she couldn't see any real reason why she should. At last, she smiled. "That's kind of you. Thanks."

"My pleasure," Garber replied. She expected him to go back to his desk to retrieve his things, but instead, he lingered close by, almost hovering, as she packed up her papers for the night. As she picked up her purse and jacket, she noticed that she and Garber were the only ones left on the floor.

They headed downstairs, passing the vacant front desk. Garber's car was parked in the adjoining lot. As Asthana followed him to the shabby Renault, she watched him out of the corner of one eye. She thought that he had grown increasingly distant over the past few days, as if he had something else on his mind. Still, it had been an exhausting three weeks for everyone at the agency, so it wasn't surprising that the strain was starting to show.

When they arrived at the car, Garber unlocked the passenger door, then went around to the driver's side as she got in. Sliding behind the wheel, he started the engine and backed out. As they headed for the front gate, he said, "Listen, do you mind if we make a slight detour? It's a place I sometimes go to think. There's something I've been meaning to ask you—"

"Sounds serious," Asthana said, keeping her tone light, although she was surprised by the proposal. "Is everything all right?"

"Everything's fine. It's just that we haven't had a chance to talk in a while, and I want to get your thoughts on something." Garber halted at the gate. "Look, it's up to you. I can just take you home, if you like—"

Asthana looked over at his face, which was in shadow. On most nights, after such a long day, she would have declined, but she sensed that there was more to the request than he was letting on. "I can't stay out too late."

"I know," Garber said, making a right onto the street. "This won't take a minute."

After going another block, they turned onto the Albert Embankment, then continued to Nine Elms Lane. As they drove along the Thames, the lights of the city cold in the distance, Asthana began to feel vaguely uneasy. Instead of talking as freely as she usually did, she found herself staring out the window at the river, glancing occasionally at the man behind the wheel. Garber, for his part, drove in silence, speaking only once, to ask if she wanted the heat on.

In the end, after five minutes or so, he turned onto a side street, where he maneuvered the car into a space under a shade tree and shut off the engine. "Here we are," Garber said. "What do you think?"

Asthana, seated in the darkness, looked out the windshield. Around them, unlit buildings stood shoulder to shoulder along the street. As far as she could tell, they were alone. Up ahead, however, against the lowering sky, she could see four white chimneys, rising into the air like the monumental legs of an upturned table. It was the Battersea Power Station.

Looking at the station, despite her wariness, Asthana had to admit that it was beautiful. High above, she could just make out the birds winding in tight circles overhead. She kept an eye on them, hoping to spot a falcon among the gulls. Falcons, she knew, sometimes made their nests in the brickwork of the station, mistaking it for the cliffs that had once been their home.

When Garber spoke again, there was a strange tone in

his voice. "You know, they're planning to build offices and apartments here. They've been trying to modernize it for years, ever since the plant shut down. I think they should leave it alone. Keep it the way it is now."

Asthana noticed that his eyes remained fixed on the smokestacks. "Keep it as what?"

"A temple to power," Garber said flatly. "A reminder of what really makes the world go round."

For the first time since they had left the office, he turned to look at her directly. She was unsettled by his air of intensity, which she had rarely seen before. "What are you talking about?"

Garber turned back to the plant. "Look at Russia. As long as Russia controls the supply of power to Europe, there's never going to be political change, no matter what someone like Chigorin thinks. Powell seems to believe he's a potential target, but I don't buy it. Do you?"

"Chigorin has certainly made enemies in the intelligence services," Asthana said carefully. "He's threatened to destroy them for good—"

"But he'll never be able to do it. Don't you see? Chigorin is popular in the West, but even if he decides to run for office, he doesn't have the same kind of support back home. He'll never win an election or be in a position to influence policy directly. As much as he talks about smashing the intelligence services, he isn't a real threat. Gaztek doesn't care if he cobbles together a coalition. As long as they control the flow of gas to the rest of Europe, the regime is safe."

"You may be right," Asthana said, although she still wasn't sure where this conversation was going. "But you don't need to win an election to influence things. The world is changing. A man like Stavisky, the whistle-blower, can affect government policy just by posting a few documents online. Chigorin seems to be coming around to this fact, at least from what I've heard."

"From Powell, you mean?" Garber shook his head. "Cornwall is backing him for now, yes, but she's just looking to buy time with the Home Office. As soon as she has enough to protect the agency, she'll cut him loose. Even I can see the writing on the wall—"

Asthana began to understand why Garber had wanted to have this conversation away from Vauxhall. "Look, I agree with you that this investigation has made some mistakes. But there's no question that someone is scared of what we might find. They planted a bomb in my car. It could have taken me out instead of Wolfe. You can't ask me to ignore that."

"But there are problems there, too," Garber said. "The more I think about it, the more that bomb bothers me. Look at how they put it together. It's the easiest thing in the world to stick a few pounds of explosive and a tilt fuse under the driver's seat. Instead, for no good reason, they wire it relay fashion, so half the bomb doesn't even go off. As if it was meant to fail."

Asthana turned to look more closely at Garber. "But what would be the point?"

"Maybe somebody is trying to implicate Russian intelligence." Before Asthana could object, Garber went on, saying, "Hear me out. Let's say that someone wanted us to make the connection to Russia. They use plastic explosive that could be easily traced to an intelligence source. They time the blast to coincide with a series of killings that all but advertise an intelligence angle, so that someone like Ilya can see it from a mile away. They even tie it in with this alleged plot against Chigorin, who seems like an obvious target, even if he isn't. The result looks exactly like an intelligence conspiracy. But it's something else entirely."

Asthana had listened to this speech in silence. "All right. So what is it, then?"

"I don't know," Garber said. "But I think someone is trying to tie Russian intelligence to a plot that doesn't have anything to do with it. Or perhaps one branch of the security services is trying to implicate another. You know that the military side, the GRU, has no love for its civilian rivals at the FSB. There's only so much money to go around. If I'm right, they're just toying with us."

"Powell wouldn't agree with you," Asthana said. "What has he said about this?"

Garber looked at the birds circling overhead. "I haven't told him about it yet. I was hoping that you and I—"

He broke off. Looking down, he was visibly surprised to see the knife buried up to the hilt in his side.

Garber looked up again at Asthana, who had taken the Spyderco knife silently from her purse. Before he could speak, she stuck the knife in deeper, then withdrew it, taking him by the hair in almost the same motion. Pulling his head back, she drew the serrated blade smoothly beneath his chin, cutting his throat.

The rest did not take long. Asthana watched, face expressionless, as Garber bled out, his eyes wide and fixed on hers. Mouth falling open, he tried to raise his hands, but they fell to his lap. She had been careful to sever the carotid arteries, so it took only a few seconds for the fall in pressure to render him unconscious, the blood pulsing down the front of his shirt and pooling on the driver's seat.

Asthana waited until she was sure he was dead. Then she wiped the knife on a clean corner of Garber's shirt and set it on the dashboard. Around the darkened car, the street was silent and deserted.

Taking the phone from her purse, she dialed a number from the list of recent calls. After a few rings, it went to voicemail.

"Hi, Devon," Asthana said tonelessly at the end of her fiancé's recording. She looked up at the smokestacks in the distance. "Sorry to do this to you, but it looks like I'll be working late again—"

37

The next day, at a few minutes before ten, the cruise ferry docked in the south harbor of Helsinki. At half an hour after sunrise, the temperature was only slightly above freezing, but Karvonen stood bareheaded as he looked out at the city. It was the first time he had returned in more than a year, and as he regarded the green neoclassical domes of the cathedral, outlined above the prim buildings of Market Square, he knew at last that he was home.

At Olympia Terminal, he disembarked with the other passengers, many of whom still had bleary eyes from the night before. Leaving the harbor, he rented a car and stowed his luggage in the ample trunk. He spent the rest of the morning sightseeing, driving out to the city's central square and parking not far from the cathedral. Mounting the steps, he spent a quiet hour inside, studying the altarpiece, flanked with kneeling angels, that displayed the deposition of Christ.

Afterward, he ran a few small errands, including a visit to an electronics shop, where he picked up a soldering kit and a handful of other components. The total cost of his purchases was less than thirty euros. By the time he left, the sun was already setting, although it was barely half past three.

He went for dinner at a restaurant near the square. Stationing himself at a table in the corner, his back to the wall, he ordered his usual Lapin Kulta, along with some mussel soup and whitefish. It was only then, as he took his first swallow of beer, that he saw the woman seated alone at a table across the room.

Karvonen studied her over the top of his glass. She was young and thin, almost bony, with long dark hair and blue eyes that were the most arresting thing about an otherwise plain face. Her mouth was wide and solemn, with something of the seriousness of a child watching the world before it could speak.

At the moment, however, she was focusing on the book at her side, a collection of John Donne's poetry. When her order came, it turned out to be a kind of vegetable crepe, which she ate with a fork in one hand, keeping the book open with the other. Now and then, between pages, she would glance absently at the diners around her, but her eyes never met Karvonen's.

After finishing her meal, she settled the bill, slid the book into her big purse, and rose from the table. Karvonen paid his own check quickly, then followed her outside, leaving the restaurant a few seconds after she did. He watched as she climbed into a blue Volvo parked at the curb, keeping an eye on her as he headed for his own car. When she pulled into the street, he did the same.

It was fifteen minutes to her neighborhood, which lay in the Vantaa district. Karvonen slowed as they turned on a quiet residential street, and parked his car half a block away. He watched through his windshield as she left her

Volvo and went into a modest bungalow. Then he got out as well, pausing only to retrieve his equipment from the rear of the car.

Going up to the porch, he found that she had left the front door unlocked. He stepped inside. Closing the door behind him, he set his bag down in the foyer, then headed for the kitchen, where the light had been turned on. In one hand, he was carrying the bottle of Armagnac.

She was standing in the kitchen, her back to the door, looking out the window at the night beyond. When he entered, she spoke without turning around. "You look different from last time."

"I'm glad to say you look the same." Karvonen came up behind her and produced the Armagnac. "I hope you recognize this, at least."

She accepted the bottle, clutching it for a moment to her body, then turned. Her face remained as serious as always, but there was the hint of a smile in her eyes as she reached up and brushed the hair from his forehead. He had removed his dental plate, but his altered hairline and eyes remained. "I liked your old face better. Although I suppose it's necessary in your line of work." She thrust the bottle back into his hands. "Let's have a drink."

As Karvonen opened the bottle, she took a pair of tulip glasses down from a cabinet. After he had poured the brandy, she put a finger in her glass and dabbed it on the back of her other hand, allowing the warmth of her skin to evaporate the alcohol, leaving only the aroma behind. She sniffed at it. "It's good."

"I'm glad you like it." Karvonen took a sip from his own glass, then looked across the kitchen at her. "It isn't too late, Laila. You still have a chance to walk away. We've been concerned about your safety—"

Laila regarded him contemptuously. "We've come too far to back away now. You of all people should know this." Taking her glass, she headed for the kitchen door. "Come on. I have something for you."

She led him to a door in the hallway, which she unlocked with a key from her pocket. A flick of the light switch revealed a set of stairs leading to the basement. Karvonen quickly drained the rest of his glass, then left it on the hall table and followed her down the steps.

On a workbench in the basement sat two packages, the ones he had sent from London a week before. Taking his new knife, he sliced them open one at a time, then set their contents on the bench. The first item was a heavy metal sphere about four inches across, packed in foam that he had cut to fit it exactly; the other was a flat plastic case with a depression in which the sphere could be set. Examining the components, Karvonen nodded. "Good."

He removed his jacket, which he had left on since his arrival, and pulled off his shirt. Underneath were the two small canisters that he had carried, taped between his shoulder blades, ever since his departure from London. He motioned for her to approach. "Help me with these."

Coming up behind him, Laila gently peeled away the cross of medical tape that held the canisters in place, her hands cool against his skin. Once the canisters were detached, she studied them for a moment, turning them over curiously, then set them on the bench, next to the rest of the device.

Karvonen regarded the components. Looking at them now, he felt with sudden certainty that the rest of the plan would unfold exactly as foreseen. "You have the last item we discussed?"

"Yes, it's here." From a drawer of the bench, she produced a box, already opened, for a mobile phone. "Nokia, of course—"

Karvonen smiled at this. Opening the carton, he took out the phone, which had been removed from its inner packaging. "And the test?"

"It went as expected. The phone returned safely. And no one suspected a thing."

"Good." Karvonen set the phone down. "We'll take care of the rest tomorrow."

Half an hour later, he was alone in the sauna. It was a tiny space with a cedar bench just wide enough for two, the kind that could be found in every Finnish bathroom. In the old days, the sauna would be built before the rest of the house, so that the workers would have a place to relax during construction. Now, after his own journey, Karvonen finally felt the tension falling away.

As he ladled water onto the electric stones, watching the steam rise, he thought of his history with Laila. He had recruited her two years ago, under a false flag, after she had been identified as a potential recruit based on certain postings on a message board for the extreme right. After feeling her out online, he had spent six months cultivating her, feeding her nationalism, and plying her with gifts, until he had been flying out almost weekly from London.

Karvonen smiled at these memories. Laila believed, not without reason, that he was an officer with the Finnish Security Intelligence Service. He had provided her with more than enough documentation to convince her of his story, but knew from his own experience that such evidence was less important than the target's need to believe. Testing the depths of her rage, he had discovered that it knew no bounds, a well of anger that her calm exterior did not begin to express.

He looked down at the wooden floor, feeling drops of sweat gathering on his body. Most of Laila's family on her mother's side had been killed in the air raids on Viipuri, which had been leveled by thousands of Russian bombs. The city had been erased, but its memory lived on, fueled by her mother's stories, in much the same way that the war had been a part of his own childhood.

Once the initial groundwork had been laid, it had been surprisingly easy to persuade her of the necessity of their mission. In her passion, and her hate, he saw possibilities that the rest of this timid country left unfulfilled. And in his more honest moments, she reminded him of something he had long since forgotten, a fierce loyalty to homeland that came before all else, no matter what the cost.

As he reflected on this, the door of the sauna opened. He looked up to see Laila standing before him, dressed only in a light silk robe. A glass of Armagnac was in her hand. With her eyes on his, her face still solemn, she let the robe drop, first from one shoulder, then the other, until it fell to the floor.

Underneath, she was naked, her body slender like a girl's, with a slight boniness to the firmly muscled hips. Her hair was loose, and it came down to the middle of her back. The breasts were not large, but pleasingly shaped, and he saw her smile for the first time as she inverted the tulip glass in her hand, the amber liquid flowing in a glistening stream down the front of her body.

Karvonen hesitated for a second, watching as she stepped into the sauna, her sweat already forming in bright pearls. As the liquor on her body evaporated in the heat, he could smell its perfume drifting up from her smooth skin, filling the small space with the aromas of apricots, figs, vanilla. He knew that if he bent his head forward only a few inches, he would taste it on his tongue.

For another moment, he paused, uncertain of where this fit into the plan. At last, however, as she reached out to run a hand through his hair, he ducked his head and surrendered to all she had to offer.

38

The following morning, Ilya went to church. When the door of his cell was unlocked, he lined up with his fellow inmates on the middle landing, in front of a barred gate beneath a cube with a view of all four spurs. Through the glass walls of this enclosure, which was called the bubble, the guards watched as the gate was opened and the prisoners marched out along the linoleum floor.

After a body search, Ilya headed with the others into the chapel. It was a fairly large space of red brick, twenty paces square, with two hundred plastic chairs for the congregants. At the front of the room stood the chaplain, a stocky figure in a threadbare suit, along with a drummer, a girl with a guitar, and three gospel singers in robes. Behind them was a mural of the Last Supper, painted years ago by a convicted murderer, with the disciples modeled on the faces of other inmates.

At the rear of the chapel, which was rapidly filling, Grisha was seated next to a small, dark man with a beard. When Ilya caught his eye, Grisha nodded, then gestured to a vacant seat directly in front of him. Ilya made his way to this row, then took a seat and waited for the service to begin.

Around him, the room rang with the voices of prisoners greeting friends from other spurs. After enduring this din for several minutes, the chaplain called for silence, threatening to send anyone caught talking straight to the segregation ward. Then he intoned the morning's prayer: "The glory of the Lord shall be revealed, and all flesh shall see it together—"

During the prayer, Ilya kept his eyes open, continuing to look around the room. The congregation, he had noticed, was divided into two distinct sections. Toward the front of the room, the first nine rows were mostly black, and they joined in loudly as the hymn began. The last eight rows, a mix of races, consisted of men with their heads bent, not in prayer, but in whispered conversations, as messages were exchanged and drugs passed from hand to hand.

When the last notes of the hymn had died out, the chaplain began the sermon, on the theme of the cursing of the fig tree. As he did, Ilya heard Grisha speak from behind him: "Now, then. This is Osman."

Ilya turned his head slightly. Osman, the tea boy from the adjoining spur, was a few years younger than he was, with an intelligent face flawed by a scar that ran from the corner of his mouth to his temple. When he grinned, the scar deepened into an extension of his smile. "Pleasure, mate."

"Good to meet you," Ilya said quietly. "Did Grisha say why I wanted to talk?"

"Sure he did." Osman leaned forward, so that the top of his shaved head nearly rested on Ilya's shoulder, and said in a low voice: "You want to hear the word on these killings, am I right?"

Ilya nodded. "Grisha says that you've heard something about the murders."

"Just rumors, mostly. You can't believe all you hear in a place like this. But people are talking, as they will." He lowered his voice further. "Campbell's demise set some tongues wagging. Plenty of Yardies here, you know—"

"Yes, I know," Ilya said. "So what are they saying about Campbell's death?"

"That it was the spies. Normally I'd call bullshit, because I don't see why they'd want to take out a Yardie armorer, right? Later, though, when they got that one in Finsbury Park, I started to wonder. That wasn't you, was it?"

Ilya had to smile at this. "No. I didn't kill them. But I believe it was the same man."

"That's what I said. A stone assassin, which makes me suspect the stories are true. Whoever did this was a cold bastard. Trained, lethal, smart. Which doesn't sound like spies to me. Sounds more like former military."

Considering this point, Ilya saw that there might be something to it. Military intelligence was a world apart from the civilian agencies, and it was better at working overseas. "Any talk about what the killer might do next?"

"Plenty of talk, but nothing I'd credit," Osman said. "But here's what I figure. These military guys don't do nothing without a good reason. The target will be someone who threatens them. If I were trying to figure what this lot was up to next, I'd keep my eye on whoever they hate most—"

As he listened, Ilya was reminded of something that Wolfe had said. "Ever hear of the Dyatlov Pass?"

"Never heard of it, mate, but I'll keep my ears open." Osman coughed. "Assuming, of course, that you can fix a few things for me as well. Maybe we can have a word about this soon—"

"Of course," Ilya said, knowing that his position, as a remand prisoner, gave him advantages that were not readily available to the general population. He glanced back up at the chaplain at the head of the room, who was winding down his sermon, and reflected on what he had heard so far. One point in particular stuck in his mind. The target, Osman had said, would be the man the security services hated most. Which made him think of Chigorin.

Ilya looked around the chapel. Over the past few years, along with his study of scripture, he had read deeply in the history of the intelligence services, relying both on official accounts and on less traditional sources. With practice, he had become skilled at seeing traces of such activities where they had never been noticed before, and had absorbed the details of events that had previously gone unconnected. One was that of the Dyatlov Pass. But there were others.

When the sermon was over, another hymn followed, during which prisoners could receive blessings at the altar. After the inmates were back in their seats, the chaplain concluded with the traditional benediction, his hand upraised: "The Lord make his face shine upon you and be gracious to you—"

The service ended. As they filed out together, Osman gave a nod to Ilya, then lowered his voice to a conspiratorial whisper: "One other thing. Watch your back, mate. A fellow like you needs to be careful."

"Thank you," Ilya said, heading for the doors. "I'll do my best to remember that."

They filed out for another body search, intended to

uncover any contraband that had changed hands during the service, then trudged back to their cells. Osman wandered off in another direction, while Ilya and Grisha returned to their own spur. And Ilya was about to ask Grisha for his thoughts on the tea boy's words when he was interrupted by a sudden commotion.

He turned. Across the landing, on the other end of the spur, two prisoners had begun to fight. They were scrawny and black, with the thick dreadlocks of Yardies, and as each man flung shouts at the other, Ilya recognized the voices of two window warriors who spent each night yelling through the bars of their cells, trading incomprehensible insults for hours.

As he watched, one of the men got the other in a headlock, the tendons standing out on his stringy arm. An alarm sounded from above as the guards and prisoners, including Grisha, began to surge toward the fun. Ilya took a step backward to avoid the stampede, his shoulders brushing the wall, and was warily eyeing the crowd when his attention was caught by something else.

Looking up at the hexagonal bubble above the landing, Ilya saw that one of the men inside was watching him. It was the guard with glasses who, on his first day, had led him to his cell in the medical ward. And as he looked into the guard's eyes, which were fixed on his, he knew at once what was happening.

He turned in time to catch the man behind him by surprise. It was the one called Goat, whom Grisha had warned him about three days ago. For a second, the other inmate hesitated, the two of them facing each other in silence. Then he lunged forward with a snarl, the gleam of a razor visible in his hand.

Without thinking, Ilya took a step back, just in time to avoid the worst of the forward slash. An instant later, he felt the cloth of his shirt part, then the skin. Hot blood began to stream down his chest, a shallow wound, but enough to turn the world red as Goat came in again.

Ilya, his pulse blooming, sensed the attack as much as he saw it, and brought up his forearms to block the back slash. He felt a sting like a shaving nick as the razor cut open his right arm. With his left hand, he took hold of Goat's wrist, the one with the razor, and managed to lock both hands around it as he threw the other man against the wall. Faintly, he heard shouts, although he wasn't sure whether they were directed at him or at the fight across the landing.

Goat's head hit the wall with a thud, the razor falling from his grasp. As Ilya released him, the seconds seemed to tick by quite slowly. Seeing the razor at his feet, he picked it up, his fingers closing around its plastic handle.

As soon as the razor was in his hand, time returned to its normal speed. Hearing the shouts and echoes on the landing, Ilya knew he had only a few seconds to get the answers he needed.

He went over to Goat, who was on his back. Kneeling, Ilya took him by the hair, then slammed the other man's head against the ground, hard enough to feel the floor vibrate. "Did Vasylenko send you?"

Goat drew back his lips and tried to spit, although most of the saliva fell back on his own forehead. Ilya, feeling the seconds slip away, slashed him across the face, opening up his cheekbone. Rolling his eyes upward, Goat hissed out a few syllables: "It wasn't Vasylenko—"

Ilya leaned in, razor almost touching the white of the

other man's eye. Behind him, he heard footsteps. "Who was it?"

"I don't know his name," Goat gasped. "I was paid for the job. They said they would help my family—"

Ilya stared at him. He was about to ask another question when he felt himself seized from behind by several pairs of arms. A voice came hot in his ear: "Drop it, you fucking shite!"

Feeling the arms around him tighten, Ilya complied. The razor fell from his hand. Before it had time to strike the floor, he felt himself lifted up bodily, his head pushed down, legs bent up and back. The world tilted sideways as he was hauled off by the guards, who shouted for the others to keep away.

He was dragged into another room, a strip cell, that stood off the main landing. As he was held down, his face shoved toward the floor, he felt cool air touch his flesh as his shirt and jeans were cut off with scissors. His chest and right forearm were sticky with blood.

There was a click of steel as they put him in wrist locks, then bent his legs behind his back again. Ilya felt a leather belt encircle his waist, then more hands pry his limbs backward as his wrists and ankles were cuffed, leaving him unable to move. He flashed briefly on the binding of Isaac, but then even this pleasingly ironic image fell away as he was carried back outside.

The lights on the ceiling bounced overhead as he was dragged down a second set of stairs, the guards puffing around him, and taken into a part of the block he had not seen before, a place smelling of sweat and human waste. With his face to the floor, he heard a door being unbolted and swung back, then allowed himself to be thrown into a final cell. It was the segregation ward.

Ilya lay curled up on the floor, still trussed, the cell door sideways in his field of vision. In the hallway, a cluster of guards was outlined against the light. He heard their last words before the door closed: "Fucking animals—"

The door swung shut, plunging the cell into darkness. He lay on the ground, his cheek pressed against the concrete, breathing the unspeakable smell. Blood was gathering on the floor beneath him, his body aching all over, and it only ached more badly as he began to laugh.

39

When Wolfe entered the segregation ward, she found that it was not quite the dungeon she had expected, but a plain tiled hallway with an institutional feel. The air smelled of bleach, as if someone had given the floor a hasty scrub before allowing her inside, but the faint stink of human dirt still remained.

The guard on duty led her to a cell halfway down the hall, rolling an office chair with one broken caster. He parked the chair in front of the door, then opened the Judas hole so that she could talk to the man inside. After asking whether she needed anything, he left, locking the gate behind him.

Wolfe sat down. In spite of the drugs she was taking, her neck and shoulder ached, and her arm was still in a sling. For now, though, she pushed her discomfort away and looked into the Judas hole. "Ilya?"

There was no answer. From here, she was unable to make out the cell's interior, but she sensed that Ilya was listening. She waited another moment, then said, "I'm trying to get you out of here. You did quite a number on the guy with the razor. But I hear he came after you first."

More silence. Wolfe glanced at the guard, who was out of earshot, then turned back to the cell. "I came to tell you a few things. We believe that we're dealing with an intelligence plot to kill Victor Chigorin. We don't have the full story yet, but it has something to do with a covert action called Operation Pepel, which took place in Turkey in the late fifties."

Wolfe waited for a response, which was not forthcoming. She had spent a long time debating how much information to share with Ilya, and despite his misgivings, Powell had signed off. The next part, however, was painful, and she had trouble keeping her voice level as she continued to speak:

"We think that one of the officers at my agency was passing information to the Russians," Wolfe said, the words still strange in her mouth. "He's disappeared. Judging from travel records, it looks like he's left the city, but then the trail goes cold. We've searched his files, and what we've found indicates that he was acting as an informant. But I still don't know what to believe."

She paused, remembering what they had learned so far about Garber. Even now, a full day after the revelation, it was still hard to comprehend, and the agency was in a state of shock. Garber's car was gone, and his credit card and identification documents had been used to buy a train ticket to Lausanne, although it seemed likely that he had disembarked at an earlier station.

Along with a great deal of other incriminating material, a search of Garber's computer had uncovered detailed information, its source unknown, about Chigorin's itinerary. As a result, the agency had decided to embed an officer into the grandmaster's entourage. Powell had volunteered to fly with them to Helsinki, and other measures were being put rapidly into place, but nothing could disguise the severity of the leak. Asthana, in particular, had taken it hard—

A quiet voice broke into her thoughts. "Did you find out about the cow's horn?"

Wolfe, startled, looked through the opening in the door. Beyond it there was nothing but blackness, but as she regarded the hole more closely, she could see something moving in the dark. "I did. Do you want to talk about it?"

There was no answer. She waited a beat before speaking again, although she had been preparing for this moment ever since their last meeting. "A shofar is the ritual horn used in the synagogue," Wolfe began. "It can be made from the horn of a ram, or a sheep, or even a non-kosher animal. But never a cow."

A long pause. At first, Wolfe thought that Ilya had lapsed into silence, but before she could go on, he said, "Yes. Even here, you see, the rabbis are afraid of the ox's face. But why?"

"Because of the golden calf," Wolfe said. "They were ashamed of it. Nothing that recalled a cow or calf was allowed into the temple."

After another pause, Ilya spoke softly. "Now, at last, you're close to the heart of the matter. That ancient humiliation. Painful after so many centuries. Taken as proof that the Israelites were unworthy of God's love. Yet the story itself is strange. Even in the original version, you can sense the author rushing past it. Something about it clearly terrified the rabbis. They erased every trace of it they could find. But what was it that made them afraid?"

Wolfe did not reply at once. She knew the answer, or thought she did, but even now, it was not something she wanted to utter aloud. Only the hope of what else Ilya might say allowed her to continue.

"The story doesn't make sense," Wolfe said at last. "The Israelites had just been delivered out of slavery. They had seen God himself at the Red Sea. Yet they gave up on him so easily, as if all those miracles weren't enough." She hesitated. "Unless, of course, they worshipped the golden calf, not in spite of what they had been shown, but because of it."

Even in the darkness beyond the door, she could tell that he was listening. "Go on."

Wolfe wanted to hurry past this part of the argument, but she forced herself to speak slowly. "So there's a tradition that the heavenly chariot, the one Ezekiel saw, was present at the exodus from Egypt. It's mentioned in a psalm, and it was associated with the exodus in the cycle of readings in the synagogue. Some commentators even say that God used the chariot and the four living creatures as a weapon against Pharaoh. Which makes me wonder—"

She slowed, then halted. Even after straying so far from her own faith, she regarded what she was about to say as close to blasphemy. "Which makes me wonder if the golden calf, the one the Israelites worshipped, was the ox of the *merkabah*. Or that the rabbis were afraid that it was."

"A very interesting possibility," Ilya said quietly. "And does this explain anything?"

"Yes. It explains why the rabbis were so afraid of Ezekiel's vision, and why it was retouched to remove the ox's face and the calf's foot. They didn't want anyone to suspect that when the Israelites worshipped the calf, saying that it was the god who had delivered them from Egypt, they might have been close to the truth. That the calf was a reflection of something real."

Ilya was nothing but a voice in the dark. "And you know the point of this story?"

Wolfe had expected the question. "I think it means that when God shows himself, we aren't always ready. Our own eyes can mislead us. Even if he appeared like he did at the Red Sea, we wouldn't understand it, unless we'd already found the answers on our own. That's what a midrash is. An investigation he wants us to make first. Even if we hate him for abandoning us in the meantime."

In the brief silence that followed, Wolfe realized that she had been describing herself. If Ilya sensed this, however, he did not mention it. "Yes. For the unprepared, the revelation simply fades away. It doesn't matter how powerful it is. The proof, we are told, is from the exodus from Egypt. Which is what happens when a vision, or lesson, is granted to those who aren't yet ready to understand."

Wolfe sensed that she had passed a test. "And you're saying that I'm still not ready?"

"Few of us are. Ever since the golden calf, God has spoken in riddles. Or not at all. That's why the rabbis look past the words of scripture. Not at the words themselves. We can't trust our eyes or ears. It's a mistake to wait for God to speak. He exiles us from his presence because his face might drive us mad. As it did with the rabbis in the orchard. Or those hikers in the snow—"

Wolfe sat upright in her chair, which slid backward. "You mean the Dyatlov Pass?"

Ilya fell silent again. Wolfe strained to see into the darkened rectangle, her mind racing. The only time she had mentioned the Dyatlov Pass to Ilya had been after his arrest. He had clearly recognized the reference, but instead of telling her what he knew, he had shared a different story. And as she thought now of the rabbis who had entered the orchard, she saw the connection at last. "Are you saying that the hikers saw something that drove them mad?"

After another pause, his voice came again from the darkness, farther away now, as if he had retreated from the door. "I am not saying anything. Not yet. But I want you to tell me why you've taken such an interest in this."

Wolfe hesitated for a moment before responding. "They were Morley's last words."

"I see," Ilya said. "And what do you think the real mystery is, after the distracting elements have been stripped away?"

Wolfe scrambled to catch up with this new line of questioning. "It isn't as strange as it seems. I don't know how much you know about the incident, but most of the hikers' injuries could have been caused by a fall down the ravine. The woman's missing tongue might have been degraded by the microbes in her own body. Their orange skin and gray hair may have been a misinterpretation of the mortician's work, or a story passed along until it changed into something else—"

She stopped, afraid of overwhelming him with information, but his next question implied that he knew as much about the incident as she did. "How do you explain the radiation?"

"It might mean nothing." Wolfe cast her mind back to

278 / Alec Nevala-Lee

something that Lewis had told her the day before. "Radiation was found on only one woman's coat, and it looks like radioactive potassium, which was often used in classroom demonstrations. All the hikers were students or graduates of Ural Polytechnic, so it's possible that they were just exposed to it in the lab. The one thing I can't explain is the lights that were seen in the sky that night—"

"That troubled me as well, when I first read of it," Ilya said. "But you're overlooking the simplest explanation. All the accounts agree that the snow that night was heavy. In a snowstorm, it would have been impossible to see anything near the pass. Which implies that the reports of lights—"

"—were fabrications or mistakes." Wolfe saw his point. "So they were just another story. Something added to the accounts of the incident long after it actually happened. A rumor. Or a misunderstanding."

"And it does nothing but distract you from the fundamental question. Which is—"

"—why nine experienced hikers just abandoned their tent," Wolfe said, finally seeing the full picture. "And why they couldn't return to it."

"Exactly." He paused again. "You mentioned that the victims were all associated with Ural Polytechnic Institute. That's in Yekaterinburg. Formerly known as Sverdlovsk. What do you know about that city?"

"Not a lot," Wolfe said, trying to remember what little she had read. "It was a closed city, with ties to military industry and engineering."

"Yes. They produced tanks, armaments, nuclear rockets. There was also a biological weapons facility. It was built after the war, using information from the Japanese germ warfare program. I once went there myself. Many years ago. On an errand in another lifetime—"

Before he could finish, Wolfe rose from her chair, which rolled backward and struck the wall behind her. At the end of the corridor, the guard glanced up, but she ignored him. "You're talking about Kamera."

She took a step toward the cell, then another, until she was only a few inches from the Judas hole. Through the opening, she smelled the stink of old waste and sweat, and knew that it had to be much worse on the inside. "The poison laboratory of the secret services. They made the poison you used when—"

Wolfe stopped. A memory appeared in her mind, with terrible clarity, of a man in a hospital room, skin peeling away, eyes glassy with dementia. What had happened to Anzor Archvadze had been bad, one of the worst things she had ever seen, but somehow, she sensed, this was worse.

Looking into the cell, she thought of the nine hikers who had perished in the snow, and what they might have seen before they died. A waking nightmare, something terrible enough for them to tear open their tent and rush into the cold and darkness. Then, with a chill, she thought of Morley's last words, and the possibility that the recent murders had been carried out to assemble a device. She bent closer to the hole. "Is this what Karvonen is building?"

With startling suddenness, Ilya's face appeared in the opening, just a few inches from her own. She stared. He had been badly beaten. There were streaks of dried blood on his face, and one of his eyes had swollen shut, but the eye that remained open was fixed on hers.

"Remember the lesson of the calf," Ilya said. "The truth isn't always what your eyes are telling you. It isn't always in words. You'll be tempted to take it by force. But sometimes you need to surrender. Isaac, they say, saw the chariot when he was bound to the altar, ready to be sacrificed. Which means—"

Wolfe saw him fall silent, and feared that he would only turn away again. "Yes?"

"That anyone who loves God truly cannot ask for his love in return." With that, Ilya withdrew into the darkness, and no matter how much she called, he would not say another word.

40

When Powell returned to the jet's main cabin, his mind was already made up. He was flying across the continent in a corporate jet that had been placed at Chigorin's disposal by one of his wealthy supporters. The Bombardier aircraft was divided by a bulkhead into two sections, one with regular seats for press and staff, the other with a fully equipped conference space. For obvious reasons of convenience and safety, the grandmaster disliked flying on Aeroflot.

In the conference area, Chigorin and Stavisky were seated close together, speaking quietly, with the grandmaster's assistant and security chief stationed nearby. As Powell entered, Chigorin glanced up from his computer, seeming to notice the urgency in his face. "What is it?"

"I was hoping that we could speak privately," Powell said. "It's a matter that concerns you directly."

After a pause, Chigorin told his staff members to leave, although Stavisky remained where he was. As the others filed past, Powell caught a suspicious glance from the security chief. He knew that he was not entirely welcome here. They had allowed him to join the entourage on the condition that his presence remain a secret. Otherwise, they feared, it would play badly in the state media, which was always eager to portray Chigorin as a tool of foreign interests.

Once they were alone, Powell related what Wolfe had told him over the phone, which was that she suspected Karvonen of preparing to deploy a psychotropic weapon. Chigorin and Stavisky listened to his account patiently, breaking in with the occasional question. When he mentioned the possible involvement of the Soviet poison program, he saw them exchange glances.

"I know it seems hard to credit," Powell concluded. "But it's the only hypothesis that fits the information we have. And we have reason to suspect that a similar weapon is being readied against you now."

As he spoke, he felt his voice catch slightly. The discovery of the grandmaster's itinerary on Garber's computer had only confirmed what everyone already feared. He had been passing information to the intelligence services, and now he had vanished, perhaps because he sensed the agency closing in. It was even possible, Powell thought grimly, that he intended to join Karvonen himself.

Chigorin was looking out the window, which displayed a view of tufted clouds. "So what do you recommend?"

"I'd strongly advise you to rethink your plans," Powell said. "If I were Karvonen, the conference in Helsinki would be the perfect place to make my move. It's inconvenient, I know, but you should consider canceling your public appearances, at least until we know more about his intentions."

Turning away from the view, Chigorin looked at Stavisky. For the second time, Powell saw an unspoken message pass between the two men. At last, Chigorin gave the other man a nod. "Tell him."

Powell glanced over at Stavisky, who had been listening in silence. "Tell me what?"

Stavisky leaned forward in his chair. "We received another batch of materials from our source last night. At the moment, we're still examining the documents. But there are certain similarities to what you've said."

"In particular, a few of the files talk about a poison program," Chigorin said, reaching for his tablet computer. "It's common knowledge, of course, that such programs existed, designed to develop toxins for biological warfare and assassination. But the documents we have just received, if genuine, imply that such research was far more extensive than was previously known. And they directly implicate Yuri Litvinov, the current head of the FSB."

Chigorin handed him the tablet. Looking at the screen, Powell saw that it contained a list of documents in Russian, twelve in all. "And this has something to do with Operation Pepel?"

"Apparently it was their first great success," Stavisky said. "Although we still don't know what it was."

Choosing a document at random, Powell opened the file, which turned out to be another photocopy, a security seal stamped on its first page. "What kind of poison program are we talking about?"

"Based on the files we've seen, it was hugely ambitious," Stavisky said. "It was the predecessor to a research program called Project Bonfire—"

"I've heard of it," Powell said, studying the file. "An effort to create a toxin weapon."

"Yes. It has been widely discussed in histories of the

poison program, but we never knew much about earlier projects, until now." Stavisky gestured toward the tablet. "What we have here is the first conclusive evidence that these programs go back at least to the period after the war. And Litvinov and other members of state security were directly involved."

"As I said, we're still trying to verify the files," Chigorin said. "But what they reveal is consistent with what you've just told us. There was a neurological weapons program at Yekaterinburg, based on Japanese germ warfare materials captured in Manchuria. And it appears that the researchers there, including Litvinov, engaged in extensive testing on human subjects."

Powell felt the pieces come together. "So the Dyatlov Pass could have been a test."

"It isn't mentioned in the files," Stavisky said. "But, yes, it's possible. According to the documents, human tests were authorized by Litvinov himself. And he wasn't the only one. There are dozens of names, many of them ranking members of the security services. So you can see why our contact was so anxious to put the information into our hands. The question now is what to do next."

Looking between the two men, Powell understood the excitement in their eyes. The documents that they had received, if authentic, could be a weapon of tremendous political significance. "What do you intend to do?"

"I say we post them online," Stavisky said flatly. "If the security services are trying to put a similar operation into effect, the smartest thing would be to make these documents public at once."

Chigorin shook his head. "We need to be careful. Once we've finished confirming the files, we can proceed. Although—"

As the grandmaster broke off, Powell sensed that he was torn between the obvious opportunity and his natural caution. The poison program was an issue of great emotional power, and the revelations would be enough to shake the security service to its foundations. All the same, going public with a false story would be equally damaging. Chigorin finally turned to Powell. "What's your opinion?"

Powell, who had not expected to be consulted, considered his response carefully. "I can't recommend anything without more information. I need to see the files first. If you agree to release the documents to my agency in advance of their publication, I can take a closer look."

Stavisky was visibly displeased by this, but Chigorin nodded. "Done. What else?"

"I still believe that it's dangerous for you to attend the conference in Helsinki," Powell said. "The machinery for an operation is locking into place. Our best guess is that it involves you. But the choice is yours."

Chigorin was silent for a moment. Finally, he stirred and said, "No, the choice is not mine. At least not mine alone." Turning to the door of the conference area, he raised his voice. "Felix, come in here, please."

A moment later, the security chief appeared at the door of the bulkhead. "Yes?"

"There's been a slight change," Chigorin said. "We will land in Helsinki, then file a revised flight plan for departure tomorrow. I won't be attending the conference, although Stavisky can remain behind if he chooses. I don't want any formal announcements. As far as the world knows, I'm still on schedule. But I'll be flying to Moscow in the morning."

The security chief frowned at this. "Can I ask why we're making the change?"

Chigorin glanced at Stavisky. "I need to speak with the leaders of the coalition. We'll schedule a meeting at my apartment in Arbat. But we can discuss this later. In the meantime, please tell the captain."

The security chief nodded, then headed for the cockpit. Once he was gone, Chigorin turned to Powell. "This is your decision, of course, but I would like you to come with us. If you prefer, you can fly home from Helsinki. But your presence would be welcomed in Moscow."

Powell was surprised by the request. As he considered it, he was aware of Stavisky's eyes on his face, watching him suspiciously. He was about to decline the offer, knowing that he would be needed at home, but then saw that he really had no choice. If Wolfe could get so close to Ilya, he thought, then perhaps it was time for him to make some new friends as well. "I'll come."

"Good," Chigorin said. "I'll arrange for the documents to be sent to your agency."

"I'll let them know, then." Powell rose and headed for the front of the plane, taking out his phone to call Wolfe. It would be good for her, he thought, to work on something tangible for a change. When he read her reports, it struck him that the creatures of Ezekiel's vision, with their four monstrous faces, were far less terrible than what men could do to themselves.

Dialing her number, he brought the phone to his ear. As he did, he felt the plane shift, and his eye was caught by the view from the window. The clouds had parted, and in the distance, as perfect as a child's scale model, he saw the city below. They were descending to Helsinki.

41

That night, Karvonen began to make his final preparations. Word of the change in plans had reached him that afternoon. Now that the timeline had been moved up, it was tempting to hurry, but instead, he forced himself to slow down, focusing entirely on the task at hand.

Seating himself at the bench in Laila's basement, he laid the components across the table, under the magnifying lamp. He would be working from memory, since the original plans had long since been destroyed. Before consigning the film and prints to the fire, however, he had studied them closely, to the point where he could almost perform the necessary steps in his sleep.

In any case, this part of the process was not difficult. He took the cell phone that Laila had provided, slid off the battery door, and removed the internal battery and card. Using a small screwdriver, he unfastened the screws holding the body together and pried apart the plastic case, exposing the phone's inner workings. Inside, nestled in a protective metal brick, was the speaker, no larger than a hearing aid. He pried this out as well, revealing a pair of leads.

Using the soldering kit that he had purchased two days before, he connected the leads to a pair of wires, marking them carefully. He snapped the case back on, threading the wires out through an opening in the center. Then he put the phone back together, allowing the wires to hang freely.

Among the electronic parts that he had bought upon his arrival was a small thyristor, a component that would continue to conduct current until its power source was shut off. He soldered one of its pins to a battery pack, which had a switch that could be slid off or on, then attached the wires from the phone. A second set of wires went to a pair of alligator clips.

Karvonen studied the result. What he had put together was a very simple detonator. When the phone rang, a pulse was sent through the leads to the wires. Current would pass from there to the thyristor, creating a latching circuit. The current thus generated could be used to activate any number of things, including the device that he had assembled, which he now brought out from under the bench.

Most of the assembly was already done. The night before, he had locked the two canisters into place inside the gray plastic sphere, the top hemisphere of which was threaded so that it could be unscrewed and removed. Then he had mounted the sphere to the plastic case that contained the remaining components, as well as the magnets that would later be used to secure the device.

As he prepared to wire everything together, he heard three knocks on the door at the top of the stairs, then the sound of a key in the lock. He glanced up as Laila's slender legs came into view, followed shortly by the rest of her. She approached the workbench, then halted. "Is it done?"

"Not quite," Karvonen said. "Sit down. There are a few things I need to show you."

Laila pulled up a stool, watching as he made the final adjustments. A pair of labeled wires already protruded from the base of the device. He attached these wires to the clips from the detonator, then used electrical tape to bind the whole thing together, including the phone.

Karvonen took a moment to regard the result. It was, in fact, not exactly a thing of beauty, its three separate pieces cobbled together with layers of tape. From an aesthetic point of view, it offended his Finnish eye for elegance in design. It was typical, he thought, of the vulgarity of the Russian mind, like the bomb that had been thrown at Tsar Alexander.

All the same, he knew that there were sound reasons for using this particular method. And the device's beauty was somehow increased by the fact that so many men, and one woman, had died for its sake.

Laila, as if sensing the importance of the moment, spoke softly. "Can I hold it?"

"Of course," Karvonen said. He handed it to her gently, watching as she enfolded it in her hands. "Is everything ready?"

Laila answered without taking her eyes from the device. "The weather report calls for snow. I was afraid it would delay the operation, but it looks like everything will be on schedule."

"I'll show you what to do, then." Taking back the device, he indicated the switch on the battery pack. "You need to slide this to the *on* position before placing it. Otherwise it won't work. The magnets at the bottom will lock it inside the mix manifold. I'll make the call when the time is right."

From the floor beside the workbench, he took a padded nylon case. He slid the assembled device inside, closed the case, and handed it to Laila. Then he cleared the bench of materials and followed her upstairs.

A quarter of an hour later, he accompanied her outside, the nylon case in one hand. It was still dark. Walking her to the Volvo in the driveway, he put the bag on the front seat, then waited as she got behind the wheel. Earlier, she had changed into work clothes and tied back her hair.

Karvonen stood next to the car as she started the engine. Before driving off, she rolled down her window, letting in some of the cold. Even in the darkness, he could make out the gleam of her eyes. "Goodbye, then."

"Goodbye." On an impulse, Karvonen leaned down, his hand stroking the back of her sleek head, and kissed her on the mouth. It was an unplanned gesture, like that of an actor in the middle of an extended improvisation, but as he sucked in the warmth of her lips, he knew that it was the right one.

After a few seconds, he pulled back. Laila was looking at him with the same solemn expression as before. For a moment, he felt something pass between them, more charged than any of their sessions of lovemaking. Then she rolled up her window, put the car into gear, and drove off, the device still on the front seat.

He stood in the cold, watching her lights recede, until she had disappeared around the corner. Then he pulled out his phone. Although it was past midnight in London, his handler answered at once. "Are we on schedule?"

"Yes, we're set to go." Karvonen headed into the house, locking the front door behind him. "She just left for work. I'll close things down here and check in later. Is everything ready on your end?"

"It will be. Don't concern yourself with it. And don't forget to take care of the girl."

Karvonen halted in the foyer. At first, he wasn't sure that he'd heard correctly. "What are you talking about?"

"The girl knows too much," the handler said patiently. "She can't be allowed to live. You know this as well as I do."

Going into the living room, Karvonen found himself looking at a framed picture on the mantelpiece, a portrait of Laila, in her early teens, standing next to her mother. Deep down, he realized, he had always known that this order would come. "She doesn't know anything about me."

"It doesn't matter. We can't afford to take any chances." His handler paused. "I need to know that you will do what is necessary."

Karvonen, standing in the center of the room, remembered his vow, sworn years ago, never to shed the blood of another Finn. Closing his eyes, he felt an unaccustomed anger, sensing that his handler had been planning this moment all along, knowing that it would serve as a final test of loyalty.

His bag lay on the floor next to the sofa. Opening it, he removed the pistol that he had retrieved from the weapons cache. Then, going up to the mantelpiece, he turned down the photograph of Laila and her mother.

"All right," Karvonen said at last. "I'll take care of it. As soon as she gets back from the airport—"

42

Ilya sat in his latest cell, back to the wall, listening to the muffled groans of the prison around him. His eyes were closed, which did not make much of a difference in the darkness. The cell's furnishings, which he knew by heart, consisted of a horsehair mattress, a steel washbasin, a toilet without a flush, a single sheet, and a blanket. There was no mirror, which was perhaps for the best.

For most of the past day, it had been fairly quiet. The guards were treating him better, or at least were not actively abusing him, which he suspected was thanks to a few choice words from his last visitor. Wolfe, he could see, was stronger than he had supposed. She was still handicapped by her belief in the system, but her faith was not as unquestioning as he had initially assumed.

At the moment, however, he had an uneasy feeling he had forgotten to tell her something. He had shared everything he knew, or at least everything he thought she might find useful, but a nagging doubt remained that he had left out something important. And now that he had so much time to himself, it seemed sensible to try to figure out what this was.

Ilya rose from his seated position, limbs aching, and

began to pace slowly around the cell, as if tracing an invisible labyrinth. His arms and legs were sore from being wrenched backward by the harness, but he forced himself to continue. He had learned long ago that it was no good to ignore pain. Pain, in itself, was no more instructive than any other aspect of life, but it was foolish to disregard something that was so central to human experience.

The restraints, now gone, had reminded him of the binding of Isaac. Abraham, in a test of faith, was commanded to sacrifice his only son as a burnt offering. He dutifully cut a bundle of wood and went with young Isaac to the peak of Mount Moriah. There he bound his son to the altar, and he was already brandishing the knife when an angel intervened, telling him that his faith was strong and that his descendants would outnumber the stars. The offer of a ram, its horns conveniently caught in a nearby thicket, would be more than enough of a sacrifice.

There the narrative ended, but the story, with the questions it raised about God's love, had continued to trouble the rabbis. Isaac, they argued, had bound himself happily to the altar, overjoyed at the prospect of obeying two commandments at once. Even more intriguing was the tradition, which Ilya had shared with Wolfe, that Isaac, under the knife, had seen the work of the chariot.

Such faith, Ilya thought now, was far beyond his own capacity, even in his younger days. It took more courage than he possessed to choose the passive way, where illumination was given only to those about to die. He had always taken the active path, like those cabalists, obsessed with seeing God, whose pursuit of the divine had been compared to storming the gates of heaven.

Looking around his darkened cell, with its stale stink of

shit, he was freshly disgusted by the vanity of such desires. It was a foolish man indeed, he thought, who believed that he could look into the uncreated light and live.

Ilya continued to pace, the pain warming his joints. Ezekiel himself had warned against such presumption. The prophet spoke of Melkarth, the king of Tyre, who had dwelled in paradise, wise and beautiful, like the cherub whose wings covered the mercy seat. Yet he had set himself up in the house of God, and for that, he would be punished by death.

This was the secret meaning of the cherubim, the angels who animated the wheels of the chariot. Wheels had been carved as a warning on the entrances to sacred groves, like the garden of Eden, which was guarded by an angel in the form of a burning sword. The proper punishment for trespassing in such places was to be burned alive, the flames kindled by a wheel of fire. *Therefore will I bring a fire from the midst of thee, it shall devour thee, and I will bring thee to ashes upon the earth—*

Ilya halted. He sensed that an important insight was just out of reach, the answer to a question that had been haunting him. Standing there in the darkness, his eyes still closed, he thought of fire, of ashes on the earth, and of a name Wolfe had mentioned before leaving. Operation Pepel. *Ashes—*

A second later, he saw the full picture at last. Opening his eyes, he swore to himself. Now that all the pieces had fallen into place, the answer was obvious, and he felt like a fool for not having seen it before.

As he considered what to do next, however, he was brought up against the facts of his situation. Wolfe was the only person capable of acting on what he had to say.

Anyone else would dismiss it outright. And he had no way of contacting her without access to a phone.

At once, he understood what he had to do. In this cell, without light, it was difficult to tell the time, but he knew that he did not have long.

The mattress sat in the corner, a blanket and sheet laid on top. Kneeling, he took the sheet in his hands, feeling for the edge, and tore off a long strip, using his teeth to start the tear. He did this again and again, until he had six strips in all, each about eight feet in length. Then he braided three of them tightly together, his fingers moving rapidly in the dark.

Once he had finished braiding the first set of strips, he started on the next. As he completed the second rope, he heard a door in the corridor being unbolted and opened, and then the sound of footsteps. Someone was coming.

Ilya gathered up what was left of the bedsheet, folding it to hide the ragged edge, and tossed it onto his mattress. Taking one of the makeshift ropes, he tied it into a slipknot, leaving a loop the width of a man's shoulders. Then he tucked both ropes behind his back and sat down.

A moment later, the door of his cell was unlocked and swung back, casting a trapezoid of light across the floor. Standing just outside was a hefty figure with glasses, a metal tray balanced in one hand. It was the guard who had brought him to the medical ward on the day of his arrival, and who had looked down impassively from the bubble as Goat crept up with the razor.

"Now, then," the guard said. "You know the routine. Hands where I can see them—"

Ilya held out his empty hands. The same drill was repeated each afternoon. The guard on duty would bring in the tray, check to make sure that Ilya had done no harm to himself or the cell, and retrieve the tray from the day before. Technically the process was supposed to involve two guards, but due to staff cuts, this aspect of the procedure was usually neglected.

Coming inside, the guard set down the tray, which bore a tin cup of water and a plate of unidentifiable food. The tray from the day before had been placed, as instructed, to one side of the door. Picking up this tray, the guard cast an indifferent glance around the cell, then wrinkled his nose. "Stinks to high heaven in here. Don't see how you can stand it. Cheers, then—"

With a wink, the guard turned back toward the open door. When he was a step away from the hall outside, Ilya rose silently behind him and slipped the noose over the guard's neck.

The guard squawked, dropping the empty tray, which fell with a gonglike clang to the floor. Before he could make another sound, Ilya swung him hard, using the rope as a sort of hackamore, and knocked him against the wall. The guard's forehead bounced off the bricks, and he fell stunned to the ground.

Moving quickly, Ilya yanked off the guard's tie, which was secured only by a clip, and used it to bind the other man's hands behind his back. The second rope went around the guard's legs. Then Ilya slammed the door shut and propped up his horsehair mattress, creating a crude barricade.

Ilya heard shouts from the far end of the corridor. He went back to the guard, who was lying on the floor, facedown, and braced his foot against the man's ample back, taking the end of the noose in his hands.

As he did, the Judas hole slid open. Looking up, he saw a second guard's white face staring through the slot, which was just above the mattress. "The fuck you think you're doing?"

"It's quite simple," Ilya said, still holding the end of the rope. "All I want is a phone."

43

"So I've been looking into Project Bonfire," Lewis began. "It started as an attempt by the Soviet Academy to develop weapons based on regulatory peptides, which are substances that can alter the mood of human subjects, causing panic and fear. Moreover, because they're based on naturally occurring substances, they can't be traced in the body, at least not with conventional methods."

"Which means that we're looking at a perfect assassination weapon," Cornwall said. She was seated behind her desk, the blinds of the office drawn, the door closed. "Assuming that it works."

"We think it does," Wolfe said, standing by the whiteboard, which was covered with names and dates. "Judging from the support they gave this program over more than forty years, they must have thought it was promising."

"Promising isn't good enough," Cornwall replied flatly. "Not when you're asking me to make a call like this."

"I know." Wolfe turned back to the whiteboard. Her arm was still stiff, but at least the sling was gone. She had been in this room for hours now, along with Lewis and Asthana, who was going over stacks of files at the conference table. The clock was ticking. Powell had called a few minutes ago from Helsinki, where he was boarding Chigorin's plane for Moscow. By now, he would already be in the air.

Wolfe was aware of the strangeness of the situation. For reasons of diplomatic discretion, Powell could not be seen advising an opposition leader, but he was also in a unique position to influence what Chigorin did next. The more intelligence they could give him, the more useful his advice would be. Given the delicacy of the circumstances, however, only the four officers here, along with a solitary member of the Home Office, had been briefed on the real state of affairs.

She studied the whiteboard, on which she had roughed out a chronology of the documents that had been received and translated so far. "At this point, I don't think we're going to find a smoking gun. All we have is a preponderance of evidence pointing toward human testing."

"I'm not sure I agree with you," Asthana said, looking up from her notes. "Even with what we have here, too much material has been lost or destroyed. It's hard to know where all the pieces fit."

"But we know that the program spent years trying to obtain information on neuropeptides, which are the kinds of toxins we're talking about," Lewis said. "We also know that they focused on myelin toxin, a poison that attacks nerve fibers in the human brain. It's all here." He fished a photocopy from the pile on the table. "Lab animals, including rabbits, were strapped to boards, fitted with gas masks, and sprayed with the toxin in aerosol form. They developed signs of paralysis and neurological changes, including dementia. And the next step was human testing."

"But, you see, that's the problem," Asthana said. "The tests you're talking about took place in the eighties. That's thirty years after Operation Pepel. Some of these documents are from even earlier."

"True," Lewis replied. "But what we're looking at is the end result of a long process. After the war, Russia went searching for Nazi or Japanese scientists who had done work on poisons and truth drugs. They were developing strains of anthrax or plague that would affect the brain. At the very least, we have an uninterrupted chain of experiments going back to the early fifties. And the tests were planned and carried out by the civilian arm of Russian intelligence."

Looking at the timeline on the whiteboard, Wolfe was reminded of something that they had discussed only in passing. "What about the Dyatlov Pass? Could these poisons have been responsible?"

"Well, consider the evidence." Lewis took out his folder on the Dyatlov Pass. "If this was a poison, how would it work? The speed of onset points to some kind of aerosol, like the poison used by Project Bonfire. Evidently it went off inside the tent, so it must have been delivered by something the hikers were given or picked up along the way. And its effects were strong, at least at first."

Wolfe saw where he was going. "But they were only temporary. Once the hikers left the tent, there's evidence of rational behavior. They started a fire and took clothes from their dead companions. The poison wasn't enough to kill or drive them insane outright. It just scattered them."

"Which doesn't rule out its use as an assassination tool," Lewis said. "The researchers may have concluded that the poison was only effective in a confined space, which is consistent with an aerosol as well."

Cornwall broke in. "Let's move to the main point. Could Karvonen be preparing to use this kind of weapon?"

Lewis seemed unsettled by the intensity of the deputy director's gaze. "I can't rule it out. The delivery system would not be difficult to assemble. The hard part would have been acquiring the poison itself."

"It might have been easier than you think," Wolfe said. "We know for a fact that poisons like this have appeared on the black market. I've seen the results myself. Given the background of Morley's bodyguard—"

Even as she spoke, Wolfe heard a low vibration rise up from the table in front of her. Glancing down, she saw that her phone, which she had set among the files, was ringing. "Sorry," Wolfe said, picking up the phone and bringing it to her ear. "I'll get rid of whoever this is—"

For the first confused second, she heard nothing but stifled voices. "Who is this?"

When the man on the other end finally answered, it was the last response she could have expected: "It's Ilya Severin."

"Ilya?" Wolfe looked at the others, who had resumed their work, but now were turning to stare. She moved into the corner, lowering her voice. "Where are you calling from? What's going on?"

"A long story," Ilya replied. "I don't have much time. But there's something you need to hear. About the Dyatlov Pass—"

Faintly, on the other end, she heard another string of shouts. "What about it?"

Ilya began to speak more quickly. "Something about it always seemed strange, even beyond what we discussed. The choice of victims. They were a random group of subjects in a remote location, yes? Difficult to control or observe. Which makes me think that the test was arranged at the last minute. That the scientists were forced to make do with what they had."

"It's possible," Wolfe said, although she didn't see why this insight had seemed so urgent. "I'll keep that in mind—"

"You aren't listening," Ilya said, impatience appearing in his voice for the first time. "Why would they be in such a hurry to arrange a test on that particular day? It must have been because they had a deadline. An operation that could not be postponed. You see? They conducted the test because something important was coming. A special action. An assassination. In Turkey."

"Operation Pepel," Wolfe said, seeing his point at last. She glanced at the whiteboard, on which the name of the operation had been written with a question mark. "But if it was an assassination, who was the target?"

"If I were you, I would look at the prime minister at the time," Ilya said. "Menderes, I think his name was. And if I'm right—"

He broke off. From the other end of the line, there was a sudden crash. Wolfe covered her free ear with one hand, trying to hear. "Ilya?"

"I'm sorry," Ilya said. "I need to go." And with that, the telephone went dead.

Wolfe lowered the phone, sensing that the others were watching her. When she turned around, she found that Asthana, in particular, was looking at her intently. "What was that about?"

"I don't know," Wolfe said, holding up a finger for time. "Something's happening at Belmarsh. Listen, I need you to look something up. It's the name of the prime minister of Turkey in the late fifties, something like Menderes. Tell me if he was assassinated or died in office."

As Asthana opened her laptop, Wolfe redialed the last incoming call, which went to an automated voice mail message. She hung up, then called the main number at Belmarsh, but heard nothing but a busy signal.

From the conference table, Asthana spoke up. "I've got it. Adnan Menderes was the prime minister of Turkey throughout most of the fifties, before he was executed in a military coup."

Wolfe headed to where Asthana was seated. "Any connection to the Dyatlov Pass?"

"No," Asthana said. "He was killed more than two years later. And he was hanged, not poisoned. So—"

"Wait," Lewis said, pointing to the screen, which displayed a biography of Menderes. "Two years earlier, a plane with Menderes on board crashed just outside Gatwick. It was a special flight from Ankara, carrying Turkish officials for the signing of a treaty in London. The entire crew was killed, but Menderes and most of the other passengers survived."

Wolfe leaned toward the screen, scanning it quickly.

"You're right. The reason for the crash is unknown. The last communication was nine minutes before the plane went down in the woods three miles from the runway. There was no sign of technical failure or pilot error. And the date—"

"—was February 17, 1959," Lewis finished. "Twelve days after the Dyatlov Pass."

"So what are we saying here?" Asthana asked, looking at the others. "That this crash was a failed assassination?"

Cornwall, coming from behind her desk, bent down to look at the screen as well. "It isn't entirely out of the question. Russian intelligence has always been active in Turkey. Menderes was moving closer to the West. So it's possible that this crash was an attempt at regime change."

Wolfe tried to think. "Okay. So let's say that the Dyatlov Pass was an improvised test of a weapon that was used two weeks later. What would happen if you put this kind of poison on a plane?"

"It's perfect," Lewis said. "A plane is a confined space with a recirculating ventilation system, so it's an ideal place for an aerosol weapon. And from what we've seen, it works very quickly."

"So maybe it was used to take out the crew," Wolfe continued, leaping ahead to the next step. "Just the crew, not the passengers. It affected the pilot badly enough to cause a crash, and none of the crew survived to describe what had happened. It wouldn't show up in an autopsy. The delivery system would be hard to find in the wreckage, if you weren't looking for it. Not in that kind of crash—"

Wolfe went pale. The last piece fell into place, appearing in her mind with shocking suddenness, so that she had to grip the table to steady herself. She knew. It had been right in front of her all along. And as she pulled out her phone, her heart pounding, she feared that she was too late to stop what was already coming.

44

Powell was in the conference area at the rear of the jet when his phone rang. Because it was a private plane, passengers could do whatever they liked with their phones, and ringtones had been going off periodically throughout the cabin since their departure from Helsinki. He checked the display. "It's a colleague of mine. Sorry, but I should probably take this."

Chigorin only nodded, then returned to his work. The grandmaster was seated at the long conference table, along with his security chief and assistant, going over plans for the meeting in Arbat. Stavisky, who had remained behind in Helsinki, was being patched in. Powell headed for a remote corner of the cabin before answering his phone. "This isn't a good time. What's going on?"

Wolfe's voice was unnaturally tense. "Alan, I've been going through the documents that Chigorin provided, and there's something you need to know right now. Has the plane taken off yet?"

"Yes, we're over Russia." Powell glanced back at the others. "Is something wrong?"

"I hope not, but listen to me. You need to land as soon as possible. I think that Operation Pepel was a plot to kill Adnan Menderes, the Turkish prime minister. They put a neurological poison on his plane and caused it to crash. The Dyatlov Pass incident was a dry run for the real operation, which took place two weeks later. You understand? *The target was his plane*—"

Powell saw the connection immediately. "So you're saying that the poison itself—"

"—was never meant to kill on its own, but to drive its victims mad long enough to be fatal," Wolfe finished. "In the Dyatlov Pass, they died of exposure. But if you put a poison like this on a plane—"

"I understand." As Powell considered the implications, his blood ran cold. Looking at his watch, he saw that an hour remained until they were scheduled to land. "All right. I'll call back in five minutes."

"I'll be here." Wolfe hesitated, as if wanting to say something more, then only said, "Good luck."

"Thanks," Powell said, and hung up. For a second, he remained standing at the bulkhead, trying to gather his thoughts. Oddly enough, he felt no fear, only a daunting sense of the difficulty of what was to follow, as he turned back to the others, saying, "I need to talk to the captain."

Something of the moment's urgency must have been visible in his face, because he saw that he had Chigorin's full attention. For the first time, he caught a glimpse of what it must be like to be seated across a chessboard from the grandmaster. "Is there an emergency?"

Powell weighed his response for a fraction of a second. "Yes. Please come with me."

Chigorin gave a nod to his security chief, who followed them as they moved through the passenger cabin to the cockpit. There were twelve people on board, Powell recalled, including members of the staff and crew. As he passed the nearest window, he found that all he could see was a layer of cloud, while far below, he knew, lay the vast expanse of Russia.

They entered the cockpit, where the captain and copilot were stationed at the controls. Both men were in their forties, professional and trim, and they had been in Chigorin's service for years. As the passengers appeared at the door, the captain looked back in surprise. "What is it?"

Powell saw that he had no choice but to dive in. "There may be a destructive device on board. Based on what I've been told by a colleague, we need to land this plane right now."

Chigorin's security chief eyed him distrustfully. "You're talking about a bomb?"

"No." As he spoke, Powell kept his eyes fixed on Chigorin, who was the one he really needed to convince. "A neurological device. We believe that Operation Pepel used a similar device in an attempt to kill the prime minister of Turkey, Adnan Menderes, by bringing down his plane—"

"—which went down just after the Dyatlov Pass incident," Chigorin said, grasping his meaning at once. A strange smile crossed his face. "Yes, of course. How stupid not to see it before. And you believe it was the same weapon?"

"I can't be sure," Powell said, seeing that the others had no idea what the two of them were talking about. "But if a similar weapon is being used against you now, we can't take any chances. From what I know about these toxins, they act fast, and they can either be inhaled or absorbed through the skin. Which means that it's possible that we've already been exposed."

The security chief was glowering at him. "This is a trick," he said to Chigorin. "I told you that we shouldn't have let this man on board. This is only an attempt to keep us away from Moscow—"

"I don't think so," Chigorin said quietly, his eyes still on Powell. "I think he's telling the truth. If he is, we need to get on the ground as soon as possible. Dmitri, what do you think?"

The question was directed at the captain, who had listened in silence. Now he turned to Powell. "This poison. It is an aerosol?"

"That seems likely," Powell said. "It could be in the air we're breathing right now."

"Then we go to oxygen." The captain spoke calmly to the copilot. "Yevgeny, deploy masks with the toggle down. One hundred percent."

His face grim, the copilot turned a knob on the console, which set the masks to deliver oxygen from the on-board tanks, without being mixed with cabin air. Then he hit the deploy switch. "Done."

Reaching out, the captain turned on the intercom, saying evenly: "Ladies and gentlemen, please take your seats. Because of an unexpected ventilation issue, oxygen masks have been deployed. Flight attendants, please assist the passengers, then return to your stations." He switched off the public address system. "I'm initiating a descent to ten thousand feet. Yevgeny, please go back and confer with the others. I will check our options for landing."

As he spoke, he removed the oxygen mask from a stowage cup over his shoulder and slid it over his nose. Powell followed the others out of the cockpit. As he did, he felt the plane shift slightly as they started their descent.

Moving through the cabin, he saw that the other passengers had taken their seats, oxygen masks in place. Several looked frightened. As he passed, Chigorin smiled. "Don't worry," the grandmaster said in Russian. "This is only a temporary problem. We'll know more soon."

In the rear conference area, the masks were already deployed, swinging like pendulums from their plastic lanyards. The copilot had brought a binder from the cockpit. As the others gathered around, their masks turning them into a group of strange acolytes, he flung it open. "If they put an aerosol device on the plane, it has to be in the ventilation system. The question is where."

Finding a schematic of the ventilation system, the copilot began to point out various features. "I'll be quick. Bleed air, from outside the plane, flows through the engines to the air-conditioning packs, and from there to the mix manifold and cabin. You with me so far?"

Chigorin, studying the diagram as if it were a chess problem, nodded. "I follow you."

"Now, if the device is located upstream, so to speak, from the mix manifold, we can bypass it using the ram system, which is an alternate source of air from the outside. But if the device is in the mix manifold itself, our only options are to disable it or depressurize the cabin."

"We can't take any chances," Powell said. "We need to depressurize the cabin now."

The copilot shook his head. "We can't. Not above ten thousand feet. Once we've descended enough, we can flip a switch and open the outflow valves. But we won't be at a safe altitude for another few minutes."

Chigorin took this in. His face was very still. "Where do you think it would be?"

The copilot wiped his brow with the sleeve of his uniform. "If it were me, I would put it in the mix manifold."

"So would I," Chigorin said. "We need to depressurize as soon as possible. But we should shut off the other systems first."

"All right." Rising from his seat, the mask still on, the copilot went to the bulkhead phone. Bringing it to his ear, he dialed the cockpit and said, "We're switching to ram air. Turn off the air conditioner packs and bleed system."

The captain's voice came over the speakers in the rear cabin. "Done. Recirculation fans are off as well. And I've looked into our options for an emergency landing. We're thirty miles from Krechevitsy Air Base, near Novgorod. It's our best chance. Shall I divert?"

Chigorin nodded at the copilot, who spoke into the phone again. "Yes. We'll divert."

"Making course change," the captain said. "Yevgeny, I'll need you up here now."

Hanging up the phone, the copilot turned to the door. Before he could leave, Powell spoke. "Wait. Just because we're breathing oxygen doesn't mean we're safe. If this substance can be absorbed through the skin, we can't take the risk of further exposure. We need to look for the device."

"I agree," Chigorin said. "Is there any chance that we can reach it from the cabin?"

"Not if it's in the mix manifold," the copilot said. "There's no access from here. But if there's a separate trigger mechanism, it may be visible." He looked Powell over, as if sizing him up. "If you really want to do this, you'll need a way to breathe. Please follow me."

The copilot removed his mask and headed back to the cockpit. Powell took a lungful of oxygen, then pulled off his own mask and followed, holding his breath as he passed through the cabin.

In the cockpit, the copilot put on another mask from the stowage unit next to his seat, then went to a plastic case mounted on the bulkhead. As Powell watched, still holding his breath, the copilot yanked away the cover and let it fall to the floor. Inside was a sealed bag with a personal breathing apparatus inside, which he pulled out. "It goes over your entire head," the copilot said to Powell. "You'll be able to move around the cabin. Understand?"

Powell nodded, watching as the copilot pulled a tab to open the bag and removed the breathing gear, which consisted of a visor and transparent hood. Following the copilot's instructions, Powell ducked his head forward and put his hands into the neck seal, guiding the hood over his head. Then the copilot arranged the base of the hood around Powell's neck and shoulders, took hold of the straps at the corners of the visor, and pulled them sharply outward.

At once, Powell heard a rustle as the starter candle went off and the mask was filled with oxygen. As he inhaled, the copilot pulled the straps back, securing the breathing cone to Powell's face. "How are your glasses?"

Reaching through the fabric of the hood, Powell adjusted the earpieces at his temples so that his glasses sat more comfortably. "They'll do."

The copilot smoothed down the neck shield at the back of the hood, making sure it was airtight. "Listen carefully. The mix manifold is underfloor at the rear of the cabin, just before the equipment bay. You can't access it directly, but if there's a separate trigger, it's probably there. Got that?"

Inside the hood, with the rest of the world muffled by plastic, things seemed curiously peaceful. "Yes. I'll do what I can."

The copilot took a seat next to the captain, then extended a hand to Powell. *"Udachi."*

"Same to you," Powell said, returning the handshake. Then he headed for the rear of the plane, groping his way forward. As he entered the passenger cabin, his heart still thudding, he forced himself to remain calm, knowing that the next few minutes would be crucial—

—and it was only when he looked at the others that he saw he was already too late.

Powell halted and stared. The words came without warning. "No," he whispered. "Oh, no—"

In the rows to either side, the passengers were buckled securely into their seats, masks in place. Looking from one face to another, Powell saw a cabin attendant, eyes wide, staring at something unseen. She was screaming. Next to her, Chigorin's assistant wept, her hands clawing at her face. When she lowered them, he could see the bloody tracks left by her nails.

"No," Powell said again, and began to move numbly toward the rear of the plane. He could hear the blood thundering in his ears, the rustling of the hood like a chorus of voices.

At the entrance to the aft cabin, he halted again, and felt another wave of despair, so wrenching that it seemed to knock him off his feet. For a moment, he found himself hoping that this was only a dream. But everything around him was too bright, too real, the cabin flooded with merciless light.

Chigorin was seated at the table, along with his security chief. His face was rigid with horror. When Powell turned to look at the man seated next to him, his own horror grew complete.

The second man at the table was no longer the security chief. Now it was his father.

Powell fell to his knees. Now Chigorin was gone as well. His father lolled backward in both seats, bleary eyes turned in his direction, begging and mocking. Both pairs of eyes were bloodshot and filled with rheumy tears. "Alone," his father croaked. "Left me to die alone—"

Raising his hands to his face, Powell tried to squeeze his eyes shut, but found that he could not. A black cloud was swirling before him. At first, he thought it was a fire, and that he should take the extinguisher down from the bulkhead, but when he looked closer at the cloud, he saw that it was alive, full of crawling things with claws and insectile skins.

A freezing horror took hold of him. He told himself that it was just a vision, a dream. Then, tearing his gaze away, he saw the bulkhead standing temptingly to one side. Rearing back, he lunged forward, his right hand clenched, and punched the wall as hard as he could.

Red and orange pinpoints danced before his eyes, an explosion of pain that cleared the smoke. He looked down at his knuckles, which were bleeding, and noticed, wonderingly, that he had broken his hand. Then he turned and saw that Chigorin and the security chief were back in their seats. His father was gone.

Rising, he began to fight his way to the aft section,

which was only a few steps away. From behind him rose the sound of weeping and screaming. His heart was hammering, the plastic of the hood pressing like a living thing against his face. He gradually became convinced that something unspeakable was lurking in the corner of his vision, just barely out of sight.

He saw that the black smoke was gathering again. Now it looked like it was entering the hood itself, a living thing, its tendrils drawn into his lungs with each pull of respiration. He could feel it on his face. "Not real," Powell managed to whisper. *"None of this is real—"*

Powell broke off. A shadow had fallen across the floor. He did not want to look up, did not want to face this final outrage, but finally, as if compelled by a force outside himself, he slowly raised his eyes.

A monstrous figure stood before him, the height of a tall man, so that it had to stoop to fit itself inside the confines of the jet. The first thing Powell noticed was that it had the wings of an eagle, its feathers filthy, spreading from one side of the cabin to another. He saw that its nails were long and yellow. Then, raising his eyes, he saw its face at last, and felt his sanity depart.

It was a cherub, the living creature of the *merkabah*, and it was real. It had four faces, arranged like the conjoined heads of cephalopagus twins. One was a man's face, twisted and contorted beyond recognition. Another was that of an eagle; the third, an ox. But worst of all, facing him, in place of the lion that Ezekiel had seen, was the leonine face of his father. His father was grinning.

Powell collapsed. Inside the hood, he could feel his hair standing on end; then he heard a faint musical tone sounding from nearby. With the last shred of his old self, he realized that it was his phone. But then even this knowledge fell away, and as he looked up at the creature that loomed above him, feathers stinking and falling from its wings, he saw the eagle's beak drop open, showing its black tongue, and the sound of the phone was lost in its sudden scream.

With all his remaining strength, Powell tried to crawl forward. Even as he did, the moment he had been expecting finally came, and as the world tilted sideways, he began to laugh. It was too late. The plane was going down.

45

Earlier that morning, a man named Ivan Suvorov had crept quietly downstairs, trying not to wake his wife. He was dressed warmly, in long johns, a denim shirt, a fleece coat, and a green knit hat, while his feet were encased in the thick felt boots, or *valenki*, that were traditional footwear in this part of the world. Because it promised to be a wet day, he paused at the door to put on his galoshes.

Outside, it was bitterly cold, but the old pensioner felt quite cheerful as he trudged to the pickup truck parked in front of the house. He slung his pack and folding chair into the rear bed, then opened the passenger's door so that his dog, an aging husky, could hop into the front seat. Closing the door, he went around to the driver's side and slid heavily behind the wheel. Then he started the truck and headed for the road, driving toward the river Volkhov, near the city of Veliky Novgorod.

A few hours later, he was seated in a folding chair on the surface of the frozen river, warming his hands in his oilskin muff. Looking out at the forest that ran along the river's margin, its rows of pine and alder trees crusted with snow, he exhaled deeply, the breath rising from his nostrils in two tidy streams of vapor. The dog was curled up at his side, its nose thrust into its tail for warmth.

The old man coughed, feeling the cold spread through the convolutions of his lungs. It had been a quiet morning. So far he had caught nothing but smelt, none of them more than a few inches long, and a couple of perch, which he had stuffed, still twitching, into the canvas sack by his chair.

Ivan was beginning to think about lunch, which would consist of a generous slice of salami and a swig of vodka, when he heard a low drone from overhead. He looked up just in time to see a plane heading his way, a sleek white private jet with wing tips slanted upward into pointed winglets, so that from this angle, it looked something like a fish itself.

His first thought was that the plane was heading for the air force base, which was ten kilometers away. He had barely enough time to notice that it was coming in far too low and fast when it passed directly overhead, so close that he could see the individual rivets on its underside, as well as its stowed landing gear. For a second, he was in its shadow. Then it dove past, barely clearing the trees on the other side of the river, and crashed into the woods.

Feeling the ground shake from the impact, Ivan leapt to his feet, his chair toppling backward. The dog, startled, jumped up as well. Ivan stared in disbelief as the plane slid onward, suddenly clumsy, not slowing as it plowed into the treetops. Branches exploded like gunshots. The plane seemed to skate briefly across the surface of the forest, with two almost symmetrical clouds of dust billowing to either side, then fell abruptly out of sight. At once, a cloud of inky black smoke, shot through with fire, mush-roomed up from the woods.

Ivan gaped at the crash, his aged heart thumping, knowing at once that this was the greatest and most ter-rible sight that he would ever see. Then, leaving his gear behind, he began to run across the icy expanse of the river, his galoshes kicking up clods of slush. As his dog ran beside him, yelping and howling with excitement, Ivan made straight for the pillar of smoke pouring up from the trees. Even from here, he could feel the heat on his face.

III

"I take it, Watson, that you have no longer a shadow of a doubt as to how these tragedies were produced?"

"None whatever."

"But the cause remains as obscure as before."

—Sir Arthur Conan Doyle,
"The Adventure of the Devil's Foot"

War had now been declared in Heaven . . . The Devil was Nabu, pictured as a winged Goat of Midsummer; so that the answer to Donne's poetic question about the Devil's foot is: "The prophet Ezekiel."

—Robert Graves, *The White Goddess*

46

Here, then, was another cell, in a part of the prison that Ilya had not seen before. His new room had two doors, an outer one of solid iron with an observation slit, and an inner door with a grid of steel mesh. Three of the four walls were made of reinforced concrete. The fourth consisted of a sheet of bulletproof glass, through which one or more guards currently watched him at all times.

At the rear of the cell stood a toilet and shower, allowing him to wash up without rejoining the general population. He was in the shower now, a trickle of warm water coming down over his head. The flow was activated by a metal button in the wall, which released about ten seconds of water each time it was pressed. It wasn't much, but he was grateful for the chance to wash the dried blood from his body. In the end, the guards had not beaten him too badly.

At last, reasonably refreshed, Ilya emerged from the shower and toweled himself off, keeping his back to the guard who, he knew without turning, was watching him through the glass. His clothes, the same he had been wearing for the past two days, had been folded and draped across the back of his chair. He pulled on his shirt and jeans, remaining barefoot. For some reason, they had taken away his shoes, which had been set outside the cell door.

He had just finished dressing when he heard steps approaching from the end of the corridor. A second later, the cell's outer bolt was withdrawn with a grating rasp, and the door swung open to reveal a guard carrying a folding chair. "Visitor," the guard said without looking at Ilya, who was watching from inside the cell, his hair wet. "Just be a moment, then."

The guard set down the chair and left, keeping the outer door open. Ilya took a step closer to the mesh, glad that Wolfe had returned. After their last conversation, which had been abruptly cut short, he had grown increasingly concerned that he had failed to give her enough information. He had shared his suspicions about the plane crash that had nearly killed Menderes, an incident he had pondered more than once while exploring the history of the security services, but as bright as she was, he wasn't sure whether she had made the final connection.

It was only then, as he waited for Wolfe to appear, that he noticed that the guards were no longer watching through the glass. And as he turned back to the door of his cell, suddenly suspicious that this visit was not what he had expected, he found himself face-to-face with Vasylenko.

He took a step back. As Vasylenko came up to the mesh and lowered himself into the chair, Ilya saw that the old man's hands were empty, but he was still inclined to keep his distance. The door's metal gridwork was too fine to admit a knife, but it would not stop a gun.

Vasylenko, evidently noting his concern, spoke quietly in Russian. "You disappoint me, Ilyushka. If I wanted to hurt you, there would be easier ways than coming here myself. Although I doubt that anyone would protest much, since you've hardly endeared yourself to the guards."

Ilya saw his point, but he still kept well away from the mesh. "What do you want?"

The old man gave a slight shrug. "It's association time. We're allowed to visit old friends. I thought I would pay you a call." Vasylenko indicated the chair inside the cell. "Sit down. It's been too long since we truly spoke."

Without lowering his eyes, Ilya took a seat, the cardboard chair creaking beneath his weight. For Vasylenko to come here would have required a substantial bribe, but he still didn't know the reason. "If you want to see me, here I am. Now tell me why you're really here."

"I wanted to find out what became of you. For such a righteous man, you have the reputation of one whose thoughts turn naturally to violence. You insist on making things so hard for yourself. And all for nothing." A gleam appeared in the old man's eyes. "You haven't heard?"

Seated in his cage, far from the rest of the world, Ilya had a foreboding of what was to come. "Tell me."

"Chigorin's plane went down two hours ago." The *vor*'s voice was regretful, though a hint of amusement remained in his eyes. "It crashed in the woods near Veliky Novgorod. No word so far on survivors. It was a noble effort, Ilyushka, but in the end, you were just a few hours too late."

Ilya remained silent. He felt no horror at the news, just a sickening inevitability, as if he had known all along that this was where the story would end. At last, he looked at the old man, who was watching greedily for his reaction. "I would have done nothing differently. If you think otherwise, you don't know me at all."

Vasylenko smiled sourly. "I expected no less. But there are things that even you fail to understand. Your life is joined with mine. If I deprived you of certain things along the way, it was only what was necessary for you to become what you were destined to be. You should be thanking me for this."

As he listened, Ilya found himself remembering the house of his youth, now a tomb, the man and woman inside fallen into a dreamless sleep. "I never wanted to become anything. A man should only seek to be a man."

"But you wanted to be something extraordinary," Vasylenko said. "There's no point in denying it. You saw yourself as the last of the righteous. A tzaddik. I didn't put the idea in your head; I only had to use it. It made you more dangerous than a man to whom cruelty is second nature. Cruelty was something apart from you, so you embraced it as a test. Am I wrong?"

"No," Ilya said, thinking of the faces that still haunted him. "All I can do now is correct the balance."

Vasylenko shook his head. "It's too late. No matter what Wolfe might have told you, you can't bring back the dead, no matter how long you spend in the valley of dry bones. I know you better than you imagine. You're drawn to her, see something in her that you've lost in yourself. But she is as powerless as you are." He paused. "What has she told you about Chigorin?"

His tone remained offhand, but something in his words made Ilya look at him more closely. Through the mesh, which cast a grid of shadows on Vasylenko's face, the old man's expression had not changed, but a note of hunger had entered his voice. Ilya wondered what this meant, the most recent question still hanging in the air, and then, suddenly, he understood.

The Chekists, he saw, were as confused about the situation as anyone else. Chigorin's plane had crashed, yes, but the forces at work were so obscure, and the secret services so impenetrable, that even Vasylenko's contacts weren't entirely sure why. To respond, they needed more information. And if they were truly looking for answers, they might be willing to offer him something in exchange.

All these thoughts flashed through his mind in a fraction of a second. Vasylenko was still waiting for his response. Ilya took another moment, then said carefully, "She told me that Chigorin was about to receive a trove of classified files. That the Chekists were anxious that none of these documents see the light of day. But there's more to it than that, isn't there?"

Vasylenko leaned back, the grid of shadows falling away from his face. "I don't know what you mean, Ilyushka."

"Someone came after me in Spain. I know now that it wasn't you. But I also gave the gangs there no reason to want me dead. Unless my presence threatened their plans in other ways."

"It's possible," Vasylenko said, with apparent carelessness, though Ilya knew that the old man's mind was working intently. "I no longer have any interest in Spain. A new breed has taken over. Anyone willing to make deals with the beasts in Transnistria is not likely to respect the thieves' code. In any case, they have pledged their allegiance to another faction."

Ilya sensed his meaning. "Military intelligence. Not your friends, but their rivals—"

"I did not say that," Vasylenko replied sharply. "I am only reminding you that the world is changing. The thieves are no longer what they once were. I should know. I was there at the beginning. Now we're nearing the end. And as much as you hate us, I know that you will bear no love toward our successors."

As Vasylenko spoke, he shifted in his chair, bringing his face into a shaft of light. Looking at him now, Ilya saw nothing more than a man in his seventies, aging, endangered, and weary. "So why was I targeted in Spain?"

"An old dispensation is giving way to the new. The gangs, I imagine, are cleaning house. If they had found you at another time, they might have left you alone, but perhaps they thought it safest to remove you from the picture. After all, you have a reputation as a dangerous man."

Trying to see beyond the *vor*'s words, Ilya caught a glimpse of some dark machine, a process, begun long ago, that was only now reaching its culmination. "What are they planning?"

"It doesn't matter." Vasylenko drew back again, retreating from the light, so that he was nothing but a voice in the shadows. "By now, there is no point in looking further. All you've done has been in vain. And there is nothing that anyone can do to prevent what is happening already."

47

On the third floor of the airport office tower at Helsinki, an incident command center had been hastily assembled. As Wolfe entered the room, the officer who had escorted her from the gate pointed to a tall man in the corner, who was talking rapidly into a telephone. "That's him."

"Thanks," Wolfe said, weaving through the crowded conference space. Although she had been in Helsinki for less than a quarter of an hour, it already reminded her, oddly, of Salt Lake City. There was a sort of Swissness to both cities, orderly and humorless, and the only real difference, as far as she could tell, was that everyone here was drinking coffee.

As she approached the man in the corner, he slammed the phone down. Eero Harju, she recalled, was a lead investigator for the Accident Investigation Board, the division of the Ministry of Justice tasked with looking into all aviation, rail, and maritime accidents. Working her way up to him, she held up her badge. "Hi, there," Wolfe said. "We spoke on the phone. I'm—"

Before she could continue, Harju spoke over her head, asking something in Finnish of an investigator at the other end of the table, who was on the phone as well. Covering the mouthpiece with his hand, the second investigator shook his head. Harju turned to Wolfe. "Stonewalling on the Russian side," he explained in English. "They aren't telling us anything."

Wolfe followed Harju as he went over to a laptop. "So there's no word on survivors?"

"We're waiting on the Ministry of Emergency Situations," Harju said, bending down to his computer screen. "They're playing it close to the vest. I wish to Christ the plane had gone down here—"

It was a strange sentiment, but Wolfe knew what he meant. Since she had last checked, two separate investigative commissions had already been announced in Russia, and while they had pledged their full cooperation to foreign agencies, their actions told a different story. "What about the site?"

"Sealed off. They aren't letting anyone in or out. The rumor is that they're afraid of contamination." He glanced up from the laptop, looking at her closely for the first time. "Hold on. You're the one who said there might have been poison on the plane. What do you know about this?"

"Nothing conclusive," Wolfe said, trying to keep the discussion moving. "Do we at least have images of the crash?"

"No footage yet. I'm told they've recovered the flight data and cockpit voice boxes. Troops from the military base nearby have been called in. There's already concern that they'll seize confidential opposition documents." Harju shook his head. "No oversight at all. It's a real mess."

As she listened, Wolfe could only share his frustration.

She wished, not for the first time, that she had been allowed to fly to Russia. In the tense early minutes after the crash, with her fear for Powell's safety channeled into anger and impatience, she had pushed hard to go to the accident site. An investigative team had been assembled to advise on the response, including a pathologist from the Royal Air Force, and Wolfe had felt that her place was with them.

In the end, however, Asthana, who spoke better Russian, had been sent instead, and Wolfe had been ordered to Helsinki. She had hustled to catch a charter flight from Heathrow, and had made good time, spending just over two hours in the air. All the while, as she scrambled to keep up with events on the ground, Asthana's final words, just before their departure, had echoed in her mind: "Don't trust anyone. Remember what happened with Garber—"

Now she turned back to the lead investigator. "Look, we need to focus on the situation here," Wolfe said. "The device that brought down the plane was planted by a Finnish citizen, a man named Lasse Karvonen. And it's almost certain that he had help at the airport."

The other investigator, who had been listening intently, broke in. "We don't know that for sure. We don't even know if there was a device at all. And if there was, it might have been planted in London."

Looking at the two men, Wolfe felt the political machinery already locking into place. She took a breath, willing herself to be patient. "Listen. Karvonen's background implies that he was chosen for his contacts in Finland. I think he's here. Tell me, please, who had access to the plane."

Wolfe saw an exchange of glances between the two investigators. Finally Harju motioned her over to the laptop, where he called up an airport directory. "It spent the night at a fixed-base operator. They provide ground services for private planes. Police are already checking the employees."

Studying the screen, Wolfe saw that this was the only place where the device could have been planted. "I want to see it for myself."

"Fine," Harju said, more quickly than she had expected. "I'll have someone run you over now."

A few minutes later, Wolfe found herself in the backseat of a van, being driven to the ground handler's office at the airport's southwest corner. Outside, it was bitterly cold, with a rumor of snow on the way. She suspected that Harju had granted her request mostly to get rid of her, which was fine.

As they drove across the tarmac, her driver silent behind the wheel, she was left alone with her thoughts for the first time since her arrival. Events since the crash had unfolded with a nightmarish clarity, and at times, she had felt close to being overwhelmed by despair. And the only way to keep it at bay, she knew, was to work all the harder, like the good Mormon she had once been.

They pulled up at an office in the shadow of the hangar, the parts department set off to one side. Wolfe climbed out of the van, the wind stinging her face, and headed in. Beyond two sets of sliding doors lay a waiting area, its television set turned to coverage of the crash.

At reception, she was met by the operations manager, a bulky figure with a key card hanging from his neck. Looking into his fixed, glassy smile, Wolfe saw that he was having one of the worst days of his life. "I called a minute ago. You said you could show me your files?"

"Yes, of course," the manager said in halting English. "Please, right this way—"

He ushered her over to the reception desk, where a group of workers was staring at a second television, their eyes wet. In a back room, Wolfe caught a glimpse of an airport police officer, who was speaking with another employee. "The police are interviewing everyone?"

"Yes. Talking with workers one at a time. The rest were asked to come from home." The manager indicated a stack of files on the counter. "You can go through these if you like."

Wolfe looked apprehensively at the mountain of folders, which was nearly two feet high. "Is there anyone on staff with particular experience with air-conditioning or ventilation?"

"A few. Let me see." The manager thumbed quickly through the files, coming up with a stack of five. "These are the ones. But none of them could have anything to do with this—"

"Thanks," Wolfe said, cutting him off. She studied the names. Four men, one woman. This was a start. Then she opened the files and saw that they were, of course, in Finnish. She swore silently to herself, then wrote the names down. "Were any of them here last night?"

"Yes, at the usual time," the manager said. "None are here right now. The mechanics usually come in later. You need me to translate?"

Flipping through the indecipherable pages, Wolfe thought of something that Ilya had said. Words would only betray her. You had to look past the words, with their easy but misleading answers, to perceive the underlying reality. "Not yet. I want to see where they work."

334 / ALEC NEVALA-LEE

334 / Alec Nevala-Lee

"Of course. Follow me." The manager headed for a set of doors at the rear of the office, glancing down briefly at her thin sweater. Just before the exit, they passed a rack of hats, jackets, and other souvenirs, each embroidered with the ground handler's insignia. Reaching out, he took down a thick purple parka and handed it to her. "Take it. On the house, yes?"

After a moment's hesitation, Wolfe took the parka and put it on. It was implausibly hideous, but as she pulled it around her, she found herself grateful for its warmth. "Thank you."

With a smile that seemed less forced than before, the manager unlocked the door and led her outside. Heads lowered against the wind, they crossed the tarmac and approached the hangar, a blue-and-white structure with room for three planes. Going up to the side, the manager unlocked the door with his key card. Wolfe noted this. "You keep records of who goes in and out?"

He opened the door and motioned for her to go first. "We checked. No record of anyone entering while the plane was here. But there is a maintenance door in the back. If you have a key, you can go in without a card."

Wolfe headed inside. "And do most of the workers have access to a key?"

The manager nodded as he followed her into the hangar, which was clean and deserted. Two private planes were parked inside, the third space ominously vacant. Around the edges of the floor stood forklifts and pallets, with a cluster of rolling tool chests at the center. On the wall, a digital sign in two languages marked the number of days without an accident. Its display was blank.

As they crossed the concrete floor, Wolfe asked, "How

hard would it be to access the plane without anyone knowing?"

The manager seemed to consider this. "Possible at night. Planes can be left alone for hours, unless they need repairs. This one did not." Evidently troubled by his own words, the manager cleared his throat uneasily as they mounted a set of steps to the second level. "Here we are."

Wolfe looked around. They had reached an upper floor of the hangar, set against the wall, with a row of lockers and cubbyholes. The doors of the lockers were closed, but on the shelves above, there was a jumble of work boots, tools, and manuals. She stared at the mess, trying to see past the objects to their absent owners, hoping that something, anything, would give her a sign—

She paused. A book on the shelf had caught her eye. Extending her hand, she slid it out and studied the spine. The title, *Rukouksia Sairasvuoteelta*, meant nothing to her, but the author was John Donne.

Something about the book bothered her, as if she had seen it somewhere else. "Whose locker is this?"

The manager frowned at the book. "Laila Saarinen. She's one of our mechanics—"

Wolfe remembered the name. It was one of the five employees, and the only woman, with experience working on ventilation systems. And as she looked at the book now, she recalled at last where she had seen it before.

She closed the book, already reaching for her phone. Her heart began to pound as she turned to the manager, remembering the books on Karvonen's shelves, and dialed the airport police. "It's her."

48

The soil in the garden was stiff with frost, so it took a few tries before the spade finally broke through. Karvonen took up clods of the hard earth until he had made a hole about eight inches deep, then propped the shovel against the side of the house and tossed in a handful of components, followed by his phone. Finally he doused the whole thing with lighter fluid and threw in a match.

Feeling the soft push of warmth against his face, he knew that he had waited too long. He should have taken care of Laila hours ago, when she had first returned from the airport. By then, any role she had to play in the operation had been concluded, and there had been nothing to gain from delaying. Yet he had been seized by an uncharacteristic indecisiveness, causing him to postpone things to the point where it was threatening to interfere with his plans.

He thought back to her happiness earlier that day. She had looked at least ten years younger, as if all the old weight of anger and resentment had been transferred to the device on the plane. To an extent, he had shared in her joy, although he knew from experience that this lightening of the spirit never lasted.

Even so, after he had placed the call that activated the device and made the rest of the process inevitable, he, too, had felt exhilarated. He had done what no other man could do. At times, it seemed that he had willed this entire operation into existence, carrying it out down to the last detail. And although news of his crime would soon travel to all corners of the world, there were aspects of what he had done that would never truly be known, except by his handler and, to an extent, by Laila.

This was why he felt so tenderly toward this girl of his former country, who knew so much about him and yet so little. After the call had been made, instead of killing her, he had, unforgivably, made love to her again. And as he remembered this now, he found that he could still smell her on his skin.

As the flames began to die down, Karvonen saw clearly what he had to do. Once the phone and other components had been reduced to a pile of ash and melted plastic, he took up the spade once more, tossed a few shovelfuls of earth across the smoldering residue, and tamped it down so that no trace of the hole remained. Going back into the house through the rear door, he noticed that a few flakes of snow were drifting down from overhead.

Inside, the house was empty, with Laila dispatched on a minor errand. Glancing at the clock, Karvonen saw that she should have been back by now. Part of him hoped, oddly, that she had fled on her own, saving him the trouble of taking care of her. He thought about calling her from the phone in the kitchen, but instead, he set about performing his last few necessary tasks.

He began by packing up his equipment. The Sig Sauer

was still nestled snugly in the holster under his coat, while his *puukko* knife hung from his belt. Bringing the shotgun out from behind the sofa, he loaded it, then slid it into its carrying case. In a country with one firearm for every two citizens, the gun itself would not attract attention, but the shells would raise questions. He had carefully poured wax into the cartridges, turning them into a lump that would explode inside a man's body.

Karvonen had just finished stowing the gun when he heard the sound of a car pulling up outside. Going over to the window, he looked through a gap in the curtains and saw Laila emerging from her Volvo.

Before she could catch him watching her, he turned away from the view. Taking off his coat, he set the bag with the shotgun next to the fireplace, although he kept the pistol in its shoulder holster. Last of all, as he heard the key in the door, he reached out for the photograph on the mantelpiece, which he had turned down, and restored it to its proper position.

The door opened as Laila came inside, the shoulders of her jacket lightly dusted with snow. As she stamped her boots on the threshold, Karvonen went up to her. "What took you so long?"

"I had to wait in line at the station," Laila said, removing her coat and unwinding her long scarf. "But we're set for Oulu."

"Good." Karvonen shut the door. As instructed, she had gone to Helsinki Central and bought a ticket for a train headed north, using her own credit card, ostensibly to create a false trail.

"I've been listening to the news on the radio," Laila said, kicking off her boots. "Rumors are flying about the crash. Someone in Russia—the deputy prime minister, I think—said they're sure it was pilot error, even though no investigation has taken place at all. Can you believe it?"

Karvonen heard indignation in her voice, as if she was furious at being deprived of full credit. "It doesn't matter. The real story will come out soon. By then, both of us will be gone."

Laila turned to him, reaching up to clasp her arms around his neck. "Now can you tell me where we're really going?"

Karvonen smiled and freed himself gently from her embrace. "I'll tell you once we've left the city. Don't worry. We've prepared a new life for you. You've done · well today, and if you like, we can put you to work on other projects. But there's something you need to do for me first."

He led her by the hand to the bathroom, the door of which was slightly ajar. Pushing it open, he revealed the sink, on which he had placed an assortment of barbering supplies and hair dye. Most of these items had been purchased half an hour ago, on a quick trip to the drugstore. He had decided that the bathroom, which would dampen the noise, would be the safest place.

Laila looked into the bathroom with evident uncertainty. "You want to cut my hair?"

"Just as a precaution," Karvonen said soothingly. "It will be easier if we do it now."

She hesitated. Karvonen knew that she was proud of her long hair, which was perhaps the most attractive feature of an otherwise unremarkable face. At last, however, she went inside, her expression set, heading for the sink. Following her in, he shut the door softly behind them.

Once they were alone together, he found himself, to his surprise, cutting her hair for real. After spending so many years in fashion, he had naturally picked up a few tricks, so it was with a practiced air that he dampened her hair with a wet comb, then went to work with the scissors, gathering and cutting it one section at a time. Laila herself said nothing, her face closed off, so that there was no other sound in the room except for the quiet snip of shears.

As he combed and cut, Karvonen regarded the process as if he were working on a photograph, just another act of retouching. A few tiny alterations, he knew, were enough to transform a particular face into something quite different. The changes did not need to be radical. A clone stamp here, an airbrush tool there, and you had a different woman altogether.

When he was finished, however, he was displeased to find that the haircut only made Laila seem younger and more trusting. The face that stared at him from the mirror was, in fact, that of the girl on the mantelpiece, the one whose eyes had troubled him so unaccountably. "Are we done?"

"Not quite," Karvonen said. He set the scissors on the edge of the sink, then picked up the package of hair coloring. Pulling on the gloves, he prepared the dye according to the enclosed instructions, combining the ingredients in the larger bottle. As he did, he caught a faint whiff of something chemical, like ammonia, which reminded him of the darkroom.

Karvonen told himself again that this would mean

nothing. Like erasing a picture, which, once gone, was only a memory. Then he turned to Laila and smiled. "Close your eyes."

Laila obeyed. And it was only then, when her eyes were finally shut, that he put down the bottle and drew his knife.

49

Wolfe was in the front seat of the police van, headed for Laila Saarinen's house, when the news came over the radio. Her blue-and-white Volkswagen Transporter was following a pair of unmarked trucks carrying the tactical unit, barely visible through the snow, which was growing heavier by the second. Although it was only three in the afternoon, the sun was already going down.

Behind the wheel of the van sat a senior constable, Timo Lindegren, of the Helsinki police. He was a big, friendly officer, red in the face, dressed in his winter field uniform, which consisted of a fur cap and coveralls tucked into black boots. A junior officer sat in the backseat, his manner quiet and respectful. Since identifying Laila, Wolfe had sensed the attitude toward her subtly changing. Even Harju, the airport investigator, had asked her to call in an hour for an update.

In the meantime, she had been closely following the reports on an English radio station, and it was the latest dispatch that caught her attention. Reaching out, she turned up the volume: "—refused to comment, although a state commission has been announced to investigate the allegations—"

Lindegren, who had been focusing on the road, glanced over at her. "What is it?"

"It's Joseph Stavisky," Wolfe said, listening to the broadcast. "His site has published files implicating Russian intelligence in the crash. I was wondering when they would be released."

As the broadcast continued, the announcer stated that several news outlets were reporting that a neurological device had been used to bring down the plane. After noting that a number of public figures had called for the resignation of the head of the FSB, the station shifted to another story just as the van slowed to a stop. Lindegren shut off the engine. "We're here."

Wolfe looked out the windshield. Up ahead, through the falling snow, she could see a quiet residential street with modest houses and ample lawns that were already turning to fields of white. Laila's home, the layout of which they had studied using plans from the municipal office, stood just up the block, a yellow house with a frosted hedge. A Volvo was parked out front.

Opening her door, Wolfe climbed out of the van, grateful for the jacket she had obtained at the airport. The other officers climbed out as well, flakes of snow adhering to their eyebrows and caps, and positioned themselves along the empty road. This was the outer perimeter, with a second one set up at the block's other end. Farther up, Wolfe saw officers from the tactical unit descending from their vans, preparing to get in place for the raid.

At her side, Lindegren held something out. "Here. I thought you might need this."

Wolfe, turning, was surprised to see that he was handing her a sidearm, a Glock 17 in a shoulder holster. With a smile, she accepted it, removing her jacket to put it on. It was the first time she had worn a gun in nearly a year, and as she pulled it into place, she realized only now how much she had missed it.

Taking a pair of binoculars from Lindegren, she turned to regard the scene up ahead. Around her, the street was deathly quiet. For a moment, she could see nothing except the curtain of snow. Then picking out a dark figure moving against the whiteness, she saw that the tactical team was almost in place.

Wolfe tracked them through the glasses. The Finnish special operations unit, known as the Karhu team, or the Beagle Boys, consisted of veterans of the Helsinki police. She watched as the entry team, a stick of four men, slid noiselessly into place. Whenever the snow parted enough for her to see what was happening, she noted that they were dressed in helmets and hardshell, their carbines fitted with flash suppressors. Farther back, a perimeter team had taken up position behind the cars at the curb, the scopes and breeches of their rifles swathed in black fabric.

At her side, Lindegren had grown silent, watching tensely as the entry stick mounted the porch. Leaving a spare body shield and fire extinguisher on the steps, they stacked up at the door, two on the knob side, a third covering them from behind, with the breacher ready to come forward with the ram.

The street grew still, so quiet that Wolfe could hear the officers beside her breathing. Looking into the snow, which fell so noiselessly, she had just enough time to hope that Karvonen was there and the girl still alive when, through the binoculars, she saw the lead officer give the signal to move.

The breacher came up, the battering ram in both hands, and swung it forward. As the door splintered and fell open, the sound was muffled by the distance, so that his actions seemed oddly delicate. Then the breacher stepped back, clearing a space, as the second officer flung something through the gap.

A loud crack and burst of light came through the open door as the flashbang grenade went off. With a shout, the entry stick rushed inside, except for the breacher, who stayed back to serve as a doorman. At once, the radios came to life, the static bristling with voices in Finnish.

Wolfe lowered the binoculars, her hands numb inside their gloves. As she looked at the house up the street, she heard another burst of radio chatter. "What are they saying? Is he there?"

Lindegren was listening attentively to the radio. "No," he responded at last. "There's no sign of Karvonen. But they've found something else." He looked up. "I think you'd better go inside."

Without waiting to be told again, Wolfe handed him the binoculars and began to run toward the house, kicking up divots of the fresh snow as she went. It took her only twenty seconds to cover the distance, the wind rising around her, but when she reached the front steps, she had to wipe particles of ice from her eyes.

Wolfe entered the foyer, which was very cold, the snow blowing in through the broken door. An officer of the perimeter unit, his rifle pointed toward the floor, motioned for her to come forward. She followed him down the hallway, the carpet of which was covered in boot prints of slush. At the end of the hall, she halted before the bathroom door, which was guarded by a pair of officers.

She looked inside. On the floor of the bathroom, handcuffed to the sink, was Laila Saarinen. Laila was glaring at them. She was alive, but furious, and as Wolfe stared, she began to spit and curse angrily.

Wolfe lowered her eyes. Scattered on the tile were an assortment of bottles and other containers, evidently swept from the sink in anger, and small commas of freshly cut hair. Taking in the sorry scene, and the woman at the center of it, Wolfe saw at once what had happened. She turned to Lindegren, who had appeared at the door. "I need to talk to her now."

Lindegren nodded. "Okay. You can take the lead, if she'll listen. I'll be back soon."

As the rest of the unit resumed their search of the house, Wolfe knelt next to Laila, who had lapsed into a murderous silence. "Laila, my name is Rachel Wolfe. You speak English?"

Laila only glowered back, her eyes like knives. A second later, she gave a curt nod.

"Good," Wolfe said. "I know that this is hard for you. But I need you to tell me where he is."

No response. Laila turned away, looking around the bathroom, as if taking it in for the first time. Watching her, Wolfe felt a strange stab of pity. Laila had been responsible for an act of horrific violence, but in the end, she had been discarded, the glory she had envisioned gone. And as Wolfe looked at the other woman now, she saw that she could use this.

"Listen to me," Wolfe continued, speaking as gently as

she could, although she knew she was running out of time. "I know it must hurt, but you need to help us. He promised to take you with him, didn't he?"

More silence. Hearing footsteps, Wolfe glanced up and saw Lindegren standing in the doorway, a pair of bolt cutters in his hands. She stood aside as he came into the bathroom and said something to Laila, who did not respond. Opening the bolt cutters, he set their jaws around the handcuffs and cut the chain in two. Before Laila could move, he neatly locked a second set of cuffs around her wrists and hauled her up. He turned to Wolfe. "What now?"

"Bring her to the living room," Wolfe said. "There's something I want to show her."

Wolfe let them go first, then followed them to the front of the house. The living room was freezing, a drift of snow gathering in the foyer. Catching the eye of an officer standing a few steps away, Wolfe gestured at the broken door. "Could you please do something about this?"

As the officer went to fix the door, Wolfe turned to Laila, who was seated on the couch with Lindegren standing behind her. A television set stood in one corner. Picking up a remote from the coffee table, Wolfe fumbled with the controls, then finally managed to turn it on. As soon as a picture appeared, she began scrolling through the channels, looking for something that she could use.

At last, she found a news program with a man being interviewed in English. It was Stavisky. Judging from the backdrop, he was still at the energy conference taking place elsewhere in the city, and as she turned up the volume, she heard a note of exhaustion in his voice:

"—but the evidence is overwhelming," Stavisky said, his haggard face looking into the camera. "This crash was the work of the Russian security services. They've targeted an opposition leader who threatened them, with a weapon they've used before. We have documents to prove it. And although we need to wait until all the facts are in, I believe that Yuri Litvinov will have to resign."

"You see?" Wolfe said quietly, her eye on the screen. "I don't know what he told you, but this man, Lasse Karvonen, was a Russian assassin. He's been responsible for at least four deaths already. Maybe you thought you were helping your country, but all you did was allow Russian intelligence to take out a member of the opposition. He used you. Just as he's used other women. You aren't the only one."

When she turned to Laila, she saw hot tears flowing down the other woman's cheeks. She had guessed right. This wasn't a knowing collaborator, but a woman who thought she was hurting her country's enemies, even as she was playing into their hands. And while Wolfe knew that it was important to tread carefully, a voice in her head insisted that she press this advantage now.

Keeping the television on, Wolfe sat next to Laila. She thought briefly about putting an arm around the other woman's shoulders, which had begun to heave silently, but in the end, she simply said, "If you want to make things right, you can start here. Tell me where Karvonen is."

After a long pause, Laila answered in a shaky voice. "I don't know where he went."

Wolfe glanced at Lindegren, who was watching them closely. "What did he tell you?"

"That he was an agent with Finnish intelligence," Laila said dully. "He wanted me to help him. I believed it. I thought I was going after Russia at last. After all they had done to this country—"

"You did what you thought was right," Wolfe said. "We don't need to talk about that now. But what did he say when he left?"

"He said that we were going away together. That they would give me a new life, a new name." Laila wiped her eyes. "Then, in the bathroom, he took out the knife. He forced me to my knees and cuffed me to the sink. And he said that he was sparing me because I was a Finn."

Wolfe was struck by this. It was an unexpected side to the man she was hunting, the first sign he had shown of anything like mercy or tenderness. "And did he say where he was going?"

Laila shook her head. "No. I don't know where he is. Except—" She paused, then turned to Wolfe. Although she had regained some of her composure, her face was still as pale as death. "I know the name he's been using to travel. I saw it on his passport. It says *Dale Stern*—"

50

Karvonen was behind the wheel of his rental car, his wipers pushing away the snow, when he began to reconsider his plan. He was nearing the bridge that led to the Katajanokka district, his radio turned to news of the crash. Outside, traffic had slowed and the sky had grown dark, his headlamps illuminating the endless waves of white that stood between him and the canal.

His destination was the passenger harbor at the other end of the island, from which he would take a Viking Line ferry to Stockholm. Karvonen, who was no fool, had not discussed his plans with anyone else. With the operation over, his handler would be tempted to tie up any loose ends. As a result, Karvonen had resolved to lie low until he had taken additional measures to ensure his own safety.

All the same, he had already compromised his safety in at least one significant way. Looking out at the rear lights of the car before him, he thought of his last encounter with Laila. Even as he drew the knife, he had experienced a strange failure of nerve. Instead of cutting her throat as planned, he had taken out the handcuffs, which he had bought on an impulse on an earlier excursion. Perhaps, he thought now, he had known all along that he would falter.

As his car finally crossed the bridge that spanned the canal, creeping forward in the snow, he saw that traffic ahead had come to a standstill. Although it was hard to make out much of anything in the storm, he saw the flash of hazard lights. Looking more carefully, he observed a number of police vehicles parked across the road. Behind them, carpeted in snow like the hulking remains of dinosaurs, were two trucks that had skidded and crashed.

To his left, through a gap in the snow, he saw that he had reached a side street. For a moment, he weighed a possible detour. Then, signaling for a turn, he headed away from the main road.

Moving forward at a crawl, he took in his surroundings. On his right was the park, beneath the looming shadow of Uspenski Cathedral, which stood on a spur of rock. To his left ran the canal, with the lights of government buildings visible across the water. Picturing the layout, he saw that if he continued north, he could skirt the island, eventually working his way down to the terminal, which would be faster than inching through traffic.

It was only then that he noticed the vehicle in his rearview mirror. Looking closer, he saw that a Black Mary, a police van, had detached itself from the accident scene and was now just a few lengths behind. Karvonen turned his eyes back to the road, then glanced at the mirror again. The van couldn't really be following him. He had done nothing to attract its attention.

A second later, the van flashed its blue lights, and he

heard the squeal of the siren. He cursed softly to himself, then eased over to the side of the road, his hands tight on the wheel.

Behind him, the van parked as well, then shut off its siren, although its lights continued to flash. Karvonen studied the van in the mirror. It was hard to tell, but there seemed to be only one man inside. The officer did not emerge at once. Instead, he remained behind the wheel, visible only in outline, although it looked to Karvonen as if he was talking on his radio.

Karvonen glanced from side to side. They had halted in an area only a few steps from the entrance to the park. The street ahead was empty. Through the snow, he could see the outlines of a deserted café. Aside from the sound of his radio, which he now switched off, everything was silent.

At last the door of the van opened, and the man behind the wheel climbed out. Karvonen watched in the mirror as the officer shut the door, then came closer, a flashlight, turned off, in his hands. As the officer approached, Karvonen kept an eye on him. Very slowly, he reached up and unzipped his jacket partway. Then he put his hands back on the steering wheel.

When the officer was close enough, Karvonen pressed the switch on his armrest to roll down the window. With snow and cold air already beginning to drift through the gap, he gave a nod to what turned out to be a junior constable. "Good evening. Anything wrong?"

"Hands on the wheel, please," the constable said, turning on his flashlight. Karvonen squinted into the glare. Even with his eyes half shut, he could tell that this was nothing but a kid in winter blues, not yet thirty, the customary Glock holstered at his side. After looking him over for another moment, the constable turned the light off. "Please step out of the car."

Karvonen gestured at the storm, as if the other man had failed to notice it. "Is this really necessary? If I've done anything wrong—"

"Please step out of the car, sir," the constable said flatly. "And keep your hands where I can see them."

After a pause, Karvonen opened his door and, with the air of a man who has resolved to be helpful, climbed out of the car, hands raised. Feeling snow trickling down his collar, he relaxed his face into an expression of harmless goodwill. "There must be some kind of mistake."

The constable, standing three paces away, put a hand on his sidearm, but did not draw it. "Is your name Dale Stern?"

Karvonen's smile only widened, but he knew at once that his cover had been blown. "Yes, that's me."

"Turn around and put your hands on top of the car," the constable said. "Slowly."

"All right, but I still don't see why." Karvonen began to turn, his eyes passing unhurriedly across the scene. The street was still empty. There was no sign of movement in the park. After noting all these things, he completed his turn, then made as if to put his hands on the roof. Instead of doing so, however, he simply slid a hand into his jacket and drew the gun from its holster.

He pivoted back, gun already cocked and raised, and found himself looking into the constable's startled eyes. Before the other man had a chance to move, Karvonen pulled the trigger twice.

The sound of the shots was swallowed up by snow. A

pair of holes appeared in the constable's thick jacket, one at the center of his sternum, the other an inch or so lower. The two men stood eye to eye for another moment. Then the constable crumpled to the ground.

Karvonen holstered his pistol. At first, looking down at the body, he did not quite understand the line he had crossed. All he could think about was the constable's final question. The police knew the name on his passport, which meant that they also knew his car. To get out of the city, he would need to abandon the vehicle and find another way to the harbor. From here to the terminal, he estimated, was half a mile by foot. Meaning that he had to leave now.

He turned away from the dead man. Behind him, the driver's-side door was still open. Reaching inside, he unlocked the rear door and opened it. On the backseat lay the carrying case with the shotgun inside. He pulled out this bag and slung it over his shoulder, then shut the door.

Karvonen was about to head around to the trunk when the rear passenger window disintegrated. He turned, his mind just catching up with the sound of the gunshot, and saw that the constable was lying on his stomach in the snow, looking up at him, his elbows braced against the ground. The constable's face was pale, his grip on the pistol wavering, but there was a grim determination in his eyes as he aimed the gun as best he could and fired again.

The second shot was closer. Karvonen felt the breath of the bullet against the side of his face as another window shattered. The constable readied a third shot, correcting his aim by a fraction of an inch, but by now

Karvonen's own pistol was out, and it was with a sense of something like incredulous indignation that he raised the gun and put one last bullet through the constable's head.

With that, the constable collapsed a second time, his strings cut. The fresh streak of red visible against the snow caused something inside Karvonen to snap. His gun still in hand, he went up to the dead man and kicked the Glock away. Then, furious, he began to kick the body itself, its limbs flopping uselessly against the ground, making angels in the powder.

"You idiot," Karvonen hissed at the countryman he had killed. "You stupid *shit*—"

He kicked the body harder, his anger rising as he perceived the full meaning of what he had done. A third kick sent a dart of pain arrowing up his right leg. He cursed, sensing that he had hurt something, but was still about to deliver a final kick when he heard shouts in the distance.

Karvonen looked up. For an instant, the curtain of snow parted, giving him a view of the scene on the other side of the canal. Across the narrow slice of water, a row of figures was yelling and pointing in his direction.

"Good," Karvonen said to himself, knowing that he was dangerously on the verge of losing control. Holstering his pistol, he shouldered the bag with the shotgun and headed away from his car, the headlights of which were still blazing into the darkness. Following his first instinct, he headed uphill, moving into the park. With every step, the pain in his leg increased.

He forced himself to think. The ferry terminal was to the east. Up ahead, veiled by snow and wind, he could see the outline of the cathedral, a tower of brick, its copper spire topped by an onion dome. As he looked up at it now, he saw that if he continued in this direction, he would end up at the far end of the park. From there, he could proceed to the harbor.

As he limped onward, however, he began to have second thoughts. The snow made it difficult to move quickly, and the pain in his leg was growing worse. What was only half a mile on the map began to feel much longer. And it was only a matter of time, he knew, before he was discovered.

An instant later, through the snow, he saw something so strange that it seemed like a hallucination: a door set into the bedrock at the base of the cathedral. It looked like the entrance to a modern office, except surrounded by blocks of irregular stone. Staring into its glowing rectangle, Karvonen realized that he knew exactly what it was. And it gave him an idea.

He went up to the door and looked inside. Through the glass, he could see a brightly lit space with chairs and a reception desk. After only the shortest of pauses, he opened the door and entered.

Behind the desk, a secretary was on the phone. When he tried to get her attention, she looked him over doubtfully, then raised a finger and turned away, signaling that he would need to wait.

Karvonen was in no mood to be patient. Lowering his carrying case, he opened it and took out the shotgun. He raised it and, aiming at random, fired into one of the frosted partitions behind the desk.

The partition shattered, the fragments raining to the ground in a long tinkle of glass. With a gasp, the receptionist spun in her chair, eyes wide, and let the phone drop from her hands.

"I apologize for the disturbance," Karvonen said, shotgun still raised. "But I'm afraid I'm in a bit of a hurry—"

51

When the news came over the radio, Wolfe sensed the change in mood at once. She was in the backseat of the police van, riding next to Laila, whose legs and wrists were shackled. For the past few minutes, as they made their way through the storm to the nearest station, Laila had been brooding and silent, but now, hearing the latest dispatch, she sat up suddenly in her seat. Wolfe looked at the two officers in the front of the van. "What's going on?"

"It's Karvonen," Lindegren said, listening to the alert as he drove. "He's killed a policeman—"

At the news, Wolfe felt her dismay click forward another notch. "What happened?"

Lindegren unhooked his radio from the dashboard, asked a question of the dispatcher, then listened to the response. "It was near Uspenski Cathedral," Lindegren said, replacing the mike. "The constable pulled over a car matching the description of Karvonen's rental vehicle. That was the last anyone heard from him. It looks like Karvonen shot him three times with a handgun."

"So he's killing Finns now." Wolfe looked over at Laila, whose face had gone white. "What about his car?"

"Sounds like it's still at the scene," Lindegren said. "Witnesses are saying he escaped on foot. Police have sealed off the park near the cathedral. The Presidential Palace is just across the canal, so security there is already moving in. Though if there's any justice, our men will find him first."

In his voice, Wolfe heard a helpless anger, which she also saw in the junior officer's face. "How far is it?"

"Ten minutes, if we hurry." Lindegren glanced out the windshield. "It won't be easy in this weather. Still—"

Wolfe said nothing, sensing that Lindegren didn't need much in the way of persuasion. Finally, without a word, Lindegren reversed the van at the next intersection, turning back the way they had come, and used his radio to report that they were heading for the cathedral.

As they pressed onward, their progress slowed by the snow, Wolfe remembered that she owed Harju a call. Fishing out her phone, she dialed the number that the investigator at the airport had provided, although she assumed, based on his silence, that there would not be any news.

She was wrong. "I have an update on survivors," Harju said, speaking over the din of the incident command center. "Chigorin is alive. The fuselage broke in half on impact. The crew at the front of the plane was killed, but Chigorin and at least a few others at the back survived. He's badly injured, possibly paralyzed, but I'm told that they think he'll make it."

Wolfe stared out at the storm, unable to believe the news. "What about Powell?"

"I don't know." The lead investigator's tone was apologetic. "Please understand that the situation is in great confusion, and we're still waiting for a list of names. The Ministry of Emergency Situations is supposed to give us an update soon. I'll call you back when I know more."

He hung up. Wolfe pocketed her phone, then turned to the others. "Chigorin made it. He's going to survive."

As she related what the investigator had said, she began to feel something like hope. She noticed, however, that the others did not seem as elated by the news, while Laila had withdrawn again into sullen silence.

Ten minutes later, they arrived at the scene of the shooting. In the shadow of the cathedral, barriers had been set into place, and officers milled around the area like strange snowmen in their fur hats. As Wolfe got out, she saw a cluster of cadets from the Presidential Palace, armed with rifles, awkward in their overcoats and white spats. The snow was falling more thickly than ever.

Wolfe and Lindegren headed for the heart of the scene, their badges out, leaving Laila in the van with the junior officer. Up ahead, beyond the barricades, she could make out the body of the constable, already dusted with snow. In the faces of the policemen around her, she saw the same impotent rage as before, and knew that none of them would hesitate to take Karvonen down.

Lindegren waved at a cadet stationed nearby, evidently a friend. As the cadet approached, crystals of ice adhering to his coat and hat, Lindegren greeted him in Finnish, then indicated the woman at his side. "This is Rachel Wolfe from London. She's been tracking your killer."

The cadet gave her a short nod, then gestured at the van. "Who do you have here?"

"A material witness," Wolfe said. "We were taking her to the station when we heard the news."

As she spoke, she shot a glance at Lindegren, who appeared to understand. Given the mood of the crowd, it would be wise to conceal the fact that Laila had been Karvonen's accomplice. Lindegren turned back to the cadet. "What can you tell us about the search so far?"

The cadet jerked his head toward the cathedral. "Witnesses saw him going into the park. We're trying to track him, but snow and wind are erasing his footprints, and there are too many people on the scene. The cathedral has been evacuated. We're searching it, but there are a lot of places where someone like this could hide. The dogs should be here within the hour."

"We can't wait that long," Wolfe said. "I need to see it now. Can you take me there?"

The cadet glanced at Lindegren, who nodded. After returning to the van, where they told the junior officer to drive Laila to the station for booking, they headed into the park, the cadet marching ahead of them. Looking over her shoulder, Wolfe caught a glimpse of Laila's face through the van's rear window, her features pale and grim. Then the van was gone.

Wolfe turned to the cathedral, which was barely visible through the veil of snow. She tried to see it as it might have looked to Karvonen, fleeing from the scene of this latest murder, and saw that it was both the most obvious destination and too prominent a hiding place. In this storm, she thought, he would head for the nearest visible landmark, but she wasn't sure whether he would stay there.

A second later, lowering her eyes, she saw what appeared to be an office door set into the bedrock at the cathedral's base. "What's that?"

The cadet looked where she was pointing. "Data center. It's built in an old bomb shelter under the cathedral. We've checked it. The door was already closed and locked when we got here—"

Wolfe went up to it anyway. Trying the door, she confirmed that it was locked, then shaded her eyes and looked inside. Beyond the glass, the interior was dark. As her vision adjusted, she began to make out the outlines of a reception desk, unoccupied, and a few empty cubicles.

She was about to turn away when she noticed the glint of something on the floor. Taking out her penlight, she directed its beam through the doorway, illuminating a scatter of broken glass. Looking more closely at the other side, she saw that one of the frosted partitions near the reception desk was missing.

Behind her, the cadet was growing impatient. "We should be going. They'll be missing us back at the—" Before he could finish his sentence, he broke off, startled, as Wolfe drew her gun. "What are you doing?"

"Cover your ears," Wolfe said, and fired once, shooting out the door's glass panel. Knocking away the remaining shards with her elbow, she reached inside and unlocked the door. "Come on."

She opened it and went into the data center, which at first glance seemed deserted. As she and the others entered the facility, guns drawn, she saw the receptionist's vacant chair, as well as an adjoining bicycle room. Beyond the reception desk was the main floor, also empty, lit only by the glow of computers. Fifteen flat-screen monitors were arranged in a semicircular console at the center of the floor, in front of a large projection screen.

"Someone should be here," Wolfe said, checking the room. "A center like this should always have someone on duty. Unless—"

She paused. From the hallway to her right, there came a muffled shout. Heading for the noise, she swung around the corner, gun first, and found herself at the closed double doors of a conference room. It had been chained shut with a bike lock. On the carpet, there was a pile of cell phones. She went up to the door, keeping her back to the wall. "Who's there?"

A chorus of Finnish voices resolved themselves into the words of a man speaking in accented English. "We're all here," the man said. "He took our phones and locked us inside."

As he spoke, he pushed the door open a fraction of an inch, which was as far as the chain would allow it to go. Wolfe looked in. Through the gap, she saw the flushed face of a man in short sleeves, with several others standing behind him, making five in all. As the officers went to find something to break down the door, Wolfe spoke into the opening. "Where is he?"

"Gone," the man said. "But he took Antero with him. Our project manager with Helsinki Power. The doors have electronic access, so he needed someone to let him into the tunnels—"

"Tunnels?" Wolfe asked. An alarm bell began to go off in her head. "What tunnels?"

Before the man could respond, Lindegren and the cadet reappeared, each carrying a fire extinguisher in his hands. Wolfe stood back as they began hammering at the doors, alternating their blows, until one of the handles finally broke. Tossing the extinguishers aside, they undid the loosened lock and unwound the chain, allowing the doors to be opened.

As the workers filed out, Wolfe went up to the man who had spoken through the door, who turned out to be the chief engineer on duty. "I need you to show me where this man would have gone."

"Of course." While the others retrieved their cell phones and began giving statements to the cadet, Wolfe and Lindegren followed the engineer into the hall. Leaving the main floor, they entered a room lined with row after row of computer servers, each locked inside a separate orange cabinet. The room was clean, climate controlled, and filled with the low hum of data processors.

"This building was carved out of the bedrock during the war," the engineer explained, leading them into the bowels of the facility. "It was originally built as a refuge for city officials during Russian bomb raids. A few years ago, we leased the space. Down here, our servers are safe. Since we're underground, we can use seawater to cool the machines. And the excess heat goes here—"

Rounding a corner, they entered an area where the walls gave way to bare rock, the marks of the tunneling tools still visible. Across the rough gray stone were bolted sets of horizontal pipes, from which Wolfe could hear the murmur of running water. Up ahead was a metal doorway. The engineer unlocked it, then beckoned them inside. "Watch your step."

Wolfe went in, with Lindegren close behind, and followed the engineer down a set of stairs. Looking around, she saw that they were on a catwalk lit by a grid of fluorescent tubes, with a network of pipes and ducts snaking across the walls. Directly in front of them, a spiral staircase descended down a rectangular shaft, leading into the caverns below.

"This is where the water ends up," the manager said. "The district heating network, seventy meters underground. Forty kilometers of tunnels, delivering heat to the rest of the city. This is where he wanted to go."

Examining the floor at the edge of the shaft, Wolfe noticed a set of drying boot prints. The marks, she saw, had been made by someone who had recently been in the snow. And they had been left not long before.

Wolfe stared down the spiral staircase, which wound into unfathomable depths. She didn't want to go down there, but saw that there was no other way. "The man who was taken hostage. Who is he?"

"A recent hire," the engineer said. "He works for the energy company. I don't know him well. But he has a wife and child—"

Looking into the darkness, Wolfe knew that Karvonen, who had already shot one man today, wouldn't hesitate to kill his hostage as well. As she reflected on this, she heard the sound of footsteps, and saw that the cadet had joined them on the catwalk. He seemed about to say something, but when he looked down at the darkened rectangle, he fell silent instead.

A map of the tunnels had been posted to the wall. Wolfe tore it down and handed it to Lindegren. "Are you coming?"

After a pause, Lindegren nodded grimly. He turned to the cadet. "Call it in. I want police stationed at all access points to the surface. And I'll need a Karhu team brought in to sweep the tunnels. Tell them to bring dogs." He turned back to Wolfe. "You're sure you want to do this?"

"No," Wolfe said. She turned toward the stairs. "But I don't think we have a choice."

She began to descend, the metal steps ringing beneath her feet. As she headed down the shaft, she wanted to pray, but found that she no longer knew how. Instead, she raised her gun and kept it pointed into the darkness, seeking comfort of another kind, as she and Lindegren passed into the tunnels under the city.

52

Karvonen moved down the tunnel. A few steps ahead of him, marching at gunpoint, was the project manager he had enlisted to guide him through this underground world. The tunnel along which they were passing was wide enough to drive through, with sleek heat and water pipes running along the rock walls. Lights were set in the ceiling every twenty feet, making the tunnels easier to navigate, but they also left him feeling dangerously exposed.

The project manager was a stout man with a bald head, and he puffed heavily as he led Karvonen to the access shaft. From time to time, he would comment nervously on their surroundings, as if giving a guided tour: "What we see here is only part of the system. The data center opened just a year ago, and is already generating enough heat for five hundred homes—"

Walking behind him with the shotgun, Karvonen barely listened. This was the kind of man he despised, servile but humorless, navigating his little world like a rat in a maze. Karvonen was more interested in the maze itself, with its odor of stone and faint rumble of pumps and turbines. He had already noted that the heat pipelines ran along one side of the tunnel, with cooling pipes on the other, which would allow him to maintain his bearings.

Otherwise, it would be easy to get lost. Helsinki, he knew, was riddled with kilometers of these passages. With historic buildings on one side and the sea on the other, the city was unable to expand in the usual fashion, so instead, it went straight down, excavating caverns and tunnels in the bedrock that lay so close to the surface. The result had been a secret city, an underground reflection of its sister above, and while the expansion was justified for practical reasons, Karvonen sensed that there were also darker impulses at work.

A city, he thought now, plunging deeper into the tunnels, was something like a man. Every great city was driven to explore the underworld, building its shadow house in order to grow. And, as with men, it was only through a journey into the darkness that it could reach its full potential.

Karvonen belatedly noticed that the project manager had slowed. "What's wrong?"

"We're here," the manager said. He pointed to a utility corridor up ahead. "See?"

Karvonen followed the gesture with his eyes. Past a pair of fire doors, he saw a set of metal steps, which seemed to lead to the surface. "Stay here. I'm going to check it out. Don't you dare move."

He crept forward, keeping the shotgun raised. Reaching the doors, he went inside in a low crouch, leading with the barrel, and found that the room was empty. The stairs lay directly in front of him. Leaning back, he saw that they spiraled upward until they reached a second level, perhaps twenty meters above, where his view was obscured by the landing overhead.

With his shotgun pointed toward the ceiling, Karvonen waited, listening. Around him, he heard the whisper of unseen machines, the movement of water in heating pipes, and then—

From somewhere above came the ring of footsteps. It was hard to tell how many men there were, or whether they were workers from the energy company or something else. A moment later, however, he heard the crackle of a radio, the words impossible to distinguish, and then, more ominously, the barking of dogs.

Karvonen backed away from the stairs, his shotgun still trained on the opening above. "We can't go up," Karvonen said without turning. "They're sealing off the shaft. I need you to—"

Too late, he heard footfalls on the stone floor. He turned, bringing the shotgun down and around, just in time to see the project manager fleeing up the corridor, panting as he ran. A second later, he was gone.

Karvonen's finger tensed briefly on the trigger, then relaxed. A shot would only give away his position. In any case, keeping a hostage now would only slow him down, when he had to act even more decisively than before.

Leaving the utility corridor, he returned to the main tunnel. The project manager was nowhere to be seen. With his free hand, Karvonen reached for the fire doors and swung them shut one at a time, closing off the entrance to the stairs. Then, looking around the tunnel, he tried to figure out his next move. There were access points to the surface every two or three hundred meters, but the shafts from the main passage were probably blocked off by now.

Directly ahead of him, three pairs of doors opened onto a set of side tunnels leading away from the main passage. After a moment's indecision, he chose one at random, and with the shotgun raised, he went in.

As he pressed onward, he tried to keep heading east, which would eventually take him to the passenger harbor. Here the tunnels grew narrower and darker, some lit only by a row of fluorescent tubes along the ceiling, while others were not lit at all. He passed through one door, then another, checking each corridor as he went, moving as noiselessly as he could.

After a minute had gone by, and he had yet to see an access shaft, he slowed his pace. Looking more closely at the tunnel, he saw that the pipes on the walls had switched places. Now the hot water pipes were on his left, with the cooling pipes on the right, which implied that he had doubled back somehow.

Karvonen lowered his shotgun, trying to decide what to do. His pulse was higher than before, but he forced himself to remain calm. The safest course of action, he concluded, was to stick to the side tunnels and work his way to an access shaft that had not yet been sealed, moving as quickly as possible.

With this in mind, he continued up the tunnel, where he found himself facing another set of doors. In the end, he chose the darkest passage, trusting that it would protect him, and headed onward, moving away from the light.

It was at that moment, unknown to him, that Wolfe and Lindegren emerged from the stairwell, some distance away, that led from the data center down to the first underground chamber.

Wolfe swung into the room, pistol first. It was empty. Taking in her surroundings, her legs aching from the descent, she saw that they were in a cavern with floors of stone, its walls lined with scaffolding and construction equipment. Up ahead, a set of fire doors opened into another chamber, with doors on either side leading into machine halls and tunnels.

Looking around, Wolfe realized that she had entered an underground labyrinth, and that Karvonen could be anywhere. A glance at her phone was enough to confirm that she no longer had a signal.

At her side, Lindegren brought out the map of the tunnels, which he had rolled up and tucked into his pocket. Across the laminated schematic, there ran a network of energy and service corridors. Lindegren pointed to a thick gray line moving north from the cathedral. "This is the main tunnel, I think. It goes three kilometers north to Katri Vala Park, where the primary heating and cooling plant is located. From there, it leads to the rest of the network."

Wolfe followed the line with her eyes. "Karvonen will stay out of the primary tunnel. It's the first place anyone would look." She tried to put herself in Karvonen's position, studying the map as he might have, then pointed to a tunnel leading eastward. "Here. He was on his way east when he was pulled over. I think he was heading for the harbor. If he has any choice, he'll keep going that way."

She could tell that Lindegren had his doubts about this, but even the slenderest possibility was better than nothing. He rolled up the map again and slid it into his pocket. "All right. Follow me."

Drawing his sidearm, he headed for the passage to their right, with Wolfe following close behind. Under her feet, the floor was damp with moisture, which ran in dark gray fingers across the stone. She hoped that the tactical units were in place. Their only real chance of finding Karvonen lay in closing off the shafts to the surface and doing a systematic search of the tunnels, and without a larger team, it would take a miracle to find him and his hostage alive.

Reaching the end of the corridor, they swung around the corner, timing it silently so that they moved in together. Nothing. They continued onward, Lindegren leading the way, keeping close to the pipes. As they diverged from the main tunnel, the passage grew darker and lower, though the ceiling was still too high for her to reach. Out of the corner of her eye, Wolfe saw cautionary signs posted on the wall, admonishing her sternly in Finnish.

At the end of the passageway, there was another door. Lindegren checked it, then motioned her forward. "Come on."

Going inside, Wolfe found that the tunnel had opened into a larger machine room. In the darkness, she could see two rows of concrete pedestals about the height of her waist, each supporting a horizontal gray drum connected to the ceiling by a pair of white pipes. She didn't recognize the machines, but thought they were transmission pumps of some kind, and was about to ask Lindegren about this when his chest exploded under a shotgun blast.

Wolfe fell back as her face was sprayed with blood and bone. As Lindegren crumpled to the floor, dead, she caught a glimpse of a figure at the other end of the room, just the outline of a man in the shadows, but before she could raise her own gun, she heard Karvonen rack the shotgun again.

As the spent shell fell to the floor, she dropped, ducking behind a pedestal just before Karvonen fired a second time. The blast, deafening in the confined space, struck the pedestal a few inches from her face, sending chips of concrete flying. She felt shards cut her on the cheek, stinging like insects, then heard the pump action of the shotgun cycle once more.

A second spent shell clattered to the ground. A pause. Then nothing but silence.

Wolfe was behind the pedestal, her back to the concrete, her gun in a high grip with two hands. Karvonen was somewhere behind and to her right. In front of her lay Lindegren's body, the pistol still clutched in his fingers.

The silence deepened. Karvonen, she knew, was waiting. Wolfe strained to hear the tactical unit, but there was no sound. By now, she hoped, they would have posted men at the access shafts, preparing to clear the tunnels. She suspected that Karvonen knew this too.

Behind her came a quiet footstep. Another. Wolfe wanted to risk a glance around the pedestal, but she forced herself not to move. Instead, she tried to put herself in Karvonen's place. If he was all the way back here, she realized, he was lost. He would be desperate to keep moving. And he would not hesitate to kill her.

Pinned behind the pedestal with blood, not all of it hers, trickling down her face, Wolfe found herself remem-

bering what Ilya had said. Sometimes it was best to surrender, like Isaac bound to the altar. And as she considered
the body lying next to her now, she knew what she had
to do.

Wolfe felt a rush of despair. She wasn't ready for this,
not by a long shot, although she'd had her whole life to
prepare for it. Then something shifted inside her, like a
mechanism finally clicking into place, and she found herself praying. Not formally, in words, as she had been
taught to do, but mutely, in thought and action, as if
prayer were as inevitable as breathing, whether God existed or not.

Ten yards away, at the other end of the room, Karvonen held his shotgun at eye level, watching for signs of
movement. He had used two shells, leaving four in the
magazine. It was darker than he would have liked, but the
strip of white tape he had laid along the barrel made it
easier to sight.

He knew that the woman was still here. From the
glimpse he had managed before she ducked down, he
also knew that she was armed. A pistol against a shotgun
wasn't much of a contest, but all the same, he had to be
careful. And as he looked around the machine hall, he
recognized at last where he was, and realized that she was
standing between him and his best way out.

In the shadows, about thirty feet away, lay the legs of
the man he had killed, with the rest of the body concealed
by the pedestal. Part of him was glad that he could not
see the man's face, but another part no longer cared. Two
of his countrymen were dead at his hands, and a day ago,
he would have mourned this. But now, with the suddenness of all great revelations, he saw that such trifles had

ceased to matter, and that he was no longer really a Finn at all.

A nation, he understood, was nothing. A man was an island unto himself, an exile in his own country, and by now, he had shaped and revised himself into something even more. It was a transformation that had been under way ever since he had sat at his grandfather's knee as a boy, determined to carve out a destiny of his own. And it seemed only fitting that it would reach its full realization here, in this underground world, which reminded him so much of the darkroom.

He was still coming around to this newfound truth when a voice rose out of the darkness. "Karvonen?"

Karvonen, suspecting a trick, pointed his shotgun toward the source of the sound. One good blast, he knew, would take off most of the woman's head, and his pressure on the trigger increased only slightly as she spoke again: "Karvonen, I'm coming out. Listen to me. My name is Rachel Wolfe. I'm a special agent with the Federal Bureau of Investigation. Before you do anything else, you need to listen to what I have to say. I'm getting up now."

A shadow emerged slowly from behind the pedestal. Sighting across the strip of tape, Karvonen saw that the woman had removed her jacket and was holding it away from her body. In her other hand, she held her pistol, grip outward, in a position of surrender. Her eyes were fixed on his.

"If you kill me, you're throwing away your best chance out of here," Wolfe said as she came into full view. "A tactical team is sweeping the tunnels right now. You know this. To get out of here alive, you need a bargaining chip. Something to trade. And that's me."

Karvonen, still wary, kept the shotgun up. He spoke quietly. "Put the gun on the floor. Then slide it this way."

Wolfe obeyed. Keeping her eyes on him, she knelt and set the gun down, arm fully extended, and slid it in his direction. The pistol skated across the floor and came to a stop at his feet. Once it was there, Wolfe put down her jacket, then straightened up. "You've got the gun. Now we can talk."

Karvonen took a step forward, leaving the pistol on the floor. Eye to eye with Wolfe, he took another step, considering his situation. Like it or not, she had a point. If the police were searching the tunnels, he could only escape with a hostage. It would be easy enough to use her to get to the surface. Then, once he was safely away from the city, he could kill her at his convenience.

He drew closer, the blood sticky under his feet, until the body of the officer came into view. When they were a few steps apart, he lowered the shotgun. "All right. You take me to where we started. And then—"

Karvonen paused. Looking down at the officer's body, he saw that the holster at the dead man's side was empty, as were his hands. The gun that the man had been carrying was gone.

He understood, too late, that he had been tricked. With a snarl, he turned to Wolfe, shotgun rising, but before he could pull the trigger, he saw the muzzle flash of the second gun, the one she had just drawn from the back of her belt. Two heavy blows struck him in the chest, one after the other, and then he was on his back, staring up at the darkened ceiling.

Wolfe came forward, covering him with the pistol she had taken from Lindegren's hands. Karvonen was on the floor, bleeding from two gunshot wounds. At least one had entered his heart.

Going up to him, she kicked the shotgun away. It slid across the concrete, where it struck the base of a pedestal and skidded to a stop. Wolfe knew from the earlier shooting that Karvonen had a handgun as well, but she couldn't see it. She thought it might be in a holster under his jacket.

"Keep your hands away from your body," Wolfe said, her voice strange and thin in her ears. "I'm placing you under arrest—"

In the distance, faintly, she heard footsteps. For a moment, she thought that they were just her imagination, but then she heard the crackle of a radio, and she knew that the tactical unit was on its way.

She looked down at the man before her. Karvonen's lips were pulled back in a grimace of pain, but from this angle, it looked like a smile. His eyes were on hers. He was grinning a bloody grin.

Before she was aware that she was going to say anything, Wolfe heard her own voice, although its tone did not seem to be hers: "You failed. Chigorin is alive. All you've done has been for nothing."

Karvonen laughed, then began to cough. Blood and sputum ran down his chin, the red startling against the whiteness of his face, and Wolfe knew that he was dying. At the very end, though, before falling silent, he managed to speak, words that would haunt her long after she had emerged from these passages to return to the world above: *"You don't know how wrong you are—"*

53

At St. Pancras Hospital, near King's Cross, a rehabilitation center had been established in the southern wing. Much of it was devoted to a therapeutic gym, a large colorless room stocked with weights, roller machines, and treadmills. In the corner, a television played a reality show with the sound turned down.

A patient was working on the parallel bars, which folded away from the wall. As he paced back and forth, his therapist, a small round woman in a red polo shirt, gave him encouragement and suggested modest corrections to his gait. The patient was careful not to push himself too hard, knowing that good habits were more important than strength, but today, he put extra effort into his routine, knowing that he was being observed from nearby.

Finally, when his workout was finished, the therapist complimented him warmly, saying that he was taking good steps. As the patient lowered himself into his wheelchair, he was approached by the woman who had been watching from the doorway. It was Wolfe. "How are you doing?"

"As well as can be expected," Powell said. He turned to his therapist. "Do you mind if we talk in private?"

His therapist smiled blandly and left. When he turned

back, Powell saw that Wolfe was looking at him with un-usual tenderness. He had been hoping to put a better face on his condition. For the past six weeks, out of misguided concern, he had been kept in the dark, and he was ex-tremely tired of it.

All the same, when he looked down at his ravaged body, he couldn't blame the others entirely. There was a cast on his right hand and a splint on his left leg, with a snug body brace holding the rest of him together. For the first two weeks after the crash, he had been under seda-tion, and he was still on more drugs than he cared to re-member. They helped with the pain, at least to a point, although his throat was constantly sore after having been intubated for so long.

He had spent more than a month at the burn unit in St. Petersburg. As soon as his mind was clear enough, having a great deal of time on his hands, he had carefully studied his charts. He had been brought in with second-degree burns across his back and legs, as well as various internal injuries and fractures. For a week, he had breathed through a ventilator, a pump inserted into his stomach to reduce the swelling, and had endured re-peated surgeries on his ankle, along with a series of skin grafts. Even now, whenever he tried to rest, he felt the constant itch of healing tissue.

If he was grateful for anything, it was for the ventilator hood he had worn as the plane went down, which had protected his face and lungs from the fire and smoke. This, above all else, had saved his life.

Of the twelve people on the plane, only four had sur-vived. Both pilots had perished, as had Chigorin's chief of security. A flight attendant had escaped with severe burns and internal injuries. Chigorin's assistant was still in intensive care. And while the grandmaster himself was expected to live, it had been widely reported that he would never walk again.

After his return to London, Powell had found that the greatest change was not physical but mental. He still had flashbacks from the poison, but on the whole, they were bearable. Throughout it all, a core of himself had remained constant and sane, and as a result, he no longer feared his father's dementia, even after confronting it in terms that he would not soon forget.

One consequence of the poison had taken him by surprise. It had subtly changed his perception of life. No longer did existence seem as orderly and logical as before. Instead, even with his sanity restored, it seemed full of signs, mysterious affinities that struck him wherever he turned. Seeing the world through a madman's eyes had taught him the limitations of his old, more rational self, and this realization had been a crucial factor in his most recent decision.

Now, shifting in his wheelchair, he turned to Wolfe, who had been waiting patiently. "In case you're wondering, there's nothing wrong with my mind," Powell said. "I'm tired of asking for straight answers. Cornwall keeps putting me off. I hope you aren't planning on doing the same thing."

"That isn't why I came," Wolfe said. She had lost weight since their last meeting, and she still bore the marks of her recent exertions, although at least her hair was growing back. "I was hoping that if I told you more, I could convince you to change your mind. What have you heard?"

"Only what I see on the news." Powell gestured at the television, on which the reality show was still playing. "Occasionally, when I can get someone to change the channel, I see Stavisky. He's milking this, isn't he?"

"To a point. He's pushing for further disclosure. With Chigorin in the hospital, he's the default opposition leader. There are rumors that he'll be running for president in the next election."

"I always knew he was too ambitious to stay put for long." Powell looked down at his body brace, made of hard black plastic, which was cinched tightly to his chest and sides. "I imagine that the attack has given him plenty of ammunition against the current regime."

"Yes, you would think so," Wolfe said. "But as a matter of fact, we were wrong."

Powell, who had begun to wheel himself around the room, came to a halt. "Wrong?"

"About everything. This was never about Chigorin at all. At least not in the way we believed."

In her face, Powell saw a look that he recognized, but he wasn't sure where he had seen it before. A second later, it seemed to him that he had glimpsed it in Ilya's eyes. "You'll need to explain what you mean by that."

"That's why I'm here. I owe you that much." Wolfe paused. "It doesn't matter what I say, does it? You aren't coming back."

"No," Powell said. "But it doesn't mean I don't want to be tempted. Walk with me."

He began to wheel himself slowly around the gym. Wolfe followed at his side, giving him plenty of space. "I began by thinking about something that Ilya told me. He said that Karvonen staged his crimes like a man who wanted to be noticed. If you want to hide a body, you don't set it on fire. And you don't take out your enemy in a plane crash that makes headlines around the world. Which made me wonder if the crimes were deliberately designed to draw attention to themselves."

Powell began to understand. "In order to implicate the intelligence services."

"Yes. More specifically, civilian intelligence. You know Karvonen's background. He was an army paratrooper from a family with a strong military history. Which implies that if he allied himself with the intelligence services, he'd be drawn to the military side. So I dug deeper. And I found that while civilian intelligence has been squeezed by the recession, its military counterparts have done rather well. Look at Gaztek. A few years ago, it received government authorization to raise its own troops. Archer, I think, told you about this—"

Powell remembered his conversation with the founder of Cheshire. "Yes. He said that they were training soldiers to guard the pipelines."

"But the authorization only reflects what has been happening for years. Gaztek has always been a state unto itself, with its own private army, which meant that it also needed its own intelligence division. They began by consulting on security, but before long they had grown into something more, a private intelligence arm that answered to no one and stood to earn billions illegally. And because they were originally brought in for their military expertise—"

"—they would have come from military intelligence," Powell finished. "The GRU."

"Right," Wolfe said. "Which has always competed for

power and resources with the civilian agencies. The balance shifts one way, then the other. With its access to Gaztek's assets, military intelligence became the more powerful of the two. A situation that their civilian rivals couldn't tolerate."

Powell felt the back of his neck begin to ache, as if a realization were gathering there. "They wanted a larger piece of the pie."

"Or all of it. From what I understand, the civilian side was preparing a proposal, with the backing of Yuri Litvinov, to reorganize Gaztek's intelligence division under its control. Billions of dollars were about to change hands. When military intelligence realized that they were in danger of losing their stake, they decided to take out their rivals altogether. Of course, to bring down the head of a rival intelligence agency, it had to be something spectacular—"

"Like the murder of an opposition leader," Powell said, bringing his wheelchair to a stop. "In a way that would implicate Litvinov."

"Which is exactly what happened." Opening her purse, Wolfe removed a thick folder, which she handed to Powell. "We've reconstructed the device that Karvonen assembled. It consisted of a point source disseminator, obtained by Campbell, and an electrical detonator, built by Akoun, who had worked as an engineer for an Algerian affiliate of Gaztek. The idea was to make a device that would immediately cast suspicion on civilian intelligence."

With his unsteady fingers, Powell paged through the file, which included a number of blurred schematics. "And the poison?"

"That was the hardest part," Wolfe said. "It had to be a weapon that could only have been developed by the poison laboratory of the civilian security services, using a method that had been linked to Litvinov in the past. To get it, they made a deal with the security consultant at Cheshire, a former intelligence officer. Morley was their point man. In the end, he agreed to provide the poison in exchange for a share of profits from Gaztek's operations in Spain."

Powell closed the folder, his eyes already smarting from the effort. "So instead of trying to reform the company, he threw in his lot with the thieves. And nobody else at the fund knew?"

"That's how it looks. Morley was the only one who knew enough about the Spanish operation to structure the deal. The intelligence arm had already established shell companies to siphon off profits. The fact that they were opening for business soon only made the plan more urgent."

Powell saw another connection. "Which explains why they went after Ilya. They were clearing the decks in Spain. If they had found him at another time, they might have left him alone, but given the stakes, and his reputation—"

"—they decided to take him out," Wolfe concluded. "Which only succeeded in turning him against them. He was the first to realize that this was an intelligence operation, although he was following a trail that had been carefully prepared. Karvonen deliberately used methods, like burning bodies with potassium permanganate, that would implicate civilian intelligence after the fact. The same was true of the bomb in my car. They always meant for someone to notice the signs. In fact—"

Wolfe paused. "In fact, it's possible that Garber was supposed to make the connection. He was in an ideal position to influence the case. But until we find him, we won't know for sure."

For a moment, they both fell silent. Powell had never completely come to terms with the fact of Garber's betrayal, which seemed so unlike the man he had known. One day, he thought, he would learn the rest. In the meantime, however, Garber had evidently disappeared for good. "And the rest of the plan?"

"It went precisely as intended," Wolfe said. "Chigorin's plane crashed on schedule. The fact that he survived was inconsequential. Once the device was found in the wreckage, it would cast suspicion on civilian intelligence, causing a scandal in which Litvinov and his allies would be forced to resign. If they had left it at that, it might have worked. But they were just a little too clever."

Powell resumed wheeling himself around the room. He had already guessed the rest. "The leaked documents. They were fake?"

"Some of them were," Wolfe said, walking at his side. "That's the beauty of it. We don't know the identity of the source, but our best guess is that he was Karvonen's handler. He took a trove of real intelligence files and inserted a few forged documents that would tie the security services to the poison program, surrounded by so much authentic material that their accuracy wouldn't be questioned."

"And what about Operation Pepel?" Powell asked. "Was it really an attempt to bring down the prime minister's plane?"

"I don't know," Wolfe said. "Personally, I doubt that

the security services were involved, but I can't be sure. The same thing is true of the Dyatlov Pass. It may have been a weapons test, but there's no proof. Karvonen himself was the forger. And nobody ever would have known, if it hadn't been for Renata."

Powell's wheelchair slid to a sudden halt. "Renata Russell. The photographer?"

Wolfe nodded. "That's the part that nobody expected. Renata was heavily in debt. By the end, she was getting paranoid, and thought that her own employees were passing information to her creditors. When I tried to put myself in her place, it occurred to me that she might have been keeping an eye on them. And what I what found, when I checked her files, was that she had installed remote monitoring software on the computers of everyone on her staff."

Powell smiled slightly, feeling the final piece fall into place. "Including Karvonen."

"That's right," Wolfe said. "It was really quite elegant. The program sent her periodic updates on his email messages, as well as screenshots from his computer at home. After a while, when it became clear that he wasn't working for her creditors, she stopped checking the updates, but the program continued to function even after she was dead. We found it last week. It's a complete record of Karvonen's activities, even though his computer was destroyed. We're still going through it all—"

Wolfe paused as Powell's therapist came back into the gymnasium, giving them an apologetic smile. "Sorry to interrupt, but I'm afraid it's time for our Alan to have a bit of a soak."

"Hydrotherapy," Powell explained to Wolfe. "I need to spend two hours in the bath."

As the therapist wheeled him out of the gym, Wolfe accompanied them to the door. "Karvonen's handler is still out there. I've asked to remain at the agency for as long as it takes to see this through. And I'm sorry to hear that you're leaving. You're sure about this?"

"It's time," Powell said simply. "I don't know how useful I'm going to be in the field these days. And the more time passes, the more I doubt I was ever suited for this kind of work. You're better at it than I ever was."

He saw a look of surprised pleasure pass across her face. "You know that isn't true."

"I've never understood that Mormon modesty of yours. It's unbecoming. Besides, I'm not leaving the game entirely. There are better ways of chasing down these connections. I may still have a few surprises in store."

"I heard a rumor about that," Wolfe said. "They say that Cheshire offered you a job."

"We'll see. I'm going to wait for the outcome of the investigation. But I might be useful there. They have the resources I need to pursue these connections outside the usual channels, and they certainly have the motivation." Arriving at the door, he turned to face Wolfe. "The world is too complicated for the old ways to work. Wheels within wheels, you might say—"

Wolfe only smiled at this. After promising to visit again soon, she stood watching as Powell left the gym.

Once he was gone, Wolfe turned and headed out of the hospital. As she made her way outside, she found herself thinking of the one thing she had neglected to mention, knowing that Powell would only misunderstand it. His survival, it seemed to her, had been a miracle, although she was no longer sure what this meant. All she had was a silent conviction that there was a larger pattern at work here, one she couldn't describe in words, which was, perhaps, for the best.

Life, she was beginning to see, was a process of investigation, with the world itself as a text. She was no longer sure what she believed, and, if pressed, would have said that she believed in nothing. All the same, she also knew that it was necessary to live as if God might still show himself if she looked at the world in the right way. Wolfe didn't think her mother would approve of this position, but she would at least accept it, now that they had begun to talk again.

Outside the hospital, it was gray and damp, a sign that London, at least, remained true to its underlying nature. Wolfe descended the southern steps, where a solitary figure was waiting with an umbrella. "How did it go?"

"Powell's doing fine," Wolfe said to her friend. "But I don't think he's coming back."

"That's a shame," Asthana said. As they turned aside together, heading away from the hospital, Wolfe saw a faint smile on her new partner's face. "But perhaps it's all for the best. I'm looking forward to working with you—"

EPILOGUE

*For there are no poetic secrets now ... Such secrets,
even the Work of the Chariot, may be safely revealed
in any crowded restaurant or café without fear of the
avenging lightning-stroke: the noise of the orchestra,
the clatter of plates and the buzz of a hundred unre-
lated conversations will effectively drown the words—
and, in any case, nobody will be listening.*

—Robert Graves, *The White Goddess*

A few weeks later, Ilya was ushered into the glass interview room at Belmarsh. He had been expecting
to see Wolfe, or perhaps his own advocate, and was surprised to find himself standing before a plump young
man he had never encountered before. The man rose
from his chair and extended a fat hand. "Pleased to meet
you. I'm Owen Dancy, Vasylenko's solicitor."

Ignoring the proposed handshake, Ilya sat down
warily. As the guard left the room, locking the door,
Dancy lowered himself into his seat again. "They've been
treating you well, I trust?"

"Well enough," Ilya said. This was true, as far as it

went. Wolfe had arranged for him to be reintroduced into the general population of the prison, and they had declined to prosecute some of his more recent charges. All the same, he was still awaiting trial for the murder of Lermontov, which was scheduled to begin before the end of the year. "What do you want?"

"Only to talk. It's high time we were introduced." Dancy gave him what seemed like a genuine smile, the deep folds of fat crinkling around his eyes. "I was quite impressed by your role in uncovering the plot against Chigorin. I assume that you've heard the latest developments in the case?"

Despite his natural distrust, Ilya was always interested in news from outside. "What developments?"

"Oh, elements of the military side are talking—anonymously, of course. It appears that the plot was inspired by the Moscow apartment bombings, another instance of the secret services committing a crime and blaming it on a convenient enemy, at least if you credit what people say. There's nothing new under the sun."

Dancy leaned back in his chair, which groaned beneath his bulk. "But there were aspects of the plan that were rather inspired. The choice of target, for one. Chigorin's presence on the plane would have led to a halfhearted investigation, because the government would have suspected that it was somehow responsible. You see, they couldn't be sure that they *didn't* do it."

Ilya gave a nod. This was a point that had occurred to him before. "And the balance of power?"

"Shifting, naturally, back to the civilian side," Dancy said. "It seems that the FSB will benefit greatly, at least in the short term. In the meantime, military intelligence has been correspondingly discredited."

"So the Chekists are on top again," Ilya said. "Your employers must be pleased."

Dancy's smile widened. "You should be pleased as well, my boy. I know that for you, all these acronyms look the same, but that isn't necessarily true. The world is a thorny place. If I were you, I would take a moment to ask myself if I had chosen the proper opponent."

Ilya saw that they were coming around to the true purpose of this visit. "I don't know what you mean."

"I'm saying that you should concern yourself with the real sources of wrongdoing," Dancy replied. "These days, if you consider how the world really works, you'll see that a new breed of criminal is responsible for most of these evils. The thieves' world isn't what it used to be. If the thugs in Transnistria are making deals with anyone, it's with the new generation, which cares nothing for the old ways, only money. You should be going after them, not the dying remains of the *vory*. And I can offer you a chance to get them where it hurts."

Ilya was beginning to glimpse the other man's intentions. "What are you offering?"

"To serve as your solicitor," Dancy said simply. "I feel that we can be of use to each other. Although you realize, of course, that there's no chance of acquittal. The evidence is far too damning. I've wondered for a long time why you didn't just make a deal, and I don't think it's misplaced pride. I suspect, rather, that it's curiosity. You want to see what will come up in a trial."

Ilya saw that Dancy was more intelligent than he

seemed. "If my case is hopeless, then why should I accept?"

"Because there are things I can share with you," Dancy replied. "A public advocate won't understand what you really want, but I do. And I have access to information you might find interesting."

"Knowing who your clients are, I have no doubt of that," Ilya said. "And in return?"

"We get you." Dancy's round face grew suddenly serious. "You see, my boy, a war is coming, between two great factions of the security services. A game of chess, if you like. The military side has been weakened, but only temporarily, and the stakes are higher than you can imagine. They amount to nothing less than the future of Europe. And I think we can use you."

Ilya looked across the table at the solicitor, who seemed in earnest. "And if I refuse?"

"I won't bother you again," Dancy said. "If you accept, I can begin to tell you more."

For a moment, Ilya was struck by the incongruous side of this offer, which had been set before him with such solemnity. "You haven't explained one thing. What you hope to get in return."

"You're a valuable man. We're hoping to profit from your insights, and perhaps from your experience." Dancy hesitated. "How you found a man like Lermontov, for example. It seems to us that you must have had help—"

Ilya pointedly avoided the implied question. "What does Vasylenko think of this?"

Dancy took a moment before responding. "Vasylenko is a useful man," he said at last. "There are those on the outside who still respect the thieves' code. As such, he is still of value. But he also has his limitations. There are others involved, with much at stake, who have taken a great interest in the Scythian. You're part of the game, whether you like it or not. And I suspect that you still have a role to play."

Ilya sensed that the solicitor was speaking honestly enough, though he also knew that there was another element to the proposal. "If I agree, it would also make it easier for you to keep an eye on me."

Dancy granted the point. "Of course. You aren't a man we want out of our sight." He spread his large hands. "So what do you say?"

"I'll think about it," Ilya said. Catching the eye of the guard beyond the glass, he signaled that he wanted to be let out. A second later, the door was unbolted and opened from the outside.

As Ilya rose from his chair, Dancy spoke without looking up. "You know, there are times when I think you went to the tournament knowing you were likely to be caught, but were prepared for this, if it brought you closer to Vasylenko." Dancy lifted his eyes. "Am I right?"

"If I were as smart as that, I never would have come back to London," Ilya said. Then he turned aside, leaving the solicitor alone.

Ilya followed the guard back down the hallway, passing through the gates that led to his own spur. As he walked, he considered the implications of the meeting. An offer from a lawyer always contained more than it seemed, like an optical illusion, or the meanings of words in scripture. But as he waited for the guard to unlock the gate of the secure area, he was struck by one detail of their exchange.

Vasylenko, the solicitor had pointed out, was a useful man. There were those on the outside who, because of custom or tradition, would follow him. Within these walls, however, he was less useful. And when Ilya set this fact against Vasylenko's advanced age, and the fact that the old man did not want to die in prison, it made him wonder what else these men had in mind.

He followed the guard up the metal steps, then waited as the door of his cell was unlocked and drawn back. The guard stood aside as Ilya went in, then wordlessly shut the door.

Ilya looked around the cell. When his eye fell on his books, he found himself thinking of Wolfe, who had brought him these two volumes. These days, whenever his thoughts turned in her direction, he saw that he had been wrong about her. In some cases, perhaps, you could find justice as a part of the system, as long as the system did not become a part of you.

And for all the assistance he had rendered to Wolfe, he also knew that he would never be allowed to leave this place. Dancy had been right. There would be no chance of acquittal.

Going to the shelf, he took down one of the books. It was the collection of midrashim that he had carried to the chess tournament, bringing it with him just in case. Studying the cover now, he thought again of scripture as a house of locked passages, a key set at random before each door. Then, opening the book to a page he had marked, he began to read from the commentary on Manasseh.

Manasseh, Ilya knew, was a king who had killed the

prophet Isaiah and raised pagan altars within the temple, sins that later generations had blamed for the destruction of the kingdom of Judah. Among his other outrages, he had dedicated a chariot and horses to the god of the sun, which is why, much later, Ezekiel had not included a horse in his vision of the chariot. Instead, the wheels had turned by themselves, showing that God had followed his chosen people into exile.

In the end, however, Manasseh himself had been taken as an exile to Babylon, where they had bound him with fetters and led him by a ring in the nose. After his return, he had reassumed the throne, repented, and given up idolatry. And his reign of more than fifty years was the longest in the Bible.

The rabbis had been disquieted by this story, which seemed to reward a sinful king. What made him worthy, they concluded, was not study or righteousness, but chastisement. His suffering had brought him into the kingdom of God when the study of scripture could not.

Closing the volume in his hands, Ilya stood there for a moment, then went over to the sink. Here, by the toilet, was the only part of the cell that could not be seen through the Judas hole in the door.

On the edge of the sink lay a safety razor. Ilya set down the book, then picked up the razor and extracted the blade. Taking the book in his other hand, he carefully slit open the base of the spine. Then, reaching inside, he removed what he had put there the night before his arrest. It was a lock-picking kit, with a torsion wrench and four picks, that he had taken from Brodsky's flat.

Ilya weighed the picks briefly in his hands, then inserted them into the binding again and put the book back on the shelf. He did not need them yet. One day, however, they might prove useful.

Because even in a life of exile, he thought, there was always the promise of return.

ACKNOWLEDGMENTS

Many thanks, as always, to my agent, David Halpern; to everyone at the Robbins Office, especially Kathy Robbins, Louise Quayle, Arielle Asher, and Micah Hauser; to my editors, Mark Chait and Danielle Perez; to Kara Welsh, Talia Platz, Jessica Butler, and the rest of the team at New American Library; to Jon Cassir and Matthew Snyder at CAA; and to Dave Daley, Gardner Dozois, Alla Karagodin Holmes, Alexandra Israel, Jesse Kellerman, Ian King, Trevor Quachri, Stanley Schmidt, Jesse Wegman, and Stephanie Wu. Thanks as well to my friends in Chicago, New York, and elsewhere; to my family; to all the Wongs; and to Wailin.

Don't miss the next novel by
Alec Nevala-Lee,

ETERNAL EMPIRE

Available from Signet in 2013.

Arkady arrived at the museum at ten. When a guard in white gloves asked him to open his bag, he unslung it from his shoulder and undid the top flap. The guard ran a penlight across the main compartment and thanked him absently. Arkady nodded and took the bag back again, careful to keep it upright. Then he continued into the entrance hall, past the masonry piers and urns of flowers, and headed with the other visitors into the Metropolitan Museum of Art in New York.

On this weekday morning, half an hour after opening, the museum was not especially crowded. Looking around the bright domed space, Arkady took in the flocks of tourists and children, the retirees and art students, and, above all, the guards in their white shirts and black ties. He had known that the search of his bag would be perfunctory, but he was more concerned by another detail. The guards at the doors only rarely carried guns, but today one was wearing a sidearm.

A few minutes later, he was climbing the grand staircase, a visitor's pin secured to his bag. Instead of passing under the arch into the main line of galleries, he turned and went down the hallway of drawings to his left. Later accounts would emphasize his dark complexion and Uzbek features, but in reality, he was simply a slender, rather handsome young man of medium height, with something of the bearing of a former soldier, which was precisely what he was.

He continued into the next wing, a gallery lined with statues by Rodin and Bayre, the famous sculptor of hunting scenes. Most of the visitors were filing toward the far end of the hall, where a special exhibition was taking place, but Arkady headed for a door to one side. Security footage would later reveal that he hesitated only briefly before crossing the threshold.

Inside, the gallery was quiet, with a single pair of visitors in sight. It was a large red space with a parquet floor and a bench set beneath the skylight in the ceiling. As Arkady went in, he noticed a guard in a blue polyester suit standing in the doorway to the next room, her back turned.

He had visited this gallery twice before. Without looking, he knew that the walls were covered in canvases by Ingres and Gericault, with one particularly notable portrait, of an elongated nude glancing back over one shoulder, hanging directly across from him. To his left was the work he had come to see, but he did not look at it yet. Instead, he pretended to study the canvas beside it, a painting of a woman being abducted by two men on horses, as he waited for his moment to come.

At last, the other visitors drifted out of the room. Aside from the guard in the doorway, he had the gallery to himself. Keeping her uniform in his peripheral vision, Arkady turned away from the picture before him, his heart quickening, and approached his true object of desire.

It was not a work likely to catch the eye of a casual viewer, a small oil painting, thirteen by twenty inches, depicting a landscape of low mountains. In the distance lay a body of water, perhaps an inland sea. A few groups of figures in pastoral clothes were scattered across the composition. At the center, a woman, naked from the waist up, was milking a mare with a white stripe down its nose.

But the most striking figure was a man lying before a crude hut, clearly out of place among the rest. He was leaning on one elbow against the sloping ground, his body draped in a loose robe, and his head was bowed, as if he were brooding over the remembered geography of a faraway land.

It is not impossible that Arkady Kagan, as he stood before the painting, felt some kinship with this model of exile, so far from home, cut off from those he knew and loved. A second later, however, the feeling passed, and he noticed that the guard in the doorway was gone.

Arkady looked around the gallery. He was alone. It was sooner than he had expected, but he had no choice but to move now.

Opening the side pocket of his shoulder bag, he removed a folded magazine, which was held shut by a pair of rubber bands. Inside was a flat glass bottle the size of a pint flask. Arkady unscrewed the top, allowing a puff of white vapor to escape, and turned back to the picture. He gave it one last look, staring into the face of the exiled poet, and before he could lose his courage, he took a step back and flung the contents of the flask at the painting.

It would later be determined, from the pattern of splashes, that he had swung the bottle three times. The restoration report would note in passing that if the work had been doused with water at once, it might have been saved, but the guards had been understandably reluctant to act without further instruction. By the time the conservators arrived, the acid had eaten through to the underlying wood, carbonizing the oils and leaving three unrepairable holes.

But all that lay in the future. As soon as Arkady had emptied the bottle, he let it fall to his feet. From his jacket pocket, which had not been searched, he drew a hunting knife. Unsheathing it, he went up to the picture, his eyes smarting from the fumes as the acid cooked its way through the pigment, and lunged forward, plunging the knife into the top of the painting above the central mountain. Then he pulled it down, using both hands, in a long vertical slash, slicing through the image of the distant sea and gouging the wood beneath.

He took a step back, breathing hard. His plan, at this point, had been to drop the knife and go to the bench at the center of the room to calmly await arrest. Indeed, he might well have remembered to do this, altering everything that followed, had he not heard a startled gasp from behind him.

Arkady turned. Standing in the doorway was the guard from before. For the first time, he saw that she was surprisingly young, with a sheaf of brown curls pulled back from her forehead. He saw her eyes flick toward the painting, taking in the damage, and then dart back to meet his own.

If the guard had shouted for him to stay where he was, he would have done so gladly. Instead, as she looked at him in silence, he was suddenly overwhelmed by shame.

Before she could say anything, he turned and walked away, the knife still clutched in one hand. Behind him, the stream of melting paint was flowing down the wall, pooling in a black puddle on the parquet floor.

Leaving the room, Arkady found himself back in the main gallery, but he did not return the way he came. Instead, he headed to the right, ignoring the elevators, and passed into a pair of galleries devoted to Cypriot art. Beyond this was a staircase, which he took, his pulse thudding somewhere up around his ears. As he rounded the landing and continued down the next flight of stairs, a cooler part of his brain reminded him that the alarm would have gone out by now to the museum's communication center, which had a direct hotline to the police.

He descended to ground level and entered the splendidly renovated galleries of Greek and Roman antiquities, his footfalls echoing on the floor. Around him, visitors were staring, but he ignored their looks and pressed on past the headless statues. Only a hundred yards lay between him and the outside world.

Up ahead, where the galleries gave way to the entrance hall, a guard was speaking into a handheld transceiver. When he saw Arkady, his eyes widened, and he lowered his radio with a shout: *"Hey, you—"*

Arkady went past him without pausing. Part of him knew he should halt, but instead, he pushed his way through a knot of startled visitors at the ticket desk. The only way out was through the main doors.

Passing the coat check to his right, he heard more shouts, but he kept going. The exit was forty steps away. Beyond the row of stanchions, he could make out the light of the summer day outside.

He was nearly there when he heard another shout, the meaning of which became clear only later, and felt a pair of blows strike his chest.

Arkady became aware of two things at once. The first was that he was still holding the knife, which he had intended to leave in the gallery. The second was that he had been shot.

Looking up, he saw a guard standing before him, his face pale and disbelieving, his sidearm drawn. For a second, the two men stood eye to eye. Then Arkady glanced down at his chest. With his free hand, he touched the patch of warmth that was already spreading across his shirt, and then he fell to the floor.

Arkady rolled onto his back, the knife falling from his fingers at last. In the ceiling far above, he saw one of three circular skylights, which reminded him, curiously, of the three holes that had been left by the acid. Feeling nothing but a strange satisfaction, he closed his eyes to that perfectly white sky, the blood pooling across the floor beneath him, and breathed out for the last time.

In the aftermath of his death, there would be rumors of a racial component in the decision to open fire, leading to a number of protests. Ultimately, however, an investigation would determine that the guard in question, a museum veteran of ten years, had mistaken the knife in the other man's hand for a gun. Since the situation had given him ample reason to regard Arkady as dangerous, the shooting, it concluded, had simply been a regrettable accident.

Afterward, the press would compare the incident to other famous cases of art vandalism, including one notorious episode three years before in Philadelphia. And while some wondered why the dead man had ignored the more celebrated portrait by Ingres in the same gallery, surprisingly few ventured to guess why he had chosen to attack that particular work, a painting by Eugène Delacroix: *Ovid chez les Scythes*, or *Ovid Among the Scythians*.

Also available from

Alec Nevala-Lee

The Icon Thief

A controversial masterpiece resurfaces in Budapest.
A ballerina's headless corpse is found beneath the
boardwalk at Brighton Beach. And New York's Russian
Mafia is about to collide with the equally ruthless
art world...

Maddy Blume, an ambitious young art buyer for a
Manhattan hedge fund, is desperate to find a priceless
painting by Marcel Duchamp, one of the most
influential artists of the twentieth century. A gruesome
cold case thrusts the FBI into a search for the same
painting, with its enigmatic image of a headless nude.
And an insidious secret society is intent on reclaiming
the painting for reasons of its own—and by any
means necessary.

**"Smart, sophisticated, and has enough fast-paced
action to keep anyone up past midnight."
—*New York Times* bestselling author
Paul Christopher**

S0420